Praise for *This Was Not the Plan*

"*This Was Not the Plan* starts out as a funny and sharply observed campus novel and then deepens into a thought-provoking examination of the complicated and always thorny politics of abortion. Daphne Uviller is a shrewd and compassionate writer, able to imagine a wide variety of intersecting lives and outlooks, and find humor in even the darkest moments."

—Tom Perrotta, author of *Election* and *Tracy Flick Can't Win*

Praise for *Super in the City*

"One should not simply read *Super in the City*; one should gobble it up like candy. This is particularly intelligent candy, mind you—but don't let that stop you from indulging in a big old sack of fun."

— Elizabeth Gilbert, bestselling author of *Eat, Pray, Love*

Praise for *Only Child*

"Honest, insightful, and entertaining…a great read."

— *Time Out New York*

Also by Daphne Uviller

*Only Child: Writers on the Singular Joys and Solitary
Sorrows of Growing Up Solo*
co-edited with Deborah Siegel

The Zephyr Zuckerman Series:
Super in the City
Hotel No Tell
Wife of the Day

THIS WAS NOT THE PLAN

A NOVEL

DAPHNE UVILLER

Library of Congress Control Number: 2024935043

ISBN (paperback): 9781662948176
eISBN: 9781662948183

For Sacha

ONE

Sylvia Tanisman squinted into the spotlights and tried not to flinch at the television cameras that zoomed and hovered like wild animals closing in on their quarry. Clutching her Tony medallion, she garbled her sincere thanks, forgetting the acceptance speech she held, damp and crumpled, in her quivering hand.

The play that had catapulted Sylvia to momentary fame was *This Is Not a Test*. When her agent reluctantly showed her the script, Sylvia was contributing to the household income by directing the occasional *SVU* episode at home, and regularly flying out to LA to direct *The Big Bang Theory* and *The Good Wife*. She accepted against the advice of her agent because Nathaniel was becoming too delicious to be away from for long, and because Leah, at the time, was entering the jaws of kindergarten. It seemed prudent for the mother to be around each night in case of… Sylvia wasn't sure what. Early onset of mean girls? Inability to glue popsicle sticks? It was virgin territory.

This Is Not a Test surprised everyone involved by moving swiftly to Broadway, remaining sold out seven months into the future, and sweeping the Tonys. Ethan and Sylvia indulged in a hotel suite the night she won the award for Best Director of a Drama, allowing themselves—which turned into forcing themselves—to stay at the after party until two in the morning. Yawning and glancing at her watch every few seconds, Sylvia wondered aloud how the celebrities did it.

"Nannies and cocaine," Ethan posited.

Determined to sleep in, they managed to remain unconscious in their plush rooms at the St. Regis until seven thirty. Bleary-eyed prisoners of monstrous habit, they surrendered, grabbed a cab, and at eight thirty were greeted at their Upper West Side duplex by the guarantors of their gene pool, who were preparing to head off into the world of finger paints and counting by tens.

Sylvia's husband, that dear, sweet man with whom she was perfectly, exceptionally matched, let her bask in her triumph all that long awards night, the whole next day, and even the following night. It wasn't until the second morning, after they'd had a solid seven hours of sleep, that he poured fresh coffee into a Zabar's mug, cocked his head sympathetically, and told her about Lisette, a fellow partner at Pantheon Architext, Ltd., who was, at that very moment, leaving her husband.

Leaving her husband for Ethan.

And so Ethan would be leaving Sylvia.

"I'm so, *so* sorry and sad, Sylvie."

Sorry sorry Sylvie Sylvie sad sorry so so.

This being a millennial dumping by an enlightened man, he would, he assured her with an earnest frown meant to convey responsibility and concern, remain fully fifty percent involved with the kids. Plus (he hurried through his rehearsed list of mitigating factors), he would not withdraw any financial support, though, of course—and here he dared to smile—she'd probably be flooded with offers and bring in plenty of her own money now. Sylvia gripped the kitchen counter as it dawned on her that Ethan thought his bombshell would be buffered by her Tony Award, rather than negate it entirely.

"Mommy, what do I wear today?" Leah croaked in her kindergartener's pack-a-day voice, bumping her way down the stairs on her butt. Ethan's quiet announcement was still ricocheting off the tiles. They'd poured hours of their lives into making sure those tiles were locally sourced, an absurdity that loomed large and nearly made Sylvia snort.

"Shorts and a T-shirt," they replied in unison, as though their sun-dappled kitchen had not just transformed into a black hole.

Leah twirled into view. She had dressed herself on this sweltering June day in pink sweatpants and a long-sleeved sweatshirt in a darker shade of pink.

"Why do you even ask?" Sylvia snapped, her shock temporarily blunted, as it would be repeatedly in the coming months by the immediacy of the kids' needs.

"But I want to wear *these.*" Leah revved her voice, preparing for battle.

"Ethan? Could you please—?" Sylvia raised her palms in surrender, and backed out of the room.

There was no question that Ethan was the better parent. More patient, sillier, less prone to yelling, more willing to see things from the perspective of an energetic three-year-old and a self-certain six-year-old. He knew the words to most Peter, Paul and Mary songs. It continually surprised Sylvia to discover in how many ways she did not match up with the adult she'd assumed she'd become.

Sylvia headed toward the stairs, her fingers trailing the wall, afraid to rely on just one sense to convey her away from This Thing. It was utterly absurd that Ethan would commit this preposterous, unthinkable act on a Tuesday morning, the kids not yet gone to school, and so there was no need to stick around to hear the rest of his consolation prizes. Either this was not happening or it would need to happen in a different way.

No. This was, of course, *not* happening. A hallucinogen had been injected into him last night, or into her, or an electromagnetic, planetary phenomenon had occurred, one that would be reported on the news as having caused all manner of unbloody but devastating domestic tragedies, most of which would be remedied by nightfall.

She ascended the tight spiral staircase to check on Nathaniel, who had last been spotted naked and constructing a spaceship out of old bubble wands. Halfway up, she realized that there was absolutely no way Ethan had said what she thought he'd said. Smiling, Sylvia shook her head, realizing this was a dream from which she merely needed to wake, and headed back down to the kitchen to start the scene again.

There was the oil painting of a shack they'd bought on a trip through Suriname, a piece of art they now understood was offensively colonialist for them to own. There was the Steuben vase neither liked, but was too expensive to get rid of. The low bookshelves they'd spent an entire weekend refinishing together. The round teak side table they'd raced to Ho-Ho-Kus to grab off of Craigslist, panicked by a high-pressure seller. Atop it was the family photo so paradigmatically A Family that people said it looked like it came with the frame. This was the apartment they had moved out of for fifteen months to urban-camp with toddling Leah so that Ethan could produce the wood, steel, and recycled plastic manifestation of their infrangible union. Their survival of the renovation acquired a smooth narrative: his skill and exquisite taste coupled with her tendency to refrain from micromanaging had amounted to bitter-free home improvement.

Leah passed by again, arms outstretched, and her hand fluttered over her mother's.

Sylvia returned to the kitchen for Take Two.

"You convinced her to change her clothes?" She smiled warmly at Ethan.

"Sylvia."

Take Two progressed exactly the way Take One had, and by lunchtime it was clear that Sylvia was embarking on a life she'd never wanted.

TWO

Meg Croyden once saved a life. Actually, twice, but she didn't count the first time, which was when she called 911 on Gemma Maillard, who had smoked some weed laced with acid and was in the 7-Eleven bathroom methodically taking a knife to each of her fingers.

No, Meg saved her own goddamned life in ninth grade the moment she crashed her mother's car. Meg's head split open and her guts spilled out and she was pinned and stuffed and sewed back together like a sock puppet. Two hundred thirteen sutures if you counted the internal ones, which she did. Her pelvis was jerry-rigged together, and her clavicle was now partly constructed of plastic. She was Frankenstein's monster (yes, Meg knew the difference between Frankenstein and his monster).

Right up until she stole her mom's car and made the speedometer shudder to ninety-five, Meg had been robbing her mother blind. AnneMarie was a billing clerk and receptionist at a dentist's office in town. A salaried job to be proud of, not hourly. Benefits, not overtime. The real deal, something she never expected to get without a college degree. The job should have paid well enough to support a family of two, but it didn't.

Not when one member of the family was stealing most of the money to shoot up. AnneMarie was in such denial about what was happening right under her nose that she declared she must be really bad at finances. A billing clerk. Bad at finances.

"I'm such a ditz," her mother would say in what was maybe some kind of leftover helpless come-on that used to work for women. So in addition to working eight thirty to five every day including Saturdays, she had to pick up shifts at Michael's on Sundays, overseeing manic birthday parties in windowless rooms, coming home covered in glue and glitter—a close cousin of tar and feathers, in Meg's opinion.

There was ample opportunity to find AnnMarie's money, as skanky Gemma pointed out nearly every day after school.

"Just go act like you're looking for a scarf," Gemma said one stiflingly hot Wednesday afternoon in September, just a few weeks into their high school career. She draped herself across the armchair and stuck her hand in the waistband of her jeans, like a guy. Through heavily lidded eyes, she gazed vacantly and somehow also expectantly at Meg.

"Why the fuck do I need to act if she's not even here?"

Gemma shrugged. "It'll make you feel better."

Psychology from a teenage smackhead.

"Why a scarf?"

The fact that Meg stalled even a tiny bit proved there was some kernel of a decent person inside her that didn't want to be doing this. It's not like it was hard work finding the money. Her mother kept cash in her top dresser drawer, and didn't miss the twenty Meg took twice a week.

AnneMarie was overly trusting, yes, and she was definitely smitten with Jesus H. Christ, but it was also a fact that she was a drunk. She didn't think she was a drunk because her beverage of choice was port, like the rich people drank, but Meg knew that five glasses of anything every night was not, as her mom said, "a little cap to my day." AnneMarie's specious logic went like this: port was upper-class and upper-class people who drank port never acted drunk. Therefore, she was not a drunk.

While gingerly sipping at her fourth or fifth Taylor Tawny of the night, AnneMarie often took a sentimental trip through the memento boxes she stored in the front closet. Meg had rummaged through them countless times herself, looking for clues as to why she was the horrible person she was. The boxes held birthday cards from AnneMarie's church friends ("Happy birthday to you, Jesus surely loves you!"), dozens of copies of *Ladies' Home Journal*, envelopes full of expired Clipper coupons, and paper-clipped stacks of utility bills, scrawled with notations of her pleas to the gatekeepers of cable and electricity to extend a grace period. She often didn't put away the contents of the boxes until the following weekend, when she wasn't so "tired."

On this particular Wednesday, Meg did her usual rounds of AnneMarie's stashes: she checked the level of the port to gauge when her mother would next need to restock, then she checked the freezer to estimate how long it would be before she'd have to go the supermarket. Meg's calculations indicated that she would be able to get away with forty dollars from the cash stash. She was on the verge of stepping over the contents of the boxes to make this happy announcement to Gemma when she glanced down and spotted a bank statement with a giant number on it. Not as in the font was giant. As in, the number value was giant. Gargantuan.

Meg reached down and pushed aside an Optimum downgrade alert and a B&E Electric and Gas warning notice. She pulled out the statement, which was stapled to a Xeroxed copy of a check that was made out to her mother. The bank statement and the Xerox were dog-eared and the creases were linen soft from folding and refolding. How many times over how many years had her mother taken out this document?

Seeing her mother's name—AnneMarie Croyden—printed on the same page as the number $75,000 stopped Meg in a way that absolutely nothing else could have stopped her drug-fueled hunt. That kind of money, all in one sum, did not figure into their lives. It was an impossibility. There was no distant but wealthy relative who could bail them out when something went wrong. No windfall from a slip-and-fall settlement. No inheritance from her grandfather other than his debt.

"Meg, yes or no?" Gemma whined from the other room. "I'm gonna get sick if I don't get some in the next hour."

Maybe Jane or Mark Prisker would know what this check meant. Those were the names at the top of the check. Jane and Mark Prisker lived at 17876 Woodbury Circle in Endicott, New York. Or they had fourteen years earlier.

And maybe Jane and Mark Fucking Prisker would know why her mother's bank statement showed a deposit of this unimaginable amount of money followed by a withdrawal of the same amount and then a zero at the bottom.

Endicott was barely half an hour away. Meg charged out of the room and shoved the forty dollars she'd found into Gemma's hands.

"Go," Meg told her. "Merry Christmas." A flicker of

confusion and then a half smile.

"Yeah, right." Gemma squinted at the roaring air conditioner, which Meg wasn't supposed to have turned on, to save money. "Wait, you're really not coming?" Gemma shifted from foot to foot, flicking the two twenties together, not hiding her excitement over double the money and half the users. She wasn't so bad at math.

"Just remembered something I gotta do," Meg said.

"Okay, I'm out." Gemma slapped her palm against Meg's and left. Meg waited to see whether Gemma would even remember to close the front door—she did—and then parted two slats in the blinds to watch her go. She had the intense, driven walk that broadcasts "I'm a user!"

Meg didn't have a plan. She had an address, tunnel vision, and the extra set of car keys she'd excavated from the kitchen drawer. She tucked her flip phone in her front pocket and took off on her bike. Thinking back, Meg was impressed with the multistep planning she pulled off: she could have decided to bike all the way to Endicott, which would have taken over an hour on the back roads. But she was filled with a sudden, insane certainty that she'd been cheated out of seventy-five thousand dollars. Driven by the conviction that there was more where that came from, Meg headed for Imbroglio and Perez, DDS, dropped her bike on the pavement next to her mother's rusty green Hyundai, and hurled herself into the driver's seat.

The house at 17876 Woodbury Circle was ridiculous. It was a mini White House and Meg hated it immediately. Hated Jane and Mark Prisker immediately. Circular gravel driveway, columns that supported nothing, hedges grown only to be reined in: all stuff that screamed *money to burn*. Meg left the car idling in front of the door, jumped out, and leaned on the bell. She wasn't high, but the prospect of having enough money to stay high for the rest of her life was nearly as good as the actual thing.

It was ninety degrees out and humid. Meg was wearing stained shorts and a grubby tank top and hadn't showered in a couple of days. The opposite of beautiful to begin with—scrawny, with a huge forehead and a nonexistent jawline, like whoever made her forgot to carve out the angle that makes a neck distinct from a chin—Meg was sweaty and greasy and her fields of acne were in full flower.

The woman who opened the door looked like the client in a bank advertisement. Perfect dark brown bob with a few streaks of silver, capri pants, and a sleeveless silk top that showed off unwobbly arms. She was as well maintained as her landscaping, but there was no hiding the fact that she, too, was naturally ugly. Deep-set, narrow eyes, a grotesquely large mouth filled with oversize teeth, all on a face that was far too long. Did she know she was ugly, or had she fooled herself?

"Are you Jane Prisker?" Meg said by way of a greeting.

The woman closed the gap in the door a few inches so that she was peeking more than facing.

"I'm sorry?"

"I'm sure you're sorry. Are you Jane Prisker?"

"Are you Rodrigo's daughter? I explained to him that he'll get paid on the first of every month." She looked flat-out repulsed.

"Do I look like Rodrigo's daughter? I'm AnneMarie Croyden's daughter, and if you're Jane Prisker, then tell me why you gave my mother seventy-five thousand dollars."

The color drained from the woman's face, and Meg had the presence of mind to stick her foot in the door before it closed.

"If you don't let me in, I'm going to stand out here and scream until the cops come."

The woman quickly stepped back to let Meg in, her eyes darting between the girl and the beater still rumbling in her driveway. When she closed the door, there was such silence and coolness that all Meg wanted to do was lie down on the smooth blond floor and rest every muscle. She rarely encountered this kind of quiet. Meg was accustomed to incomprehensible yelling in the middle of the night, sirens penetrating the thin walls of her house, cars backfiring that were indistinguishable from occasional gunfire, a steady beating on the nerves. But you could be healthy and strong with this kind of peace enveloping you. You could say no to Gemma, no to Troy Cutler and Baxter Fenster, whom Meg regularly blew for smack, tell them to fuck off, tell them never to utter your name again. You could, maybe, kick the urge, and do something like have an apple with peanut butter and do your homework and read a book without feeling like you also had to keep an invasion at arm's length.

"Did your mother send you here?" With the door closed, the woman wasn't as worried about Meg screaming. There was probably even a silent alarm button. Meg had lost her advantage.

"How do you know my mother?"

The woman shook her head, weighing her response.

"I don't," she said. "I mean, I don't anymore. We barely knew each other a long time ago." She watched Meg warily, as though to see how this would sit.

"Bullshit, barely knew. You gave her seventy-five thousand dollars. Or more."

She took a step back.

"More? Was there more?"

"No! That was it!"

"But you did give her the seventy-five. Tell me why."

Jane Prisker had been cornered, and Meg felt dark elation.

"Is she here?" Jane asked. "Is AnneMarie in the car?"

"No."

"Who drove you?"

"I drove myself."

"But you're only—"

They both waited.

"How do you know how old I am," Meg said rather than asked.

"I have no idea how old you are," she said defensively. "You just look too young to drive."

"You know how old I am, don't you? I was born a few days before you gave my mom that money. *Why?*" Meg pressed.

Jane Prisker studied Meg, and Meg boldly held her gaze. What did she do all day in this sprawling house? She looked like she was in her fifties, though maybe she was older and money kept her looking younger. She was too old to have any kids to look after, and it didn't seem like she'd just come home from work.

"Do you want something to drink?" Jane Prisker asked reluctantly.

Meg did. Meg desperately wanted a drink, a sweet drink, a cold, sugary lemonade, which she imagined there was a pitcher of in this woman's fridge, but Meg didn't want to owe her anything. So Meg said no, and the woman's shoulders relaxed at the thought of not having to watch Meg put her lips to one of her glasses.

"Actually, yeah," Meg amended abruptly.

Somewhere in that moment, though, Jane Prisker had found her courage.

"Actually, no," she said. "You have to leave. This was never supposed to happen, and that was the deal."

"The *deal*?"

She shook her head.

"What deal? What wasn't supposed to happen? How do you know my mother?"

The woman stepped around Meg and opened the door. The wall of heat made Meg want to cry.

"No!" *Please don't make me go.*

"If you leave now, I won't press charges."

"For what? I haven't done anything! I rang the bell and you let me in!"

Jane Prisker faltered.

"If you wanna make a deal," Meg told her, "pay me to go away."

The woman crossed her arms, a scowl settling over her ugly features. "That's what I did the first time."

A tremor shot through Meg, and she knew she would pass out if she didn't sit. There was a useless chair to the side of the door, an uninviting antique with a hard, polished back and an overstuffed seat. Meg perched on the edge and lowered her head between her legs.

"But I've never been here before," she mumbled.

Jane Prisker—this really was Jane from the check—stood in front of Meg, so close that Meg was looking straight down at her beige heels. Who wore heels around the house? Jane crouched down and put her mouth near Meg's ear.

"You were born in the bathroom upstairs. That was the last time you were here."

Meg drew in a breath, forcing it down her closing throat.

"Go ask your mother where the money is. Or your father. I believe he was the last one to get his hands on it." Jane allowed herself a cruel guffaw. "But I will not have you people threatening me. So get the hell out of my house and don't any of you ever come back here."

THREE

Many years ago, the McClanahan family had gone out to dinner to celebrate Bethany's eighteenth birthday and her upcoming departure for college.

Caroline Byrne McClanahan had purchased for her daughter a beautiful, and not inexpensive, gold cross inlaid with tiny pearls. It was small and delicate. Bethany had turned into a rather big girl, and so Caroline tried to find styles on the QVC that would make her look more feminine. Christopher was in charge of the birthday card, and he had picked a perfect one:

> *God is all around you, in front of you and behind you.*
> *Feel His hand on your shoulder.*
> *Happy Birthday!*

Caroline thought it was judicious of Christopher to have picked one that didn't have an actual Bible verse on it; a direct, more modern message was the way to go with Bethany.

They were all four together, which was so rare by then. Bethany was a senior at Our Lady of Perpetual Help High School, and she had her own life. She was busy with choir and girls' Bible study and the volleyball team. She'd gotten a scholarship to Thomas Aquinas and would be moving out soon. Caroline was full of pride, the good kind. And she was proud of herself for not picking a fight about how little Bethany had been to church lately. As her daughter pointed out—on the very few occasions Caroline did bring it up—she lived by Christ's word every day at school, and Caroline could hardly argue with that.

It was a good time for the McClanahan family. Even Jonathan was finally showing some promise. He was still a quiet boy, sullen even, but his parents chalked that up to adolescence. After he failed to meet the standards of Perpetual Help and was encouraged to go to the local high school instead, he realized, after trying out some of the vocational curriculum, that he was adept at repointing bricks. So Caroline insisted that *he* continue to attend church. While they were glad to save the money on the private school, Caroline and Christopher worried constantly about Jonathan's soul, mixed in among the others, many of whom had not been saved. Of course, Caroline was all for diversity and acceptance—as a Christian, she loved all of God's children—but she'd never been entirely clear on how to balance her open heart with the need to make sure her own family was saved. She would muster up the courage to ask Father Flechette at the next Bible study, though she was nervous about asking a dim question that would make it seem like she didn't understand the Scripture.

It was a Friday night, and they were all to meet at the diner. Caroline had come from a Sepulcher Sisterhood Mother's Day lunch planning meeting, and Christopher had come straight from work. Bethany would be coming from volleyball practice and Jonathan from the jobsite where he was apprenticing. Caroline hoped they would each clean themselves up before dinner, but she would of course accept them in whatever state they arrived. Caroline herself had taken care for the occasion. She'd even applied a bit of the lip gloss she kept hidden in the back of her nightstand.

Steven, her favorite waiter, showed her and Christopher to their table. Bethany had arrived before them, which unsettled Caroline. She had wanted to set the scene, have the gift box waiting, the table unmarred by activity. Bethany had already begun doodling on the paper placemat.

"Happy birthday, Bethie!" Caroline sang out.

Bethany offered a smile, but didn't stand up. Caroline leaned awkwardly over the table, and felt the corner dig into her thigh. That would leave a bruise. She reached for Christopher's hand, but he was already sliding into the booth, next to Bethany. Caroline sat down alone across from them. Jonathan, of course, wasn't there yet. She hoped he would show up. Punctuality and scheduling were not high priorities for him. And now that he was getting rides from a friend, a senior at the high school who had his license, he always had a ready excuse—it was someone else's fault.

"I know what I'm getting," Bethany said.

"But there's so much to choose from!" Caroline wound up addressing this to Steven the waiter, who was leaning over to fill her water glass, and he dipped his head in acknowledgment. Steven had been serving them for as long as they'd been coming here, tolerating the college students at breakfast and looking forward to the civilized families at dinnertime, as he liked to say. What would it be like to wait tables at his age, which was about her age? To be on your feet all day?

"How's my girl?" Christopher said, putting an easy arm around their daughter. Bethany leaned into him, Caroline noticed. So often, it seemed, Bethany found a way out of Caroline's embraces.

Bethany shrugged.

Caroline made a show of turning the pages of the oversize menu. She fingered a spot of melted plastic obscuring a description of the spinach salad.

"Anyone heard from Jonathan?" Caroline said lightly.

No one answered, so she looked up.

"Anyone?" she repeated.

Bethany and Christopher shook their heads, identical movements that irked Caroline.

"Do you think we should wait to do presents?"

Bethany looked at her with something that seemed, to Caroline, like pity.

"Am I going to have to talk to myself all evening?" Caroline joked.

"I'm sure Jonathan didn't get around to getting a gift," Bethany said, "so you may as well give me yours now."

Why did these family dinners never follow the script in her head? Caroline regarded her daughter and cast about for a compliment. Bethany had been a beautiful child, but now, everything from her haircut to her sullen expression obliterated any trace of loveliness.

Caroline was reluctant to produce the necklace.

"Let's wait a little longer," Christopher said, saving her.

Steven returned. Caroline peppered him with questions about the pasta special, then settled on the fish special. Christopher ordered the steak. Bethany ordered the soup and salad combo.

Caroline piled the menus and handed them to Steven. She regarded her husband and daughter expectantly, but Christopher's and Bethany's attention was drawn to the television above Caroline's head.

"Helloooo," she tried.

Their eyes dipped down to her.

"It's the bishop stuff," Bethany said.

Caroline inhaled to protest, but Christopher shook his head ever so slightly at her. Did Bethany speak this way on purpose to hurt her? The death of His Eminence Archbishop John Joseph O'Connor, consecrated by His Holiness John Paul II, dismissed as *bishop stuff*? Caroline choked with the effort of silencing herself. The school had suspended classes the day following His Eminence's death to honor the man who had fought for the working people and preserved the sanctity of the St. Patrick's Day parade.

Caroline released her breath through pursed lips, every mother a martyr.

"May he rest in peace," Christopher said.

Bethany drummed her fingers on the table. Her nails were bitten down and dotted with the patchy remnants of purple polish. How did she get away with that at school? Caroline had been unable to monitor Bethany's appearance because, for all of her senior year, Bethany had been up and out before Caroline had emerged from her own bedroom. She was thrilled that her daughter was so involved in Perpetual Help's activities, but entire days could pass where she saw only Bethany's closed door—"Studying!"—and her dirty plate in the dishwasher.

She'd also stopped helping Bethany conform to dress code because the withering looks her daughter bestowed on her were intolerable. Leave it to the school—thank God for the school!—to take care of these things. But had no one said anything about her short hair? The ugly boots? Obviously, there was nothing to do about the acne, but it seemed to Caroline that Bethany welcomed the disfigurement. In any case, the medicated unguents Caroline bought for her were stashed, unopened, under the kids' bathroom sink.

"Who do you think they'll pick?" Caroline asked.

"For another bishop or whatever?"

"Archbishop," Caroline corrected, but nodded hopefully.

Bethany shrugged and let her eyes drift back up to the television.

Caroline pleaded silently with Christopher for help. He shifted on the banquette, resisting the draw of the screen.

"Well, there's talk of a South American," he offered.

Caroline grimaced and was dismayed that at that moment Bethany looked at her, catching the uncharitable if involuntary reaction.

"That would be lovely!" she exclaimed and brought her napkin to her top lip, hoping to pass off her face's treachery as an itchy nose.

"There's also talk of another Pole."

"Well, that would be good, too."

Steven returned with their soup, depositing in front of them a bowl for Bethany, and a modest cup each for Caroline and Christopher.

"Enjoy."

He bent slightly at the waist and took two little steps backward—an elegant gesture but a risky one—before turning to tend to his other diners. Caroline dipped her chin to her chest and clasped her hands in her lap. Christopher and Bethany followed suit, and the incomplete family was silent. She nudged Christopher's foot with hers, wishing the head of the family didn't need reminders to lead.

"Blessed are you, Lord our God, maker of heaven and earth and Father of all your people," he intoned. "Bless this food and grant that all who eat it may be strong in body and grow in your love. We give thanks for blessing us eighteen years ago today with our wonderful Bethany. Blessed are you, Lord our God, forever and ever."

Caroline smiled, anchored once again. She surveyed the restaurant and spotted Lauren Chumley, with whom she sorted clothing donations once a month. Lauren, eating with her newlywed daughter, Lila, waved cheerfully.

Still no Jonathan. She dipped her spoon, scooping toward the far side of the cup.

"So," she said, pausing to let the soup cool, "I thought it would be fun to go shopping for dorm supplies. Sheets, a hot plate, a toaster, curtains. Did you get the suggested list yet?"

Bethany shook her head.

Please Lord, please let my daughter speak to me. Why won't my own flesh and blood utter a single word to her mother?

"I'm not going to Thomas Aquinas."

Caroline put her spoon on the saucer and adopted a politely confused smile.

"Of course you are," Christopher said, and blew across the top of his cup.

"I'm not." Bethany moved her jaw from side to side in a way that reminded Caroline of the adults who boarded the special bus on their corner each morning.

"Are you getting married?" Caroline asked, bewildered and hopeful.

Bethany guffawed and stared balefully at her mother.

"I'm going to New Paltz."

To Caroline's relief, Christopher guffawed right back.

"You're not going to New Paltz," he reassured all of them. "You have a full scholarship to Thomas Aquinas College, and that is where you'll be matriculating in the fall." He punctuated the declaration with a definitive slurp of soup.

"I have a partial scholarship to New Paltz."

Caroline swelled with an urge to smack her daughter, anything to stir that impassive, pimply face.

"Well, we're certainly not paying the rest." Christopher laughed, confident this information would extinguish his daughter's absurd conceit.

"You don't have to. I saved up the rest."

Caroline crossed herself, ignoring her daughter's fleeting sneer.

"We've never talked about SUNY New Paltz." Caroline kept her tone light. She was on a peak, blindfolded. One step forward, backward, sideways, and Bethany would be gone.

"I talked about it and you shot it down," Bethany said.

Caroline sat back on the banquette and dabbed delicately at her neck with the heavy paper napkin.

She recalled no such exchange. She would have remembered a discussion about that breeding ground of abominations across the river, funded by her own tax dollars. She occasionally included those deceived students in her prayers, knowing they could find salvation if they could escape the clutches of their infidel teachers.

"Bethie," she implored, looking back and forth between her daughter and her husband, who, for once, looked as flabbergasted as she felt. At least, Caroline thought, she and Christopher were in this one together.

"Hi, all," Jonathan said, managing to infuse the two meager syllables with sarcasm. He plopped down on the corner next to his father. Why? Why would he squeeze onto that side? Was she so repulsive to her children? She glanced across the room at Lauren, ashamed of her family's three-against-one seating arrangement.

"Jonathan, sit here," Caroline hissed sharply by way of greeting, touching the expanse of vinyl-covered bench beside her.

Her children exchanged glances.

"Happy birthday, Busy B," Jonathan drawled. He blew his sister a kiss, then made an exaggerated, sloppy show of pulling himself up and reinstalling next to his mother.

"You missed appetizers," Caroline said, knowing it was exactly the wrong thing to say.

"But you didn't miss the big news," Bethany told him.

"Bethie is having a little fun at our expense," Christopher told their son, inviting him to join the correct faction. "Says she's going to SUNY New Paltz instead of Thomas Aquinas.

I have one thing to say about that. Ha." Christopher laid his spoon beside his bowl.

"Cool," Jonathan said, reaching past his mother for an oval of bread.

"It is not cool!" Caroline cried out.

"It's also not the big news," Bethany said.

Caroline laid her head back against the banquette. "No?"

"No," Bethany told her with a baleful stare. She appeared to relish the slow torture she was inflicting on her parents. "The big news is that I'm gay."

There was a moment of silence and then Christopher smiled.

"Is that so?"

"This isn't a joke."

Steven appeared and inquired about the quality and progress of their soup course. Caroline and Christopher shooed him off with reassurances.

"Well," Caroline said carefully. "If it's not a joke, then we will find you conversion therapy immediately. I'm sure Father Flechette can help us." She was pleased by how calm she had kept her voice, how practical she was sounding in a crisis, despite her pounding heart.

Bethany raised her eyebrows and glanced at her brother. "Uh, yeah, no."

Even though she knew it would make her look weak, Caroline glanced at Christopher. He would know what to do. But Christopher was swallowing repeatedly, his Adam's apple bobbing away.

"Uh, yeah, yes," Christopher managed.

"You will not be allowed home unless you undergo conversion therapy!" Caroline blurted out. Christopher turned to her in surprise.

Being Bethany's parents had bewildered them daily, but nothing had prepared them for this. Caroline didn't believe her daughter really required conversion therapy, because she didn't believe Bethany was really gay. No one was *gay*, except maybe for a few perverted types on the edges of society, some people who had had terrible things happen to them as a child or college students wanting attention. It was a fad introduced by the liberal media, the current manifestation of the devil's work. What Bethany needed was prayer and salvation.

"Bethie, honey," Christopher pleaded. "You need to be saved."

Caroline exhaled.

"This is exactly what I expected," Bethany announced, appearing cheerful for the first time that evening. For the first time in years, if Caroline was honest. "That's why I waited until today to tell you. Eighteenth birthday and all, so…" She smirked at them. "I packed before dinner, just in case."

Caroline gasped. "You did not."

"Oh, I assure you, Mother. I did."

"Bethie, no!" Christopher tried again, and Caroline found herself unexpectedly disgusted by his weakness. *For God's sake, don't plead. Be a man.*

If Bethany thought she could shame Caroline and Christopher by confronting them with their predictability, she had another think coming. That her daughter knew she wouldn't be permitted to live at home only confirmed that Caroline had set an example by remaining steadfast in her own devotion to God. If it hadn't been for an unsettling feeling that Bethany was orchestrating this family schism, Caroline would have been completely secure in her righteousness.

After that awful night at the diner, Caroline and Christopher prayed constantly for Bethany's salvation. They knew what a thing of beauty it would be when Bethany accepted Jesus into her heart. Caroline often reminded herself that she missed her daughter terribly, that she was suffering as a mother, but she found she rose earlier in the mornings, noticed the house felt lighter and friendlier since the ever-present dread of an encounter with the sullen teenager had dissipated. She didn't know where Bethany had slept the night after she announced her ridiculous news, nor did she know where her daughter slept a single night after that.

Over the next eleven years, Caroline learned this: Bethany had attended high school graduation and graduated from SUNY New Paltz in four years with a bachelor's and a master's degree, though Caroline didn't know in what subjects. She knew nothing else about her daughter's whereabouts or whatabouts, as she called Bethany's evil proclivities, and neither did Christopher—or so she'd thought. She had never stopped searching a crowd for her, but she suspected she was as likely to avoid her daughter, should she spot her, as embrace her. She wondered whether she'd ever see her again. That would be God's decision.

For over a decade, husband and wife had agreed: the Lord's wishes were crystal clear. Christopher frequently claimed he was heartbroken and Caroline said, of course, so was she. Christopher often broached the topic of forgiveness, and Caroline wholeheartedly agreed that once Bethany returned to the fold, they would forgive her. Christopher would regard her silently, which she took as agreement. She never thought he would choose Bethany over her. Choose Bethany over God.

And then one day, he left a letter on her nightstand:

Dear Caroline (he'd never adopted an endearment for her),

I have prayed and prayed about this, and I don't think God meant for me to be away from our daughter any longer. A man has a responsibility to the fruits of his loins, and I have shirked mine long enough. I have forgiven Bethany (alarming to read her name; their daughter had been only "she" and "her" for many years), *but I know that you have not and that is OK. You are stronger.*

Yours in Christ (not love),
Christopher (not Chris)

FOUR

Caroline crossed herself and murmured "Amen" with the rest of the congregation. On this late spring day, the entire town was redolent with new grass, lilacs, and evaporating rain. Inside the Church of the Holy Sepulcher the wooden pews were warmed by sunshine flooding in through the high windows. A beat behind everyone else, she retook her seat, stealing glances at the familiar congregation.

Caroline wriggled her bottom and glanced around, passing it off as a neck stretch. She could count on two hands the number of times she'd sat by herself at church over the past three decades. Christopher had always been by her side, and she felt exposed, as though she'd left her coat at home on a chilly day.

Maureen Murphy caught Caroline's eye and tilted her head sympathetically. Well, that *was* kind of her. Maureen was president of the Sepulcher Sisterhood, and while she was certain the mother of five would never pass judgment on another, Caroline had been avoiding her and most of the other members. She was battling feelings of shame, which was plain silly. Christopher was the one who should be ashamed, abandoning their family, breaking their contract with God.

Today was the one-month-iversary of the day Christopher moved out. Thirty-four years of marriage, two beautiful children, and he had given up.

Caroline swallowed and quickly returned her attention to her Bible, knowing her suffering was all part of His glorious plan. But this, the Seventh Sunday of Easter was a low point, the hardest test He had ever given her. She took a breath and focused on Father Flechette. He had chosen a reading from Corinthians to begin.

We are afflicted in every way, but not constrained;
Perplexed, but not driven to despair;
Persecuted, but not abandoned;
Struck down, but not destroyed;
Always carrying about in the Body the dying of Jesus,
So that the life of Jesus may also be manifested in our body.

It was truly miraculous, Caroline marveled, how Father Flechette always, but *always* spoke about something that was relevant to her. It was proof of sacerdotalism. Caroline really liked that word, being that it was so specific. It was reassuring, grounding, evidence of the righteousness of Catholicism. Priests are essential—*essential*—mediators between God and man. The word wouldn't exist if it wasn't true.

Caroline ran her thumb over the Bible's cover—smooth leather, embossed with her initials, a gift from Christopher on their twenty-fifth anniversary, observed with a Marriage Intention at the church—letting Father Flechette's deep voice bathe her thoughts with today's sermon, entitled "You Can't Untie a Knot with Gloves On."

She was going to have to get a job, a paying job. She was not embarrassed about this. Not at all! She'd always been a strong woman, and she would take care of herself with the Lord guiding her every step of the way. She'd run a household for thirty-four years. She was certain that being a good employee wasn't a whole lot different: organizing, coordinating, people skills, adaptability when soccer was rained out or a snow day meant the St. Valentine's celebration was postponed and something had to be done with the four pounds of freshly sliced strawberries prepared for making a heart-themed snack. Even though she'd dropped out of the College of Saint Elizabeth to marry Christopher, Caroline could balance a budget with the best of them. When Christopher was asked to retire early from IBM and before he found work as the operations manager of Midland Overall Company—had his ego never recovered? Was that the problem?—she had stretched their dollars so that their kids had never wanted for any necessity.

> *May He give you the desire of your heart*
> *and make all your plans succeed. —Psalm 20:4*

Caroline pressed her lips together in quiet pleasure. She *would* find a job! She lifted her head in triumph and this time caught the eye of Dotty O'Donnell, who gave her a you've-got-this thumbs-up. A swell of warmth washed through her. She was so touched that these women—sisters!—had kept track of her struggle. It was perhaps a touch embarrassing, but she would follow up on their overtures. She'd always wanted to be closer to them, but shyness had won out. Now, God was telling Caroline it was time for her to put old insecurities to rest. When He closes a door, He opens a window. Christopher was gone, but she would open herself up to friendships in a way she never had before. Caroline gave Dotty a thumbs-up in return, feeling better than she had in weeks.

Where *was* Christopher anyway? Surely, he wouldn't stop attending church altogether. Would he attend a different one? Caroline flushed at the thought, realizing that she had hoped to see him today. That was a whole other boat of shame she hadn't even considered, that he would join a different congregation in order to avoid her. He wouldn't. He couldn't. Give up a church after thirty years? Of course, he'd given up their even longer marriage.

An hour later, with the rest of the congregants, Caroline concluded the final verses of "Here I Am, Lord." She rustled about, gathering up her purse, savoring the warm breeze wafting in from the open door when a sudden motion in the aisle made her brace for conversation.

Maureen reached her first, with Dotty on her heels.

"Caroline!"

Caroline recoiled from their energized sympathy. There was such a thing as support, to be sure, but there should also be solemnity with regard to a faltering marriage.

"I'm so sorry," gushed Maureen. She was petite, verging on gaunt, with a prominent brow. Her gaze was intense.

"Thank you," Caroline said stiffly. "I'll be fine."

"Will you? We are here for you, you know," said Dotty, who stood too close, always did. "This must be so hard on you."

Caroline nodded, feeling exposed.

"Are you tempted to see Bethany now? Because I don't know that that's wise," Maureen advised, narrowing her eyes to broadcast deep concern.

"Bethany?" Caroline weighed this tactic. Christopher had left her because of their disagreement over Bethany, and she'd figured that father and daughter were back in touch. She certainly didn't think seeing her estranged daughter was her next move.

"I would definitely be tempted," Dotty said seriously. "God will forgive your temptation, but he will reward you for resisting. And he won't reward Christopher for caving."

"You're a strong woman," Maureen added so automatically that Caroline doubted the woman's sincerity.

"I can still resist seeing Bethany," Caroline said, hoping it sounded like a sacrifice, when in fact, it had been a sinful relief to break off contact with her own flesh and blood over a decade earlier.

"Well, of course, but the baby? You're a grandmother now—assuming it's Bethany's and not, you know, the other one's."

Caroline briefly saw spots.

"The other one's," she repeated dumbly. Baby. Grandmother. She grasped the back of a pew and pursed her lips to exhale.

"It's the other one's?" Maureen exclaimed, her mask of concern slipping for a moment to reveal prurient interest.

"No, no, I mean…" What could she possibly mean? "I mean I don't know," Caroline nearly whispered.

"Really?" Maureen looked shocked, then quickly recast her expression as awe. "That's so strong of you to—to, you know, stay so far from it."

"I don't know if I could do it," said Dotty mournfully, unhelpfully.

"How did you hear?" Caroline was careful to sound neutral.

Maureen and Dotty exchanged a glance.

"Caroline, it's on Facebook. Everyone knows."

FIVE

"People like us don't *divorce*," Sylvia's friend Ruth scolded the day after Ethan's bombshell.

Ruth Takeshiro had yet to encounter an occasion on which to lower her voice. The crammed-together tables of B&H Dairy, the minuscule lunch counter in the East Village, proved no exception. The customer two feet away glanced over her shoulder. Sylvia flashed an apologetic smile, but there was no avoiding the broadcast play-by-play of her imploding life.

"So, what, you're kicking me out of your marriage club?" Sylvia shot back. "Fine, Ellie and I won't let you into our One Dead Parent club." She ripped a piece of challah, limp under its burden of butter.

"We have weekly meetings," Ellie Pruitt confirmed through a mouthful of borscht.

"I'm *serious*," Ruth insisted.

"No, you're not," Ellie defended Sylvia. "You're ridiculous."

"*No.* People like us—products of married parents, educated, late to marry—we go to therapy. We struggle. You do a Hillary."

"Hey," Sylvia urged quietly, hoping to lower the volume on the conversation. "I'm sorry I'm disappointing my demographic. If he'd given me any kind of option whatsoever, don't you think I'd be on a couch right now? I would consider forgiveness as a possibility—someday, after I'd strangled him—but it turns out there's nothing you can do when one of you just wants out. We've always told the kids that this family is *not* a democracy, but apparently even I don't have a vote."

The customer at the next table shifted, clearly listening even though all Sylvia could see was a headful of spiky hair with pale pink tips, and a cross tattooed at the nape of her neck.

In retrospect, Sylvia was mortified by her and Ethan's marital arrogance. The afternoon Leah came home from PS 87 in a bewildered panic, having lately been introduced to the concept of divorce by a classmate, Sylvia had conspiratorially promised her that it could never happen to their family. Not *would* never. *Could* never.

To Sylvia's mind, there were three components of this insurance policy, only one of which was the fact that she and Ethan were in love and in trust. That was first and foremost, certainly, but bolstering that bond was the power of inertia. The amount of paperwork and friend realignment and offspring reaction and real estate adjustments and narrative redirection were all things neither of them had the energy for. And finally, the ultimate underwriter of their policy was the powerful force of overly involved in-laws, fully cross-pollinated in their loyalties. In the unlikely event of even a shadow of a threat to the marriage, Sylvia figured that the thought of his mother's fury would stop him in his tracks.

Sitting in B&H with their droopy bread and heavily dilled soups, she could already see how the hue of her connection to friends would change because of the split from Ethan.

"So she adds *divorced* to her adjectives," Ellie said to Ruth. "She's still award-winning director, fabulous mother—"

"Ha," Sylvia cut her off.

"Whatever. Adequate, food-providing mother. Excellent friend. Devoted daughter and sister."

Sylvia pushed back her chair, needing space between herself and Ruth's intensity.

"You're not even fighting for him!" Ruth burst out.

"Ruth, stop. Don't put this on Sylvia!" The tips of Ellie's ears were bright red with indignation, and Sylvia was grateful to her, but deflated.

"I'm sorry. I know this affects all of you," Sylvia told Ruth with a generosity she didn't feel. "But I don't fight unwinnable wars."

"Bullshit." Ruth balled up her napkin and threw it at Sylvia. "How the hell do you know a war is unwinnable until you've tried fighting it? You fought like hell for your sister, right?"

"And lost!" Sylvia protested. "She lives in *Oregon*, for Christ's sake." The departure of her beloved Maddie from New York a year earlier had been like a first divorce.

"I realize that," Ruth said, irritated. "The point is that you did everything you could to persuade her to come back before giving up."

"I'm never giving up on her," Sylvia said automatically.

"Exactly!" Ruth pounded on the table with her small fist, then raised her palms as if to ask whether anyone at the table besides her was in her right mind. The tattooed, pink-tipped woman turned surreptitiously to glance at them again.

Sylvia leaned back and undid her hair from its clamshell

clip, then put it up again. She regarded the collection of ancient signs hanging over the grill—Rice Pudding 10¢ and 2 Hot Dogs 25¢ Every Tuesday—and was momentarily comforted by the knowledge that the world plodded along and didn't care about her problems.

"Do you think Ethan was jealous of how much I miss Maddie?" she asked, surprising herself. She wasn't certain the thought had ever crossed her mind.

When an immediate dismissal of this suggestion was not forthcoming, she looked at her friends, who were having a silent conversation with each other.

"Seriously?" Sylvia said. "Come on. Come *on*. My marriage wasn't that vulnerable. Was it?"

"I don't think your marriage was that vulnerable," Ellie ventured. "Well, I don't know for sure, honestly, but I do think your attachment to your sister was—is—that strong."

"Oh God." Sylvia put her head in her hands, and when her hands couldn't hold the weight of this new possibility—that she had failed to balance her attention between her husband and her sister—she crossed her arms on the table and laid her head between them.

Sylvia owed her life to Maddie. Literally. Maddie was an easy, calm child and so attracted to the babies in the playground that their parents, who'd been planning to stop at one, couldn't help but give their sweet girl a real, live dolly. What a rude surprise Sylvia was, prone to tantrums in her early years, and then to posturing in adolescence. It was as if it took three parents to deal with her, taking turns handling the phases. Her father fanned her love of theater, but wouldn't tolerate her superficial assumptions of moral rectitude: Sylvia's harangues about recycling, energy conservation, animal cruelty, and a brief flirtation with veganism ("Vegetarian, okay, but vegan? Vegan is an eating disorder!"). Although he made a living as a green builder, her formative grasping was to him an irritating experiment in grandstanding.

Sylvia's mother was more forgiving of these trial personalities, but couldn't stand the subpar choices of boyfriends—they scared her to her core, made her feel that her second-born lacked the most important kind of judgment. So when Ethan and Sylvia announced their engagement at the beyond-hope age of thirty-five, her brow furrowed less often. Ethan was steady, easygoing, successful, in the same field as Sylvia's father, and taller than Sylvia. Sylvia's mother, feminist laurels be damned, was discomfited by shorter men.

With Maddie, Sylvia was only and simply loved. She was weirdly like a grandparent in her unwavering, uncomplicated, nonjudgmental love for her little sister. From an early age, Maddie was enamored of photography, and as long as she had her Canon F-1 slung around her neck like a talisman, she was immune to whatever tensions were flaring up among the rest of the family. When a tempest had run its course, Maddie would emerge and suggest to Sylvia that they ride their bikes around Washington Square Park, where they were frequently escorted past turf skirmishes by a considerate drug dealer.

So when, one day four years after she graduated from Cooper Union, Maddie returned their parents' car from a Fairway run and left it parked too close to a fire hydrant, and discovered it had been towed and went to the pound on the West Side Highway to retrieve it and met Jason, who was also there to reclaim his car, Sylvia was blindsided. Maddie and Jason, after safely stowing their cars in a nearby garage, headed a few blocks south to watch helicopters whirl away from the Thirtieth Street landing pad. Then they strolled north along the river. They talked, they walked in silence, they talked again, and walked so long that they found themselves back at Fairway on 125th Street. They were married four months later, and Sylvia was abruptly no longer her sister's number one.

Was this really the root of her failed marriage?

"Can I blame Maddie for being such an abnormal sister and thus fucking up all my understandings and expectations of future relationships?" she asked her friends.

"Sure," said Ruth, a fan of tidy explanations.

"Uh, no," corrected Ellie. "Your marriage was fine until Ethan fucked it up."

"Isn't the party line that it takes two to tango?"

"Name one thing you did wrong. Does Ethan even think you did anything wrong?"

He didn't, but Sylvia wasn't so sure. Of all the many worsts, one of the worst casualties of their split was the fraught rereading of the previous decade. Should she have worked less? Worked more? Cooked more? Laughed more? Listened harder? Dressed better? If she had stopped in at his office with dinner when he was en charrette, would he have had no opportunity to fall in love with lusty Lisette? If she'd changed her last name, would they have worked out? Sylvia had stumbled upon a new form of exquisite torture. Divorce was a black light on a marriage—every previously invisible flaw suddenly shone bright.

"Have you prayed about it?" their next-table neighbor

asked. She turned fully in her seat to face the trio, and while she appeared to be sneering, the expression was more likely the unfortunate result of a nose whose tip extended well beyond its nostrils.

"Uh-oh," Ellie said quietly.

"Excuse me?" Ruth said, umbrage already in her voice.

Sylvia put her hand over Ruth's, though her own blood pressure had already perked up.

"Jesus has all the answers."

"Quick, ask him what nineteen times three thousand fifty-six is," Ellie said.

"Jesus is dead," Sylvia said.

The interloper smiled knowingly. "Jesus died for your sins and was resurrected. Marriage between a man and woman is sacred, and everything in the world should be done to preserve it. I advise all having trouble to start by praying."

"You do know you're in the East Village, right?" said Ruth.

"I sure do," said the punk preacher, unfazed. She extended her hand and flashed a big smile, which did little to alleviate the auto-sneer effect. "My name is Faith Christian and I'm running for city council."

"I thought you looked familiar," Ellie said doubtfully. "You were a country singer?"

"I surely was."

"And now you tell teenage girls not to get abortions."

"Oh, Christ," Sylvia said, slumping in her seat. This? Right now? Perhaps there was, in fact, a god and she had angered it.

"That's but one of the many things I do to make the world a better place," Faith said, besting them merely by keeping her cool. "I am also a proponent of healthier food in our children's schools, government support for drug user rehabilitation, and after-school activities for teenagers."

"I'm sure kale salads and basketball club will stop teen pregnancy," Sylvia said.

"It's a start," said Faith.

"Oh, definitely a start," Sylvia said. "Very admirable. I just wonder how many of those teenagers' babies you've adopted. Or whether you're underwriting all the babysitting so the young mothers can continue school." Once again, Sylvia unclipped her hair, raked her hands over her head, and reclipped it.

Faith smiled knowingly, the smile of the willfully ignorant and irredeemably certain. "God does not want those babies to die."

"You do know," Sylvia said, "that God is the biggest abortionist of all?"

Sylvia succeeded in startling Faith.

"What do you think a miscarriage is?" Sylvia demanded. "It's a natural abortion. One in three conceptions miscarry because"—she used air quotes here—"God decides it's not meant to be. Throw in stillbirths and the great spaghetti monster's rate rises even higher. But then, I'm sure you don't take antibiotics or anything, because it's God's will that you get a tooth infection or a UTI. I mean, you just accept it and suffer, right? Or, actually, is it Jesus's will? Remind me," Sylvia said, feeling a trickle of sweat wind its way between her shoulder blades, "what *is* the difference between Jesus and God? I mean, I know there's the whole father/son thing, I get that, but why should someone accept Jesus if they're already praying to God? Is it a package deal kind of thing?"

Faith made a big show of stoically collecting herself. She

inhaled, drawing up her shoulders and settling them back down. When she looked as though she might be ready to venture a reply, Ruth said, "Consider this a dry run for meeting your constituents."

Faith Christian stood up, gathered a ratty knapsack from the chair beside her, and squeezed past them. She dropped some money on the counter and left, the bell on the door jangling in her wake.

Sylvia felt faint, the way she always did post-adrenaline rush, and she cursed herself for not being made of tougher stuff. Her pulse felt as though it would burst out of her neck, and tunnel vision was setting in. She turned sideways in her chair, and dropped her head between her knees. Ellie rubbed her back.

"I'm sorry, Syl."

Sylvia just shook her head, but that only made her feel dizzier.

"Miss?"

She opened one eye and found the busboy crouching in front of her, offering a wet cloth.

"You don't look good." He mimed putting the cloth across his eyes and then handed it to Sylvia. It was the perfect offering until she noticed the gold cross hanging around his neck.

"Oh," she said, feeling the adrenaline start to kick in again. "I'm sorry…I hope I didn't…I didn't mean…" What did she mean? It was fine for him to wear a cross, but not Faith Christian?

Well, yeah, in that it was fine for him or anyone to wear it as long as they didn't proselytize. Sylvia accepted the cool cloth and leaned back to drape it over her face.

"Please," she heard him say, "Christian lady don't leave no tip."

SIX

Meg turned the wrong way up a one-way street, making a garbage truck swerve and take out the side mirror of a parked car. A cascade of tenor honking and yelling erupted from the truck as she turned at the next corner. She was trying to figure out how to get back on the highway and dial AnneMarie all at the same time, but the phone kept slipping from her sweaty hand. The air conditioner was broken—it had never worked—and the oven-hot wind blew through the open windows.

She found the entrance ramp, cut off a jeep, and raced on, not bothering to check the lane she was joining. She pressed hard on the gas pedal, the wind now roaring in, and her mother finally answered her phone.

"Meg? I'm sorry I'm not home, sweetie! My car was stolen! Meggie, where are you? What's all that noise?"

"I have your car, Mom."

"What! Meg, where are you?"

"I'm in Endicott."

Nothing.

"Did you hear me? I'm in Endicott. Ever been there?"

"You're *driving*? Meg! Pull over right now. Right now! I'm coming to get you."

"How? How are you going to get me if I have your car?"

"Meg! Stop driving this second!"

"Don't you want to know what I was doing there?"

"Meg!"

"It sure didn't look like a fucking convent, Mom!"

The jeep Meg had cut off was on her tail now, flashing its brights and honking. She used her steering hand to flip it off, which made her swerve, which made the car back off.

"What? Meg? You're scaring me! Please pull over!"

Meg pressed harder on the gas, and a plug of satisfaction settled into her chest.

"I was born at Our Lady of the Facelift? In a fucking bathroom? You squatted in a fucking bathroom and then told me I was adopted? What the fuck, Mom? And where's all the money? Where's the money? I want it!"

Meg banged the steering wheel, glaring bullets out the front window at nothing, sweat in every crevice. She passed every car, swerving between lanes to get ahead so she could go faster, faster. She wanted to drive to oblivion, drive until Gemma and Troy and Baxter and her shit-brown house and her pathetic, drunk mother vanished, wanted to drive until she wasn't ugly, until her father came home and said he missed her and that he was sorry.

"Meg, pull the fuck over and I will answer all of your questions!"

AnneMarie never cursed, not ever. Meg yanked the wheel to one side and ground to a halt on the shoulder. Horns wailed and faded.

"Meg?"

"I'm stopped."

Both mother and daughter were breathing hard.

"You *are* adopted. That's not a lie. You were the most wanted baby in the world, and God meant for you to come to me and your dad. Do you understand that, Meggie? Do you? It's very important that you understand that, because that's the only thing that matters here. The rest of it is just details."

Meg put her mother on speakerphone and balanced the phone on one mottled, pasty thigh. She leaned back and crossed her arms.

"Details," Meg repeated, but her mother thought it was a demand.

"I'm telling you, I'm telling you. Just. Let me just catch my breath. You scared the heck out of me." She exhaled loudly through her mouth, and it sounded to Meg like she was deciding what to say. "Where exactly are you right now?"

She was fishing! She was still going to evade.

"I'm exactly about to pull back onto the highway if you don't tell me every last fucking detail."

"Stop cursing, Meggie," AnneMarie said sharply. "Okay. I used to clean houses, to pay for the dental admin course. I worked for a couple of families in Endicott, and one of them was the Priskers."

She paused, waiting to see whether she could have gotten away with keeping that bit to herself.

"Yeah. I just had the pleasure of meeting old Jane," Meg told her.

AnneMarie exhaled again. This time it was wobbly.

"Right. Jane. Okay, so. Jane had a daughter, a teenager, I forget her name."

"No you didn't."

"Right. The daughter was Alexa—"

"That's a fucking soap opera name."

"I swear to the Good Lord, Meg, if you don't stop with that mouth…"

"I'll just keep driving."

"The daughter was Alexa," AnneMarie continued quickly. "She was fifteen. She was very, very heavyset. I only met her a few times. She was usually at school, so I didn't know much about her, but, Lord help her, she got pregnant. I don't even think she knew she was pregnant."

"What! That's such bull— Such crap."

"No," AnneMarie said sharply, on firm ground now that she was telling the truth. "No, it's not. It happens all the time, these big girls, no one can see it, they're in denial or don't know how babies get made, or I don't know, because no one in the family talks, not like you and me."

Oh God, the fiction this woman lived in. Meg almost felt sorry for her, but she'd been in training for years not to.

"Alexa was fifteen, and one day she was home sick from school with terrible stomach cramps. Groaning away in the bathroom. I was cleaning the kitchen, but I could hear her. I remember thinking it sounded much worse than a stomachache, so I went partway up the stairs to see whether I could help. Mrs. Prisker was outside the door, with the phone, about to call an ambulance. And, then, well, you know."

Meg sat straight up in disbelief. "I know? I *know*? I know absolutely nothing."

Except she did know. Of course she knew.

AnneMarie had flown down the stairs, grabbed a paper clip from the writing nook in the kitchen, unfurled it, and hurried back. She pushed past Jane Prisker and popped the lock on the bathroom door. She pushed it open to find Alexa in the fetal position on the marble-tiled floor. Attached to her by a bloody rope was a howling, full-term, muck-covered baby lying atop a pile of Wamsutta gray bath towels. In an attempt to ameliorate the situation, Alexa had pulled used linens out of the hamper, rather than sully the ones hanging on the rack.

Jane promptly collapsed into AnneMarie's arms. Why are rich people so much more faint of heart than poor people? Does it depend on how they became rich? Like, maybe the ones who inherit it or who marry it are weak, but the ones who've had to work for it are tougher. And maybe Meg's mom was strong in that moment either because someone had to be or because she was poor and simply couldn't afford to pass out.

Jane came to after a few seconds, rage apparently propelling her to consciousness. She began to bellow at her daughter, even as the girl and the infant—*the infant*—were both howling. Not an ounce of sympathy, AnneMarie recalled. Not a hint of awe at the miracle that had just taken place. She had placed a hand tentatively on Jane's arm, hoping to help her see, like really *see*, but Jane recoiled from AnneMarie's touch as though it were as loathsome as the scene before her.

"Meggie," AnneMarie's voice drifted up from the phone on Meg's lap, "it was like the whole world was bathed in light. I knew. I knew you were mine."

For a moment, there on the side of the road, Meg almost bought her version. AnneMarie didn't lie. She may have spun things her own way, but that didn't mean she was lying. Meg knew she believed what she was saying.

"Why couldn't you just tell me that? Why couldn't you tell me the truth? It's not so different from a teenage girl in a convent."

"It's not, right?" she said in a rush of relief Meg didn't yet feel she deserved.

"So why?" A spotted fawn emerged from the woods, its nose in the grass, and Meg honked. It looked around, uncomprehending, then resumed grazing.

"It…she…you have to understand. You saw her, saw where they live…Mrs. Prisker?"

"Don't call her that. You're not her servant!"

"Okay, okay. Jane. Jane and that family, their daughter having a baby was just not something they could handle. But we could. Your dad and I wanted you."

"But why couldn't you tell me?" Meg pressed.

AnneMarie hesitated.

"Mrs. Pris—she made me promise not to. That's all, honey. She just didn't want anyone to know, and you can understand, right? You can understand I had to keep a promise, right? And we wanted you so badly, it was all just so perfect."

"Daddy didn't want me," Meg reminded her.

"That's not true, Meggie, not true at all."

Meg closed her eyes against the lie.

"We've been over this. Men leave. It's what they do. It had nothing do with you."

The fawn stood right at the edge of the highway, oblivious to cars that were swerving away from it.

"I can't remember him."

"Meg, please tell me where you are so I can come get you. You're lucky you haven't been arrested."

Meg bashed the horn again with her palm. This time the deer didn't even look up. It was acclimating to danger and noise right before her eyes. Why was it alone?

"Mom, what was the deal you made with Jane?"

"Deal?"

"She said she paid you to go away."

"That's crazy," she said quickly. "Of course she didn't pay me to take you."

"So you took me, and she gave you seventy-five thousand dollars, but the two aren't connected."

"Meggie," she said after a pause. "It's very expensive to raise a baby. She knew I wouldn't be working for her anymore, that diapers and formula cost, that—"

"So you spent it all on diapers?"

"What? Yes, diapers. And formula. And clothes. Toys. Food."

"All that cost seventy-five thousand? There was nothing left over?"

"Yes! You'll see when you're an adult. Life is expensive."

"But…"

"Honey, let me come get you."

Meg laid the phone on the passenger side and reclined her seat. She breathed deeply, calmly. She felt like she could fall asleep.

"I don't believe you."

"Well," AnneMarie said hesitantly, "you don't have to believe me. It doesn't change the fact that it's true."

"You know what I think is true?" Meg closed her eyes.

"I think Daddy got a look at that check and took off with the money. Ditch the screaming baby, take the money. Who can blame him? I would've done it, too."

AnneMarie said nothing.

"Did he leave you anything, Mom? Like even beer money?"

"Honey. Please tell me where you are."

"Let's make a deal. I'll tell you where I am after you tell me that Daddy took that money."

"Never mind, Meg. I'm coming to find you."

"In what car?"

"Meg, *please*."

"Jane knew Daddy took the money. How did she know?"

"Meg, stop this!"

"You went back and asked for more, didn't you?"

In the silence that followed, Meg reached over and ended the call. Then she ratcheted up her seat and looked around, clear-headed, peaceful. The deer retreated into the woods. Traffic hummed past.

Meg put the car in drive, checked her rearview mirrors, signaled, and pulled on. She slowly depressed the gas pedal, picking up speed. Thirty, forty, fifty, sixty, seventy. Eighty. Eighty-five, and the car began to shake. She merged into the left lane, speeding along inches from the cement median.

She pressed the gas pedal all the way to the floor of the car and then swung the wheel to the left.

SEVEN

Caroline fidgeted with her Timex, happening to glance at it while she did, but telling herself she wasn't. Her wrist was itchy, that was all.

Caroline was fourteen years old in October of 1973, and she was restless. She fingered the purple flyer peeking out of her Bible, listing the church's activities for the month. Teen group was once a week, and the day had finally come around again. Caroline fervently hoped no one new would join. They were just the right size. Three girls and four boys.

Ten more minutes.

People rustled around her, and she quickly stood to sing the last hymn before Father Garvey's closing remarks. Was it a sin that, although Caroline really did enjoy and take comfort in the hymns Father Garvey chose, she found them less exciting than Father Gilhool's?

Be still my soul, the Lord is on thy side
Bear patiently the cross of grief or pain
Leave to thy God to order and provide
In every change He faithful will remain

See? She chastised herself. Very comforting, very important. Father Garvey's sermon this week had been titled "Faith in God Makes Molehills Out of Mountains." Caroline had gotten the gist after the first couple of minutes. Predictably, he had launched into one of his favorite harangues: the Willis Tower in Chicago. He thought it showed hubris that it had topped out to become the tallest building in the world. Caroline thought it was kind of groovy, but figured he knew better.

And don't worry—whatever is going to come
Just tell God every detail
And the peace of God that no one
Understands will come to you
No, don't worry
Just tell Him every detail and His peace will come to you

Everyone sat. Caroline thunked down in her pew a little sloppily, and Mother's elbows tightened to her sides in disapproval. Father Garvey also managed to work in something about a sacrilegious decision by the Supreme Court earlier in the year that made all nine judges murderers. It seemed to Caroline that he needed to take his own advice about mountains and molehills, but maybe she just didn't understand. Father Garvey had soft jowls and red-rimmed eyes, so you didn't want to spend too much time looking at him. Which meant you mostly listened, but he spoke in a hypnotic rise and fall that made it hard to focus on the actual words.

Not so with Father Gilhool. Just thinking his name sent

an electric shock to right below Caroline's belly button. She thought his name again. Yep, there was that shock again. It was hard to get it to go a third time, but after a few minutes, she'd be able to surprise herself and get that feeling. She leaned forward slightly in her seat to catch a glimpse of him, but her view was blocked by a pillar.

Father Gilhool had feathered hair and perfect skin and energy, so much energy. God's love emanated out of all his perfect pores. He was the one who had started the teen church group, and he was the one who decided there was no reason why the group couldn't be trained to do the work of Jesus: Caroline and her peers would be the first teenagers in Dutchess County to be certified in CPR and First Aid. They would actually save lives. Father Gilhool was the face of modern Catholicism, that's what Mother said. Daddy only grunted, but Daddy's participation in conversations these days was limited to two subjects: the latest bombings by the IRA and Riggs's plan to go up against that faggot Billie Jean King.

Finally, *finally*, Father Garvey said, "Lord Jesus Christ, you said to your apostles: 'I leave you peace, my peace I give you.' Look not on our sins, but on the faith of your church, and grant us the peace and unity of your kingdom where you live forever and ever."

And the congregation said, "Amen."

Caroline bounced her foot up and down, and her mother stilled her with a hand on her knee.

"Caroline," she reprimanded softly.

And Father Garvey said, "Thanks be to God. May almighty God bless you, the Father, and the Son, and the Holy Spirit."

And they said, "Amen."

Caroline blew out her breath as quietly as she could.

And he said, "The Mass is ended, go in peace to love and serve the Lord."

And the congregation said, "Thanks be to God!"

And then it was time to go be with Father Gilhool.

Caroline hurried along the aisle to the side exit, smiling at knowing parishioners who were pleased with themselves when they saw teenagers in the congregation being good Christians.

Down in the activities room, overheated because of its shared wall with the boiler room, chubby Jenna Lou was already tearing open packages and laying Hydrox cookies on a plastic platter. Caroline raked her fingers through her hair, fluffing it as best she could. First in her list of prayers each night was a plea for thicker Farrah Fawcett hair. She'd worn her favorite outfit, a collared yellow satin blouse tucked into a brown plaid wool skirt. She'd fought hard to get Mother to agree to satin; only after she'd consulted Father Garvey and gotten his assurances that it wasn't an invitation to sensuality, whatever that meant, did she let her daughter buy it. Caroline would have to make sure to steer clear of Jenna Lou's chocolate-licked fingers.

Father Gilhool hustled in, and Caroline's breath caught. He'd taken off his robe, and was wearing dungarees and a T-shirt that said Anti-Nam, Ma'am. Caroline wasn't allowed to go to the movies, but she'd seen posters for *The Sting*, and it was hard not to notice the resemblance to Robert Redford, especially in the lips.

Father Gilhool's face lit up when he saw them, and Caroline felt herself rise to a whole new level of wakefulness, one that her fourteen-year-old self rarely attained. Behind him was dopey, gawky Michael Riordan, who was gangly and mostly silent, and his sister Kathleen, who made up for his silence. Caroline braced herself for the onslaught of the rest of the group, but no one else came.

"Ladies!" he boomed to Caroline and Jenna Lou, and his voice was like something you could drink. "We've got a smaller group today. The other Mikes and Edward are in the basketball tournament. Louise has a 4-H meeting. Just us chickens."

Caroline's heart sank. That meant (this) Michael and Kathleen would be paired up, and she'd be put with Jenna Lou. When there was an odd number, someone got to pair up with Father Gilhool for First Aid activities, and it hadn't yet been Caroline.

"With so many missing, I'm thinking we should hold off on training, do something else. On the other hand, you guys showed up, and so if you want to continue, I think that's fair. What do you think?"

They were scheduled to practice wrapping tourniquets on each other, so Caroline was ready to vote for holding off on the chance that at the next meeting they'd have an odd number. She wondered if Jenna Lou had been doing similar calculations, because she said, with an edge of disappointment to her voice, "Yeah, let's just wait for them."

"Hang on, you know what?" Father Gilhool continued, either ignoring her or not hearing her. "Let's get started on CPR! It takes a lot of practice hours, and you guys can help teach the others next time."

He unlocked the supply cabinet with a key he retrieved from above the doorjamb and looked over his shoulder to wink at them. Just like that, they were trusted allies.

Father Gilhool pulled out a nearly life-size female doll with yellow-red hair, permanently closed eyes, and thin, almost nonexistent lips. The semblance of a mouth opening was about the creepiest thing Caroline had ever seen.

"Guys, say hi to Annie."

Without thinking, the group did as they were told, and dutifully intoned "Hi, Annie," then laughed nervously at themselves.

"The story is that one of the doctors who created her had a daughter named Annie who drowned," Father Gilhool told them. "And that he created this doll for training so no one would ever feel as helpless as he did. It's unclear how much is true, but the face itself is modeled after a girl who drowned in the Seine in Paris. That part I think is true. Either way, you all are going to learn how to save someone's life who has collapsed from a heart attack or for some reason has stopped breathing! Cool, right?"

"Excuse me, Father Gilhool?" Kathleen raised her hand. "You didn't yet assign us the reading on this, so we're not going to know what to do."

"Absolutely accurate." He beamed as if she'd said something wonderful. "You're going to go home and read it after today. But I teach by doing, so that your muscles and reflexes and tendons and nerves all learn what to do, and then the reading will cement what you've learned with your bodies."

"Okay," Kathleen said doubtfully. "It's just that I learn a lot better by—"

"Kath," Father Gilhool interrupted. "This isn't school. This is fun. It's a risk-free place to learn a new way, right?"

Caroline nodded vigorously as if it were her he was trying to persuade.

"So," he continued as Kathleen opened her mouth to answer. "Let's talk about clearing airways first."

"Shouldn't we pray first?" Kathleen still managed to say.

Caroline thought a flash of impatience crossed Father Gilhool's face.

"Absolutely. No, better, let's sing! Let's sing as loud as we can to bring Jesus into the room with us, to have him guide us as we learn how to save his flock. Yes?"

"Yes!" the teenagers cheered. And so he led them in "The Joining of Jesus and Me," Caroline's all-time favorite hymn, sung, more or less, to the tune of "Aquarius":

When the world is too much for me
And abandonment is all around
Then Jesus will come to me
And we will become one flesh

This is the joining of the Lord and me
The Lord and me!
This is the joining of the Lord and me
Our flesh and blood are one!

Acceptance and understanding
Care and protection
Love and acceptance
Jesus takes me as I am!
Come to me, Jesus, and I will come to you!

Caroline was breathing hard by the time they finished, having belted the last line without any self-consciousness. She felt as if she'd been dancing or running or…singing!

"Far *out*!" Father Gilhool looked around proudly. "That was a great suggestion, Kathleen. Okay, are we ready to learn how to save a life?"

"Yes!" they shouted.

Father Gilhool knelt on the rug and showed them how to shake the doll and say, "Annie, Annie, are you okay?" It took a while to progress past giggling. He cradled her neck in one hand and gently tilted her head so she could breathe around an obstruction. Then he demonstrated how to pinch her nose and breathe into her mouth. Caroline realized she was holding her own breath when he lowered his mouth to Annie's, not believing he would really touch his lips to the doll's lips. She glanced around and quickly exhaled when she saw her own dumbfoundedness grotesquely reflected: Michael was bug-eyed and even more red-faced than usual, Kathleen was working her chapped, flaking lips between her teeth so that it looked like she might bite a piece off, and Jenna Lou was simply gaping.

Caroline reined in her senses, remembering that she was not watching something dirty. Quite the opposite.

"Okay, who wants to try first?"

There were no takers.

"Come on, guys, you all have to go. What are you afraid of?"

To everyone's surprise, most of all her own, Caroline's hand shot up.

"Caroline, great!" Father Gilhool patted a spot on the rug

beside him, and she knelt down, close enough that his bare arm brushed her sleeved one. His heat passed through the satin to her skin. "Okay, remember what to do?"

Caroline looked down at Annie. The doll was creepily passive, and Caroline had an urge to jam her elbows into the soft, rubbery flesh, to do something to make Annie stop staring mutely. Quickly, Caroline lowered her face to the doll's, intent on covering its disgusting, inviting mouth with her own, when Father Gilhool grabbed her arm.

"Whoa! Whoa! You're skipping a few steps!" He laughed as Caroline jerked up, her face prickling with heat. The others tittered. "Remember, what's the first step?"

Caroline drew a blank, and Father Gilhool looked bemused.

"Annie, Annie…?" he prodded.

"Oh yeah," Caroline said, unable to look at anyone besides the doll. Her disgust for the doll increased now that it was the cause of her embarrassment. She took hold of Annie's shoulders and shook. The head thudded heavily backward against the floor.

"A little more gently," Father Gilhool suggested.

Caroline shook Annie again, alarmed at how the whole body shifted.

"Annie?" she queried halfheartedly.

"A little louder."

"Annie, Annie!" she said.

"Good, keep going."

"Annie, can you breathe?" Caroline asked. "Annie?" She waited a beat, suddenly remembering her part in this play. "Call 911!" She tilted the head back—gently this time—and peered into the mouth to inspect whether there was anything obstructing the airway. Finding nothing, she remembered to swipe two fingers through the soft mouth. "Nothing in there," she said firmly. Finally, Caroline pinched the nose and bent her head over once again, feeling all eyes on her.

"Oh, wait!" Father Gilhool said, and Caroline was certain the despair she felt showed on her face. What had she done wrong now? But Father Gilhool grabbed a paper towel and Windex from the cookie table. "I forgot to wipe down her mouth," he said sheepishly. "Can't aid and abet germs!"

He removed whatever trace of him was on Annie, and Caroline felt a swell of disappointment.

"Okay," he said. "Continue. You're on a roll! Sorry about that."

Caroline didn't want to continue, but knew she had to finish. Again, she pinched Annie's nose and put her mouth over the doll's and suddenly experienced the same sensation near her belly that she had whenever she thought or heard Father Gilhool's name. Caroline perked up: that was the familiar feeling of Jesus coming into her body. Suddenly, the connection between Jesus's work and their own right there in the basement was clear. She relaxed, all the hostility toward Annie evaporated.

Caroline breathed into her mouth, and the doll's chest rose and fell.

"Good, good!" Father Gilhool said.

He made Caroline run through it one more time, then wiped down Annie's mouth and asked who was next. This time, everyone raised their hands.

After they'd each taken a turn, Father Gilhool checked his watch and concluded that they had plenty of time to begin learning how to do chest compressions. He demonstrated with Annie, tracing the arches of her rib cage with his fingertips to locate her sternum, then placing the heel of one palm two fingers' width beyond the base of the sternum. He rose up high on his knees, put his other palm over the first one, and pumped in quick, violent motions. He encouraged the four teenagers to feel their own rib cages, then instructed them to pair off and find the proper position on their partner.

Caroline and Jenna Lou glanced at each other nervously. They'd known each other since before they were born, as Caroline's mother liked to say, but had never had a whole lot of use for each other. Jenna Lou didn't have any friends, and Caroline was afraid that would rub off on her.

"Here," Jenna Lou said, and lay down in front of Caroline, her thin curls fanning out to frame her splotchy face. She tugged on her own plaid skirt, which caused her blouse to spring from the tether of the waistband. A roll of pale flesh surfaced, and she didn't notice.

"Um," Caroline said.

"What?"

Caroline pointed at Jenna Lou's midsection. "Would you...?"

Jenna Lou peered over her chest—it was a source of debate among the eighth graders at Regina Coeli whether those were boobs or fat—without lifting her head. This gave her many more chins. She shrugged, which made her blouse swim higher, and put her head back down.

Irritation overtook Caroline. Had she no pride or decency, no sense of deportment? Caroline yanked the shirt down herself.

"Hey," Jenna Lou protested.

"No one wants to look at that," Caroline muttered.

"What?"

"Nothing. Lie still."

Caroline jabbed at the region where she thought her partner's ribs should be, and Jenna Lou convulsed with a shriek of laughter.

"Lie *still*," Caroline repeated, annoyed.

"It tickles!" Jenna Lou said in a high voice.

Caroline waited with theatrical impatience for the girl to collect herself.

"Okay, okay," she said, wriggling herself into a calm state of mind. "Go."

Caroline's hands were still safely above Jenna Lou when she burst out laughing again, her shirt riding up, her belly jiggling, her face growing redder, her eyes disappearing into fleshy, scrunched cheeks.

"Get up. You do it on me."

She rolled over on her side and hefted herself up. "You'll see," Jenna Lou said, still giggling despite herself, swiping at her eyes with the back of her hand.

Caroline lay down brusquely, smacked her heels together, arms stiff at her sides like a horizontal soldier, showing Jenna Lou that she meant business.

But when she saw the girl loom over her, she started laughing before Jenna Lou's hands had even begun their descent.

"See?" Jenna Lou said, both defensive and relieved. "It tickles just thinking about it."

"Having some trouble over here?" Father Gilhool observed.

Caroline looked over at Kathleen and Michael. He was lying on the floor while his sister delivered a bossy monologue at him.

"We can't stop being ticklish," Jenna Lou explained.

"Ah, yes, a common obstacle," he said, the corners of his mouth pulling down in amusement. "Here, try again."

He knelt beside Jenna Lou, his knees suddenly at the side of Caroline's ribs. Her pulse quickened, and she fought to breathe easily. She got a whiff of his breath drifting across her, warm and fresh. "Okay," he said. "Show me how you're doing it."

"I haven't even gotten clo—"

"Okay, okay, here, let's do it together." He grasped Jenna Lou's index fingers and middle fingers and dug them firmly into Caroline's sides. He rapidly slid them upward, along her rib cage, until his hands met at the top. He put two of Jenna Lou's fingers between Caroline's breasts then placed his palms over her palms. Things got crowded, which is why, Caroline, supposed, his knuckles wound up pressing into her nipples.

"Got it?" he said to Jenna Lou, who was speechless. "Let's do it again."

Slowly this time, firmly, he slid and positioned, and again four hands were kneading around Caroline's newly sprouted breasts. His fingers, large and confident, easy to recognize, nudged the small mounds and grazed the nipples, which hardened and strained painfully against her satin blouse, the thin bra doing nothing to tame them.

"Okay, and one more time. You're really getting the hang of it!" Again, trace, position the palms, and then a hand cupped and squeezed Caroline's right breast and suddenly she felt like she'd peed in her underwear. Her eyes flew open—she'd shut them tight in anticipation, disbelief, excitement, confusion—and she was mortified, but Father Gilhool was beaming and Jenna Lou looked flushed and happy and Caroline realized that no one would be able to see a few drops of pee through a wool skirt.

She also realized it wasn't pee. It felt like an overflow of the warmth that had suffused her bloodstream in the past few minutes and quickly reached every last knuckle, ear tip, and kneecap.

"Stealth," Father Gilhool advised. "If you do it quickly and deliberately, it doesn't tickle." He patted Caroline's arm and lurched back onto his heels. "All right, let's see how Kathleen and Michael are faring."

"Wait!" Jenna Lou said plaintively. "I didn't get, I mean, Caroline didn't get a turn trying on me. Can you show her on me?" Her yearning was so obvious that Caroline was embarrassed. To her delight—which also embarrassed her—Father Gilhool said there wasn't time.

They spent the rest of the hour pumping Annie's chest. Caroline thought Michael would melt right then and there out of sheer mortification. She'd never seen a face turn so red. When his and Kathleen's mom appeared at the top at the stairs, ten minutes early, Michael flew up the stairs without a word. Mrs. Riordan said something sharply under breath and a faint "Thank you" flitted down as he disappeared.

Caroline and Jenna Lou helped Father Gilhool clean up, not that there was much to do. They moved slowly, waiting each other out. There were cookies to seal up, and a few kids' toys still scattered around from the nursery school group that used the basement during the week.

Finally, Father Gilhool locked Annie in her closet and headed to the bottom of the stairs. He looked over his shoulder, his hand on the light switch.

"Thanks, girls. Looks better than when we got here. Consider yourselves dismissed." He grinned at them warmly.

"My mom can't actually get me for another hour, so is it okay if I stay down here and read?" Caroline was well aware that she was supposed to have let Father Gilhool know this change of plans at the beginning of teen group.

Jenna Lou looked crestfallen. She lived walking distance from the church. There was no reason for her to stick around.

"Sure, sure," he said absently. "But wait upstairs so I can lock up down here."

He gestured for the girls to go ahead of him. Jenna Lou trudged upstairs, and Caroline followed, her eyes locked on the heels of the girl's rainbow-striped sneakers.

Jenna Lou took her time putting on her coat. She licked her lips and looked up toward the apse, then departed, disappointment weighing down her steps.

Caroline was pretty sure she was alone in the building with Father Gilhool. She imagined them praying together, kneeling side by side in the first pew, or maybe even right up at the altar. She imagined how focused she'd be, how close to Jesus she would feel. Would he suggest it? It would make a lot of sense.

"Okay, you have a book, homework?" he said, heading away from her. "You're good out here?"

She all but crumpled on the spot from disappointment.

"Mm-hmm," she managed.

"Great. I'll be in here, so just give a shout when you leave. Great work downstairs," he added over his shoulder, disappearing into his office.

Caroline gazed at the paintings on the ceiling—Jesus washing the feet of a beggar, Jesus bleeding from the cross—and willed herself to feel awe and inspiration. She would connect to God on her own, which really had been her intention all along. She shuffled along the pew toward the center aisle, too chicken to approach the altar alone. She wasn't even sure she was allowed to go up there.

"Hoo," Caroline said quietly, to hear the echo, then blushed. She pulled down a kneeler and crossed herself. She said the Apostles' Creed and then the Our Father and three Hail Marys, then looked at her Timex. How was it possible only five minutes had passed? She wished she really did have a book or homework with her.

Father Gilhool strode out of his office and glanced her way.

"I'm going to make some tea. Want some?"

Caroline's heart soared. She nodded and awaited an appreciative comment about her praying.

He tilted his head in the direction of his office. "Go wait in there. I'm just raiding Father Garvey's stash. He has much better tea." There was that conspiratorial smile that made her toes warm.

She sidestepped back to the aisle, and cautiously entered

his office, a place she'd been inside only once before. It was paneled in dark wood and had plush burgundy carpeting that made her want to remove her shoes. The overhead lights were dimmed, and there was a bright pool of light on his desk, encircling piles of dittos and a gold-etched Bible. The wall was covered with framed diplomas and photographs of Father Gilhool with other priests. Caroline perched at the edge of the puffy red leather couch and worried the sunken buttons of the cushions with her fingers.

Father Gilhool came in, his lower lip caught between his teeth, concentrating on holding aloft two steaming cups. He kicked the door closed gently behind him.

"Alrighty!" He set down the mugs on his desk and fished out an array of tea bags from his back pocket. "Apologies for the poor presentation," he said sheepishly, holding out the choices. Caroline selected a cinnamon packet.

"So. How's tricks, Caroline?" Father Gilhool sat down beside her on the couch.

"Um, good," she replied into her cup. She felt like she had won a private audience with a movie star.

"Are you enjoying teen group? Do you think kids are liking it?"

He was looking to her for reassurance! Man, he was a sweetie pie.

"Oh, absolutely!" Caroline gushed. "We're all super excited to get trained in First Aid and, you know, CPR, and all that."

"What about the other activities?" He squinted at her uncertainly. "Do you think I'm striking the right tone? I mean, I know I'm not so far off from being your age, but still, I'm older." He laughed nervously and she wanted to hug him. "Do the other activities seem cornball or, you know, just bogue?"

"No way!" she exclaimed. "You pick the best hymns, and the rap sessions are really helpful, you know, connecting our experiences to Jesus's and stuff." A drop of hot water splashed onto the couch, and she quickly mopped it with her skirt.

"Thank you," he said earnestly. "That means a lot to me. It's just such a privilege to be able to serve this amazing community, and you guys are just so…" He inhaled deeply and closed his eyes. "Just so good. You know? I'm inspired by how committed to Jesus you are, to His word." He opened his eyes suddenly and looked into hers. Her hand threatened to tremble. She'd imagined him talking to her like this and looking at her like this so often that she had a hard time understanding it was really happening. "Can we pray together?"

Caroline nodded vigorously, not trusting her voice.

He took her mug and placed it with his on the desk. Then he grasped her hand, and they knelt in front of the couch. She tried to redirect her attention away from their intertwined fingers, but could barely focus on his prayers.

"Oh, Lord, know that we strive to grow in knowledge. Witness our faith under the mantle of Mary, Queen of Heaven. We proclaim that the kingdom of God is at hand in our families, our community, and the world. Animated by this faith, we work together with loving hearts and helping hands to serve the Lord."

He inhaled and exhaled deeply and was silent for a moment. Caroline did the same. He continued. "We pray for peace not only in our lives, but in the lives of those less fortunate than us. We pray for the returning vets and for the oil embargo to end. We pray for the soul of our president and for the starving children in Africa."

Caroline glanced at him. His eyes were tightly closed, and he was a million miles away, thinking about saving the world, his pure heart working, focused completely on helping others. She was abandoned in the wake of his goodwill.

But then he put his arm around her shoulder and kissed the top of her head. She sighed gratefully and leaned in, smelling him. She couldn't help herself. She loved him. *No!* she thought in horror. That wasn't possible! That wasn't okay. But still she gave him a quick hug, needing to feel her arms around him just once.

He hugged her back. They held each other and swayed a little on their knees.

"You know," he murmured, "we worship with our words, but the Lord designed our bodies for worship, too. Do you know how to show your joy for the Lord with your body?"

Caroline shook her head, rubbing her nose in his shoulder.

"Can I show you?"

She nodded, her heart pounding. Still holding her tight with one arm, he took one of her hands and guided it down along her hip, then up and under her skirt. He pressed her fingers between her legs and gently circled them around that spot that she touched in the darkest of night, in her bed, with her sheet, which she truly did only because she was itchy or hot.

"This is the highest respect you can show to God. Do you feel the ecstasy?" he whispered.

Caroline couldn't speak. She was picturing Jesus washing her feet, Jesus running his hands up her legs, Jesus gazing at her. This was Jesus making her feel this way, Jesus snatching sense from her mind, taking the words from her mouth. Father Gilhool rubbed harder and faster, and she cried out, her body convulsing. She collapsed into him. She felt him go rigid, heard him grunt, and then he hugged her.

"You've experienced the glory," he whispered into her ear. "Isn't it beautiful?"

She nodded into his shoulder again, realizing she was panting. He pulled her back and looked into her eyes.

"Do you know why you were able to feel that joy?" he asked.

She shook her head.

"Because you pray hard, and you are a good, kind Christian, and you live as the Bible tells you to."

And Caroline realized then that it wasn't Father Gilhool she loved. It was Jesus, and she was *supposed* to love Jesus! She beamed at Father Gilhool in relief and pleasure.

"The others, though, Caroline, they're not at this point yet. They wouldn't understand this higher level of prayer. Can we keep this between us for now?"

Even before he'd said it, she'd sensed that this was something private and special. She hadn't planned on telling anyone anyway. She had no desire to share Father Gilhool's special prayer. It was special. She was special.

"Yes." She beamed at him. "That was…great."

He squeezed her shoulder and stood, extending a hand to pull her up, sealing their partnership.

"Caroline?" They heard a faint voice from outside the office, and an almost imperceptible darkness flashed across his face. He flung open the door.

"There you are, Mrs. Byrne!" He greeted Caroline's mother with a wide smile, and she, who rarely smiled, was startled enough that she returned it. "We're saving on heat, keeping the door shut."

"Wise," she approved, then squinted disapprovingly at her daughter. "Caroline, are you coming down with a fever?"

Caroline and Father Gilhool prayed together nearly every week, and she looked forward to Sundays more than ever before. On the rare occasion when her mother could pick her up on time from teen group, she was bereft and grumpy and her mother made sharp remarks about American teenagers. But Caroline was rarely without a Bible in her hand, and her mother's approval of her was generally on the rise. There was a peace to Caroline's days she hadn't known before. She cheerfully threw herself into schoolwork and after-school activities. Her grades were steadily climbing, and she was gaining a reputation with the teachers as a good student and a dependable member of the mentoring club and the bake sale committee.

Caroline enjoyed these activities, but lived for that hour alone with Father Gilhool in his office on Sunday afternoons. They always chatted for a while. He'd ask her about school, about ideas she had for teen group activities. She did her best not to be impatient, but all she wanted was to pray with him. *We are one body, one body in Christ.* Their prayers were going longer and longer and had gotten more intricate and more joyous. There were so many ways to feel the glory. And then one day, after about two months of praying like this, he asked Caroline if she truly understood that he was a messenger of the Lord and whether she wanted to feel Jesus actually enter her body.

She did. She wanted that more than she'd ever wanted anything in her whole life.

He told her it might hurt at first, like the nails going into Jesus, but that she could think of it as a glorious kind of suffering. It did hurt. It both hurt and it was heaven and she knew just how Jesus felt on the cross. And after the first time, their worship didn't hurt at all. It was stunning, breathtaking, and once Jesus was inside her, all she could think of was getting him inside her again and again. Father Gilhool was thrilled with her spiritual progress, and she loved their secret. She loved that she was prayerful enough, dutiful enough, *Christian* enough that she had reached this level of devotion. She doubled down on Christian mentoring, hoping to bring others to her level of salvation.

Watching Father Gilhool succumb to the spirit, as he called his shuddering transformation, was beautiful once she stopped being embarrassed by it. She was the only one who got to see him like this. Jesus would leave her body, and then Father Gilhool would kind of howl-grunt, his face contorted with ecstasy so deep it looked like suffering.

There were weeks when Caroline would beg Father Gilhool to let Jesus impale her, but he wouldn't. They would still find joy, but she was disappointed. It wasn't during the week when she wore her Kotex belt—Jesus loved her blood because it was his blood—but always the week after.

And then one Sunday in March, shortly after Caroline turned fifteen, Father Gilhool and she sang alone together:

*Let all mortal flesh keep silence
And with fear and trembling stand;
Ponder nothing earthly minded,
For with blessing in His hand,
Christ our God to earth descendeth,
Our full homage to demand.*

*King of kings, yet born of Mary,
As of old on earth He stood,
Lord of lords, in human vesture,
In the body and the blood;
He will give to all the faithful
His own self for heavenly food.*

Father Gilhool ran his hand down her waist and hip, and then up and down again. "No belt?" he whispered.

"Nope."

"All done?"

"No," she whispered back, as she began to feel the presence of Jesus. "I haven't needed it in a while."

Father Gilhool's hand stopped moving. He pulled away from her slightly.

"How long?"

She tried to tug him back, but he kept a few brutal inches between them.

"How long?" he repeated and her eyes flew open. She'd never heard this tone of voice. It wasn't warm and sweet or loud and laughing. It was small. Scared.

"Um." Caroline was flustered, unsure whether he was

really asking her about her…about *that.* She blushed and tried to think. "Around Valentine's Day? I think?"

He pulled back and his face darkened.

"What's wrong?" she pleaded. All she wanted was for them to do what they always did, to pray, to move together. Why was today different?

"It can be dangerous not to get your period."

Why on earth was he talking about *that* disgusting thing? The spirit was slipping away. This wasn't how it was supposed to go. Why was a holy man talking about something he should never be talking about?

"Dangerous?" she repeated.

Father Gilhool looked at her, and for a moment, something slipped away, and in its place was something that, many years later, Caroline would understand had been incredulity.

He licked his lips then kissed her gently. Oh, how she loved his kisses. She felt safe and perfect and beautiful then.

The following Sunday, when her period still hadn't come, Father Gilhool took her to a doctor he said was a good friend of his. He told Mrs. Byrne that he valued her daughter's opinion, and that Caroline had been working so hard in teen group that he wanted her to accompany him to three caterers to sample menus for the church's spring fling. Caroline had never seen her mother agree to something so quickly. The more Father Gilhool took her under his wing, the more her mother approved of her. Caroline was so excited about the food-tasting adventure, she nearly forgot about the doctor's visit. Restaurants were a rarity for the Byrne family, and when they did go to the diner, their budget limited her to a choice of the same three items each time: hamburger, pancakes, or spaghetti alfredo. She tried to imagine foods she'd never tasted, but could picture only the raw fish she'd once seen presented as an example of a foreign food in a textbook. Her heart soared at the thought of driving side by side next to Father Gilhool, to nearby towns along country roads. Maybe they'd stop and pray along the way.

The doctor, a slight man with sparse, oily hair, unlocked the darkened office himself. There was no receptionist there, no nurse. Father Gilhool said they should be very grateful to his friend for opening up for them on a Sunday. Caroline didn't say a word from the moment they entered to the moment they left.

"You're very lucky to have Father Gilhool as a mentor," the doctor said sternly, roughly guiding her into a supine position on the examining table, then clapping a mask over her nose and mouth. "He's very unjudgmental. Now breathe deeply and this will all be over."

When she woke up, she was dizzy and had wrenching cramps, which the doctor had warned her about. He said it would feel like a heavy period, and even in her drugged stupor, she felt herself blush.

"Am I okay now?" Caroline tried to say, but her tongue wouldn't form clear words.

"Thank you," she heard Father Gilhool say.

"She's lucky she got herself into trouble this year and not last year."

"As if that would have made a difference to you!" Father Gilhool laughed.

"Just would have charged you more. Hazard pay." The doctor returned the laugh and clapped Father Gilhool on the back. "You're a good man, taking these little whores under your wing. Almost gives me faith in the cloth again!"

Caroline and Father Gilhool left the doctor's office and drove around for a few minutes or a few hours; Caroline slept the whole time.

When he dropped her off at home, it was twilight, the sky streaked with pink and orange.

"Mrs. Byrne, I'm so sorry, I think Caroline is coming down with something. She got very groggy a little while ago and looks flushed. I think she needs to rest."

"The flu is going around," Mrs. Byrne agreed, studying her daughter.

"I hope she didn't catch it from me. I was feeling a little low earlier in the week."

"Oh, I'm sure she didn't, Father Gilhool," she gushed. "Thank you for taking such good care of her!"

"We had a good time, didn't we, Caroline?"

And Caroline thought but didn't ask, *When will we go see the caterers?*

EIGHT

Being adopted turned out to be a great topic for a college essay. Meg started with a visual: "The first thing I do at any new doctor's office is draw a line through the family medical history pages. I'm a blank slate."

So she stretched the truth a tiny bit. But going back to the Priskers with a clipboard and asking them to fill in her genetic history? Not happening. She never saw them again and hoped she never would. No, that wasn't true either. One day, she was going to make sure they knew she got a full scholarship to college, a college that *U.S. News & World Report* ranked way higher than the one Alexa—her *birth mother*—went to. And she did it without a penny from them.

When the doctors finally let Meg emerge from the medically induced coma—which, by the way, she would highly recommend for heroin withdrawal, since all the sweats and cravings happened while she was unconscious—she rejoined a world in which she couldn't feed herself, had tubes to drain away her piss, wore a diaper, couldn't walk, couldn't read or watch TV because her vision was too blurry. She was bored out of her mind. A nurse suggested audio books; Meg wasn't much of a reader and didn't know where to begin, so she

Googled "tenth grader books" and stumbled upon a superior education. *To Kill a Mockingbird, Invisible Man, Ethan Frome, The Bluest Eye, Portrait of a Lady, A Raisin in the Sun, The Catcher in the Rye.* One afternoon, Meg awoke from a nap—though awake and asleep were more or less indistinguishable during that time—having dreamed, of all things, that she was a princess on a submarine and was making everyone on board laugh. Not laugh *at* her; they were laughing because she was being funny, something Meg had never been in all her fourteen years. She'd also never imagined herself as a princess, not even when she was young and the Little Mermaid was busy returning to the sea. The levity of the dream compelled her to take a break from *Sister Carrie*, big downer, and pick something that looked lighter, something that was not on the list of recommended reading.

Meg selected an audio book that had a picture of a princess on the case cover. As she began to listen, she glanced guiltily toward the door of her hospital room, embarrassed that she'd been drawn to such a silly, girly cover. The book was called *Elizabeth I*, and Meg had had no idea it was a biography. She'd never read a biography before and, after this introduction to the genre, she was hooked. Soon she was able to read again, print on paper, and she devoured the life stories of everyone from Jim Henson to Malcolm X, from Genghis Khan to Menachem Begin. Stories that were true? That left you knowing useful shit? History through someone's personal experience? Why hadn't anyone told her, *really* told her about these? Meg was so pissed that her school didn't teach history through biography she decided she would refuse to go back to school even if she was ever able to. Certainly not to Barton

High, where the teachers had so clearly abdicated their responsibilities. Or just sucked.

Once Meg stabilized, the hospital staff persuaded her mother to go back to work; presumably, they had an interest in her maintaining her excellent health insurance. Meg knew her mother would never in a million years admit it, but those were the best months the two had ever spent together in Meg's entire life. The accident had put an end to their money struggles because Meg could no longer steal from her mother. AnneMarie no longer had to work at Michael's, and for the first time in years, she had nearly every weekend off, and she rested. Second, she finally knew where her daughter was every minute of every day, so the worrying was over: unlike every other parent in America, she was a hundred percent sure all the time that Meg was not getting into trouble. Third, she was Meg's only company. No one came to visit, so they became each other's entire world. Maybe because of all this, or maybe because she swung a deal with God, she stopped drinking. She could've had her port in the hospital. No one would have cared; there's no rule against drinking in a hospital, not like smoking. But she gave it up.

AnneMarie would arrive at five fifteen every evening and settle onto her cot with a magazine or a word search in her lap, to show she wasn't pressuring Meg into conversation. But Meg, starved for human interaction, was excited to see her mother and talk to her. AnneMarie rose to the occasion, regaling her daughter with stories about the patient who refused to stop chitchatting during her appointment and the one who adopted a British accent only in the minutes after her procedure was finished, but she didn't mind when Meg drifted off.

Meg had never seen her mother so peaceful. Happy. She'd never seen her mother happy. In the first few weeks after regaining consciousness, Meg couldn't stay awake for too long, but eventually she'd float back to the surface and find AnneMarie still there, contentedly hunting the names of geological formations or US presidents, eating soup she'd brought for her dinner. Meg was still getting fed through a G-tube because her esophagus had been damaged, so no soup for her (a reference she wouldn't understand until she saw *Seinfeld* reruns in college). After the second month, Meg was able to watch most of a twenty-five minute sitcom, and the two became fans of *The Office*, like every other normal person in the nation. For the first time in her life, even though she was immobilized and infant-like, Meg felt like she was a regular citizen, like she was part of something. At nine o'clock, AnneMarie would zap off the TV, help her daughter rinse out her stinking mouth, and empty her urine bag. Then she'd grasp the railing of the bed, kneel beside Meg, and they would pray together.

Yeah, Meg prayed. At first, she only pretended to pray because it was too exhausting to say no to her mother. She kept her eyes open and guiltily watched AnneMarie, feeling as though she were spying on her. Then she found her mother's calm focus was catching. And appealing. She gave it a try, and before long, Meg was praying with sincerity. She even started buying into the whole Jesus thing, convincing herself there was a sentient being at the other end of the line, tuning in. Seriously, if ever there was a sign: the fact that she lived? That she didn't hurt anyone else when she turned the wheel into the median? Meg came to be grateful she'd crashed, to see it as the second chance that it was. She was uglier now than she'd ever been, but at least now there was a reason; it was no longer just a bad roll of the genetic dice (ugly Alexa, ugly Jane). There was nothing else to do, nothing else she *could* do except learn. Meg didn't know if she was smart before the accident; being smart was no way to win friends in Barton so she'd never tried it on for size. But now, though she wouldn't have admitted to anyone—not that there was anyone around to admit anything to—it was interesting being interested in things.

If that wasn't proof of a plan by Someone smarter than Meg, then she didn't know what was. On top of everything else, she got only six months' probation, an eight-o'clock curfew, and mandated counseling, which was all laughable because the sentence was handed down when she was unconscious. The counseling wasn't even drug counseling, because she wasn't high at the time—remarkable—and it wasn't even for suicidal tendencies. It was for being underage and stealing her mom's car and taking it for a joy ride. Everyone figured, well, yeah, if a fourteen-year-old drives a car, she's gonna crash it. It all worked out in this perfect circular logic.

The cool thing about smashing herself was that merely surviving became this big old laudable accomplishment. How often in your life do you get cheered for getting a fork to reach your mouth? For peeing in a bed pan? For getting vertical when the staff figured she'd be horizontal for eternity, first in a bed, then in a grave, maybe sooner rather than later? And when Meg actually took some shaky steps, the nurses brought in a cake. People talked about how brave Meg was, how determined she was, what a fighter she was, and the thing is, none of it was true. She was just doing what there was to do. Surviving was a pretty fucking low expectation that even Meg could meet.

But she started to believe the hype, and then the hype started to be true. (More circular logic, but a good kind.) Suddenly, Meg was a Hardworking Kid. The school district was obligated to pay for a home tutor, and it was a girl from Buffalo, Wendy, who'd just gotten a master's from Syracuse and was way smarter than any Barton teachers. So, yet another bonus: Meg got a top-quality teacher trucked in just for her. Before the accident, she never thought about the quality of her education—what a wonky-ass, meaningless phrase for people who lived in different worlds from Meg's— but now, she understood. And it was even sweeter that no one else understood.

Meg crashed her mother's car in the fall of ninth grade. Wendy started coming in February, when Meg was back home and could focus her eyes for decent stretches of time. Wendy continued coming for all of tenth grade and even eleventh grade, though by the spring of tenth Meg could easily have gone back. But why would she return to that wasteland one second before the school officials stopped paying Wendy? By then, Meg knew all about college. She knew it was a place she could go, *should* go; she knew it was her right to apply, and she knew it could help her get away from Barton forever. Meg understood that she was worthy of leaving.

When Meg returned to the hallowed halls of Barton High for twelfth grade, limping on a cane, she was both cocky and terrified of how her cockiness would be received. Which she now knew was a paradox. Just knowing that was called a paradox helped fuel her cockiness so that it won out over the terror. (She put that in her essay, too.) She hadn't laid eyes on Gemma, Baxter, or Troy in three years, and hadn't thought about them much since. Now, they loomed large, as magnetic pulls to be resisted. So she was pleasantly surprised when she saw how tiny and spaced-out Gemma was—had she always looked like this?—and discovered that she and Troy no longer spoke to each other, and learned that Baxter had dropped out of school altogether.

Meg figured everyone else would still see her as the strung-out loser she'd been, but in fact, while she was lying in the hospital with applesauce dribbling down her chin, she had grown a reputation as a badass: for stealing the car, and also for crashing it, and, in particular, for surviving. Again, big credit just for breathing in and out. People forgot she wasn't a victim, that she'd done this to herself. She easily placed into honors classes, where even the teachers seemed to have bought into the mythology of Meg Croyden's rebirth story. They were relieved that Meg was on track to be a success, or at least not another failure, and the fact that she was scarred and limping added to the image of the smart kid who was above it all, who didn't bother with things like crushes, dating, messing around.

Mrs. Sherry, the gym teacher who got an extra stipend for being the college guidance counselor, said Meg was selling herself short. The way she saw it was that Meg had been smart to begin with, and then she finally let the smarts out of their dark cellar and brought them into the sunshine. Meg said that made it sound like her intelligence was in a bunker, kidnapped by some letch, and Mrs. Sherry said, "That's exactly what happened."

It turned out that the honors track did have slightly

better teachers, and kids who could sometimes communicate in more than grunts. So Meg kept learning and got it into her disfigured head that she could maybe not just go to college but go to a fancy college no one from her school had ever even considered.

Mrs. Sherry and some other teachers suggested Meg apply to SUNY Cortland, where the occasional valedictorian managed to matriculate. This was a giddy vote of confidence since, primarily, Barton High was a feeder school for Tioga County Community College. Most kids went there for a few months, if they went at all, before getting pregnant, dropping out, and going on welfare. Meg decided to apply to Cortlandt, definitely. But while watching movie after movie with her mother, her favorites had been oldies set on idyllic college campuses, like *The Sure Thing* (she wanted to be the nerdy girl, not the sure thing girl) and *Good Will Hunting*, even *Animal House*, *Legally Blonde*, or the very old movie *Love Story*, which had the added benefit of the sick girl. Embarrassed, Meg began picturing herself studying in a tiny dorm room and meeting friends for frozen yoghurt at midnight. She wanted to be around kids who weren't former drug addicts from Barton.

Mrs. Sherry was unfamiliar with many of the schools on Meg's list.

"Isn't Williams down south?" the guidance counselor asked, frowning at the folder Meg had assembled. "I don't think you'd feel at home in the South."

"No," Meg said, trying to strike the tone in which a teenager can correct an adult. Deferential, but certain enough to convey factual accuracy.

"Harvard? Yale?" she asked in disbelief. She'd heard of those.

"No, no," Meg said quickly. "I'm not applying there. That's the annual ranking. *U.S. News & World Report*? It's just to show that some of the schools I've picked…" Meg was at a loss. "Well, they're ranked. Like, to show they're good schools." She hunched forward and picked at the peeling laminate surface of Mrs. Sherry's desk.

In the end, with Mrs. Sherry dubious at every step along the way, Meg won a full scholarship to Linden College in Pierre, New York. It was an empty victory because no one in her backward, redneck, stupid-ass town had ever heard of it. It made it hard to brag about it or even to revel in it. She thought her mom would be proud, but she was in the same boat as Mrs. Sherry, pushing for TCC. No, they weren't exactly in the same boat, because on some level AnneMarie knew. Well, she didn't *know* Williams and Swarthmore and Haverford (*"Harvard?"* she misheard, wide-eyed), but she knew Meg was going more than a four-hour drive away.

When Meg showed her mother the acceptance letter, she gazed at her daughter as though she were already gone. Meg met her mother's eyes, feeling guilty, though for what, she didn't yet know.

NINE

Sylvia had frequently fantasized about being invited back to her alma mater as a sign of having won the institution's pride. Why her parents' pride wasn't enough, why she had to search for more approval from a third parent—the *mater*—was the guess of anyone's therapist. How many graduates have a prodigal son/daughter fantasy?

What she had in mind when she envisioned her glorious return to Linden College was being dined by the college president off a plastic tray in Toten (nicknamed Tuten) Commons, then crossing campus with her to the venerable Slaughter Hall to give a lecture funded by the rich heir to an outdoor clothing fortune. After staying overnight at Alumni House in a room with charmingly wobbly nightstands and embroidered hand towels, she would teach a master class the next day. It was a vague imagining, a compilation of misty movie scenes featuring Sylvia, charging around the base of a packed amphitheater spewing wisdom, and masses of visibly inspired twenty-year-olds, none of them looking at a phone.

What she did not get around to imagining was a low-paying gig meant to fill a curriculum gap, which she took because nothing else had come along.

To everyone's shock, Sylvia had not received a single offer of stage work after winning the Tony. Apparently, being the director of a heretical three-person play qualified her to direct only heretical three-person plays. She was pigeon-holed as "serious"—a death knell masquerading as a paean—her glossy history of directing sitcoms notwithstanding. She hoped television work would come along again, as sporadically and unpredictably as it always did, but she needed a lifeline, a dependable routine, something she'd never had in the course of her entire career. Not just an occupation, but a preoccupation to keep her thinking about something other than how she had come to be a divorced, middle-aged woman—that damnable demographic targeted by publishers, cruise lines, and Spanx.

And so here she was at an anemic departmental welcoming reception, eating cubed cheese on Triscuits in a low-ceilinged, fourth-floor office, the scent of dust, two-hundred-year-old wood, and damp stone sending her headlong on an olfactory trip of Proustian proportions. The offer to teach a playwriting seminar—something with which Sylvia had zero experience— had come just ten days before the start of classes. Academic institutions that had fired faculty during the Great Recession were now scrambling to convince paying parents that they had all areas covered.

They must have been desperate to take on a director rather than a writer to teach playwriting. Sylvia impressed this upon the department head, Mariella Corkenthorp, in the two somewhat frantic phone calls that constituted her vetting process. But Corkenthorp believed that Sylvia's freshly won Tony constituted blanket qualification, which did give Sylvia a small measure of satisfaction.

Professor Corkenthorp hefted herself across the room, her patchwork skirt falling in Christos-sized folds from her wide hips, and clicked plastic glasses with Sylvia. Mariella, at least, was genuinely glad to have Sylvia aboard if only to have a fellow real-worlder there among the academics.

"Did you sort out a crash pad at Alumni House?" Mariella asked.

Sylvia swigged some warm white wine to wash down the scratchy remnants of a cracker.

"Yep. Tuesday nights. I'll drive or train up on Tuesday mornings, hold office hours, teach Wednesday afternoon, and head home. And it's easy for me to pop up for meetings."

In fact, it would be logistical hell, but she knew that merely acknowledging The Balancing Act was career death.

"Groovy!" Professor Corkenthorp—*Mariella*, Sylvia reminded herself, *first names, first names*—had been making peace, not war, since 1968. She had come to Linden five years earlier, after earning a reputation as the grande dame of New York's downtown theater scene, mounting plays that required audiences to sign waivers and repeatedly stirring up internecine conflict within foundation boards, who feuded over whether to grant money to her incendiary projects. She and Sylvia had crossed paths a few times, and she cheerily regarded Sylvia as a sellout.

"David!" Mariella summoned another faculty member from a dusty corner, doing her best to fulfill the purpose of this desultory little gathering. "You should meet David," she told Sylvia. "David and his husband, Jay, also commute from the city."

Sylvia shone a warm, conspiratorial smile on the lanky form that approached. Gay + theater + New York City was her comfort zone, her people. She would have an ally here, or at least someone she could read clearly and speak to in shorthand. David Ketchum had a gleaming reputation as a savior of theater companies. In quick succession, he had swept in as executive producer of the Sphere, in London, and then the New York Theater Club, and, most recently, Tertiary Theaters, and escorted them with more brute force than tough love from red to black. His weekly presence on the Linden campus was meant to stanch the flood of criticism on op-ed pages nationwide that small, precious liberal arts colleges such as this one were poorly preparing students for the real world.

"Welcome," David Ketchum said coolly. No zing of brotherhood.

"Thanks. Looking forward to…" Sylvia spread the fingers of her hands as though preparing to catch a basketball. The fluorescent light caught her rings, both of which she still wore. "All of it."

"Well, if there's anything you need," he offered unconvincingly and drained the contents of his plastic glass.

"Do you commute only on teaching days?" Sylvia grasped at a connection.

"Jay and I have the same schedule as you—we stay at Basement Vistas on Tuesday nights and then go home to Brooklyn."

"Extra long commute," she remarked, hoping this would remind him that she, too, was of the city. "Wait, Basement Vistas? Seriously?"

At this, a quick half-power smile flashed. "No. Alumni House."

"Yikes. That bad?"

"No, not quite. But they do save the rooms with views for cash-bearing alums. Understandably," he added, ever the bottom-liner. "You guys are staying there, too?" he asked.

"Just me, yes." She did not yet have the fortitude to elaborate.

Mariella heard the hesitancy in Sylvia's voice, and misinterpreted it.

"I'm sure you can get along without Ethan for a night," she chided, ever the champion of fish managing without bicycles, despite having held on to the same sturdy bike herself for thirty years. His name was Harry, and he manufactured fake plants.

Until now, Sylvia's world-conquering, such as it was—a new professional venture, a successful mortgage refinance—had been possible because of the knowledge that she was deeply loved and considered. Sylvia wasn't sure who she was without Ethan in her corner. So she didn't elaborate to Mariella and David on her use of the single pronoun. It wasn't shame that kept her quiet; she evaded because a fake fortress of comfort was better than none at all.

There followed a terrible silence, a moment during which at least one of them feared that no new line of conversation could possibly be introduced, that the opportunity for a natural segue had passed, and they would stand there until someone turned the lights out.

"I enjoyed *Test*," David fired into the void.

"Thank you," Sylvia said, too gratefully. Her chest actually ached with the awkwardness of the situation, and she wondered briefly whether sheer social discomfort could bring on a heart attack. "I'm glad you had a chance to see it."

"I worked with Alma at NYTC. A bit of a sphinx, no?"

Alma Ng Sorenson was the author of *This Is Not a Test*, and when Sylvia had first read it, she'd felt as if she'd found her soul mate, her articulate self, the writer she would be if she could be a writer. Alma had taken the best of Dawkins, Hitchens, Harris, and Epstein and baked them into a deceptively profound family comedy that articulated everything that was insidious about religion. So when Sylvia finally met Alma, and Alma turned out to be wan, unforgivably uncommunicative, and wimpy, wearing her hair in a scraggly topknot that aimed for bohemian, but landed on self-abnegation, Sylvia was not just disappointed, but bereft.

"A lot of a sphinx," she answered.

"You, of all people, must know how she pulled off that feat," David persisted, his coolness gone for the moment.

"Which particular feat? There were lots." Sylvia chuckled, feeling collegiality finally permeate the proceedings.

David pulled on his upper lip with his teeth, which made his nostrils slightly bigger.

"The whopper. The Jehovah's Witness thing."

Sylvia adopted an expectant look, eager to be enlightened.

"You know. How she could write such a gorgeous ode to atheism while being a devout door-knocker."

Sylvia burst out laughing.

"Where did you hear that? I love it!" Relief flooded to her fingertips. This was an insider joke that could bring about peace, bond all three of them standing there. Mariella chortled beside her.

David looked nonplussed.

"I'm pretty sure…no? Huh. I thought it was true." David looked almost hurt, and whatever bond they'd been developing vanished. Sylvia grasped at it.

"Well, I, huh. Really?" Sylvia's compulsion not to let anyone feel bad because of anything she might say or do made her consider this preposterous hypothesis regarding Alma's religiosity. It was inconceivable that this might be true. Actually, what it was was mortifying. Was it possible that Alma had remained so uncommunicative and unreadable that Sylvia had directed an award-winning play of hers and had managed to stay in the dark about her true beliefs? Had the whole play been some kind of private exercise for Alma? A challenge to see whether she could write the opposite of what she felt? In which case, Sylvia was a pawn in the whole awful artistic experiment. In it, she represented the lip-service liberal, the atheist fool. Loathing surged through her, even as she was also in awe of her for being able to do something Sylvia never could—to understand the Other Side without agreeing with them, and to be constantly vigilant that one's generosity didn't turn into agreement.

"I'm just messing with you." David smiled coyly.

Mariella stiffened. Sylvia felt the way she had when Nathaniel was going through his "pantsing" phase, yanking at waistbands as the family attempted to cook or slip past him with arms full of grocery-filled tote bags. Indeed, David may as well have just pulled Sylvia's pants down in front of everyone. Except, unlike Nathaniel, David's dupe was fueled by cruelty, not innocent joy.

He'd intentionally sent Sylvia on a short but rocketing journey of self-doubt, purely for his own amusement. There was a certain kind of humor, at the cost of other people's dignity, that was more the province of unpleasant men than of unpleasant women, a sadistic and puerile power display.

Sylvia always started with the presumption that people were kind, and, so often, she was penalized for that. Now she felt like a fool, was instantly drained by the unreciprocated effort to be civilized, and wished she'd never accepted this job.

"So do you have plans for your downtime?" David reached past her and replenished his plate with orange cheese. Having highlighted Sylvia's vulnerability, he was now warming to her.

"Downtime?" Insult to injury. Sylvia had just added a ninety-minute commute to her already unpredictable life; she had to stay on top of a class she didn't know how to teach; she had two demanding children—demanding her attention, her time, her scheduling prowess—and spent any moments apart from them persuading her agent that she was available for work in LA at the drop of a hat.

Mariella jumped in. "Commuting faculty have the gift of family-free hours. You spend some of it prepping, but then, the world is your oyster." She spread her hands expansively.

Sylvia had been free of a family for three months. Pierre, New York was no world, and it definitely was not an oyster from what she recalled. The room felt short on oxygen.

"Right?" David pressed. "You have office hours Tuesday mornings and teach Wednesday afternoons, so you've got twenty-four found hours. It's not like you're a writer and need to hole up with a manuscript. Freedom!"

Sylvia fixed him with a frank gaze, one meant to convey, *Really? Are you really this big an asshole with a straight face?* She would pass her "found" hours lying in bed streaming Netflix on her phone and calling it professional enrichment.

She sipped at her warm wine and met David's gaze.

"Actually," Sylvia lied sweetly, "I'm swamped with scripts since the Tony. I'll use the time to pick my next project."

TEN

Unlike her mother, Meg had no idea how far away she was going. When she left for Linden College on the last day of August, she regarded herself as more or less fully formed, the only remaining task to fill her head with more information, like a glass vase that needed marbles. She pictured her cocky, ugly self, contentedly single for the rest of her life, getting a high-paying job—a lawyer with a secretary, yelling into a phone most of the day—and coming home to an apartment that she shared with AnneMarie, not having to think twice about getting HBO. The apartment had wall-to-wall carpeting and wasn't in Barton, that much Meg knew. Maybe Buffalo, maybe New York City.

So when Meg and her mother pulled up in front of Cushman Hall—whose entrance was obscured by scaffolding, making for an uncertain arrival rather than a triumphant conclusion to a journey already delayed by a flat tire around Elmira—AnneMarie was probably less surprised than Meg to find the place swarming with smooth-skinned, cheery kids in large cars without frayed suitcases strapped to their roofs. There were a lot of men around, too. Fathers. Meg hadn't pictured that part.

Her classmates were beautiful, loud, confident; these were *freshmen*? They seemed to know the place already, to know each other already. It turned out those who didn't know each other from high school—the notion of attending college with someone you knew from high school struck Meg as bizarre and horrible—had met during freshmen orientation days, which Meg had skipped. The two overnights at a nearby summer camp sounded optional, and they cost extra. She could have requested a scholarship, but the school was already giving her so much money it didn't seem right to ask for even more for something that wasn't required. Needless to say it was, unofficially, required if you didn't want to be the only freshman who hadn't learned the school song, who hadn't been inducted into the centuries-old tradition of sledding down the grassy hill behind the dining hall on oiled trays, if you wanted to show up to move-in day not a complete outsider.

Meg had imagined everyone would look like her—little, narrow-featured, brainy escapees from their respective hometowns. Together, they'd create a place where people like them ruled. That's what happened in movies. Instead, she was thrown in with a pack of shiny-haired, glowing beauties, and every last one of them had been valedictorian of their class, like Meg. But also, mysteriously, they already knew that Tuesdays were free gummy toppings night at Licks, the frozen yoghurt shop, and that if you wanted to get first dibs on reused textbooks, it was already too late. They showed up with bedspreads and posters, which Meg, too, had thought to bring, but they had brought electric skillets and whiteboards, stuff that wasn't on the suggested list—some of which was expressly prohibited—but which would make the suites suitably cozy. On top of that, they had parents who knew their way around, who knew where to get shelf brackets and rug mats. They had all arrived already knowing what to do.

By the time Meg reached the fourth floor of her entryway and encountered the hive of activity inside what was to be her home for the next nine months, she was certain that she wasn't even going to unpack. She'd tell AnneMarie this was all a mistake and that of *course* she was actually going to enroll at TCC. Meg turned to inform her, only to find a squat, muscled boy—man, she guessed they were men now—sweating under the weight of her heaviest suitcase. Someone had done them a favor, so there was no turning back.

"Meg!"

Before Meg could register anything other than *Asian*, she was enveloped by someone about her size but double the strength. Meg froze, arms paralyzed at her sides, anticipating wrenching pain. Meg and AnneMarie had never hugged before the accident, and they certainly hadn't begun after, when Meg was held together with pins. Instead, they waved at each other at close range. No one had ever held Meg this tightly, not even Baxter or Troy when they were fucking her in a flatbed in a field. Each stayed a safe distance above, eyes closed, arms fully extended, keeping points of contact to a minimum.

The hugger released Meg. She was also small and birdlike, but that's where the similarities ended. She had a cluster of moles on her neck, accentuated by a bob that framed her face like parentheses. Meg wondered why she didn't grow her hair long to hide the ugly brown bumps. She wore tight tan cords and a flowy, floral blouse. She beamed at Meg expectantly, like she was supposed to know her.

"Hannah," she reminded Meg, placing both hands on her flat chest.

"Hi. Meg," Meg said. This was the first new person Meg had met in years who wasn't a doctor, nurse, therapist, or tutor.

"I know, I know! I'm so glad you're here! Rosetta is here"—Hannah waved over her shoulder in the direction of a bedroom—"and we're just waiting on Michelle."

"How did you know I was me and not Michelle?"

"Process of elimination," Hannah said. "You were the only one who never joined the email thread. The others had photos." There was the faintest hint of a reprimand.

There had been so many emails from Linden, about courses, about the scholarship, about the orientation trip, about extracurricular clubs, about rooming preferences. Meg had tried to stay on top of what was important—academics— and she vaguely remembered a chirpy introductory email that she'd written off as nonpriority.

"Sorry."

"Whatever! You're here. In the flesh!" She reached past Meg and extended her hand to AnneMarie. "Hi. Hannah! I was a little worried about whether we'd have enough stuff to furnish the common room, but we can just go to IKEA tomorrow and get whatever we're missing. Unless you brought the coffee table and an ottoman…?" She finished on a hopeful inflection.

Meg shook her head. She wasn't a hundred percent certain she knew what an ottoman was—a footstool that you could sit on, right? Why would you need one in a college dorm?—and she'd definitely never heard anyone under the age of forty use the word.

"No problem, no problem at all," Hannah said, sweeping an anxious eye over the explosion of furniture, rolled-up rugs, suitcases, and clothes on hangers slung over every available surface.

Two short, round, grinning people who could only be parents spilled out of the bedroom from which Hannah had emerged.

"You're either Meg or Michelle! I'm Adriana Goldberg, Hannah's mom, and this is my husband, Bob."

She's adopted, too. Meg bet it went down differently from her own so-called adoption, which she had come to think of more as an unloading.

"This is Meg," Hannah confirmed.

"Welcome to Linden!" boomed Bob. "Meg, Meg, let's see if I remember. Hannah made us study. You're the one from outside Binghamton, right?" He looked over his glasses at Meg, inquisitive, cheery, bearded.

"Um, yes, and this is my mom, Mrs. Croyden," Meg said quickly, determined to catch up on whatever it was she was already falling behind in.

"AnneMarie," her mother said quickly. "Call me AnneMarie."

Meg glanced at her. In her whole life, she'd never heard her tell a stranger to call her by her first name.

"Are you a morning person, *AM*?" Adriana giggled. "Does anyone ever call you that?"

"Uh, no," AnneMarie said too quickly. "But that would be fine."

It would not be fine, but she was just as swept along by this strange tide of greetings as Meg was.

"So I'm a little worried about Rosetta," Adriana confided in a stage whisper, nodding toward the bedroom.

"She's just sitting there," said Bob.

"Sniffing a baggie with some dead leaves in it," said Adriana.

"It's potpourri," said Bob.

"I don't think it's potpourri. Potpourri sits in a basket on the back of a toilet. You don't carry it around. We're not living in a century of open sewers."

"Well, it's not pot."

"Never said it was," said Adriana. "It's more her affect that's worrieso—"

Just as Meg was suspecting that the Goldbergs used more words in an hour of conversation than she and her mother did in a week, a goddess emerged from the bedroom.

Over six feet tall, with blond hair tumbling in silken rolls to her waist, shining in a way Meg didn't know hair could shine outside of a shampoo commercial, this buxom, pink-cheeked specimen looked like she'd just taken a break from posing as Venus. Except that she was wearing jeans and holding a snack-size baggie of dried leaves to her perfect, aquiline nose.

"Hey." Rosetta nodded at Meg by way of a greeting, who found herself belatedly appreciating Hannah's tight embrace.

"Hey." Meg could match anyone in a showdown of who cared less.

"Do you know if my dad and his friend left?"

The multiple interpretations of this question left only silence. Was the friend just a friend? A girlfriend? A guy friend, like a buddy? Something else? Where was her mother? Was she asking if they'd left for good? And if they had, wouldn't she know? Wouldn't there have been a significant exchange of farewells? It seemed an intimate question for a group of strangers. Did Rosetta realize that Meg had only just arrived and would have no idea which of the many nervous, swarming adults down on the quad belonged to her?

"Ummm," Adriana offered.

"Doesn't matter." Rosetta waved her hand. "If they come back, just tell them I went out."

"Will you be back in time for dinner?" asked Bob. "You'll want to go to the dining hall as a group."

"That's okay," Rosetta said and left, taking a loud sniff from her baggie.

"That's okay?" repeated Bob. Adriana put her hands on her hips and shook her head.

"Hoo boy, this doesn't augur well. I don't suppose you can switch rooms and be with Meg? Michelle hasn't arrived—"

"Mom," Hannah groaned. "Stop it. We've known her for two hours. She's probably nervous. And no, I can't switch. The rooms are assigned, plus can you imagine the tone that would set?"

"You're right, you're right," murmured Adriana. "Oh, I just wish."

Meg tried to swallow the idea that she looked like the better option.

"Regardless, you two will go to dinner together," Bob said to Hannah and Meg. "And tomorrow morning, Adriana and I want to take everyone out for breakfast. So I really hope Rosetta's parents haven't left." He shook his head at his wife, and she shook hers back in agreement over the obliviousness of some people to plans they never knew about.

Meg and AnneMarie glanced at each other. A restaurant that Adriana and Bob Goldberg would select was not in their budget, and even if "take everyone out" truly meant they'd be treating, and even if it was only breakfast, it meant that the Croydens would then owe them. Meg was pretty sure a bag of Egg McMuffins was not going to cut it as a return favor.

It took Meg less than an hour to settle in. What was there to do? Arrange her minimal wardrobe, shelve her high school notebooks in case she needed to reference anything she'd picked up in Barton, plug in the radio alarm clock AnneMarie had picked up at Walgreens, arrange the bathroom caddy. She pushpinned a free calendar into the wall. There were already curtains and a desk lamp, which Meg knew would be there, because the forms she had paid attention to were the ones saying what the school would provide and what they'd have to bring or buy. AnneMarie sat on the empty bed across the room and refolded all Meg's clothes. When they could find nothing else to do, she took a small brass crucifix from her purse and propped it on the desk.

Meg had been assigned the bed nearest the window, and once the scaffolding came down, she would have an unfettered view not only of the entire freshman quad—freshperson, she had to remember to say, or frosh or first-year—but all the way across Pierre to a range of mountains in the distance. Even now, she could see them between the bars. She'd never lived above the second floor and certainly had never had access to a view like this. She allowed herself a sting of delight.

Michelle still hadn't arrived by dinnertime, so Meg and Hannah decided to head to the dining hall together, like the first date of an arranged marriage. And even though Meg's mother wasn't leaving right then—she was going to stay the night—that's when it sunk in for Meg that they would now live apart. As Hannah and Meg said goodbye to their parents outside the entryway and Meg saw her mother standing a little apart from Bob and Adriana, Meg realized she was leaving her. Which, of course, her mother had foreseen all along.

Meg's years of stealing from her mother and lying to her had receded far into the past. Since the crash, they'd been nearly inseparable, and Meg hadn't pictured what it would be like to live without her. No, that wasn't right. She'd pictured living without her—in a strange dorm room, eating at long, crowded tables in the dining hall, missing her—but hadn't pictured *her mother* without *Meg*. She hadn't thought, not once, about her mother eating alone, hadn't imagined her moving through the house by herself, going to work without saying goodbye to anyone, coming home to no one, saying grace all alone. It's not like their evening routine was so elaborate or depended so much on Meg. Mostly, it was a continuation of the routine they'd developed in the hospital, Meg doing homework, her mother doing a word scramble, followed by a movie and frozen dinner, prayers, and bedtime. Still, the thought of her mother once again praying alone made Meg's throat ache with the threat of tears.

AnneMarie waggled her fingers bravely at her daughter, and Meg realized her mother didn't know where to go to eat. If she followed the Goldbergs, would she be able to afford it? What would they talk about? Her mother didn't follow the news very closely, and mostly read her Bible. Meg hoped the Goldbergs could talk testament.

Hannah already knew the way to the dining hall, which turned out to be gothic and forbidding, and not originally designed to be a dining hall. Inside, it was as chaotic as the Barton high school lunchroom, more so because of all the stations and choices as well as the newfound dietary freedom bordering on hysteria that many classmates were embracing. Most trays were loaded down with multiple glasses of soda and a variety of desserts, often tucked next to a giant salad, an attempt at zero sum nutrition. Meg stuck to what she knew: a bowl of plain pasta, some cooked broccoli, and a glass of whole milk. She'd developed a taste for hospital food.

Hannah waved hello to a bunch of people she'd met during orientation days, and Meg attempted to stick close to her while appearing not to need to do so. She would have chosen an empty table—let other people come to them—but Hannah guided her toward a table where two girls (women?) were digging into piles of food. Hannah knew Tatiana—squat and goth, with heavy black eyeliner—from summer camp ("I never went to summer camp," Meg answered), and Tatiana had met Angel at the campus store that afternoon in the tampon section. Angel was an amalgam of features like none Meg had ever seen: caramel skin, Asian eyes, freckles, red hair. Meg thought she was very ugly, but suspected she was wrong.

Meg said little, which she hoped was okay. She tried not to think about her mother, or what she was doing or about how she'd have to say goodbye to her tomorrow. They stood to clear their trays, and Meg was gratified that even Hannah, who already seemed so comfortable at Linden, didn't know where to bring the dishes. As they peered toward the corners of the dining hall for clues, a student wearing a bright red Welcome to Linden, Class of 2014 T-shirt hurried toward them, her hair in two braids down her shoulders. Her name tag said Lisa Constantino, Senior Counselor.

"Are any of you Hannah Goldberg or Meg Croyden?" She was out of breath.

Tatiana and Angel pointed at Meg and Hannah, who pointed at themselves.

"Whew!" Lisa wheezed and bent over to put her hands on her thighs. She lifted one finger to indicate she'd be okay in a moment. Meg's first thought was that something had happened to her mother.

"You guys are hard to find!" She straightened up and beamed them the big smile she had probably hoped to lead with. "I'm Lisa, your counselor. I live on the bottom floor of your entryway, and I was supposed to be there today to greet you, to help you move your luggage, offer to take you to dinner, stuff like that, and I'm so sorry I wasn't there. I was in the dean's office most of the day, trying to work out a little problem in your suite."

Meg and Hannah glanced at each other. Meg wondered what she could have already done wrong.

"Rosetta told me you two were here." It was a small bit of intimacy that surprised Meg: disinterested Rosetta had been paying attention. She could tell someone where her roommates were. They had moved a millimeter in the direction of being a unit. "If you're done eating, can you come back to the suite with me?"

They put their plates on a conveyor belt outfitted with

shelves and headed back to Cushman, led by Lisa, who attempted small talk as they crossed the quad. Upstairs, they found Rosetta on the scaffolding winding fairy lights around the beams and crossbars.

"Uhh," said Lisa. "You're not allowed out there?"

"Okay," said Rosetta. "I'm just gonna finish this strand."

"Well, be careful. It's dark out."

"That's what the lights are for."

Lisa gave Meg and Hannah a weak smile, her lack of power laid bare.

Rosetta clambered back in through the window, one impossibly long leg after another.

"What's up?"

"Well, so this is about Michelle, your fourth roommate." Lisa locked eyes with each of them in turn. "She's not coming. Not this semester anyway."

"Why not?" Hannah asked, full of concern, as Rosetta said to Meg, "Hey, you get a single! Lucky."

Hannah glanced at Rosetta, hurt before she could prove what a spectacular roommate she'd be.

"I can't exactly tell you all the details, because they're private, but let's just say she changed her mind."

"Okay." Rosetta shrugged.

"What do you mean, changed her mind?" Hannah pressed. "Did she get in off the wait list somewhere better?"

Somewhere better than Linden? Meg couldn't imagine dithering over elite schools. You went to the place that gave you the most financial aid.

"No," Lisa said. "She just, well, had a hard time getting in the car. Let's leave it at that."

"Should we call her?" Hannah asked. "Maybe if she hears our voices, knows that we're all here waiting for her? She sounded so norm—I mean, she seemed like she was excited to come. She was going to bring the mini-fridge!"

"Do you guys want to talk about it?" said Lisa, pulling on one of her adorable braids.

"Isn't that what we're doing?" Meg asked.

"Yeah," Lisa said doubtfully. "Just, it kind of changes the dynamic, you know?"

"We don't have a dynamic yet," Rosetta said.

"True, true, but you know, you were expecting to be a quad, and now you're a triplet."

"I wasn't expecting anything," Meg reassured her. "I didn't read most of the stuff."

"That's true!" Hannah said enthusiastically. "So at least one of us didn't have a preconception."

Rosetta abruptly bent in two and stretched to touch her toes, her long hair falling in a sheet over her, like Cousin It.

"I'm fine, they're fine. I think we're good," she said into her knees from behind her hair. "And now we have a bed for guests."

"Um, okay," said Lisa. "Well, if you need anything…oh, my roommate and I are hosting an ice cream break at eleven tonight! You can meet the rest of your entryway!"

Eleven? Meg was supposed to stay awake until eleven to eat ice cream? In three years, she hadn't stayed up past ten o'clock.

They assured Lisa they weren't emotionally injured and that they'd seek out her rock-solid self if they suddenly became overwhelmed. She left, walking sideways out the door, her first test as a frosh counselor falling short of the mark.

"You guys, come out on the scaffolding with me. It's like we have a terrace!" Rosetta suddenly straightened up. "I already stocked refreshments."

Hannah and Meg both looked at the printed sign taped to the window that said Trespassing on Scaffolding Is Strictly Prohibited. There was a time when Meg would have regarded such a sign as an invitation, but now that she was held together with rods, pins, and plates, she had no appetite for breaking rules or bones.

"Oh, come on. We're stupid first-years. We'll get a rap on the knuckles if anything. And it's got to be safe enough to hold the construction workers, right?"

Hannah chewed her lip for a moment, then carefully removed the sign from the window and crumpled it. Rosetta looked happily surprised.

"Awesome. I don't know why I didn't do that first thing." She swung herself out onto a plank and reached back in to offer a hand. Hannah took it, ducked down, and hopped out. They peered out at Meg expectantly, and suddenly there was no way Meg was going to decline.

It was a cool, dry night, and as they sat on the splintery boards, peering out over the quad watching nervous groups—some of whom would stick together for life, others who would reorganize by morning—Meg let herself believe that she was actually going to be a part of this movie. The whole thing was surreal: leaving Barton, being allowed on this campus, being given a key card to the entryway. It wouldn't have surprised her one bit if Lisa the counselor had come to tell her in the dining hall that there'd been a mistake and she couldn't stay.

Until this moment, the thought of being told to leave offered relief, but for the first time, Meg saw how this could wind up being fun.

"I'm going to email Michelle," Hannah said, accepting a red Solo cup from Rosetta.

"Why bother?" said Rosetta, draining her own cup and reaching behind her for a bottle of wine. She filled Hannah's cup and her own, then held up the bottle to Meg questioningly.

Meg shook her head.

"That's cool," she said to Meg, introducing the possibility that it might not be cool. Suddenly, her baggie of leaves appeared, and she held it to her nose.

"Well, because, it's weird," Hannah elaborated. "That someone wouldn't show up to school. What *is* that?" she asked, unable to hold back any longer.

"A personalized spice concoction that keeps my appetite in check," Rosetta said, like this was commonplace. "We can't all be as skinny as you and Meg. Sounds like mysterious Michelle had a nervous breakdown. I mean, who among us hasn't? It's Darwinian. Like, who moves past the breakdown and gets here anyway."

Hannah looked shocked, but Meg nodded. Rosetta's coldness was clarifying.

"Yeah, if I'm here"—Meg surprised herself by speaking—"anyone can be here."

"Why?" Hannah said immediately.

Because she had been born on a bathroom floor, unwanted first by the body from which she emerged, and then again by the man who had signed on to be her father. Because her mother was effectively paid to take her. Because she'd robbed her for years to get high before trying to kill herself. Because she'd used heroin, not cinnamon, as an unintentional weight control regimen.

Meg was deciding which of these to say when the door to the suite opened and their families returned: the Goldbergs, followed by two people Meg presumed were Rosetta's father and sister, and finally AnneMarie, her eyes immediately scanning the room for her daughter. She deserved a better story than any Meg had been about to tell her suitemates.

"Because I was in a car accident and almost died."

"Cool," said Rosetta, and Hannah looked horrified. Already, they were a wild-woman-and-her-sidekick duo, which was either going to blossom into something funny or devolve into pain for Hannah. "I mean, didn't it clear up a lot for you? Like separate the real friends from the fair-weather friends? Show you your priorities? Or is that just a cliché?"

"No," Meg said, "you're right. It did do that."

"Was that what your essay was about?" Rosetta addressed Meg, but narrowed her eyes at the adults in the common room. Meg shook her head.

"I wrote about being adopted."

"Hey, I was adopted, too!" Hannah exclaimed.

"No shit," Rosetta said. "I hope *you* didn't write about that."

"Why?" Meg asked as Hannah's jaw dropped. She seemed to know why.

"Pretty unoriginal."

Silently, Hannah set down her cup and climbed in through the window, to the surprised exclamations of the parents. She put up her palm as she passed them, headed to the bedroom she'd be sharing with Rosetta for the next nine months, and closed the door. Bob immediately followed her and knocked on the door. Adriana headed for the window and poked out her head.

"Any idea what's bothering Hannah?"

Meg envied the well-choreographed partnership: imagine having a pair of parents who, without even consulting each other, split their duties—one to comfort, one to go investigate the source of the angst. Meg hadn't even imagined such a thing existed, couldn't have articulated it at that moment, but it got to her, that teamwork. That second parent.

"We found out our fourth suitemate isn't coming," Rosetta answered easily.

When Meg was a thief and an addict, she, too, had perfected the art of answering a tricky question with an unrelated truth. Meg watched Rosetta polish off another cup of wine and wondered whether she and her new suitemate might understand each other after all.

Adriana nodded vigorously, thinking she fully understood, and made the effort to give them a quick, inclusive smile. "You ladies bonding out here? That's good. Take your time. We had a lovely dinner with your mom, Meg. And we just bumped into your dad and your...your family, Rosetta, coming back here. Okay, I'm just going to..." She trailed off and hurried back to her daughter's bedroom.

Meg waved to her mom and held up one finger, indicating she'd come inside to save her in a moment.

"What did *you* write about?" Meg asked Rosetta. "For your essay?"

Rosetta rolled her eyes. "No, I didn't write about *that*."

"About what?"

"C'mon, like you don't know." She emptied the last of the bottle into her cup, and Meg's heart contracted a tiny bit. Had she traveled all these light-years from Barton just to wind up with another Gemma Maillard? Screw this. Screw her. Meg stood up.

"Wait," Rosetta said. "You really don't know?"

"Why would I know anything about you?" Meg said. "Is there something everyone is supposed to automatically know?" Letting her impatience bloom, Meg felt a slight power shift in her favor. Rosetta was flustered, and appeared to be weighing her words.

"About my mom? Never mind. The point is that I didn't write about her. But I did write about the stupid-ass name she gave me and how I've learned to live with it. Identity, all that bullshit. As long as you mention identity, you have a chance of getting in. Whatever. Let's go apologize to Hannah." She got up and beat Meg to the window, as if she were the one ending the conversation, as if Meg had anything to apologize for.

"Hi, honey!" AnneMarie gave a flimsy wave from her perch atop an unpacked box. She clutched a bottle of water she'd brought from home, from the stash they bought by the pallet at Costco because their tap water ran brown.

The man Meg hadn't yet met was uncorking a bottle of wine. He flashed a high-beam smile.

"Hi!" he boomed. "I'm Rick Stone, Rosetta's dad."

"Yeah," Meg said. "I'm Meg."

"Meg! Great to meetcha! Care for a drink?"

AnneMarie's eyes went wide.

"Um, no thank you." Father-daughter peer pressure. Fun.

"Meg, meet my wife, Laila. Laila, this is Meg."

Even though there was only one other person in the room she had yet to meet, it still took Meg a second to make sense of what he was saying. Rosetta's sister was not her sister. She was her stepmother.

Laila jumped up to pump Meg's hand.

"So nice to meet you, Meg!" She could have passed for a senior counselor. For all Meg knew, she *was* a senior counselor. She was mousy, and about a foot shorter than Rosetta, who strode toward her bedroom as if Laila weren't there.

"You, too," Meg said as Rosetta knocked on the bedroom door. Bob opened it, and Meg glimpsed Hannah sitting on her bed, shuddering and wiping her eyes. Rosetta looked back at Meg and rolled her eyes, then went in, performing what was apparently a regular cycle of fire-setting and damage control.

"How much money you think you gotta pony up to have a building named after you here?" Rick Stone mused loudly.

AnneMarie fingered the cross around her neck.

"My mom and I are going to finish unpacking," Meg lied.

"You bet!" He held up his glass in salutation. "AnneMarie, where are you staying tonight?"

"Here." Meg's mother looked confused.

"In the dorm? Oh, that's adorable!" Laila gushed. "Rick, we should have done that!"

Rick guffawed. AnneMarie followed Meg into her bedroom.

"Well," she said when they'd closed the door.

"Yeah," Meg said.

"Do you think I *should* stay in a motel?" she worried. "It's going to be crowded in here when your roommate comes. I can stay out in the common room," she added doubtfully. They'd brought along the air mattress.

"It's fine. The roommate isn't coming."

"What!"

"Yeah. Our counselor told us right before you guys came. Couldn't get in the car."

"Couldn't get in the car? What does that mean? Like she broke her leg?"

Meg shrugged. She could too easily imagine not getting in the car.

"Will they get someone else?"

"I don't think it works that way."

"You really think it's okay if I take the bed? What if she changes her mind and shows up in the middle of the night?" AnneMarie said, eyeing the empty side of the room. "I should sleep in the common room."

"We're safe," Meg said with more confidence than she felt, and stood on tiptoe in the closet to find the set of spare sheets they'd brought. AnneMarie put her hand on her arm.

"Don't. Don't get them dirty. I'll use the sleeping bag."

But when they laid out the sleeping bag on that bare, flimsy striped mattress, it looked so woebegone that AnneMarie silently reached for the extra sheets. Meg tossed one of her two pillows onto the other bed.

AnneMarie sat on her bed and Meg sat on hers and neither knew what to do without their pre-bedtime TV routine. They could watch something on Meg's laptop, but then they'd have had to sit really close together on one of the beds.

"Should we pray?" AnneMarie suggested, and that sounded as good an idea as any. Meg prayed only in the company of her mother. It had become a reliable fallback when silences became uncomfortably long. They knelt in front of the desk, before the cross her mother had propped there.

There was a knock on the door. It sank in a little further that Meg was no longer living alone with her mother, that she was living in close quarters with people who would knock on her door at all times.

"Yeah?" she called over her shoulder.

"Can I come in?" Hannah's voice was timid, but she opened the door as she asked. "Oh!" she said, spotting them. "I can come back!" She looked as shocked and embarrassed as if she'd walked in on them having sex.

"No, it's fine." Meg hurried to stand up. Her mom crossed herself, closed her eyes for a very long moment, and then stood up.

"Were you praying?" Hannah said incredulously.

"We were sending knee-mail," Meg's mother joked.

"What?" Hannah was genuinely confused. "Email?"

Meg laughed nervously and it sounded terrible, because she rarely laughed.

"Nothing," Meg said, and felt her mother's hurt. "Come in."

Hannah blew out her cheeks as she looked around. Her eyes rested on the extra bed.

"Wait," she said hopefully, "did Michelle—?"

"No, my mom's sleeping here tonight," Meg said quickly.

"But I don't have to, really, I can go get a hotel room," AnneMarie blustered.

They'd stayed in a hotel once before—a Motel 6—on a church retreat that was paid for by the brother of a local nun. A hotel was not in their budget, plus Meg suspected that an empty room in Pierre on move-in weekend didn't exist. She wondered whether her mom knew this sort of thing and if she didn't, how Meg *did* know.

"So, Rosetta apologized and everything," Hannah began, oblivious to their silent embarrassment. "But, oh my God, I don't know if I can handle her for a year. I really braced myself not to have any preconceived notions, you know, to make no assumptions about a celebrity kid, and figured that was why they put me in a room with her, maybe in my recommendations it came across that I'm really open-minded and low-key and everything, but…oh my God," she concluded.

"Celebrity?" AnneMarie and Meg asked in unison. Meg still didn't understand what had been insulting about Rosetta saying she hoped Hannah hadn't written about being adopted—was *she* supposed to be offended?—but the whole of the past awkward hour was abruptly overshadowed by this new information.

Hannah drew back in amazement.

"You don't know?" she said.

"No," Meg said curtly. She didn't like feeling more out of it than she already was.

"She's Judith Stone's daughter."

"Her name is Rosetta Stone?!" Meg exclaimed incredulously. "Who would do that to a kid?"

Hannah returned her incredulity.

"Judith Stone, that's who!"

"Judith Stone, the writer who's in jail?" Meg's mother said eagerly.

"Yea-ah." It was barely a step removed from "du-uh."

"For staging her own kidnapping?"

Hannah nodded vigorously, glad that one of them was dialed in to the world.

"What!" Meg said, alarmed.

"Oh my goodness," her mother gushed, "and Rosetta used to model for the covers! I thought she looked familiar! Well, not exactly her, but her hair. You know?"

Hannah did know.

"But then she refused to keep modeling," AnneMarie continued, "and they had this big falling out, and then her mother disappeared and there was this possibility that her daughter"—she looked in the direction of the door admiringly—"that *she* had done away with her, but then there were all these clues that maybe she'd been kidnapped, but it was actually a big publicity stunt for her new book, but then because she'd made all these emergency services look for her, she had defrauded the government or something, so she's in jail." AnneMarie was elated. "I mean, it was all so terrible," she added, remembering that she was a somber, righteous Catholic.

This rang a bell, but Meg couldn't get past the name.

"Rosetta Stone?" she confirmed. "Really?"

"What's wrong with her *name*, Meg?" AnneMarie sounded exasperated that her daughter wasn't joining her on this carnival ride of gossip.

"It's…" Meg began, then stopped. There was no way to explain the archeological marvel that had demystified Egyptian hieroglyphics without making her mother look ignorant. This kind of pothole had been appearing with increasing frequency; Meg had been on the lookout to head it off, and she was not going to let it happen here in her dorm room, in front of a suitemate.

"You know, the Rosetta Stone. As in…the Rosetta Stone," said Hannah helpfully. "But I mean, that's the least of it."

"How much longer does she have to be in jail?" AnneMarie asked.

"Five years!" Hannah whispered loudly. "So, I know, I really need to find my way back to sympathetic. Rosetta's going to go through all of college without her mother. I get it, it's tragic, but God, does she have to be so mean?" She issued a dramatic, puffed-cheek sigh. "I probably shouldn't hide out in here, it'll make things worse. But I can't believe I really have to share a room with her for a year. Hey, maybe we *could* ask the housing office to move around, since Michelle isn't coming. I could move in here…?"

Meg panicked. She hadn't realized how relieved she was to learn she'd have a single by default. Getting used to suitemates would be hard enough; the joy of being able to close—and lock—the bedroom door would save her. Her mother removed the lock from her bedroom door at home after the "accident," too pointless, too late, and Meg only now realized how much she'd missed being able to secure herself away from everyone else.

"Why don't you see how the first few days go?" her mom said to Hannah smoothly, surprising Meg, saving her.

"Yeah," said Hannah, unconvinced. She looked around longingly, seeing her entire college narrative dictated by the algorithms and guesswork of an anonymous housing office. The students' lifelong friendships would be shaped by not much more than a roll of dice. Her eyes landed on the crucifix on Meg's desk.

"You're Christian? Cool," she said without waiting for an answer. "You take care of the religious diversity. I provide the racial. And Michelle would have been the geographic diversity. Nebraska. Don't know her religion. Maybe she's Mormon! That'd be wild."

"Where are you from?" AnneMarie asked as Meg said, "What religion are you?"

"New York, just like you," Hannah said in a tone meant to remind Meg that she should have paid attention to the email thread. "But New York City, so, you know, Jewish."

She said it so casually.

"And what religion is Rosetta?" AnneMarie mother asked politely, allowing Meg to register this news.

Hannah laughed, as though Meg's mother had made a joke. "Okay, well. I'll let you get back to it." She backed out of the room and closed the door with conspicuous care.

Meg sank down on her bed, suddenly drained. This was too much, too different.

"I've never met a Jew," she said, "but I know they don't look like that."

AnneMarie looked shocked.

"What?" Meg said defensively. "Have you?"

"Well…of course."

"Of course? Where?" she demanded.

"Patients."

"How would you know they're Jewish if they don't have the big noses and the frizzy black hair? It's not like it's on their registration forms. Is it?" Meg added doubtfully.

"No, of course not! You can just tell sometimes, especially from the names. Gold this, Silver that, you know."

"How would you ever know that a Chinese girl is Jewish? Weird," Meg mused.

"It's not *weird*," her mother said, perching cautiously on the other bed.

"Okay, so it's not weird to you. It's weird to me." Meg wasn't ready for this to be normal.

"When people adopt," AnneMarie persisted, "the kid is the religion of the new parents, and only that religion. You know that, right?"

"I—what? Wait."

She waited.

"Who do you know who's a Jew?" Meg asked carefully.

AnneMarie wrung her hands and looked everywhere but at her daughter.

"Remember?" she said meekly. "Remember those people we talked about once?"

Meg didn't want to remember.

"No," she said.

"Yes, you do."

"We've talked about a lot of people."

"Meg."

"No."

"The Priskers. They were—are, I guess—Jews. But that means *nothing*," she hurried to add when Meg cried out. "I mean, it doesn't mean nothing, but, you know, we *like* Jews." She said this so plaintively Meg nearly put her hands over her ears. "Jesus was a Jew."

"I *know* Jesus was a Jew!" Meg yelled. "But I happen not to be! I know who I am!"

"Sweetheart…"

"I can't believe you're telling me this now. Like this"—she gestured around the room—"isn't enough. You have to tell me this…this new thing *now*?"

"But it doesn't mean anything. I'm not telling you anything worth talking about!" She was desperate for this to be true. "You're mine. You're Catholic. You were baptized a Catholic, and you will always be a Catholic. I know that, you know that, and God knows that."

She launched herself from the bed and knelt before her daughter. She grabbed Meg's clenched fists.

"I don't know why I told you that," she said imploringly. "I don't know why. When you said you'd never met a Jew, it seemed like I'd be lying if I didn't say anything. You can understand that, right?"

Meg pulled her hands away and scanned the ceiling.

"I need to go to sleep," she said.

"Isn't there an ice cream social?" her mother pleaded.

Social. What an embarrassing word. "I'm not going."

"Meg."

"I'm not going," Meg repeated. Resigned, her mother nodded and stood.

"I'm just going to…" AnneMarie trailed off. She fished her toothbrush out of her purse and left the room, peeking out the door before stepping into the hallway, as though checking for traffic.

Meg studied the bed across the room. How was it that she was here and the mysterious Michelle from Nebraska wasn't? Who could have more reason than Meg not to get in the car? Was there a chance she truly had only broken a leg and couldn't manage to start college? Meg doubted that was the case; Lisa would have told them. She was pretty certain she knew exactly why Michelle wasn't there. And where she hadn't had the courage to get here from wherever she was—a farm? A ghetto? Did Nebraska have ghettoes?—Meg had. The thought should have lifted her, but it didn't because she missed Michelle, Michelle whom she'd never met. Meg wished she could call her and tell her she understood and that they'd get through this together. But of course, Meg didn't know her, and maybe only thought she understood. She had zero experience getting through anything with anyone except her mother.

Meg lay on her bed and thought about Rosetta with her bag of potpourri and her famous criminal mother, and Hannah the Chinese Jew, and she kind of hated Linden.

ELEVEN

Meg and her mother woke the next day to metal banging on metal. It was horrible. Meg bolted upright, thinking she was still at home and that the roof was finally collapsing. Her mother mirrored her on the bed across the room, mummified in the sleeping bag. Meg pulled the heavy blue polyester curtain aside and found herself looking straight into the eyes of a man wearing a hard hat. He looked as startled as she was. She yanked the curtain shut.

"Jesus Christ!"

"Margaret Anne Croyden!"

"Well, crap, there's a man six inches away!" Her heart was pounding as much from the surprise encounter as from the shock that she had not dreamed her arrival at Linden. She was actually here.

The clanging resumed.

"This can't be happening!" Meg shouted to her mother. "Is this going to be all year?"

"What?"

Meg bolted from the bed and out of the room. She had no idea what time it was, or where anyone was, or how she was going to live in a construction site. The common room was empty, and the door to Hannah and Rosetta's room was shut. Had they left or were they still sleeping? She pulled up the window that faced the site of the failed bonding the night before. Rosetta's fairy lights were in a tangled pile on the ledge.

Meg leaned out and watched the crouching figure hammer away at one of the scaffolding poles.

"Hey!" she shrieked. "People are sleeping!"

The man whose face had all but been inside her room looked over his shoulder at her. He was weird looking, kind of young and a little scrawny. He reminded her for a second of Troy Cutler and she shuddered.

"Lucky them," he said and turned back to hammering at the pipe.

"Wait!"

He turned back, not as impatient as he could have been.

"How long is this going to go on?" Meg asked feebly.

"Well…" He let her panic for a moment. "Not long," he conceded. "The banging, I mean. We had to fix some of the scaffolding. But the rest of the work is repointing. It's pretty quiet, comparatively." Troy would never have used the word *comparatively.* "It's more of a muted chopping sound, not a banging sound. Sorry we woke the sleeping beauties. We waited 'til eight. Like the contract says."

He turned back around and resumed banging.

Meg brought her top half back into the common room and found Hannah standing dazed, looking like she'd been catapulted there.

"My parents are going to be here any minute! I can't believe I overslept!" She paused for a moment, realizing she was being drowned out. "What is that ungodly racket?"

Meg thought only moms in books spoke that way.

"The downside to our outdoor terrace." Meg held up the discarded lights. "Rosetta's going to be pissed." Actually, she had no idea whether Rosetta was going to be pissed, but it felt good to say it, like she was playing a part in a movie about three college suitemates who knew each other's likes and dislikes.

There was a knock on the door, followed by a singsong "Good morning, giiiirls!"

Hannah let in her parents, their enthusiasm and energy pouring into the suite. They stopped abruptly when they saw the girls' matching states of somnambulism.

"Uh-oh," said Adriana.

Bob tapped his watch.

"We'll be ready in five minutes, right, Meg?" Hannah said, heading toward the bathroom. "Oh," Meg heard her say. "Sorry, AnneMarie, I forgot you were here." Meg wondered how her mom felt now about having encouraged an eighteen-year-old to call her by her first name.

The day loomed long and uncertain. The Goldbergs had a schedule they expected everyone to follow, and Meg would have been content, even grateful, to follow their lead, but she knew some of the day's events would require an outlay of money: eating outside the dining halls, shopping for the ottoman she had failed to bring. It was already clear to Meg that the Stones and the Goldbergs had much bigger budgets than she and her mother did, if they had budgets at all.

Rosetta was still sleeping when they left, so Hannah dutifully left a bright pink Post-it on the bedroom door and another on the bathroom mirror telling her where they were headed. It was no small relief when the five of them set out for breakfast without the intimidating presence of the Stone clan.

The Croydens and the Goldbergs took the diagonal path across campus, which was just beginning to stir, though the exhaustion from the day before was as palpable as the humidity that had set in overnight. Bob and Adriana led the small group through the gates and across the street to the small satellite business area of Pierre that served the college community. To Meg's relief and disappointment, they pushed through the smudged glass door of a diner called Gloria's that looked as dirty and run-down as the diner called Gabby's back in Barton. Even though she and her mother couldn't have afforded any other restaurant, this was the last place Meg wanted to launch her first full day at Linden.

A short, pale woman with wrinkled cleavage and flab swinging from her stained T-shirt sleeves hurled menus at them without making eye contact.

"Gloria's been running this place since I was here," Bob announced, grinning. "She's never once said hello to me!" He said this as though it were a personal achievement. "They have the best eggs you've ever tasted, I promise!"

Meg stored away the fact that Hannah's dad had gone to college. Had gone to Linden. That Hannah had been hearing about Linden her whole life, and that none of this was new to her.

"See now, I'm pretty sure she smiled at me on my very last breakfast here, the day after graduation," Adriana teased. "My car was all packed up and I was sitting at that table over there, weeping uncontrollably."

"She was just glad to have one more Linden kid out of her hair." Bob elbowed his wife and she grinned.

The whole family had gone here?

One thing at a time. Figure out what to do about ordering. The offerings on the grubby menus were the same as at Gabby's, but the prices were nearly twice as high. Meg glanced at her mother, whose face remained expressionless as she studied the menu.

"So," Bob proclaimed, putting down his menu, "how was the first night, girls?" He beamed at Meg and Hannah, expecting to hear nothing less than a report of complete joy.

"I slept well," Hannah chirped, and Meg glanced up, feeling the expectation of an upbeat answer.

"Me, too," she said automatically, and went back to the menu. She was hungry. Did the Goldbergs remember that they'd offered to pay? And even if they did, would her mom insist on paying their share of the bill?

"You ready?" Gloria was at their booth, looking behind her, no notepad in hand.

"We are!" Bob said. "I'll have the Western omelet, with home fries and a side of bacon. Coffee, orange juice, buttered whole wheat toast."

Meg glanced at the price of the Western.

"You?" Gloria dipped her head in Meg's general direction.

"Um, one egg over easy," she said quickly and handed back the menu.

"Fries, toast?" she said impatiently.

"Neither."

"I'm starving," Adriana Goldberg announced, "so make Meg's a full breakfast and I'll eat what she doesn't eat, in addition to my own. Meg, bacon, ham, sausage?"

Meg had never splurged on the meat. "Sausage is fine, thank you."

"Great!" she said with relief, as though Meg were doing her a favor. "Bring her a juice, too. And I'll also have the full Western omelet with bacon. Thank you, Meg!"

Hannah ordered pancakes and then they waited for AnneMarie.

"Just coffee," she said lightly, handing her menu to Gloria. Gloria turned away.

"AnneMarie," Bob began, but Adriana put her hand on his and he stopped. "Well, good, we probably ordered too much—you'll help me finish what my eyes are too big for. So, Meg! Tell us about your interests. What do you think you'll major in?"

"Daa-aad," Hannah implored, just as Adriana said, "Bo-ob."

"What? I can't ask a kid her interests?"

"You can't ask us our *majors*! We just got here yesterday!" Hannah shook her head at Meg, like, *Dads—what can you do?*

"I want to be prelaw," Meg said.

There was a silence, and she wondered how she could have flubbed even that answer.

"So you want to go to law school after college—cool!" said Adriana smoothly. "You can be any major for that. Smart choice!" Someone should give this woman a pair of pom-poms.

"It's just," Hannah said. "I don't think there's prelaw here. That's kind of at…other schools. But, premed, yes!" she exclaimed as though she had misheard Meg, and Meg had been talking about premed all along.

Bob's eyes widened. "Did I hear my daughter say premed?"

"No, you did not!" Hannah bantered back.

To Meg's surprise, she was relieved when the door flew open and Rosetta strode in, sucking all attention to her as she passed other tables and pulled up a chair to the end of theirs.

"God, that fucking construction noise!" she said by way of a greeting.

Meg felt her mother stiffen beside her.

"Hey, Gloria!" Rosetta called out behind her. "Could I get some coffee over here?" She looked around the table. "Jesus, this place. Gloria, everyone here needs coffee!"

Bob's and Adriana's eyes were wide as Gloria gave Rosetta the finger while she shuffled over to the table with a full pot. She began filling cups.

"They let a ho-bag like you into this school?" Gloria said, pushing Rosetta's head forward an inch, not ungently.

Rosetta grinned, the first time Meg had seen a real smile on her.

"I'm here to make you miserable for the next four years."

"Probably take you five to finish if they don't kick you out first."

"Probably." Rosetta took a deep slurp of black coffee and sighed. "Whew. That helps. What'd I miss?"

Bob found his voice, but it was stripped of its earlier bravado.

"We were just talking about maj—I mean interests. What you girls are interested in studying."

"Ugh," Rosetta said. "My only goal is to *not* study rock snot anymore. Maybe I'll shock everyone and be an English major, read books for credit. Sounds like a cakewalk. Sorry, not PC. Cakewalk was a thing white owners made slaves do."

"I'm sorry," Adriana said. "*What?*"

Meg had decided not to say anything else during this breakfast, and her mother was clearly planning the same, so she was glad someone else was asking. *Rock snot?* She had to have misheard.

"Cakewalk. Actually, I think it was more prevalent after so-called emancipation, when actors would put on blackface and mince around being Blacks pretending to be whites. Something like that."

"No," Adriana said. "Rock snot?"

Gloria arrived with steaming dishes of grayish food.

"Oh. I did an environmental class in high school," Rosetta drawled, "and wound up writing a paper on this pollutant called didymo that covers the bottom of rivers and makes everything else die." She eyed the dishes hungrily then plunged a hand into her bag and came up with the baggie full of leaves. She took a deep sniff. "Amazingly, it doesn't come from China like every other fucking pollutant, but from the Faroe Islands."

"Remind me where the Faroe Islands are again," Bob said, tapping his chin with his forefinger.

"Off the coast of Scotland," Rosetta said from inside her bag.

"But rock snot?" Adriana repeated, then shrank back as Gloria's mottled arm reached across her to set a plate in front of Hannah.

Rosetta shrugged. "It's a nickname. It's gross looking."

"And you don't want to study it anymore?" Hannah asked.

"It was in this journal. I was first author. So now everyone thinks I'm going to be this environmental prodigy, but it was a fluke. I'm not even that interested in it."

"Okay, dig in!" Bob instructed. The eggs were greasy and

rubbery and completely unappetizing, but he was paying so Meg ate. Her mother sipped at her coffee. Meg silently offered her a forkful, but AnneMarie shook her head quickly.

Rosetta, however, pinched off a bit of Meg's potatoes and popped it in her mouth. Meg hid her surprise.

"Did you want to have your par—your dad and…join us?" Adriana asked Rosetta.

"Definitely not. I have his credit card and that's all I need. We're going furniture shopping, right?"

"That was the plan, yes," Bob said.

"What do you girls need?" Meg's mom spoke up. "We have a lot of extra stuff in our garage at home. I could bring it the next time I come up."

"Do you have a coffee table and an ottoman?" Hannah asked eagerly.

"I may have a coffee table, but I don't have an ottoman," AnneMarie said, squinting as she mentally searched their tiny, crowded garage.

"What about at your dad's place?" Rosetta asked, pinching potatoes again, this time from Bob's plate. Unlike Meg, he did not hide his alarm, but Rosetta remained oblivious.

"Rosetta," Adriana said sharply.

"I don't have a dad," Meg said.

"Single mothers are the backbone of our society," Bob said. "I congratulate you, AnneMarie. And look where you got her. That must have been a tough row to hoe."

"It was by choice," Meg blurted out. Her mother was very still. "She wanted a kid and so she went for it." She couldn't bear to be pitied by these people.

"Oh, my sister and her partner did in vitro, too! With a

sperm donor!" Adriana gushed, relieved to occupy this sphere of experience with Meg and her mother.

"No," Rosetta corrected. "She's adopted. She told us that last night."

"Even better!" Bob said and was met with an uncomfortable silence. "Just, you know, unwanted children. Needing homes."

"Okay, so ottoman, coffee table, what else?" Adriana said.

"Let's just go to Carton and Box and see what we want," Rosetta suggested.

"That's a little pricey for some student furnishings," Bob said. "We were planning on IKEA."

"How about both? Carton and Box first. It's closer."

Gloria breezed by and dropped an oily check covered in incoherent scrawls onto the table. "You all done?" she asked as she continued past.

AnneMarie reached for her purse. Bob held up his hand.

"Absolutely not. This is our treat." No one challenged him, and he regained a bit of his authority. "We're thrilled to be the ones to introduce you to the delights of Gloria's!"

The Goldbergs pretended to themselves that Gloria's had the best eggs ever when, in fact, they were the worst eggs ever. This would be the first of many self-deceiving proclamations made by Linden students and faculty and parents that Meg would witness in the coming years. Lindenites declared superlatives that patently weren't, convincing themselves that the lives they were leading were better than other lives elsewhere. Why did they need to lie to themselves about bad eggs when it was already so clear that life here was heads above what it was in the rest of the world? Why would they go out of their way to eat bad eggs when there were probably good eggs, already paid for, in the dining halls, and then say the bad eggs were good eggs?

One thing Meg did know: if she made it through these four years—a big if—she would never set foot in this rathole again.

After breakfast, the six of them piled into the Goldbergs' black SUV, the cleanest, quietest, most comfortable car Meg had ever ridden in. Bob turned on the air conditioning—none of the Croyden cars had ever had working AC—and she leaned back in the leather bucket seat in the second row and closed her eyes.

Meg and her mother were allowing themselves to be swept along because they didn't know what else they were supposed to do that morning. It wasn't clear when the parents would depart campus and leave the girls to begin their adventures solo. Tomorrow would be filled with orientation talks—everything from health and safety to understanding schedules. Classes would begin the day after that. Meg couldn't imagine how she was going to pass another forty-eight hours of this torturous, amorphous time. On the other hand, she'd seen her schedule and was dismayed to learn that most of her classes met three times a week and one class met only once a week. How was she supposed to fill the rest of her time? Surely, studying didn't take *that* long. If it did, she was doomed.

"Oh my God!" Hannah cried from the row behind her.

Meg opened her eyes to see a crowd of people holding signs, immediately identifiable as a protest of some kind. To her shock, polite Adriana Goldberg thrust her middle finger up at the window.

"God, I knew this happened, but I've never actually *seen* it," said Bob Goldberg.

He slowed down so that they could better behold the spectacle, and he rolled down Meg's window. She expected to hear yelling, but instead heard the familiar murmur of the hymn "Abide with Me."

The signs said Defund Intentional Families and Abortion Is Murder under a picture of a smiling baby, and IF Is Racist! under a picture of a smiling Black baby.

And then there was one sign, a huge one, propped on the trunk of a car, that featured bloodied, dismembered baby limbs.

"Oh, that's terrible," Meg's mother gasped.

The protesters were gathered outside a chain-link fence that enclosed a parking lot. A man and a woman, lanky and young, crossed the lot, and headed toward a blue awning bearing the familiar logo of Intentional Families. There'd been one in Binghamton. It's where everyone in Barton went to get their STDs treated.

"I know," Adriana agreed breathlessly, but Meg knew the two mothers were talking about two different things. She wished Bob would drive away, but instead he came to a complete stop and gaped as though they were at a zoo.

"They're all fucking old white men!" Rosetta spat.

"Of course they are," Hannah said bitterly.

They watched as two middle-aged women wearing neon orange vests walked from their shaded spot under the awning to greet the couple. The four of them exchanged nods and then the man turned around and shouted something to the protesters.

A frail geezer, whose clothing hung loosely off his gaunt frame, was holding a sign that, curiously, said Abortionist and featured a helpful arrow. He yelled back in a voice too feeble for Meg to make out what he was saying.

One of the vest-clad women put her hand on the young man's arm, but he broke away, and ran to the middle of the parking lot. He spun around and yanked down his pants so that the group in the Goldbergs' car had a clear view of his pimple-pocked ass framing a pair of low-hanging hairy testicles.

"Oh, good Lord!" Meg's mother cried and covered her eyes.

Adriana made a gagging noise. Bob rolled up Meg's window and stepped on the gas.

"I can't believe people would actually yell at a person going in for an abortion," Rosetta said. "Do they think that girl woke up and said, hmm, I know what'll be a fun activity today! Don't they know it's the scariest thing she's ever had to do? Do you think they know that one in three women in this country will get an abortion?"

Bob and Adriana exchanged glances in the front seat.

"That doesn't make it right," AnneMarie said quietly enough that only Meg heard her.

"You know what you girls should do?" Bob said at the next red light. "You should go volunteer and do what those women are doing. Escort patients. Show those protesters that your generation means business."

Hannah and Rosetta made matching sounds of enthusiasm behind Meg.

"How could anyone in this day and age not understand that abortion is essential to the progress of a society?"

Adriana shook her head.

"Well, I don't know about society, but I'm glad no one aborted Meg," Meg's mother said clearly.

The silence in the car was brutal.

"Mom…"

AnneMarie glared at her daughter: whose side was she on?

Meg was on her side. Of course she was on her mother's side. But she absolutely didn't want to talk about this right here, right now.

"Well," Adriana sputtered, "I mean, of course, no one means that—"

"If that teenager had had an abortion, I never would have had my wonderful Meg."

Meg thought about her years of theft and lying and heroin and juvenile sex. Wonderful.

"But," Hannah said tentatively, "I mean, you understand, right, that you can personally be against abortion, but still be totally pro-choice. Like, each woman gets to *choose* what's right for her."

"Murder is not a choice."

Meg wanted to be anywhere but in that car.

"I think we're going to have to agree to disagree," Bob said softly, as he turned past a row of boarded-up homes and headed for the entrance to Route 9, where, Meg would learn, all the nice retail was kept safely away from the failing downtown Pierre neighborhood.

"All those people were doing was praying. They are allowed to pray." Meg couldn't believe her shy, reticent mother was pursuing an argument.

"But that gruesome picture of the body parts!" Adriana cried.

"That was not right," AnneMarie agreed stiffly. "Not Christian."

"They shouldn't be allowed to talk to the patients! It's harassment. Indisputably," Rosetta insisted with particular urgency. When no one said anything, she blurted out, "If anyone had tried to pull that shit when I had my abortion, I would have decked them!"

AnneMarie mashed her lips together into a thin, tight line. "I live by God's word and He does not condone abortion."

"Well, I'm not a big fan of his, so we'll call it a draw," Rosetta retorted.

"You are welcome to go encourage women to kill their babies, but Meg will not be joining you."

Meg squeezed her eyes closed, even as she knew this was a betrayal of her mother.

"Meggie?" AnneMarie asked. Her voice was flecked with doubt.

"No. No, of course I'm not going to volunteer. I…"

"What?"

"Nothing."

But Meg had, horribly and unexpectedly, found herself thinking, *Please go home and let me start my life.*

Meg had never been to a Carton and Box before, had never set foot in any furniture store. Her mom had always found what they needed at garage sales, or rescued perfectly good items from people's curbs on garbage day. The airy two-level building was like a museum, cool and full of light, and Meg wanted everything in there. And she didn't want just one of the glasses. She wanted a stack of them, and she didn't want just one plate, she wanted *all* the plates and bowls and striped placemats and corn holders and whimsical salt shakers. Actually, she would have liked to have lived in the store. Spotting exactly what you needed at tag sales, finding something that was unchipped and clean and in a color you liked came with its own kind of satisfaction having to do with thrift and patience and perseverance. This was an entirely different kind of satisfaction, one that had to do with being surrounded by loveliness and taking a piece for yourself, even if you'd never before thought about a container designed specifically for storing half an avocado.

Meg was unable to enjoy any of it. She'd been anxious about how the shopping trip was going to work, but also a little excited. In the car, though, her mother had detonated the remainder of the day. When they got to the store, Meg and AnneMarie wandered among the dishes, separately, while Rosetta and Hannah and her parents headed upstairs to look at furniture. Meg's mother had accelerated her suitemates' bonding by distancing them from Meg.

Hannah and Rosetta found an ottoman and a coffee table, and AnneMarie said nothing further about searching her garage. Adriana came down to invite Meg to weigh in, but Meg said she'd be fine with whatever they'd picked. Her mother might have made a pretense of trying to pay at Gloria's diner, but no one even brought up the subject of payment now. Meg assumed that Hannah and Rosetta, using her father's credit card, split the cost of the purchases.

The group did not continue on to IKEA, and, except for

Adriana's occasional perky forced observations, the car was quiet on the ride back to campus. The Goldbergs remembered they had some errands to run and disappeared as fast as they could. Rosetta announced she was taking a nap and headed upstairs without thanking Hannah's parents for driving. Meg started to follow Rosetta, wondering what she and her mother were going to do for the rest of the day, since they seemed to be personae non gratae.

"Meg." AnneMarie put her hand on her daughter's arm. "I'm going to head home."

Relief flooded Meg.

"No, why?" she protested feebly.

AnneMarie shrugged. "You need to get on with things."

"I guess."

"I'll see you at Thanksgiving."

Meg's stomach clenched. "There's always the bus. I can come home before that. Or you could visit me," she added halfheartedly.

"Sure, I could do that."

AnneMarie cast her eyes around the quad. Someone had set up a speaker in a window so that jazz provided a soundtrack for the kids biking and walking along the crisscrossing pathways, for the frisbee throwers and loungers sprawled on sheets spread on the emerald grass.

"Meggie, do not forget that Jesus is your savior and your guide. You can always turn to Him."

"Of course," Meg said quickly, glancing around to see whether anyone had overheard. "You don't need to tell me that."

Her mother shrugged like a little girl and nodded upward,

toward the suite window. "Just be careful around these girls, that's all. Don't lose sight of what you know is right."

Fifteen minutes later, Meg's mother had gathered her things and left. For the first time, as long as Rosetta stayed asleep, Meg had the suite to herself. She stood in the middle of the common room.

I'm at college, she thought. *I'm a student at Linden College. I go to Linden.*

Meg tried on these identifications as she ran one palm along the wall, but Linden was designed for people whose parents had gone here and gave them credit cards and bought furniture from glossy stores on a whim. Her mother had one credit card that she kept in a block of ice in the freezer for emergencies. Dire emergencies. She had thawed it to cover Meg's hospital bills and was still paying off the charges.

Fuck them, Meg thought out of nowhere. Her old mantra. She hadn't wanted angry Barton Meg to follow her, but there was no escaping. It was a relief to allow herself that familiar fury at the world, a channel through which she knew how to maneuver expertly. Fuck them for making her mother feel out of place, for making her feel embarrassed by AnneMarie.

Meg was startled by a knock on the door. "Hello! Anybody want to go get ice cream?"

Lisa Constantino, the ardent, feckless frosh counselor.

Meg walked gently away from the door in case the floors were creaky—by the end of the year, would she know the floorboards as well as she knew the ones in her home or would she have flamed out long before?—and climbed out the window. She could hear the knocking only faintly out there.

The suite was hot and sticky, and the scaffolding offered no relief. Meg surveyed her fellow students on the lawn below and felt a wave of loathing for these people who had no idea who she was and probably would never bother to find out.

Fuck them.

Her gaze fell upon the pile of fairy lights. Why would anyone take them down? Assholes. She tossed a string of them over a beam and began to rehang them. Not as a favor to Rosetta, Meg assured herself, but so she could have a place to escape to.

"Hey, don't be startled," a voice said as Meg's body convulsed slightly.

"Jesus!" She turned to find a tall guy out on the scaffolding with her.

"But you can call me JD," he said, and Meg recognized him as the worker who'd awakened her earlier in the day. The morning felt like it had been a year ago.

"You mean JC," she said without thinking.

"Hey, she's funny." He nodded past Meg, and she followed his gaze to see a hard hat upside down on the planks a few feet away. "Could you pass me that? I'll catch shit if the foreman sees me without it."

She handed it to him.

"I was hot," he explained. "Against safety regs, but…"

"You were hot."

"I'm still hot."

Meg looked at him sharply. So he *was* an asshole. But he blushed.

"That didn't come out right. I mean, I'm hot, like you're hot, like"—he was looking around, gesturing wildly at the student-specked lawn below—"like they're hot."

Meg couldn't help letting a grunt of a laugh escape.

"I get it. It's hot out."

"Yes," he said, defeated. "I meant it's hot out." He examined the hat, but didn't put it on his head.

"Do you know who took our lights down?" Meg asked, aware of the weight and uncertainty of *our*. This guy didn't need to know she already felt like an alien among her suitemates.

"My supervisor. You guys aren't supposed to be out here."

"Maybe we put them out here for your enjoyment." Meg ducked beneath a beam and threaded another strand between two planks.

"Sure, they do a lot for the ambience around here at high noon."

Meg snuck a look at him. He looked like Barton trash, but he didn't talk like it. And, actually, he didn't look that trashy. It was just the skinniness and the pimples—not exactly style choices. Without the hard hat, she could see he didn't sport the closely shaved head preferred by every boy in Erie County. His hair wasn't as long and floppy as what the guys wore here at Linden—thank God, because those boys looked like sheepdogs—but it was a happy medium.

Thank God? Why did she give a shit about what this guy, this JD, looked like? JD: the degree she hoped to get one day, but apparently would not be able to start preparing for here at Linden. Meg shook off the discomfiting remnants of that mystifying breakfast conversation.

"Are you going to tell on me?" she said over her shoulder as she continued stringing lights, horrified by her flirtatious tone. As if her own bony, bolted-together body was any great shakes. Meg knew only that JD was the first person she'd met since arriving at Linden twenty-four hours earlier who seemed not completely foreign.

"Where are you from?" he asked, ignoring her insincere question.

"Manhattan." She glanced at him to see whether he'd buy it.

"Really?" JD's brow furrowed.

"I don't look like it?"

"Not really," he said, and Meg was startled by his ingenuousness.

"Where do I look like I'm from?"

"Townie?" he tried.

Meg thought about this. It hadn't occurred to her that there could be other people to meet in Pierre besides Linden students. People more like her. More like JD. Meg bet *his* parents hadn't gone to Linden.

"Kind of," she said. "I'm from outside Binghamton, New York."

He nodded as though he understood, even though Barton was four hours from here.

"I don't know how I'm going to survive here, among the bitches and the assholes," Meg said suddenly.

"They're not so bad, just sheltered."

His kindness toward Linden students was a rebuke. Meg's face grew hot.

"Yeah, no," she amended clumsily. "I know."

"Meg!" Lisa's moony, startled face was suddenly sticking through the window. "You're not supposed to be out here! It's against the rules." She looked back and forth between Meg and the strange man. "And sir, you're trespassing!"

"Actually, she's trespassing. I work here," JD said, unruffled.

"You—oh." Lisa spied the hard hat he had tucked under his arm.

"How did you get in?" Meg asked Lisa ungenerously.

"Rosetta…" Lisa looked behind her, but apparently Rosetta had arisen only long enough to put an end to Lisa's knocking. "Are you coming inside or not?" she demanded.

Meg opened her mouth to unleash a world of hate on the innocent, infuriating counselor. Had Lisa heard what Meg had in store for her, she would have resigned her position immediately, or so Meg liked to think. More likely, Meg would have subjected herself to tedious sessions of mediation and behavioral intervention, sentenced to a kindly, demeaning "adjustment program" Linden had in place specifically for students "like her." Meaning, students unlike those who sat on disciplinary boards in judgment of their own classmates.

"So I'll see you at seven at Angelo's, corner of College and Elm?" JD said to Meg suddenly. He turned to Lisa and let his voice singsong to a falsetto. "Funny coincidence. Meg's mother and my mother are members of the same country club!"

TWELVE

Caroline was unwrapping and restocking new tumblers, a job she enjoyed, but today her mind was racing and her hands were restless. She was afraid her distraction would cause her to drop a piece. She polished a thumbprint glass with her apron and settled it carefully on the shelf, alongside fifteen others. Displaying such an enormous number of glasses, more than anyone would ever need in her own kitchen, was called enviable abundance, and was tantalizing to customers: even though the four or ten or even twenty they'd buy couldn't re-create the clean, bright space that promoted a sense of plenty, they would still try. Caroline had learned about sales psychology from her Carton and Box employee training. It sounded sneaky, but the store was such a lovely place to be that it felt like a good deed to help customers buy its items.

"Excuse me, could you tell me where I could find the picnic plates?"

Caroline looked up and smiled automatically, but that didn't make it a disingenuous smile. The customer, a heavily made up woman about Caroline's age, looked anxious, as though a lot depended on the outcome of her request.

"You mean those melamine ones that clack when you stack them?"

"Exactly!" The woman's face relaxed.

Connection made.

"Unfortunately, I don't think we have any left because picnic plates were part of our summer inventory, but let's take a look."

It felt good to know this. Caroline had never had a body of knowledge before. There was the Bible, *of course*, and she'd mastered certain household budget tricks like the days of the month to stock up on meat at Price Chopper. But there was something so satisfying and systematic, so of-the-world about knowing the seasonal patterns of Carton and Box. She was an insider now, trained by the team leader, updated on what was arriving, what was "evergreen," and what was about to go on sale to make room for the next season.

Caroline gestured for the customer to follow her, and her train of thought picked up where it had left off. That morning, after the weekly PAIN meeting (Parents of Adult Infrequent and Nonattenders) had migrated from the chair circle to a chatty klatch around the weak coffee and powdered doughnuts, Maureen and Dotty had suggested Caroline sign up for the church trip to Albany. They were planning to lobby their representatives to cut off funding to Intentional Families. Caroline's first instinct had been to wave her palms at her new friends—they were friends now, right?—as if to say, *Not me, I don't do that sort of thing.* But, and she smiled as she relived the enjoyable moment, they hadn't let it go. They'd insisted she would have fun and learn a ton. They said she'd be a good addition to the group. Caroline had never been to the state capital, and she suddenly saw herself as having purpose and definition.

In the months since Christopher had left her, she'd become a new person, or at least she felt like a new person. She had been trying lots of new things, including getting this job at Carton and Box, trying out a new supermarket, reading the library's book club selection, and even attending the monthly discussion. (She had had nothing to say at the gathering, and was taken aback by people's strong opinions. It was, after all, just a made-up story.)

But talking to—lobbying!—senators and congressmen and whoever else they kept up at the capital was a whole other level of new. Would a politician listen to her? But if Maureen and Dotty thought she could handle it, then maybe she could. She would be someone who stuck her neck out for causes she believed in. She'd never thought of herself as having a cause, but why not? Why couldn't she be that person?

"My sister just bought a house on the Jersey Shore," the customer said, huffing slightly, and Caroline glanced back at her. She was nearly as wide as she was tall, but Caroline tried not to notice. "She was supposed to close on it at the beginning of the summer, but there was one problem after another. I should have gotten the picnic plates right when she went to contract. I don't know why I didn't."

"Well, let's see what we can find for her." Caroline wondered whether other stores also prompted these personal revelations or whether the products—the bright stacked serving bowls, the unsmudged glasses, the perfectly white plates—invited everyone to live in a fantasy world, an aspirational world, as the morning shows called it. She couldn't remember ever feeling compelled to explain the story behind her purchases at Penney's or Macy's.

"She bought the house with the money she got in her divorce. I really wanted those cute plates with the orange stripes," the woman fretted. Caroline twitched at the word *divorce*. She knew they'd run out of those plates weeks ago.

They reached the meager summer display at the back of the store. A stack of straw placemats that had been a bust were surrounded by towers of multicolored plastic wineglasses that had sold so well the store received extra shipments for the Labor Day sales. Caroline challenged herself to get this woman to buy the unpopular placemats. That's what Yuna, the team leader, always reminded them to do each morning before their shifts. "Challenge yourself!" she would cheer as the sales associates headed out of the staff room and onto the floor, though it came out "Chawenge yawsef!" Caroline had been lukewarm about Yuna at first. She was so young, and the accent made her a little hard to understand, but she was starting to appreciate that Yuna, with her impossibly shiny black ponytail and her stretchy lime-green key ring worn around her tiny biceps, felt as good about Carton and Box as Caroline did.

As the customer flipped noncommittally through the placemats, Caroline's mind darted back to the other idea Maureen and Dotty had planted. They suggested that in addition to coming on the Albany trip, which was a one-time event, Caroline should join them on Wednesday mornings to pray outside the local Intentional Families clinic. As nervous as it made Caroline to contemplate talking to politicians, she knew that they were already on her side. They needed only to be reassured by their constituency (that's how Maureen and Dotty had put it). But outside that clinic—which was downtown, in the worst, dirtiest part of downtown—anything could happen. And even though Caroline knew the Protect Life group was peaceful and only prayed, she had heard stories about angry patients and rude "escorts." People in orange vests stood outside luring in young women for abortions and cursing at the prayer group.

"I don't know," the customer said so helplessly that Caroline was overcome by a wave of disgust.

"Hmmm," she said, putting her finger to her lips to quiet her impatience. *Rise to the challenge. Change course if you have to.* "You know what everyone needs in a new house? Glasses. Even if you have some glasses, they're always breaking or you have mismatched ones. Follow me," she added quickly when the customer began to protest.

Caroline marched swiftly back to where she had been unpacking tumblers, hearing the customer huffing behind her.

Imagine these girls going inside to knowingly have a baby torn from them! Caroline knew it was wrong, almost indecent, to want to get a look at them, and she corrected herself: what was making her pulse quicken was the thought of praying for their salvation, of saving them. This, she thought as she placed a glass between the customer's pudgy fingers, could be a chance to make a real difference in a young person's life. Her own children had never been receptive to her guidance. They didn't appreciate her at all. An errant thought popped up before she could block it: her own children didn't actually like her. But these young women very well might like her and even appreciate her.

"You really think she'll like these?" the customer asked doubtfully.

"Of course!" Caroline said automatically, then felt guilty about how little thought she'd actually given to this woman's needs. She was about to suggest regular indoor placemats when another shopper appeared tentatively at her side.

"Excuse me, I'm sorry to interrupt—"

"You're not interrupting at all!" Caroline said, relieved. What a mistake it would have been to introduce a new option to the indecisive woman. "We just decided she's going to get these gorgeous glasses. Right?"

"How many should I get?" the pudgy one asked woefully, examining the glass. Caroline feared she would drop it or crush it.

"Eight," Caroline said firmly and looked to the new customer for backup.

"Um, sure," said her uncertain ally. "That seems good." *This* shopper, Caroline noticed, was wearing a small gold cross on a chain around her neck. The woman, in turn, noticed Caroline's own small gold cross, and the two shared a quick smile. Caroline felt a wave of peace flush through her and reflexively glanced upward.

The sister of the divorcée nodded in defeat.

"I'll pick them out for you and meet you at that register," Caroline instructed. This was against protocol, but she feared the sale would be derailed if she were to leave the selection to this customer. The woman trudged off in the direction of the checkout counter.

Caroline turned to her savior. "Thank you. I needed some reinforcement."

"Oh, well. Okay." The shopper—this one was slender and well-kempt—seemed thrown off guard and looked like she regretted approaching Caroline.

"Tell me how I can help you," Caroline urged. She reached behind the customer and unpeeled a shopping basket from a strategically placed stack. She began to load it with glasses.

"I don't know who to ask, but I was wondering whether there are any job openings here." Her voice rose at the end, making it a question.

Caroline hadn't expected this, and was surprised to find she felt protective of her job. As if there was a quota for middle-aged employees and she didn't want any competition. Ridiculous, she told herself, but doubted that it really was ridiculous. She was the oldest employee by thirty years.

"I don't know for sure," Caroline finally said truthfully. "Are you looking for part-time or full-time?"

"Oh, it's not for me!" the woman answered, and now Caroline was insulted by her tone of voice, which implied that she did not need a job such as this. "For my daughter." She gestured across the store floor to where a frail-looking, sour-faced girl slouched over a display of lemon-squeezers and nutcrackers that had been designed by an artist recently given a retrospective at some big museum down in the city.

As Caroline watched, two other girls trailed by an adult couple sailed down the escalator, and it became clear the customer's daughter had been keeping them in her sights. The little Asian one and the breathtaking, tall one—goodness, but she looked like something on the cover of a romance novel—had a presence that was much bigger than themselves. It wasn't that they were overly loud, or even obnoxious, but their confidence, so much confidence in such young people, was unseemly. The little one wore a Linden baseball cap and the big one wore a Linden T-shirt, and, as they headed toward the ugly girl—well, sorry, but it was true, and it didn't mean God didn't love her as much as He loved anyone else, maybe He loved her more—Caroline understood the scene before her, and her heart tightened in sympathy. The escalator girls had never once in their lives felt out of place anywhere (or, she guessed, needed a job) and the ugly girl only ever felt out of place (and always needed a job), and now here they all were at college together. And at Linden, no less. Caroline's lip curled slightly at the thought of the brainwashing that occurred daily just miles down the road from her home.

The customer fingered her cross nervously, and Caroline was flooded with compassion for this mother. She would not be able to protect her daughter from these girls.

"God will protect her," Caroline said before she realized the words had left her mouth.

The mother looked startled and then a look of relief spread across her face. She grabbed Caroline's hand.

"Thank you," she whispered. "Thank you."

Both women closed their eyes and silently prayed together. In that moment, Caroline knew that she was meant to step up, to move on to something bigger. She would go to Albany, and she would begin to go to the clinic every Wednesday. She would carry out Jesus's word.

THIRTEEN

The kid Sylvia had come to think of as Presbyterian Rastafarian for his square jaw and blond dreadlocks (given name Mason Salem) eagerly offered to read a draft of his scene aloud. She reluctantly agreed, figuring she'd have to get him out of the way sooner or later. She'd read the piece, working title "Sniffing My Fingers," and it had made her despair for the future of civilized intercourse. In this environment of infantilizing trigger warnings, she wished she could issue one for bad writing. But he was a good-natured kid, and Sylvia would do her best to guide the group through as gentle a critique as possible.

Sylvia's foray into teaching Linden students playwriting had not been going so well, even though she was as prepared as any well-intentioned poser could be. She'd spent the past month rereading Aristotle, the Bard, and McKee, and allowing Ruth and Ellie to remind her that she was, in fact, far more familiar with playwriting than the eighteen-year-olds she'd be teaching. Plus, Sylvia knew a thing or two about acting, and so she acted like a teacher. Yet no natural momentum ever gathered during the interminable two hours.

The biggest challenge, it turned out, was keeping herself focused on their writing during class, so fascinated was Sylvia by the proximity not only to these future consultants of the world, but by the glimpse they gave her into what her own children might be in a few short years. Teenagers had become foreign to Sylvia, not having had much opportunity for interaction with them since she'd been one herself, save the occasional babysitter. She considered the statement stickers slapped across their laptops—presumably the scaffolding to their identity-building—wondering at the yin-yangs, the #IStandWithIntentionalFamilies, the inarguable if oddly nondirectional truths like No Farms No Food. Mostly, she was fascinated by the (it seemed to her) misplaced confidence they oozed that made her regard all of them with caution.

"Place: an Upper West Side therapist's office. Time: timeless," Mason began.

Place: a setting that allows me to think no further than my own thoughts. Time: gratuitous existentialism, Sylvia thought, stifling a sigh.

"Gentle furnishings abound: posters from Native American museums, throw rugs, innocuous statuettes. Books are everywhere, shoved in horizontally on the shelves, in piles on the floor, threatening to topple and consume an unlucky patient. The grimy windows haven't been cleaned in a decade. In one tattered chair is DR. SEYMOUR, a large, bearded gentle bear. Facing him, on a ripped couch covered with a batik throw, is JASON, 18, snappily dressed, sporting dreadlocks."

Sylvia glanced around the room to see if anyone else was as mortified by this unabashed public display of egoism as she was. *Explain switching ID characteristics*, she jotted down. If in real life the person on whom you're basing your character is short with a tiny penis, in your writing he is now a giant with the endowments of a stallion. Most of the students were scribbling furiously, and Sylvia resigned herself to the fact that their critiques would be formed as much in their own images as the script was formed in Mason's.

The lone student not taking notes was staring at Mason as he read, her jaw slightly open in an expression that did not hide her alarm and incipient disgust. Sylvia liked this kid. She thought of her as Blue Collar because she wore her hair in a tight, unflattering ponytail, and her guarded coolness seemed genuinely self-protective, not aggressively assumed. Sylvia surreptitiously ran her eye down her cheat sheet. God help her if anyone ever saw it, though she doubted they'd be able to decipher it.

Pres Rast: Mason

Nap: Lily

Lily Changberg, a biracial beauty whose parents had combined their last names, came to each class with a semicircular crease on her forehead that disappeared over the course of the two hours. Sylvia's hunch was that she arrived fresh from a post-lunch facedown nap.

Pat: Toby

Fluid gender, wan, no muscle tone. If a student ever saw this list, there was no way they'd be familiar with Julia Sweeney's androgynous character from SNL.

Ribbed: Alicia

Sinewy, tiny, a paler shade of white than the classroom walls, Alicia always wore a black ribbed tank top to class, bright red lipstick, and sported a wild mass of blond curls that provided an eight-inch buffer between her head and the world.

Blue Collar: Meg

Meg. Right, Meg. Sylvia tried to commit this to memory. Meg had submitted one of Sylvia's favorite scenes so far, about an adopted kid confronting her birth mother. If it was based on real experience, then it would serve as a great example of a Writing Do versus Mason's current Writing Don't.

"JASON: 'So I finally had sex!' Jason holds up his hand for a high-five, but Dr. Seymour leaves him hanging."

A few gracious titters rippled around the table. Meg glanced Sylvia's way, the first indication Sylvia had gotten that anyone in the room cared what she thought. She took a chance and raised her eyebrows a fraction of an inch: it was a minimal enough gesture that if she were reading Meg wrong, she wouldn't get herself in trouble. But Meg raised her eyebrows back, and they were allied.

"DR. SEYMOUR: 'And was it with a man or a woman?'"

No way. No way would any professional shrink say this. These kids were all in therapy, Sylvia was certain. How could Mason not get at least this part to sound authentic? *Because this is fiction*, Sylvia reminded herself. *It's his fantasy.*

"Jason hesitates, runs his finger along the spine of Erik Erikson's *Identity: Youth and Crisis.* JASON: 'Both. Neither. All of it.'"

Kill me now. Moments like this, it was a Herculean task to remember why she was here, paying someone else to have the privilege of walking Nathaniel to kindergarten, listening to his running commentary on every passing person, dog, pigeon, and car, observations that were light-years more insightful than what Rasta here had on tap.

Sylvia stretched herself out of a defeated slouch and squinted through the window, trying to make it look like she was thoughtfully processing this drivel, instead of refraining from crying out to its creator to cease and desist. Her eye was caught by a metallic glint, and she found herself surreptitiously studying the hair of Ribbed. She glanced at her cheat sheet. *Alicia.* Was that a barrette stranded in Alicia's tangle of blond curls? Did she know it was there? It certainly wasn't acting as a restraint of any kind. But no, it was a square, not a barrette, like a piece of foil put in for a hair tint. Sylvia glanced away, ran her gaze around the table, and looked back. Was it possible a piece of garbage had landed in her hair and she didn't know? There was no way to find out, because if it was decorative and not garbage—though it could easily be both, an exercise in self-expression, a commentary on the nature of garbage as art—and Sylvia pointed it out, she risked offending, and who knew what the legal ramifications were for offending a student these days.

Mason's tragedy continued. "Jason pulls a banana out of his backpack and begins to demonstrate."

On the other hand, if it was unintentional garbage stuck in her hair, then it was basic common courtesy to let her know, like alerting someone to toilet paper on the bottom of a shoe, or a skirt caught up in underpants.

"DR. SEYMOUR stands and turns to the window, clearly hiding his arousal."

Alicia was expressionless. She had stopped taking notes, and was watching Mason read, one arm propped along the back of her chair. As Sylvia watched, Alicia began to twirl her hair around one finger, though *twirl* wasn't really the right word. She plunged her hand deep into the mass and made a digging motion. Her hand was close to the metallic square, but it might be days before the two crossed paths.

"DR. SEYMOUR: 'And how was it for you?' JASON: 'It was everything and it was nothing.'"

The hand moved closer to the target. Sylvia suddenly realized she was staring and abruptly shifted and looked away. She looked immediately to Meg, who was biting her lip as if to keep from laughing. Was it because of Mason's decimation of all that was holy or had she, too, spotted the garbage-art in Alicia's tresses? Her decisive turn away from Alicia made Sylvia think it was the latter.

"And that's as far as I've gotten."

Silence. Mason looked up expectantly, a cue that this was not a continuation of his assault, but, rather, its blessed conclusion.

"Okay," Sylvia chirped. "Thanks so much, Mason." She made a show of glancing at her class list, but already knew she'd call on Pat/Toby, not just because zher—the pronoun zhe used—gender fluidity nicely suited the piece at hand, but because zhe had proven to be exceptionally diplomatic. "Toby, why don't you start us off with the positive?"

Toby squinched zher nose thoughtfully. "I really like the scene setup, the description of the 'gentle furnishings' and 'innocuous statuettes.' You have a great knack for description."

Damn, that was going to be Sylvia's comment, the only positive observation she could make. There was a slight murmur of activity as many around the table crossed out similar observations.

"And it's a really powerful setup, having it in a therapist's office."

Powerful. *I do not think that word means what you think it means.*

"So that's all great."

Toby was buying time.

"I guess, well, could you tell us where you see this going?"

Mason nodded intently, scribbling notes. Was he going to forget this vanilla commentary if he didn't memorialize it? Sylvia was on the verge of one of her mini-crises, the modest panic attacks she now reliably had multiple times a day when she was up in Pierre. She'd grow short of breath, assure herself those were not chest pains, and stave off lightheadedness thinking about the utter uselessness of being there. Children were starving a few short miles from where she sat, women were being raped every second of every day somewhere in the world, and, even were she to block out those atrocities, there were years of her children's artwork to be sorted, a recipe for banana muffins with spinach stowed inside to be attempted, and dentist appointments to be scheduled. Attending to any one of those matters would be a better use of her time than being here, where she was merely feeding her hungry pride.

"I don't believe in outlining. I want to listen to my characters and see where they take me," said Mason.

The room was horribly silent. Sylvia glanced down at her roster, relieved that she could put the onus on another student while she bought herself some time.

"Dixon," she said, singling out a puffy-faced young man who had withstood a rather harsh critique of his piece, about a family called the Whites, who lived on White Street in White

Plains and were…Black. "What do you—wait!"

Sylvia looked at the list again to double-check. "Have you guys realized that we have Mason and Dixon in the same class? Like, the Mason–Dixon line! That's really funny!"

Indulgent nods let her know that she was the last to figure this out. She willed herself not to flush.

"Just kind of funny," Sylvia repeated weakly. "Dixon, what do you—?"

As Sylvia spoke, Alicia's hand made contact with the metallic square. She frowned as she extracted it.

A condom wrapper.

She gave a small, unalarmed nod of recognition and dropped the wrapper into her backpack.

Good Lord. It wasn't the screaming proof of recent, daytime sex that threw Sylvia. It was the grave hygienic implications. What the hell else was hiding in there?

"Dixon," Sylvia tried again, before anyone caught her watching Alicia. "Where, as an audience member, do you, in your gut, hope this scene will go? Brainstorm for Mason. No right or wrong."

Dixon's face projected abject fear, and she knew he wanted to see this scene go the same place she wanted it to go. An incinerator.

"Actually, you know what, forget that," Sylvia said smoothly. "Let's all do some written brainstorming on Mason's behalf. This is a good exercise, I promise. Take five minutes to sketch out some ideas, on paper. We'll have just enough time to go around and read them." She glanced gratefully at her watch. After today, they'd be free of Mason's unpalatable creation for at least another month.

Sylvia passed small stacks of only slightly rumpled looseleaf around the table, and at last there was blissful silence as everyone contemplated blank pages. Sylvia tried to rally her attention to Mason's scene, but once again found herself longing to enfold Leah in a tight hug until she let out her raspy giggle. To play hot lava—jumping around the living room furniture without touching the floor—with Nathaniel. Before her life had been overturned and its guts shaken out, Sylvia had found playing with her kids tedious. She had wanted to feast her eyes on them without actually having to play Chutes & Ladders (as it turned out, a realistic lesson in life's whiplash and undeserved changes in fortune) or Candy Land or any other number of criminally dull games. She had a distinct memory of sitting on the floor with Leah when she was new to toddling. She would bring Sylvia one stacking ring after another and Sylvia would think, *You're so freaking cute, I'm so bored, you're so delicious, I'm so bored, I want to cover you in kisses, good God when is the sitter coming.* But now, now she would do anything to spin a rickety plastic wheel with them.

Come on, Syl. Come up with something. These kids' parents pay two hundred dollars an hour for them to be here so you have to live up to your end of the bargain. She finally jotted down some suggestions for embedding the character's sexuality issue in other settings instead of addressing them quite so directly. *Give your readers some breathing room, for Christ's sake.*

A trickle of paper began to make its way to Sylvia. She gathered up the suggestions, praying there was one in there that Mason would deign to entertain.

Set the play in a French colony on the moon.

She sympathized. Anywhere but a therapist's office.

Make Dr. Seymour a woman.

Sure, why not. It wouldn't help, though.

Have Jason's parents be at the therapy session.

Good Lord: these crippled, helicoptered, overgrown babies. She'd heard stories of parents contacting professors regarding their now-adult children's troubles. It had to have started earlier, most likely in therapy sessions where the kids should have been talking *about* their parents not *with* them. Well, she was in no danger of becoming a helicopter parent, seeing as she was seventy miles away from her children. *Focus, Sylvia.* She was being as solipsistic as Mason.

At least she uses protection.

What? Sylvia frowned at the scrawled suggestion, flipped it over to see if she was missing something. She glanced up, about to ask whether someone had the rest of the comment, when she found Meg watching her with raised eyebrows and pursed lips.

If the sun had come out and she'd downed three cups of coffee, Sylvia couldn't have gotten a bigger lift or infusion of confidence. Meg had crossed the divide that shouldn't be there anyway and reminded Sylvia that she wasn't a million light-years away from these kids after all. A condom wrapper in one's hair wasn't normal, and Mason's writing sucked and should be treated—kindly—as the sciolism that it was.

Sylvia relaxed and felt a genuine smile spread across her face.

"Okay, here's my suggestion," she said, setting aside the stack of scrawled notes. "Set the scene in a hair salon. It's a traditional space for confidences, and as a set, it's not quite as…limiting."

The room murmured in agreement, and she felt a definite uptick in the students' regard for her. She dared to glance at Meg, who pursed her lips in something resembling a smile. She tilted her head ever so slightly toward Alicia, who, her hands still rummaging atop her head, remained blissfully unaware of how her wild tresses had indeed inspired some art.

FOURTEEN

It was Meg's day to present, and though she told herself she didn't care what these assholes thought, she was nervous anyway, and that just made her more annoyed. There had been times in this seminar when she seriously thought she was going to jump out of her seat and pummel a classmate. Could they not hear themselves?

In a million years, Meg would never have chosen this seminar, Intro to Playwriting, but no one had bothered to explain to her that class registration at Linden was a cutthroat race. At the end of the enrollment window, she wound up with a schedule that included nothing she had chosen: History of Math, Intro to Caribbean Anthropology, Twentieth-Century Suburban Novel, and this. Not only would she have to suffer through this weird mashup of classes, she'd have to do well enough in them so that she wouldn't lose her scholarship before she had a chance to take the classes she wanted. As it turned out, though, Meg wasn't at all bored. Weirdly, she even noticed overlaps between some of the stuff she was learning in the mathematics history class and some of the data collection methods in the anthropology class, and that kept her entertained.

But Intro to Playwriting was the one that might send her over the edge, because the students in it were so full of shit. The only reason she could get through it was because she liked the professor—they weren't supposed to address her as "professor" because Sylvia Tanisman was only a "visiting professional"—and she was sure it wasn't just because Sylvia liked what Meg was turning in. It was because Meg guessed Sylvia also thought the rest of the class were assholes.

"Okay, Meg, you're up." Sylvia nodded at her. She had encouraged the class to address her by her first name, which Meg thought was a mistake. Her classmates, with their stainless steel coffee mugs dangling off their purposely ugly backpacks, munching their barbecue soy puffs, shuffling around in knockoff Crocs—"Crocoffs"—should have to be reminded that they were not the smartest people in the room, even if only by being required to call a teacher by her last name.

But no one had asked her opinion.

Meg reluctantly pulled out the five pages she had to read aloud, and avoided making eye contact with anyone while they dug out their copies of the scene she'd written. She couldn't remember ever feeling more vulnerable, and that included being pinned down by Troy Cutler in his dad's tractor. There was nothing Meg wanted to do less and nowhere she wanted to be less.

"Place: an American suburban mansion. Time—"

"Hang on, Meg," Sylvia said. "Not everyone's ready."

Meg sat back and glowered until all the paper shuffling subsided. She swore she could feel the hate flooding out of her classmates. So she pictured JD's rough, large hand holding hers, which he'd suggested she do whenever she was riled by

Lindenites, and it almost always calmed her down.

"What's it called?" Lily Changberg squinted at a mess of papers in front of her. She routinely showed up with a dent on her forehead, which Rosetta had learned was the result of a weekly massage she received right before class. Meg couldn't picture how a massage happened and why it would cause a dent in a forehead and she wasn't about to ask. How Rosetta knew Lily Changberg or her self-care habits was another mystery. She was part of an information exchange that Meg would never be privy to.

"Untitled," Meg said flatly.

"Got it," Lily said, beaming as if expecting a reward for being perpetually adorable.

"Place: an American suburban mansion," Meg repeated, plowing through the words, daring anyone to stop her again. "Time: the present. The lights come up on a fancy front door with pillars in front of it. We see part of a circular gravel driveway and we hear the sound of a beater car coming to a screeching halt. Slamming door, angry footsteps crunching on the gravel. GEMMA enters. She is fourteen, scrawny, ugly, and angry. She presses hard on the doorbell."

Could anyone guess that this was Meg's exact story? Was it cheating that she hadn't changed a single detail except swapping out her name for Gemma's? She hadn't wanted to take this stupid class in the first place and didn't know where to begin writing fiction, so this is what she had. The only thing she planned to imagine was the bathroom scene her mother had described, and have stupid, fat, scared Alexa actually give birth to Meg onstage. A flashback. She was eager to make everyone in class squirm while she screamed labor pains during the read-aloud. Sometimes, while she'd been writing it, Meg had pictured her play being put on somewhere and Alexa and Mrs. Prisker just happening to be in the audience, writhing with discomfort and regret.

The first scene closed with her—Gemma—leaving the house after meeting The Bitch (aka her fucking grandmother).

"That's it," Meg announced, putting her pages facedown and crossing her arms. Let them tear it to shreds.

No one said anything, and Meg began to seethe.

"That was amazing," Toby said. Toby was neither a boy nor a girl, which usually irritated Meg, but right now she was grateful to him/her. Them. Meg's high school tutor had taken great pains to open Meg's eyes to proper grammar—the consequence being that abject errors assaulted her everywhere she looked—and Meg was still hoping a singular third pronoun would burst onto the scene.

She glanced at Toby suspiciously, but Toby was sincere.

"Totally gripping," Mason Salem, the idiot with whiteboy dreads, agreed.

"Can you guys give her some specifics?" Sylvia prodded.

"I like how you describe both characters as ugly, but convey how money has made one look better and poverty has made one look worse," Toby offered.

"I wouldn't call it poverty," Meg said quickly, then added, "but yeah, okay."

"FYI, instead of saying 'fancy door with pillars in front of it,' you could just call it a 'portico,'" said Alicia, twirling a finger in her Jew-fro.

Of course *she* would find a way to make Meg look stupid. Meg had disliked her and her big hair and her little tank tops and her red lipstick the second she laid eyes on her. She was above making eye contact with anyone.

"Fine." Meg rolled her eyes and scrawled "portico" across the back of a page.

"What happens next?" Dixon said eagerly. Meg glanced at him to see if he was mocking her, but he was either a great actor or a nice person. She had never been in school with a Black kid before, but understood very quickly that she was never to say things like that out loud at Linden. That kind of statement elicited gasps, and she wasn't interested in being their upstate, working-class object of fascination any more than she already was.

Meg glanced at Sylvia and she nodded encouragingly.

"So it will turn out that Mrs. P. is Gemma's grandmother. As in, her fifteen-year-old daughter gave birth to Gemma. That's what Mrs. P. means when she tells Gemma she's been to that house before, that she was born in the upstairs bathroom."

Silence.

"Wait, what?" Alicia interjected. "Why would a rich family's daughter have the baby in the bathroom?"

"But no, even before that," Lily piped up, "the teenage daughter of a rich family would never have the baby. She'd have had an abortion."

Meg felt like she'd been punched.

"The girl doesn't know she's pregnant," she said with what breath she could muster.

Alicia made a waving motion.

"What's that supposed to mean?" Meg demanded.

Everyone froze.

"I mean," Alicia said, still to the ceiling, "I know you hear about these kids who supposedly are so in denial that they don't know they're pregnant until they're sitting on the toilet with cramps and pop, out comes a baby. But come on. They know."

Meg's heart pounded.

"Some of them are f—heavyset," she caught herself. Again, dodging the verbal minefields set by the loathsome Lindenites.

"Whatever," Alicia said, barely sounding interested, which was what infuriated Meg the most. "I don't care how fat you are; you have sex, you don't get your period, come on, how dumb do you have to be?"

"Okay," Meg tread carefully, controlling her voice. "So, say she knew she was pregnant. Maybe she knew her family would try to get her to have an abortion and she didn't want one. Maybe that's why she didn't tell them."

Alicia made a pfft sound and waved her hand dismissively again. "Please. What teenager would want to keep a baby? That's ridiculous. I mean, does this take place in Kansas or something, like where everyone is a holy roller and abortion is illegal?"

Sylvia must have been able to tell Meg was about to jump out of her seat, because she spoke up.

"First of all, for what it's worth," she said, "abortion is still legal in many states. But that's not the point here." She shook her head at herself. "Let's be aware of the…*lenses* that we're all bringing to class, through which we all see. And let's try to see through each playwright's own lens. If that makes sense," she added doubtfully.

"My lens," Meg spat, "is that not every pregnant teen wants an abortion!"

"Fine," Alicia said.

"It *is* fine." She knew she sounded petulant.

"Does anyone have any other questions for Meg? Comments?" Sylvia pleaded.

"Are you, like, anti-choice?" Lily asked, ponderous as a child at a zoo.

"I don't think—" Sylvia said.

"Yes," Meg said, although until that moment, she hadn't decided. A few people gasped. They actually gasped, she would emphasize to JD later, when they were lying in her narrow, extra-long bed. Realizing she'd just cut any cord that might have still linked her to her classmates—they were all eighteen, they were all students, they were all away from home—she added, "I was adopted and I'm pretty fucking glad that idiot teenager didn't abort me."

Everyone but Lily froze.

"But that doesn't mean you have to be anti-*choice*," she persisted, unfazed. "You understand that, right? Like, *you* can be anti-abortion, but that's a choice you're making for yourself."

It was the same verbal acrobatics Hannah had performed in the car the day they went to Carton and Box. Where did they all pick up this bullshit?

"Whatever. I'm pro-life," Meg said haughtily.

"Most quote unquote pro-lifers are for the death penalty," Lily retorted.

"Those are two different things," Meg said automatically.

Selena, a Hispanic girl—again, there was a different word Meg was supposed to use—who smelled of old makeup, suddenly grabbed her backpack and ran out of the room.

"Well, I guess we know who's had an abortion or two," Alicia quipped to her fingernails. "We need a trigger warning for this convo."

"Let me see if I have this right," Meg snapped at Alicia.

"Meg," Sylvia warned.

"No, no." She waved off her teacher. "You're all pro-abortion—"

"We're not pro-abor—"

"Whatever, you're all in support of abortion, but you shame someone who's had one." Meg nodded toward the door. More brick wall silence. Silence she might never recover from in her four years here. Meg was making a name for herself on campus, right then and there, and the realization was both terrifying and exhilarating.

Fuck it: it turned out she was glad to be alive. For the first time in her life, she was actively, consciously glad that fat, ashamed Alexa hadn't aborted. This was surprising, and perhaps it was her surprise that drove her to embrace a position with a wholeheartedness that was a little too unexamined. But embracing ideas one hundred percent was a rampant disease on campus. Her classmates' stance drove her further into her corner, and it was so much easier to assume the label of being pro-life instead of examining the issue piecemeal, which Meg didn't have time for. It was delicious and invigorating to fight. If Alexa had had an abortion, Meg wouldn't have had a chance to fight. So now she was pro-life, and she knew immediately how happy that would make her mother. It would make up for a host of insecurities AnneMarie had suffered since her daughter had come to this strange place.

"My birth mother was a rich bitch just like you," Meg spat at all of them, burning the last timber of any bridge that might have remained, "with a *portico* and everything. And she wanted to keep the baby. To keep me. It's not just poor trash who want to keep their babies."

"Meg!" Sylvia exclaimed, and Meg felt awful. She liked this teacher, hadn't meant to blow up her class like this.

"You're as limited as they are," said a girl whose hair was a sheet of blond. Meg had never had the courage to engage with her, hadn't wanted to bother even learning her name, but knew it was Celia. She looked richer than the rest of them put together, like she occupied the same sphere as Rosetta.

"And *you* would know?" Meg bellowed, losing the last shred of control.

"Yeah, I'd know," Celia said with disgust. "You think you have a claim on being poor at Linden? Like you're the only one? It's not some identity we should wave around. Stop embarrassing yourself."

Meg's mouth hung open for a moment as she tried to process Celia's "they" and "we." No way was Celia in any way like her. Was she? Could she be?

Celia fixed Meg with an unforgiving glare, bringing the full hatred of the assimilated down on the head of one who threatened to unmask her.

"Really?" JD teased Meg an hour later, back in her bedroom. He traced one finger down her ribs, making every nerve stand up straight. "You're anti-choice?" He'd also grown up Catholic, thank God, though they'd mostly skirted conversations about religion. JD wasn't on speaking terms with his parents, which didn't bother her at all—two fewer people to deal with—but she suspected that's why he wasn't a practicing Catholic and that made her uncomfortable. But how much did she practice, really? Meg had grown to love praying with her mother, but then hadn't attended a single church service since arriving on campus. On top of that, she'd lied to her mother and told her she had.

"Don't use that stupid term. I'm pro-life," Meg said defensively. "Aren't you?" she asked nervously.

JD shrugged. "I think it's safe to say everyone except psychopaths are pro-life."

"But we're Catholic," she said firmly. "We don't support abortion."

"Wellll," JD said.

Meg sat up, alarmed. "What do you mean, 'well'?"

He pulled her back down and planted gentle kisses along her cheek, his lips soft, his stubble rough. "I mean, there's a whole range of Catholic. There's a whole range of what it means to be religious."

"Don't you believe in God?" She pushed him away to look at him. Her voice gave away her fear.

"The crazy, unreliable guy in the Bible? Not so much. I think organized religion has caused more harm than good." Meg started to protest, but JD spoke over her. He stroked her wrists, planted firmly against his chest, coaxing her back. "That doesn't mean I'm not spiritual. It doesn't mean I don't believe in an unseen force. And it doesn't mean I don't respect people who go to church. Okay?"

"Well, I'm pro-life," she insisted, aware that she sounded peevish and therefore uncertain. "And they all hate me for it.

It's gonna be super fun when Rosetta and Hannah hear about this."

In fact, it could turn out to be a relief, and it could set their relationship into relief, too. The three of them had achieved a tenuous peace in the suite, no one quite understanding anyone else, with Hannah the only one interested in trying. She seemed to have wanted to befriend Meg, but ultimately had more in common with Rosetta, however outrageous Rosetta and her family were. Class trumped all other differences: even though Rosetta and Hannah had wildly different backgrounds, *they* both knew how massages worked, *they* had both had SAT tutors, *they* both knew what it was like to go through airport security. They had no idea Meg had never set foot in an airport, let alone on a plane. Meg thought often of Michelle, her phantom, no-show roommate, and wondered what her days were like and whether they would have been friends or whether Meg would have alienated her, too.

Michelle's nonarrival, though, was what had allowed Meg and JD to flourish. They had a door they could lock and behind that door, yes, they could have lots of sex, but they could talk—before sex, after sex—and get to know each other in a way she'd never known another person. They could tell each other things at all times of the day or night. They could be cozy together, a state of being Meg was utterly unfamiliar with and so had never imagined attaining it either on her own or with someone else.

But about the sex. Before her accident, Meg had sex in exchange for the chance to get high or because she was already high or because she was bored. The strongest emotion she'd mustered for Troy or Baxter was repulsion. She knew she wasn't pretty, but neither were they. So after the accident, when she went from ugly to ugly and broken, she figured she'd never have sex again. She would have entered a convent if she thought she could stand being around so many women all the time. She couldn't imagine anything would work between her legs anyway. But it turned out that Meg's body was more awake than it had ever been. She could get wet, JD could get in there, and nothing hurt. In fact it felt so damned good she often had to hold back tears. JD was the first guy who didn't want anything from her, or rather, he didn't want anything from her he wasn't also prepared to give himself.

"I want to be a fly on the wall for your weekly suite meeting." JD kissed her over and over on her cheek. Meg grabbed his bare, taut ass and pulled him closer.

"Rosetta said you should be at the meeting since you practically live here."

He pulled away and studied her. "Do you think I'm here too much?"

In answer, she took his hand and clamped it around her barely there breast.

"Don't you dare come any less than you do."

JD grinned.

"Okay." He pretended to be sullen. "If you insist, I'll keep coming. And coming and coming."

"How do I know you don't like me just because you don't need to wear a condom?" Meg teased him.

"How do you know you're not anti-choice because you know you can't get pregnant?" he murmured, running his lips gently across her cheek.

The comment froze her. She didn't think it was true, but she experienced a spike of animosity toward her perfect boyfriend for chilling her certainty.

JD sensed the breach. He rolled on top of her, and placed his hands on either side of her face.

"Hey," he said. "It's me. Just making conversation."

And all thoughts of the kids in Sylvia's class ganging up on her, of her suitemates' superiority, of her mother's loneliness, and of her own daily foreignness dissipated.

FIFTEEN

Sylvia was bored, which was a sin. She had no one to meet, no friends to catch up with, not even an errand to run. And as David Ketchum had so kindly pointed out, nothing to write, no work to do. He didn't know she had no gigs to turn down. She had multiplying emails to tend to, the eternal modern albatross, but even those were nonessential.

Linden College had felt small by the end of her sophomore year, and it hadn't grown any bigger in the decades since she'd graduated. After the first two weeks visiting old haunts—the stuffy seminar room where she'd been introduced to Brecht and Shange, the beer-scented staircase where she'd had uncomfortable vertical sex for the sole purpose of adding to her quiver of collegiate experiences—and marveling at the intrusion of modernity—green-roofed, glass-walled triumphs of ecologically sound architecture crammed in between the stoic stone behemoths—she'd run out of things to do. She tried to read, but she was anxious, out of step with the rest of the world. She should have been at the height of productivity, connectivity. What the hell was she doing squirreled away in some leathery library? Without the chaos of the city to camouflage nothing-to-do-ness, Sylvia became painfully aware of how nonessential she'd become. Nonessential personnel.

Four weeks into her inglorious stint as a professor, she was dutifully paging through her backlog of *New Yorkers* in the coffee bar located in the new science building—a corporeal rebuke to the humanities—when her phone rang. *Home.* Thank God. She hurried to answer.

"Mommy?"

Her children's voices were so high, and even higher on the phone, that Sylvia could rarely identify the caller in two syllables. And if she erred, great offense was taken.

"Sweetie!" she bluffed. "What's up?"

"Nathaniel's sneaking screen time."

"Leah, please don't call me just to tattle."

"I'm not."

"Is what you're telling me going to get your brother into or out of trouble?" This neat distinction, so satisfying to adults, rarely elicited the desired outcome.

"Nathaniel's brain cells will rot!"

"So you're saying you're getting him out of trouble by saving his brain."

"Yes."

"Tell me how school was."

"Seneca's sister got tongs."

Sylvia set down her coffee mug and blocked her free ear. "Say that again?"

"Seneca's sister got tongs," Leah repeated in her croaky voice. "And her parents won't let her wear them."

"Hang on," Sylvia said. "You don't wear tongs."

"Well, Seneca's sister does. And they stick up out of her

pants so her parents won't let her wear them."

Sylvia coughed back a laugh.

"Sweetie, I think you mean 'thong.' It's a kind of underwear." She thought for a moment about how to explain it. "It's a kind of underwear you need tongs to get off, actually."

"*Really?*" said Leah, and Sylvia sensed an avalanche of misinformation ready to pound Mrs. Hartford's first-grade class tomorrow.

"No, I'm kidding!" She hurried to explain. "It's just that the words sound alike—thong and tong—and tongs are… never mind. It's a complicated joke."

It hit Sylvia then that she was essential personnel to Leah and Nathaniel. There were teachers to enforce the learning of multiplication; there were babysitters and grandparents who did the requisite indulging of screen and sugar; there were gymnastics instructors to ensure their bodies remained strong and limber. But whose job was it to parse idioms for them? Who else but Sylvia cared about the interstitial learning, the intake that happened between the scheduled teaching? They needed her. Someone needed to make sure Leah didn't say "tong" when she meant "thong." Someone needed to make sure she learned why the mistake was funny. Sylvia knew then that she must get home to them, her soft, warm mini-humans.

She looked at her watch, a beautiful, simple watch Ethan had bought at the MoMA gift shop, which reminded her of him every time she looked at it, as did a million other things. Sylvia could expunge only so many objects from her life.

"Sweetie," Sylvia said, "I'm heading to the train now. I want to see you so badly."

"I thought you were sleeping at ping pong tonight."

Ping pong. Ping pong. Sylvia's brain came up short only for a moment, and then successfully filtered "ping pong" through the Leah strainer and came up with Pierre.

"I'd rather spend three hours on the train to go home and come back here tomorrow than spend twenty-four hours here not being with you."

"What?"

So much for the math teachers.

"Never mind, sweetheart." Sylvia blew kisses into the phone and tossed Camus into her backpack, elated by this taste of freedom and autonomy. Why hadn't she done this before? The idea that she shouldn't waste her time going down and back each day to teach was absurd. Waste what time? Whose time? Sylvia was just taking up space here in Pierre.

She willed herself to stick to the speed limit as she drove along the mini-highway that allowed people to get to and from campus with minimal exposure to the poverty and dissolution of the city it bordered. She hadn't checked the train schedule, but they left every hour, and she would cross her fingers that she was closer to the next one than the last one. It felt so good to be leaving Linden that Sylvia wondered, yet again, how big a mistake it had been to come here. She wasn't offering the students anything crucial. While she knew what *made* good writing—Sylvia had an eye for picking directing projects—she didn't know how to make it herself, let alone teach it.

Sylvia circled the train station parking lot, every occupied space a barrier to her nuzzling Nathaniel's sweet neck or hearing Leah's hoarse cackle. It was a cool October day, the cliffs across the Hudson River studded with color, but Sylvia began to sweat. Nothing except those two ungrateful little angels mattered, and her focus had narrowed to them as a lifeline. Panic mounted as she circled a second time, knowing she needed to cut bait and head to the multilevel garage, but irrationally thinking that would take her farther from the front door of the train station.

She circled a third time, and, miraculously, an SUV had its reverse lights on. Sylvia let out a small yip of relief and waited. And waited. What the hell was the driver doing? It was a beastly, indefensible Escalade, an earth-murdering machine that absolutely no one needed. Wasn't the beeping from the reverse gear driving her insane? The driver would be a blond ponytail, sitting high up in her throne on her gym-toned ass, texting away to some other blond ponytail confirming the times of their mani-pedis that had to be completed before school pickup. That's the story her precious little family silhouette stickers broadcast. Four daughters (four!), a dog, a husband. Why? Why did people feel the need to post their family status on their cars? And when they divorced, did they tear off one of the relevant figures? Before her pulse climbed higher, Sylvia flashed her lights, a polite preamble to honking, but the driver was perched well above the trajectory of her beams.

The question of whether to wait for the woman to pull out or to head to the garage paralyzed Sylvia. Stay? Go? Was this infuriating moment Sylvia's fault? Was it this woman's fault? If Sylvia missed this train, could she blame the blonde? Whose fault was it that Sylvia was up here in this depressed town, hiding out in an ivory corner, misleading young minds?

She was about to slam the horn when she suddenly remembered: department meeting. There was a mandatory theater studies faculty meeting that afternoon, and so this entire mission was doomed before it began. Sylvia crumpled in her seat, even as she recognized guilty relief. In the way that her children shuddered after an escalating campaign—for a sweet, a playdate, a toy—had been nipped in the bud, some part of her was glad to be restrained from her impulse. Did the relief mean she *was* supposed to be here? That didn't sound right either.

Forget the train. Forget seeing her kids. Sylvia had to go to a meeting. Like a regular working grownup. She straightened her shoulders and pulled forward.

Just as the Escalade finally fucking moved backward.

Crunch.

At one mile per hour, the impact wasn't the stuff of movies, but the driver burst out her door and jumped down. As anticipated: a tiny blond ponytail in Lycra. Sylvia allowed herself, amid the blooming dread of the aftermath—insurance calls, repairs, delays, explanations—to relish the accuracy of her stereotyping. Was it stereotyping if the stereotype turned out to be completely accurate? Perhaps then it morphed into worldly wisdom.

Sylvia popped open the glove compartment and dug around for her insurance card. It had better be in there. That was Ethan's job, to make sure the insurance was paid up and that the new card was put in the car every year.

The driver waved both palms at her wildly, as if Sylvia was still driving.

"Oh, for fuck's sake," she muttered and opened her door.

"I'm so sorry!" she gasped. "I'll pay for the repair. Don't call your insurance company!"

Not what Sylvia was expecting. She softened immediately,

in part because of the charming Australian accent, which counteracted the ick factor of her appearance.

"Well, but we both were at f—"

"No, no! I can't have another incident on my record! My rates will go up, my husband will kill me!" *Kee-euw* me.

She saw the alarm cross Sylvia's face.

"Not like that, not like he abuses me or I'm scared of him or anything, I've just completely used up his patience with this. Please," she begged again.

Sylvia got out of her car. Given how slowly they'd been going, she was surprised by how bad it looked. The woman's behemoth, unscathed, had taken out one of Sylvia's headlights and crumpled a section of the fender.

"Okay," Sylvia said. "What do we do?"

The woman glanced at her watch and furrowed her little brow.

"Do you have time now to get it fixed? I have a guy. I can move my schedule around if you can."

Sylvia did have time. She had four hours before the meeting. Not enough time to go to the city and back, but enough time to have an adventure with an accident-prone Aussie still not used to steering from the left side of the car. Sylvia's spirits lifted at this unexpected turn of events.

Her name was Pauline. Sylvia trailed Pauline out of the parking lot and they wound their way through downtown Pierre, past the occasional house trying to survive its boarded-up neighbors, past vacant-eyed children who were, worryingly, not at school, past a well-tended window box trying to distract from the weeds in the sidewalk cracks. Sylvia knew that Pierre was not well, but she hadn't realized exactly how far gone it was; she never had occasion to travel these streets. They pulled into an auto-body shop that was indistinguishable from the ones on either side of it.

"Oh, Pauline. Not again?" someone said when Sylvia followed her into the cramped, grease-caked office.

"Oh, Tony!" she wailed, though it sounded like "Oh, Tiny!"

Tony was what distinguished this shop from the others. Tony was beautiful. Tony was straight out of a Diet Coke commercial. Tony was like James Dean in a Diet Coke commercial, if James Dean were alive to plug carbonated beverages. Tony was smooth—his hair, his skin, his T-shirt, his smile. Sylvia wanted to hug him close, feel his warm muscles, rest her face in the crook of his neck, feel his collarbone against her cheek.

Whoa. Where was this coming from?

"Can you fix her up?" Pauline implored.

"Of course I can," he soothed, glancing at Sylvia, not her car. He could fix her up. *I would like to be fixed up by you, Tiny.* Sylvia was mentally babbling.

"Can I drop you anywhere?" Pauline asked Sylvia. "I'll take you and bring you back when your car is ready. I really appreciate this."

How could Sylvia tell her that she didn't want to go anywhere with her, that this was a mini-vacation? To be in a run-down part of town, no one knowing where she was, with *her* barely knowing where she was, feeling an old, familiar stirring she'd thought was gone forever. Sylvia wanted to stay right here, outside her life.

"This won't take more than a couple of hours. We've got a couch, TV, and coffee machine on the other side of the building," Tony said, and relief surged through Sylvia.

"Will you be done by three thirty?" she forced herself to ask. The meeting began at four.

"Should be. And if not, I'll get you where you need to be."

"Oh, that's great," Pauline said, distracted by a ping on her phone. "I really appreciate this, both of you. Tony, words cannot express…"

"Go, go, I know I'll see you soon."

"I'll stop by to pay you tomorrow," Pauline singsonged, the incident already closed for her. "And…?" She looked at Sylvia pleadingly.

"Sylvia."

"Sylvia, thank you!"

She hurried out of the office, and Sylvia watched her narrowly miss getting hit by another car pulling in.

"Wow," she said.

"Yeah," Tony agreed. "I never let her give rides to the people she's bumped. Not safe."

Sylvia deflated. She'd thought he'd wanted her to stay.

"She has four kids. Very distracted all the time." He looked at the ceiling thoughtfully. "Four kids might be too many."

He reached in front of Sylvia to hold open the office door. He smelled like soap and gasoline.

"It's a liability," she agreed half-heartedly as she passed. He followed her to her car, and she pretended to survey the damage, though she was only watching him survey the damage.

"She really needs to take remedial driving lessons," he sighed.

"But this way is more business for you?"

He looked over his shoulder at the small parking lot

packed with cars facing different directions.

"You don't need the business," Sylvia concluded.

"Not really."

"So why do you keep helping her?"

"You gotta help people. Even people like her."

It was either one of the more profound statements on human kindness Sylvia had heard in a long time or she was smitten, starved for attraction.

"Is there actually a couch and coffee or were you just saving me from her?" Sylvia asked.

"No, there is," he said, crouching down to examine the smashed headlight. He ran his fingers over it gently. "Go back through the office and out the other side. You'll see it."

So much for her Pierre adventure. Sylvia should have risked another ride with Pauline.

She took her time passing through his office, looking for signs of Tony, something he'd touched, something personal. A desk calendar covered the surface of a round table in the middle of the room, partially obscured by a cactus. She nudged the plant aside: scrawled phone numbers and customers' appointments filled most of the boxes. *Maria's birthday.* An employee? Wife? Girlfriend? God, she was desperate and nosy, desperately nosy. Slapped across the door ahead of her was an EARTH bumper sticker, in which the word *ART* was highlighted in red. Now that was interesting. But why should it be interesting? she chastised herself. Did she think just because he was a mechanic, he couldn't be interested in preserving the earth, wouldn't be inclined to profess a love of art? Actually, it made Sylvia realize she wasn't entirely certain what that bumper sticker, which she'd seen many times, actually meant. As she went through the door, she let her fingers brush a bomber jacket hanging from a hook. She sniffed it; no one was watching. There was that soap and gasoline smell.

Sylvia entered a sunny, pleasant lounge with two new-looking couches and a glass coffee table. There was a black Formica countertop with a coffee machine and a basket of buttered bagel halves wrapped in cellophane plus three more cacti holding their prickly poses. A television was mounted to the wall, and she automatically reached up to turn it off. This was as good a place as any to spend a meditative afternoon. A retreat.

A sudden burst of shouts drew her attention to the window. At first, Sylvia didn't realize she was facing a different street from the one on which she'd arrived, so she thought lovely Tony was arguing with a group of people. But it wasn't him. Graying men and women, either stooped or holding canes or both, were—was Sylvia seeing this correctly?—yelling at a young woman. It was grotesque, like the classic photo of Florentine men leering threateningly at a woman so that she is forced to step into the gutter in order to pass. Except these were infirm, elderly white men *and* women intimidating a tall, zaftig Latina woman.

What the hell?

Then she saw the signs.

Abortion Is Murder

Men Regret Lost Fatherhood

God Loves Your Unborn Child

Defund Intentional Families

Sylvia wasn't surprised, then, when she spied the blue awning over the door toward which the young woman was striding: Intentional Families.

She had never witnessed this intimidation firsthand, but was all too familiar with it. She knew that people took time out of their days to stand around doing their best to turn a stranger's very hard day into a truly miserable one. These people—or people just like them—were responsible for her sister leaving her.

Maddie had finally, *finally* gotten pregnant. Though she was four years Sylvia's senior, and although she had married Jason eight years before Sylvia married Ethan, she hadn't been able to hang on to a fetus until a year ago. She and Jason depleted their savings trying every artificial means available. Of all the women in the world, it was Maddie who should have become a mother as many times over as she wanted. Finally, on the tenth try, Maddie's belly grew round, and the family spread their palms across her taut skin, feeling limbs kick and roll and scrabble.

Maddie allowed everyone to celebrate her at thirty-two weeks. Her eyes shone, and she and Jason held hands throughout dinner.

The next day, they went for a checkup and learned the baby's heart wasn't pumping properly. A closer examination revealed that the baby had trisomy 13: underdeveloped brain, missing eyes, cleft palate, cleft lips, no muscle tone, extra fingers and toes. The baby might continue to grow in utero over the remaining eight weeks, or it might die inside her. There was almost no chance it would survive beyond the first few days of life, and zero chance its truncated life wouldn't be vegetative.

For three days, Sylvia and her parents wailed and cursed, and Maddie attempted Zen acceptance: she would let nature take its course. But on the fourth day, following another sleepless night, she concluded that carrying a soon-to-be-dead baby inside her for another two months was a punishment she did not deserve. And although she lived in a supposedly progressive state, a bunch of faceless legislators had decided that she should suffer this fate, so she and Jason made arrangements to fly to Kansas, where a late-term abortion was still legal. The wheels of their plane touched down at the Eisenhower National Airport in Wichita just minutes after George Miller, the man who was to have relieved their suffering, was assassinated during a Sunday church service. They found out while watching the evening news in their Ramada Inn room that night.

So they booked a new flight the next day for Oregon, a state that did not mandate suffering, and it was there, in a small town outside of Eugene, that they finally began to mourn and move forward. But they never moved back.

Sylvia's blood boiled. Before she knew what she was doing, she flung open the door to the repair shop and strode outside into the sunshine. It was a gorgeous fall day. A scarecrow of a woman dressed in varied shades of beige caught Sylvia in her sights and marched across the street, a pamphlet in her outstretched bony hand. She was faster than Sylvia would have expected and reached her before she could skirt her. A dozen rosaries jangled from her wrist.

"Help us shut down Intentional Families?" she queried cheerfully.

"Die," Sylvia grunted before she even realized the word had escaped her lips.

"Yes!" the crone agreed in a high voice. "The babies are dying in there! They're murdering innocent babies. These poor young women go in there thinking they're getting prenatal care and then Intentional Families pays them to get an abortion. They're getting rich off dead babies!"

Sylvia pushed away the woman's arm roughly, and her nerves fired when she made contact. Her heart pumped hard, her vision narrowed, and she couldn't focus on the rest of the crowd, though later she would remember a sea of people shorter than her and very little color: drab clothes, drab hair, all in contrast to the brilliant hues of the trees around them, as if humans had been superimposed in black and white on a color background. She heard them begin to murmur behind her, and then their voices rose and they were praying in unison.

"Hail Mary full of grace. The Lord is with thee. Blessed art thou among women and blessed is the fruit of thy womb, Jesus."

Their voices followed Sylvia through the parking lot though they remained on the sidewalk. She yanked open the door and found herself in a stuffy, dim foyer. The woman with the child was going through another door, and Sylvia started to catch hold of it and follow them.

"Excuse me!" a voice bellowed from the other side of a Plexiglas barrier. "Can I help you?"

A scowling woman, her multicolored hair in elaborate braids piled on top of her head, didn't seem like she was eager to help anyone.

"Yes," Sylvia said, looking over her shoulder through the glass door. Childishly, she thrust her middle finger at them, though she didn't know whether they could see the gesture. She thought of everything these ogres didn't know about her sister, everything they didn't know about the woman who'd entered the clinic ahead of her. Sylvia thought of Faith Christian blathering her either/or nonsense. She thought of the kids she'd just seen wandering around the neighborhood when they should have been at school. Why didn't these assholes first go see what those living, breathing, abandoned children needed?

"I'd like to volunteer."

SIXTEEN

We breathe air, we shit, we pee, we eat, presumably, we sleep. This had become Sylvia's weekly incantation as she studied the protesters on their side of the parking lot fence. It was all she could come up with that they might have in common. Also: *we all own a spatula.* She knew the party line for noble people was that most human beings wanted the same things: a safe world for their children and peace on earth. But Sylvia could not believe that these fucking morons—with their plastic rosaries and crucifixes (how was praying to an image of human torture not considered sociopathic behavior?), in their thick-soled shoes and elastic waistbands, singing atonally about Mother Mary and roses in the snow, insulting patients by begging them to think about what they were doing—shared anything at all with her. They were a different species.

A woman with a tube of stretch-marked flab flopping over her dirty velour pants trudged along the sidewalk pulling a sniveling child behind her by the wrist. The old farts darted out of her path. Her waddle was wide enough that she knocked over a sign proclaiming Abortion Is Murder! The protester named Donald, a frail and nasty man who spouted some of the more nonsensical vitriol in the group, scurried to right it, sneering at the woman whose unborn baby he professed to want to save.

"We can help you!" croaked one named Maureen, leaning away from the woman.

"God loves you and he loves your baby!" added the one named Caroline from behind Maureen's shoulder.

The fact that Sylvia knew their names, but they didn't know hers, gave her a stab of unpleasant satisfaction. She knew that Donald was one of eight children, something he had told her proudly during one of their fruitless arguments down at the fence. She knew that Maureen, who had begun to spruce up her browns and tans with a lime green scarf when the weather turned crisp, was the queen bee. The other women gathered around her and hung on to everything she said. Once, when a patient's father started screaming obscenities at her, Maureen had covered her ears as if she was too much a lady to be exposed to such language. The others had followed suit, like the "hear no evil" chimpanzee. In almost any other context, Sylvia would have regarded these people as the gentle elderly, perhaps in need of her assistance crossing the street, which she would have eagerly provided. Here, they were witches and ogres.

Caroline was new to the group, and Sylvia didn't have a handle on her yet. She'd hung back at first, nervously fondling the cross around her neck, but had been warming to the action and begun to yell more. They all yell-prayed at the patients and yell-yelled at the volunteers.

Sylvia strolled down from her spot under the awning and pointed at her own bright orange vest that read Intentional Families Escort to make sure the woman with her son understood Sylvia was not one of *them.* It was common for the patients to be in such a state of anxiety, because of the protesters, that they couldn't distinguish the volunteers from the protesters, even with the fence dividing them.

"Intentional Families is racist!" Donald called out to the woman. "Thirty percent of the abortions are done on Black babies!"

"That's because thirty percent of our patients are Black," Sylvia said lightly to the Black woman as she crossed the threshold onto IF property. She opted not to remark on how unimpressive a figure thirty percent would have been as an example of just about anything. "Welcome, and I'm so sorry about them."

The woman ignored Sylvia. Her little boy began to cry.

"Hi, sweetheart," Sylvia said to him.

"You would have liked to have killed him, too!" Donald yelled. Sylvia's pulse quickened, but she pretended to ignore him.

The boy followed his mother's lead and ignored Sylvia.

"They'll take good care of you inside," Sylvia called weakly as the woman disappeared through the door.

For now, Sylvia was alone in the lot, which she disliked. Not because she was afraid of the protesters doing her any physical harm, but because it was hard for her to tune them out without someone else to talk to. Unlike Carrie, the constantly harried mother of three who insisted on coming to volunteer despite the fact that she was on her phone most of the time dealing with domestic logistical crises, or Irving, the retired wise guy who reveled in being the only male escort (he adored that term) and issued forth an unending stream of colorful commentary, Sylvia had trouble thinking about anything besides the willful ignorance of the protesters.

They embraced a binary world view that was at best stunted and at worst a crime. Like/don't like, good/bad, saved/damned. Over and over they read that one unforgivably dull and poorly written book, and lived by only the words in it because to read something else might cause them to think. They had the advantage of maintaining an absolute stance—*abortion is bad*—whereas Sylvia, who knew that abortion was *essential* and *complicated* would still never call it *good*. It's challenging to stay pithy when you live among the grays. But the grays were what responsible, thoughtful adults trafficked in. These people, she could see, were perpetual children in their fear of seeing the world from different angles. Through different lenses, as she instructed her students to do.

Sylvia paced back and forth, so close to the edge of the IF property that she could see the web of wrinkles gouging Maureen's face. They looked suspiciously like smokers' wrinkles, though Sylvia had begun to understand that even if Maureen had been a smoker in the past, this vice would not shame her. She would credit God with having given her the strength to overcome the habit, and would be elevated in her peers' eyes at having struggled and conquered a sin. Sylvia also knew it wouldn't stop her from looking down on current smokers.

She strained to capture snatches of their conversation, both eager and afraid to hear an exchange that would infuriate her. Even their quotidian conversation repulsed her because it caused her to picture them out and about, poisoning every place they went with their confident lies. These people wheeled carts down grocery store aisles and replaced vacuum bags and had sticky lint on their alarm clocks, just like Sylvia did. It was disgusting.

"We're not using the same bus company as last year," Maureen told her minions. "The bathroom was filthy."

A senior trip to the city, perhaps? Did they dare trek to the den of iniquity, even to see a matinée? Sylvia grinned at the image of them finding themselves in the audience of *This Is Not a Test*.

"Killing babies makes you smile?" Donald spat.

Sylvia strolled past the entrance to the corner of the lot as if to inspect a car, keeping a smile plastered on well past the point of comfort. She wished there was a way to be near them without her heart rate rocketing. She briefly pictured herself collapsing at their feet from the stress and guffawed; they'd step over her while hoisting their Respect Life signs a little higher.

From this corner of the lot, though, Sylvia had a clear view of Tony's repair shop, and she was visited by the distinctly adolescent tingling caused by merely thinking the name of a crush. *That* kind of heart rate rocket was okay by her.

Because at age forty-two, Sylvia had a crush. Last month, Tony had fixed her car with time to spare, and then, instead of tackling his packed lot, he'd come into the sunny room with the couch and the coffee and sat down and started talking. He was alarmingly open about his interest; Sylvia, feeling she had less than nothing to lose, didn't hide her interest either. The only thing she hid, for the first time, was her wedding ring.

She told him that while he'd been underneath her car, she'd become the newest IF volunteer, scheduled to begin escorting abortion patients the following week. Sylvia told Tony this news defiantly, presented as the litmus test that it was. Not only didn't he flinch, but he blew out his cheeks and said, "Thank you. We need more people like you out there."

He went on to give her a primer on the protesters, who called themselves Catholic, but in doing so did a huge disservice to actual Catholics. He didn't know what sect of crazy they were, but they believed the Vatican took its cues from socialists and that the pope wasn't Catholic enough. Sometimes a bald man with a long beard came with a group of girls, all of them dressed in ye olde clothes, who appeared to be his wives and not his daughters, but who were clearly of school age. For religious home schoolers, coming to yell-pray at the clinic was a top-notch field trip. Tony told Sylvia these people were also against birth control.

Sylvia nearly dropped her pod-made coffee.

"So deny them birth control, and then when, surprise, they get pregnant, deny them abortions?"

"Well, sure," he said. "You're not supposed to have extramarital sex, and then you're supposed to have as many children as they do. All while voting down welfare reform for the hungry babies who result from their ill-conceived plan."

"Ill-conceived," Sylvia commented. "Good one."

"Have dinner with me," Tony said.

Sylvia wanted to think that his invitation was not prompted by talk of extramarital sex and birth control, but it didn't matter. The following week they went to dinner in a neighboring town so that she wouldn't risk running into students or colleagues. Sylvia was so nervous that she began to shake as she entered the restaurant. She'd insisted on meeting him there, environmental carpooling be damned, because she wanted an escape hatch if it turned out all her dating instincts had vaporized during a decade of marriage. Mostly, she felt guilty, like she was betraying Nathaniel and Leah, and then felt guilty that she was letting them down by maintaining such an unempowered attitude. (*Ethan* had left *her*; she wasn't cheating on him *or* them; they were legally separated so she wasn't even committing adultery the way Ethan had, etc.)

Tony had picked an Indian restaurant, which Sylvia thought was bold partly because she was snobbishly suspicious of any ethnic food prepared outside four of the five boroughs and partly because it was heavy fare with the potential for post-prandial digestive irregularities. As she made her way inside, she suddenly wondered whether this was even a date or whether she had misunderstood and read his signals wrong, whether he was just bored with the people he knew up here and was interested in a new person to talk to—

He was at the table when Sylvia arrived. He stood up, pulled her to him, and pressed his lips firmly against hers.

"I wanted to get that out of the way now, so we can enjoy dinner without the looming tension of will-we-won't-we," he said.

"The looming tension," Sylvia murmured, ready to pass on dinner and go home with him. The goofy thought occurred to her that she would be accumulating two Tonys in one year. And this one would be more gratifying.

She gazed now at what looked to everyone else to be a grimy, nondescript mechanic's shop, but which for her was a source of pleasant chills radiating to her extremities. Tony and Sylvia had had dinner each Tuesday night since—her only night of the week in Pierre—and they had definitely made use of birth control, though Sylvia had procured condoms at a store and not from IF's freebie basket. She was now overstocked on the toothpaste and ibuprofen she'd grabbed as camouflage.

"Good for you!" Maureen yelled, and for a split second, Sylvia thought she was cheering on her newly sprouted relationship. The posse was fixated on the velour-pantsed patient, who was leaving the clinic just moments after she'd entered, no longer pulling the child by his wrist, but letting him lag a few paces behind her. "She changed her mind!" Maureen announced.

Sylvia was not allowed to say to Maureen: *Perhaps she got a flu shot. Perhaps she was there for an STD treatment. Or a cancer screening.* The protesters did not give a shit that IF provided medical care for poor people everywhere. They claimed to be the most Christian of all Christians, but made Jesus roll over in his grave with their lack of compassion for any poor who were not white, neat, and polite. And Sylvia was not supposed to interact with them at all.

"Any word uttered to them is breath wasted," Trish in human resources had counseled her. Trish wore a cross around her neck, had five children, and loved the pope; she saw her Catholicism as being in line with the mission of IF.

Sylvia hesitantly sidled up to the patient, not wanting to crowd or anger her.

"Everything okay?" she asked.

"I don't got the fifteen dollar co-pay. Drake, get your skinny ass over here," she snarled at the little boy. She still hadn't looked at Sylvia.

"What are you gonna do?"

The woman shrugged.

"You made the right decision!" Caroline yelled. That one was getting bolder.

"We can help you keep your baby!"

Right, because this woman can't scrounge up fifteen fucking dollars, Sylvia thought, *so she's definitely going to find the money to raise another child*. And these assholes would be voting down any services that might help her. What was their big plan—to have God's love feed her growing family? Was God's love magic pasta and invisible Cheerios? The woman trudged toward the gate, where the protesters prepared to swamp her with pamphlets and rosary beads, all notably inedible.

"Wait," Sylvia said urgently, and hustled up to the bench by the clinic door. She rifled through her wallet and pulled out a twenty. She likely wasn't supposed to do this, and certainly, if the woman turned out to be a camera-wearing poser sent by the anti-choice syndicate, Sylvia was in for a world of pain. But she couldn't do nothing. Well, she could have. But she chose not to. Sylvia tactically positioned herself in front of the woman and slipped her the bill so that the protesters couldn't see.

The woman took the money, turned on her heel, and headed back inside. She said nothing to Sylvia, only scolded her son once again.

"What did she tell you?" Maureen shrieked. "Don't listen to her! She's lost her way! She's one of Satan's messengers!"

Sylvia's heart was pounding so hard it actually hurt a little bit. She put her hand to her chest and reminded herself she'd done nothing wrong. She wasn't an employee, and she didn't know what the woman needed the co-pay for, only that she needed medical attention.

Irving coasted through the gate on his bike, intentionally scattering the protesters.

"Watch where you're going!" Donald scolded.

"Oh, I was. But I missed."

Donald looked confused.

"He'll be chewing that over for at least a day," Sylvia said, and Irving grinned.

"How are you darlin'?" He sailed past and parked his bike at the rack in the upper end of the lot. Sylvia and Irving had hit it off immediately. A retired IBMer, he and his wife were avid theater-goers, and his awe at Sylvia's minor fame had fast-tracked their friendship over the past month. They spent the downtime—and there was a lot of downtime; mostly, they were parking attendants—comparing plays and books. They had decided to try reading the same books and discussing them under cover of being aggressively prayed at. World's weirdest book club.

The protesters began to sing.

"Uh-oh," Irving said, pulling his orange vest over his balding head and clipping it closed. "They don't usually sing for another half hour. What did you do?"

"How did you know—?"

"I've been at this for a long time." He gave Sylvia a quick hug.

"I—"

But that moment, the same patient came slamming out of the front door again. Sylvia hurried toward her.

"What happened?"

"They said I can't have my son with me. Why the fuck they don't tell me this the first time?"

Now, at last, she looked at Sylvia. She hadn't known someone could be vacant-eyed and angry at the same time.

"I'm so sorry," Sylvia said, and she was. "They should have. I hope…" What did she hope for this woman? "I hope everything works out for you."

The woman guffawed and yanked her son away. Sylvia wondered whether she'd hang on to the twenty until she could come back. Somehow, she doubted it, and despondency settled over her. Another unwanted future ward of the state was on its way.

"Any good stickers today?" Irving asked, surveying the lot. "Ooh, what's that one?" He squinted at a pickup truck that had NRA love plastered across the back window as well as a bumper sticker with a picture of a fishing rod reeling in the words *Praise Cod*.

Sylvia and Irving parsed that one for a minute: it was a reminder that not all gun-lovers were religious. But wait, did the owner of the truck mean to be disrespectful to God or did he merely hold fishing in high regard and didn't stop to think that some might find the pun offensive? For the two of them in their orange vests, the sacrilegious joke canceled out some of their distaste for the NRA stickers. Not that the owner would care what they thought: they weren't deluded, just bored. (Weren't the protesters bored, too, or was their love of God like a TV that was always on, streaming constant entertainment?)

Sylvia had never affixed a bumper sticker to a car. How would you choose, in so few words, what to broadcast about yourself? The slogans were invitations to make snap judgments.

Some she'd seen in the parking lot over the past few weeks were mating calls (Wanna Test Drive My Vulva?), others warning signals (Do You Follow Jesus This Close?). Some revealed intransigence and tendentiousness (GO VEGAN) and others humble pride (My child is an honor student at James Madison Middle School). A depressing number were gratuitously hostile (My pit bull will eat your honor student).

The protesters, who parked on the streets around the clinic, also slathered bumper stickers on their vehicles. Predictably, theirs railed against abortion, but one also proclaimed We Support Our Priests. That one appeared on her car shortly after the latest group of God-fearing pedophiles were unmasked.

"Your friend here is working hard today," Donald yelled to Irving.

Irving looked at Sylvia, who shrugged.

"I thought people in assisted living were too old to be tattletales," Irving called back.

"She didn't succeed in killing *that* baby!"

"Another angel gets its wings," Irving said, then turned his back on them. Sylvia thought he was going to ask her what had gone down, but instead he asked, "What are we reading next? Because, lemme tell you, the freedom in Franzen's *Freedom* is the freedom not to have to finish it. So pick something else."

"I like it!" Sylvia protested.

"You're only liking the dysfunction because you're in the middle of a divorce. Trust me, you won't really like it once the dust settles."

Coming from anyone else, this would have been irritating, but Sylvia knew that this was Irving's way of keeping her best interests in mind. Also, he was on his third wife (twenty years now—this one was a keeper), and Sylvia appreciated that he was the only person in her life not treating her divorce as a tragedy. Still, she was going to finish the book.

A woman in her fifties who had entered the clinic with her daughter an hour earlier came out the front door and lit a cigarette.

"They here all the time?" she asked Sylvia and Irving, jutting her chin at the protesters.

"Just on Wednesdays," Sylvia told her, anticipating her disgusted comprehension of why this was.

She took a long drag.

"I agree with them. I don't believe in abortion."

Sylvia had heard this astonishing declaration from another patient the week before.

"They're also against birth control," she added.

The woman turned her face away to exhale, then turned back.

"You mean for themselves."

"No, for everyone. They don't think anyone should use birth control."

The woman raised one eyebrow.

"Well, I don't know anything about that, but I agree with them," she repeated. "I had an abortion and I'm here supporting my daughter with hers"—she nodded back at the door—"but I don't believe in it."

She stubbed out her cigarette on the bottom of her shoe, tucked the remaining half in a baggie, and went back inside.

Sylvia turned to Irving, ready to explode.

"I think that's the tooth fairy she's thinking of," he said.

Sylvia burst out laughing.

"I hate those kinds of patients more than I hate the protesters," he said. "'Abortion is wrong except when I need one. Everyone but me is a slut.' Let's read the new Michael Chabon and don't give me a hard time about only reading white men. They deserve to be read, too."

They spent the next five minutes debating the literary merits of the Brooklyn Jonathans—Ames, Foer, Franzen, and Lethem—and arguing over which were technically Manhattanites, before settling on Chinua Achebe's *Things Fall Apart*, whose themes they both admitted to referencing in discussions touching on colonialism, but without actually remembering any details from it.

There was a rise in volume among the protesters, and they looked toward the sidewalk to see the big woman, this time without the boy, heading toward her again. Sylvia worked hard to keep her face neutral as she planted herself near the gate.

"I'm an alcoholic," the woman announced loudly, by way of a greeting, "and I been drinking during this pregnancy and I don't needa be using up any more resources that my son, Drake, needs. I'm doing this for *him*," she finished fiercely, spitting the words over her shoulder at the white-haired posse on the sidewalk. She turned back to Sylvia. "I had to give the money to a friend to watch my son," she said pointedly.

Understood. Sylvia hurried up to the bench again to dig out another twenty. The woman followed her. Sylvia handed it over and watched her head inside a third time.

The protesters went into a praying-singing-yelling frenzy, and Irving very pointedly launched into a story about the Jamaican nurse from what he called Meals on Veels, who tended to his elderly mother in her Brooklyn apartment and who knew how to cook kosher meals. Sylvia concentrated on his story as if her life depended on it. One day, she'd master the art of ignoring the ignorant.

That evening, Sylvia had reluctantly given up a bonus dinner with Tony to allow Ruth and Ellie to train up and take her out for her forty-third birthday. She was trapped in Pierre for a mandatory all-faculty meeting the following day, and so her friends had insisted on coming. Sylvia relented because even though she didn't feel like celebrating, she also didn't want to find herself alone later that night regretting not celebrating.

She led them to Leandra's Kitchen, a protean mainstay of the Linden community that had sprung up after she and Ellie had graduated: daily, it morphed from a cozy breakfast joint to the perfect collegial lunch meeting location to a sports-but-also-candlelit bar to a low-lit dinner with cloth napkins replacing the midday paper ones. She could have taken her friends farther afield, but had a childish wish to run into some of the ruder members of the theater department—namely, David Ketchum, who continued to intimidate her—in order to show them she had a full life in New York and didn't need them.

What Sylvia hadn't anticipated was being waited on by one of her students. The three women were studying the beribboned menus when a familiar voice queried them about sparkling versus tap.

"Oh, hi!" Meg Croyden said, more cheerful than Sylvia had ever seen her in class.

"Hi!" Sylvia returned, too enthusiastically, feeling irrationally that she had something to hide. "Guys, this is one of my favorite students!"

Her outburst rang so false that she blushed, even as she realized it was, in fact, true.

A spark of distrust flickered across Meg's face.

"I didn't know you worked here," Sylvia said, mining the vein of useless chatter.

"Yeah, well. My mom thought I should take a different kind of job, you know, like, not handling other people's food, but…" She trailed off and shrugged. "I can walk here in five minutes. The tips are good." Perhaps realizing the awkward situation this observation put them in, she quickly added, "I don't know, I just, you know, like it?"

The three friends nodded energetically.

"Tap water is fine," Ellie said, firmly putting an end to the awkward dance.

After Meg nodded and slipped away, Ruth exclaimed, "An actual student! You have students! You're a professor!"

"I'm definitely not a professor," Sylvia corrected her, glancing around the restaurant and wishing, as always, that Ruth would lower her voice. Sylvia lowered her own. "That's the *one*."

"What one?" Ellie said, then remembered and her eyes widened. "Oh, the anti-choice one?"

"Yep." Sylvia wondered what Meg would think if she knew where she'd been earlier that day. "But also, the one who called out all the limo-liberal posers," she said. "She was kind of awesome."

"I'm pretty sure we would be classified as limo liberals," Ruth said.

Sylvia pretended to look around. "Huh, I've misplaced my limo."

"I'm serious," Ruth insisted. "How hypocritical can you be?"

"Excuse me?" Sylvia assumed Ruth was joking.

"Ruth," Ellie warned.

"How can you come straight from the clinic, and then find your anti-choice student charming because she calls out the students who think the way you do?"

Sylvia worked her lower lip with her teeth. "I didn't come straight from the clinic," she said faintly, with a weak attempt at a smile.

"I think there's a misprint," Ellie said, indicating the menu.

"Don't change the subject," Ruth said.

"Ruth," Ellie said again, sharply this time. "This is her birthday dinner. Save whatever it is you're working up to for another time."

"No," Ruth said stubbornly. "I'm not planning to ruin her *birthday.*" She said the word disdainfully, as if it were childish for an adult to expect special treatment. Sylvia wanted to remind her that it hadn't been her idea to so-called celebrate. "But we need to pause for a second."

Sylvia closed her eyes and summoned her patience. When she opened them, she saw Ellie doing the same. Their eyes met and they shared a wry smile.

"Okay, paused."

"It's amazing that you're out there helping patients at IF."

"It's bizarrely fun," Sylvia said quickly, to deflect any perceived selflessness.

"Fun doesn't make it less important," Ruth shot back just as quickly. "But you need to educate this girl." She pointed in the general direction of the restaurant kitchen.

"Ruth," she said. "I can't hound a student about her beliefs! First, that would make me a terrible teacher—"

"Would it?" Ruth interrupted.

"Yes, and second, it would probably get me fired!"

"So what? You just said you're not a real professor."

Ellie threw up her hands and looked to the ceiling, seeking assistance from a higher power.

"Enough!" Sylvia said.

"What would Maddie say?"

Sylvia felt her jaw drop.

Meg returned to the table with a carafe of water and a basket of focaccia and looked at them expectantly.

"A bottle of the Malbec," Sylvia told Meg quickly, and the girl headed off again. Sylvia leaned in and lowered her voice. "I think Maddie would say thank you for keeping those nasty, evil, psycho protesters away from women trying to preserve their own lives!"

"Well, duh," said Ruth, "that's the easy part."

"Excuse me?" Sylvia's pulse quickened.

"Relax," Ruth said unapologetically. "Not easy. I didn't mean easy. Straightforward. Your job there is straightforward, and you know those shit-for-brains are never going to see things any other way. But here's this scholarship kid—"

"How do you know she's on scholarship!" Ellie exclaimed.

"Look at her," Ruth said. "Oh, don't give me your PC bullshit shocked looks. Am I wrong? You can just see it. The tight ponytail, I don't know. By the end of the school year, she'll be blending in, but right now, she stands out. Look: here's this kid who's obviously really smart or she wouldn't be here, and has an absorbent, impressionable mind. You have an opportunity to actually educate her. And think of how many people—her own age, back home, whatever—she can influence. You'd be saving at least one young mind and probably a lot more from the anti-choice horror show."

Sylvia slumped back in her seat, watching Meg across the restaurant. She noticed the girl's limp for the first time. The result of the car crash she'd barely fictionalized in the scene she'd written for class? She wondered why Meg had chosen Linden and whether she regretted coming and whether her bravado in class was real or a carapace. Probably some of both. Sylvia deflated at the thought of how hard the job of growing up was and how much work Leah and Nathaniel had ahead of them.

"For God's sake, Ruth," Ellie said weakly. Ruth opened her menu again and began to scan it.

"I'm just saying, don't make this kid your little mascot. She's not some adorable spitfire. She's someone who's going to have influence. She's someone who thinks your Maddie should have been forced to keep carrying her dead baby. She's someone who might agree with the people who murdered George Miller. Now, where's this misprint?"

"Jesus, Ruth, you're like a fucking machine gun," said Ellie, who never cursed.

"'Gnocchi on a bed of *tefillin* with braised autumn root vegetables'!" Ruth shouted and began to chortle.

Sylvia and Ellie shushed her. But then Sylvia found the corresponding line in her menu and burst out laughing.

"Is it a lettuce of some kind?" Ellie asked.

"No!" Ruth howled. "*Tefillin* is the box with the leather straps that Jewish men wrap around their foreheads!"

"What?" Ellie was alarmed.

Ruth was listing sideways in her chair, cracking up. "It's a prayer thing! They put it right here," Ruth gasped, pointing to her brow. "Where the Botox goes!" She exhaled a loud, pleasure-filled aftermath sigh.

Ethan used to raise his palms generously and say, *You can't pick your old friends.* Sylvia tried to let his excellent adage soothe her now, but suddenly felt like she wasn't going to be able to get through dinner with Ruth, which was a new and awful feeling.

As if she could read her mind, as if she could tell Sylvia needed her to stop being so Ruth-like, Ruth collected herself and asked, "Are you glad you took this job?"

Sylvia bit into a piece of focaccia and in the process bit off a small chunk of cheek. She cried out and tears sprang to her eyes. She gingerly stuck a finger inside her mouth and it came out bloody. Ellie pushed water toward her, but Sylvia shook her head. She didn't want to swallow a mouthful of bloody water. She grabbed a fresh piece of focaccia and pressed it to the wound like gauze. Her friends regarded her dubiously.

"Now what?" Ellie asked, grimacing.

Sylvia fished a tissue out of her purse and stuck the bloody bread in it. She tore off a fresh piece and stuck that in her mouth.

"I'm so fucking angry," Sylvia spluttered through the bread, surprising all of them. "I'm angry all the time. I'm so angry at Ethan. It feels like he drove me to take this idiotic job, even though I know he didn't. I mean, it's not like his leaving me was why my work offers dried up, right?"

"No," Ellie said. "But he's why you jumped at the chance to be somewhere else two days a week. You know that, right?"

"I guess, although I would have taken this job even if he hadn't been a douchebag." Frustratingly, it still didn't sound right to reduce him with such pedestrian epithets. He wasn't a douchebag. He was a great guy who happened not to love her anymore. That was humiliating, confusing, frightening, infuriating. "I would have had someone to process it with. I would have integrated this whole weird poser experience into my real life. It would have been a lark. It wouldn't have felt so…"

"Freighted?" That was Ellie, of course.

"Freighted." They watched Sylvia remove the second piece of bread. It was slightly less bloody. She stuck it in the tissue and tucked one more piece inside her cheek. "Last one," she promised them.

"Maybe you *shouldn't* be escorting at Intentional Families," Ruth suggested. "I know you call it fun, but it's not really a calming experience."

"That's the best part of my time here."

"I'm sure, but…isn't it just too raw?"

"You mean because of Maddie?"

Ruth nodded.

"Maybe. But maybe I need raw. I don't know. I need that place. I love it there. Isn't that weird? I can't exactly figure it out. I mean, obviously, I feel like I'm doing something for Maddie, but it's more than that."

"You're angry, and it's prompting you to act," Ellie said, reasonable as ever.

"I know, but directing people to parking spots? Not really action."

Ellie shrugged. "It *is* action. It's control: you can't force your sister to come back east, but you can control that little bit of square footage. That parking lot is your domain."

Sylvia pulled her chin back in surprise.

"See, she's as annoying as I am, just in a different way," Ruth said triumphantly.

Sylvia felt like she and her sister were even—didn't one dead baby equal a failed marriage in the big add-up? It was time for Maddie to come home.

Sylvia was in Pierre. Her sister was in Oregon. Her kids were in New York. Her husband was with another woman. Her friends were not succeeding in providing solace. She spit the last piece of bloody bread into her tissue.

"What the hell am I doing here?" Sylvia asked them.

"Getting laid, thank God," said Ruth, just as Meg materialized at the table with a bottle of wine.

SEVENTEEN

Never in her whole life had Caroline expected to be having a discussion with a Black boy wearing shimmering purple eyeshadow.

She had stopped him—politely—on his way to IF by handing him literature that explained exactly how they killed babies inside that grim, gray building. He'd told her that he wasn't going in there for an abortion.

"Well"—she smiled, showing that she, too, had a sense of humor—"your girlfriend."

He put his hands on his hips and looked her up and down. "Lady, in case you can't tell, I don't got girlfriends." He was polite, amused.

Was he celibate?

"I go in there for the free condoms," he said.

She blushed at the word.

"To use with my *boyfriends*," he said emphatically. "I'm gay."

"There's no such thing," Caroline told him automatically. Her mind flashed, against her will, to Bethany. To the grandbaby out there. To the woman she'd never met who had torn apart her life. Jonathan had shown her photos of Bethany, but Caroline had not laid eyes directly on her daughter in eleven years. When she thought of her, Caroline still pictured the defiant eighteen-year-old at the diner.

He pinched himself and grinned. "I'm pretty sure this here's real."

"I mean, you're not gay."

"Oh, honey, there's no one gayer. This is how God made me."

"I don't believe that." A thrill pulsed through Caroline when he referenced the Lord.

"'What is crooked cannot be straightened.' Ecclesiastes 1:15, ma'am."

"That's not what that means," Caroline stammered.

"Well, what's your explanation for the fact that I love dick?"

"Maybe you love him as a friend, but God didn't make you gay. You *choose* to…do what you do."

"Lemme ask you something." He swung his weight to the other hip and looked her straight in the eye. The whites were very, very white. She had never stood this close to a Black person for this long. She could smell his breath, minty, and was reassured that he had also begun his day by brushing his teeth, just like she had.

"Go ahead."

"When did you choose to be straight?"

"I'm sorry, I don't—"

"You just said sexual orientation is a choice, so I'm asking you: tell me about the moment you decided to be straight."

Caroline looked at him blankly and was surprised to hear someone laugh. It was that new volunteer, the one who was always deep in conversation with the creepy Jew. What kind of horrid woman lurked in parking lots and eavesdropped when she wasn't busy preying on innocent girls? It incensed Caroline.

"You think killing babies is funny?" Caroline turned away from the sparkly boy and called out sharply, using Donald's line.

The woman gave her a supercilious smile.

"Were we talking about killing babies?" the woman said. Why couldn't she put on a bit of face powder or make her hair neater? "I thought we were talking about your delusion that there's no such thing as homosexuality. How about all your priests who love little boys a little too much?"

Caroline felt like she'd been punched. She knew there was a good answer, and she was embarrassed that she didn't have it on the tip of her tongue. Just like she knew there was an answer for this odd purple eye-shadowed Black kid beside her.

"Come on now, they're not all gay." Caroline recognized that voice; it was him, the big-nosed sidekick. "Some of them like little girls."

At this, the boy laughed and said "God bless" to Caroline before turning with an exaggerated flounce on the ball of his foot and heading into the parking lot. When Caroline saw him high-five the woman and the man—the so-called *escorts*, more like *executioners*—her breath caught with the betrayal. She hurried across the street to where Maureen was approaching an occasional pedestrian with leaflets and rosaries.

"Are you okay?" Maureen asked her, and for that simple query, Caroline was extremely grateful. Her friend caught her by the arm and looked at her meaningfully. "Did you have a rocky one?"

That's what they called any interaction that turned unpleasant.

Caroline nodded, embarrassed that her throat was tight, her voice threatening to betray her low threshold for confrontation. Maureen handed Caroline her leaflets and rosaries, hoisted her Defund Intentional Families sign onto her shoulder, and led Caroline away from the clinic.

"We'll circle the block," Maureen directed. "Tell me what happened." Dodging some dried dog poo, they breathed in the moldy smell of newly fallen leaves and headed toward Church Street.

Caroline relaxed. She was so pleased to have this friendship, to belong to this group. Planning the lobbying day in Albany had been more fun than she could have imagined. Days were no longer spent home alone, trying not to miss Christopher. Instead, she would hurry from work—she enjoyed saying to her fellow planners, "I finish work at two, so I'll be there right after"—and start making phone calls to encourage more church members to join. Or, with a polite yawn and stretch, excuse herself from the Dunkin' Donuts where the organizers sometimes had coffee in the evenings, saying, "I have the early shift at work tomorrow."

Caroline was the liaison with the charter bus company, becoming schooled in the labyrinthine workings of union rules. She'd had to calculate exactly how many hours their group would be in Albany, because if it exceeded a certain number, the driver would need a hotel room in which to rest. She'd had to prepare for different scenarios: whether they'd hit traffic, whether they'd be done early, whether it would take a group of twenty—or it might wind up being fifty—activists (she was an activist!) twenty or forty minutes to use the facilities. She learned that one could reserve a hotel room without paying anything, though only up until the check-in time, and she learned that there would be a waffle maker in the lobby. It was hard work, but for the first time, Caroline thought she might be penetrating the mysteries of the world beyond her own. She realized she partly had her marble-mouthed boss, Yuna, to thank for getting her started.

Still, Caroline was uneasy. In the pronounced silence that Maureen made no effort to relieve, Caroline knew what her friend wanted to hear. There was another reason, aside from her assiduous work, that her new group of friends had embraced her so wholeheartedly, but Caroline wanted to believe she would have been welcomed even without it.

A few weeks earlier, a meeting of PAIN had, atypically, whipped itself into a confessional frenzy. It had started with a parishioner named Thomas, who broke down in tears when he admitted that not only was his grown son a nonattender, but that the same son had filed for divorce from his wife. This led to a woman named Mary crying out that when she'd gone to visit her daughter in her new apartment in Queens, she'd found contraceptives in the medicine chest. Each of them was met with such compassion and understanding that others had begun to reveal their own private shames.

Sandy, in comforting Mary, admitted that she herself had had premarital sex, and while she would never entirely forgive herself, she knew that her husband and God had. (Caroline wondered how she could be certain God had forgiven her.) Terry then said in a broken voice that he thought he was an alcoholic, which wasn't technically a sin and wasn't a revelation to anyone but Terry himself, but still, the murmurings of comfort continued until Caroline, swept up in the endorphins of naked group candor, raised her hand like a schoolgirl. Her silent gesture stopped everyone, and the group turned its collective hungry attention to her. Caroline closed her eyes, felt the Lord speak for her.

"When I was young, I murdered my baby."

There was one slight gasp. In that moment, Caroline hadn't known what would become of her in this group, in this parish, in this town, but she knew that it had been God's will that she speak those words. They certainly weren't her words. She had never before articulated, even to herself, that this was what had happened on that day in 1973 with Father Gilhool. It wasn't until she spoke the words to the group that she understood that she, Caroline Byrne McClanahan, had had an *abortion*.

She began to weep. Her shoulders heaved and snot ran and she knew that that would have been the baby who would have loved her. That would have been the child who grew up to appreciate and honor her, to stay by her and care for her, to be her best friend.

"I can't help you at the clinic," she sobbed. "I'm a sinner and a hypocrite!" She hung her head, the sheer relief sapping her strength.

But then she felt hands on her shoulders and she opened her wet, blurred eyes to find Maureen crouching before her, gazing at her. (Maureen had neither an infrequent nor a nonattending adult child, and Caroline was never sure why she was in this group.)

"Caroline. You know the pain. You know the regret.

You are *the* most perfect person to pray for and talk to those women. God forgives you and He wants you to teach."

There were murmurs of agreement, tinged with awe.

And so Caroline had become the most perfect person for the Church of the Holy Sepulcher's Protect Life group. Or rather, she was trying to become that most perfect person. Quite apart from the discomfort caused by interacting with strangers, especially strangers who were apt to be hostile, she felt that she was lying by omission. Right now, as they avoided tripping on broken parts of the downtown Pierre sidewalk, Caroline knew that Maureen was titillated by Caroline's sinful past, that she wanted to hear details.

Caroline would indulge her as best she could, but was not prepared to tell a soul that it had been dear, beautiful Father Gilhool who had brought her to that terrible place with the greasy-haired man. Brought her and then refused to meet her eye ever again, let alone pray with her privately. She felt the familiar knot in her gut as she ran through the circuitous liturgy of their schism. Would she have wanted him to leave the priesthood for her? No, of course not. To raise that baby together? No, of course not! She knew that what had happened to them had been an exercise in love for God, not love like that between husbands and wives. She'd never felt that kind of passion and otherworldliness with Christopher. Her experience with Father Gilhool had been transcendent. But how could something so beautiful result in something so wrong? Was it wrong? She always ended on that note of doubt.

Over four decades later, Caroline still remained as confused as she had been during those dark months. She had never before allowed her mind to venture near that memory.

Never, before the PAIN meeting, had she even *thought* the word *pregnant* or *baby* or, for heaven's sake, *abortion* in connection with her own experience. There was so much she regretted, but she had the unsettling feeling that her regret was imperfect. Impure. Could regret be pure or impure?

She shook her head briskly, shooing away the familiar tangle. It was that awful man—Ernest? Ezra? Ira? He had thrown her with his repugnant comment about priests and little girls.

"I'm fine, really," she told Maureen. "It was that escort who said something offensive."

"Irving," Maureen said, her voice heavy with contempt. "Tell me what he said. Get it off your chest."

"Let's just say he stooped to insulting the clergy."

Maureen crossed herself quickly and kissed her fingers. "I thought maybe that boy had upset you," she said, glancing quickly at Caroline.

"No. He was strange, but harmless." Caroline wasn't at all sure he was harmless, but she didn't feel like replaying the conversation that had sideswiped her. Because of course Caroline knew now how she should have responded to his impertinent question. She should have told him that it's *not* a choice to be "straight"—God made everyone "straight," that stupid word. If you claimed to be homosexual, you were choosing to be something other than what God intended you to be. As with any other sin, you were straying. You were straying, and while God loved you just the way you were, He loved you too much to let you stay that way. If you were tempted by the sin of homosexuality, you went to confession and underwent conversion therapy. Caroline blew out her cheeks. She wished she could have thought this clearly in the moment.

"I have to learn to manage surprising conversations," she said aloud.

They rounded the corner and the wind picked up. Caroline tightened her grip on the leaflets, and Maureen braced the sign against her chest. This street was like a mini-highway that ran through town. There weren't many pedestrians, but a steady line of cars streamed off the bridge, hightailing it past the poor part of town, headed for higher ground.

"Have you told any of the patients yet about your experience?"

"Um," Caroline said, unsteady on this topic. "No. No, no."

A car honked in solidarity, and Maureen rewarded the driver with a wide smile.

"Do you have anyone to talk to about it? Have you ever processed it? Father Flechette is very good about these things."

Caroline flinched. She went to confession every single week, but couldn't begin to imagine telling him *this*. Her experience felt outside the classification of "these things." She pictured his papery cheeks and rheumy eyes and glanced sideways at Maureen to see whether she was serious. She appeared to be.

"And of course, you can always talk to Dotty or me."

Caroline gave her what she hoped looked like a grateful smile. A few weeks ago, she couldn't have imagined blurting out the incident. It would take another forty years before she said anything further about it.

The two women stepped to the side as a group of local boys, taking up the entire width of the sidewalk, passed them. All four wore enormous headphones, which were not enormous enough to keep music from leaking out of them.

"I'd like to see them when they're seventy, if they live that long," Maureen said after they'd passed. "See how their droopy drawers look with hearing aids." She shook her head.

"Excuse me?" A lovely girl, clean and bright-eyed, stood in front of them. She had an earring through her nose, but it was small and delicate. "Are you handing those out?" She nodded her chin in the direction of Caroline's fistful of rosaries.

"Yes," Caroline exclaimed, holding up the strings of beads. "How many would you like?"

"Could I have two?" the girl said tentatively.

"Of course!" Caroline peeled away a pair and Maureen beamed.

The girl noticed Maureen's sign. "Oh," she said brightly, "that's where I'm trying to get to! Could you tell me where it is?"

Maureen was nonplussed.

"Do you need pregnancy help?" Caroline ventured.

"Oh, no!" the girl said quickly and the women exhaled in tandem. "I have no intention of getting pregnant before I'm married." She smiled at their smiles, and Caroline could see her front tooth was chipped. "I thank God every day for that place. They give me free birth control." She shook her head, and the women found themselves shaking their heads along with her, instinctive politeness accidentally overriding firmly held beliefs. "I will not wind up like my mother. Ten kids. Is Intentional Families on that block?" She pointed in the wrong direction and for a fraction of a second, neither Caroline nor Maureen answered her.

"I believe it's over there," Maureen said stiffly. "Please,

though, before you go, read this. They kill babies in that place! They need to be shut down!"

The girl gaped at her briefly, and backed away from the proffered pamphlet. "Okay, well, God bless you, okay?"

"No, God bless *you*," Maureen said petulantly. The girl disappeared around the corner.

"What do you do with someone like that?" Caroline asked.

Maureen shook her head sadly and returned the rejected flyer to her stack. "Pray harder." She clutched Caroline's hand, closed her eyes, and said hastily, "Holy Mary, Mother of God, pray for us sinners, now and at the hour of our death. Amen."

"Hey!"

Caroline's eyes flew open in time to see two girls in a maroon car bearing a Linden College bumper sticker pull away from the traffic light.

"Go feed some abandoned kids, bitches!" The car sped off.

Maureen and Caroline met each other's gazes, and for the first time in her life, Caroline felt a true, deep bond of friendship with someone other than her husband. She and Maureen were suffering together, sharing a crucible, summoning God's strength at the same moment for the same reason, under circumstances that would be all but impossible to convey to someone who wasn't there with them. Caroline squeezed Maureen's hand and smiled.

"Let's go back."

It would have been faster to go back the way they came, but they braved the remainder of the block and were rewarded with another supportive honk just before they turned onto Maple Avenue.

Why hadn't Father Gilhool found a place for her to go? Caroline wondered out of the blue. Everyone knew that priests and nuns found "au pair jobs" abroad for girls that weren't au pair jobs at all—the Irish sent their girls to American convents to wait out their remaining months and vice versa. Families believed what they needed to believe, so why hadn't Father Gilhool arranged for Caroline to go away? She could have had the baby, put it up for adoption, and then found it when it was eighteen. *It*. A boy, a girl? She wouldn't be alone right now. Jonathan wasn't *gone* gone, the way Bethany was, but he called her only on her birthday and on Christmas—so obligatory as to be hurtful.

Tears sprang to her eyes, and she gasped to stave off a crying jag. There could have been a baby out there for Caroline. The enormity of the loss hit her with the force of forty years. She did feel real regret, she realized with a rush of clarity and, strangely, relief. Real, pure, genuine regret.

The clinic was ahead of them. They could see Donald and Merwin, another parishioner from their church, admiring a low-slung sports car parked at the curb. Across the street, Caroline's least favorite protester had set up in his usual spot. An obese (God forgive her) man with a long, stiff beard, he always wore overalls and was accompanied by four girls who dressed the way Caroline imagined Mennonites dressed, though she wasn't sure she'd ever seen a Mennonite. It wasn't clear to anyone whether the girls were his daughters or whether one—or more—might be his wife. It made Caroline very uncomfortable. He made them, the proper Christians, all look bad.

Even before they regained their spots in front of the entrance—not right in front, because that would be against the law and the parishioners of the Church of the Holy Sepulcher could never be accused of breaking any law, unlike the murderers inside—Caroline could hear that unkempt woman, the escort who carried herself like she was better than everyone else. Her voice had a pitch that punched through all the others.

"God is the biggest abortionist of all," she was saying to a woman who looked to be Caroline's own age. Likely the mother or grandmother of an IF victim. The mothers and the boyfriends often came outside to smoke, and Caroline had absorbed Maureen's frustration at not being able to reach them once they were in the parking lot—the clinic's private property. Caroline had heard this particularly disgusting heresy from this escort before. Conflating God's will with a sin—it was unbearable that Caroline couldn't set the poor grandmother straight. She had to have faith that most of these targets knew the truth in their hearts. The idea that a miscarriage was an abortion by God—who would swallow that nonsense? Maureen had even suggested that it might drive people back to the church, hearing such blasphemy.

All of a sudden, the escort pointed at Caroline and Maureen, and the woman she was talking to nodded. Caroline felt powerless and furious.

"Jesus loves you!" Caroline shouted.

"Well, duh," replied the woman. The escort smirked.

The trip to Albany couldn't come soon enough.

EIGHTEEN

Meg emptied the contents of her backpack onto the overturned milk crate that served as a side table, and her roommates shrieked as though they hadn't seen food in a week. At the end of the dinner shift, when Leandra's Kitchen closed, the staff were allowed to take any baked goods that couldn't be reincarnated the next day as bread pudding or some other soaked dessert. Rosetta and Hannah, having eaten dinner at the dining hall and then consumed loaded frozen yoghurts a couple of hours later, all of which was included in their meal plans, nevertheless descended on the two cheese Danishes, the oversize red velvet cupcake, and three apple twists. Free food always tasted better.

Meg and JD stood back and watched them like bemused parents.

"Aren't you going to have one?" Hannah said through a mouth full of crumbs. She had a dollop of frosting at the corner of her mouth.

Meg shook her head.

"I don't think she's eating enough," Rosetta said to JD, tearing the Danishes into pieces and making a three-layer bite for herself. The potpourri-sniffing had been replaced by actual eating, though the eating was often preceded by some sort of preparatory, disfiguring ritual such as this.

"She looks good to me," JD said, sliding an arm around Meg's waist. But then he frowned. "Are you losing weight?"

"Not a chance," Meg said lightly, though in fact her appetite had waned around the time she'd begun working at Leandra's three weeks earlier. Regular proximity to other people's half-eaten food turned out to be disgusting, but Meg didn't want to admit her mother might have been right about which job she should have taken. Also, bringing these treats home to her suitemates was one of the few generous gestures she was able to make. Meg felt certain it had contributed to the tentative peace the three girls had attained. Bringing home these nearly stale pastries made it easier for her to enjoy sitting on the ottoman the other two had purchased and more likely to stretch out on the Persian rug Rosetta's mother had managed to order from prison without consulting any of them.

"I still say no," Hannah told Rosetta, continuing the debate they'd been having when Meg and JD interrupted them. "I don't think it's fair for someone who has Tourette's to go on a silent retreat."

"But it's not their fault they can't be silent," Rosetta protested. "Plus, there's the chance that the low stress levels and meditation could get their tics under control. How could you deny them that?"

"I don't know whether this is actual or hypothetical," JD said, "but these are not the sides I would have expected you to take."

"You mean because I'm usually such a hard-hearted bitch?" Rosetta drawled.

"Well, yeah," JD said so earnestly that the three suitemates all laughed. Meg felt both happy that her boyfriend and suitemates got along and nervous that Rosetta might get it into her head to steal him away. JD had reassured her many times that this was not possible, and although Meg was not completely convinced, she sensed that if she pressed the point, she'd make it come to pass.

"It's not hypothetical," Hannah said, pinching off a piece of apple twist. "Rosetta's friend has signed up for a retreat."

"Who?" Meg asked, curious to get a load of someone with Tourette's. She could hide all her scars under clothing; what would it be like *not* to be able to hide your defects? Wait, not defects. Otherly abled? Was Tourette's an alternate ability?

"High school friend," Rosetta said, and Meg was mildly disappointed.

A text dinged on her phone, which was in a pocket somewhere in her backpack.

"Mom," Hannah, Rosetta, and JD said together, and Meg blushed. Everyone had parents and everyone spoke to their parents—well, JD was not on speaking terms with his—but they spoke to them at random times, informally. Meg's mother was so reluctant to bother her (AnneMarie's words, not Meg's) that she wouldn't call when Meg wasn't expecting it. So they had agreed on Wednesday nights, after Meg got home from work. If Meg didn't call her by eleven, AnneMarie texted to make sure it was okay for her to call. The lack of casualness, and even more, her deference, was embarrassing; Meg hadn't realized everyone had noticed.

"Yeah, yeah," Meg said, heading to her bedroom, trying to convey in those words both an indication that she understood her mother's behavior was not normal while also not betraying her. She'd been doing a lot of that balancing act since arriving at Linden. "Save me something," Meg called out behind her, even as her stomach twisted at the thought of the buttery pastries.

Meg kicked the door closed to her room, took a few deep breaths to prepare, breaths that were in their very necessity cruel to her mother, and dialed. AnneMarie picked up on the first ring.

"Hi, sweetheart," she said eagerly.

"Hi," Meg said, the flatness in her voice intended to get her mother to back down. When she did, Meg felt terrible.

"How was work?"

"Fine. It was funny, I waited on one of my professors and her friends."

Her mother didn't say anything.

"It was fine," Meg told her, not sure what the silence meant. "She tipped well."

"Well, that's good." There was a pause while AnneMarie tried to think of something to say. "Which class does she teach?"

Meg hesitated. She hadn't told her mother she was taking a playwriting class, partly because she didn't want to admit she hadn't understood how enrollment worked and so had gotten stuck with this one, but mostly because she didn't want to explain the class or how it had turned out to be her favorite. Playwriting was not an activity that had ever crossed their minds or entered their world, and Meg was afraid the mere fact of her taking it would widen the growing gap between them.

"English." They read things and they wrote things and it wasn't history, so this was barely a lie.

"Oh. Nice. And how's your activity group going?"

Irritation surged through Meg, masking embarrassment. *Activity group.* She meant the pro-life club Meg had checked out, Linden for Life. It was lame was how it was. Meg and two acne-attacked international students. At the first meeting, they'd discussed holding a silent prayer protest at the local Intentional Families clinic. Meg hadn't gone back, but hadn't told her mother that.

"Fine," Meg said. Was there a synonym for fine? *Adequate. Lovely. Tolerable. Okay.* None of them really worked.

Meg flopped on the bed and looked out at the scaffolding. Hannah, Rosetta, and JD were climbing onto it through the common room window. JD looked toward her room, but she was sitting in the dark, so he couldn't see inside. Still, he waved in her direction and then put his hand on his heart. She knew in that moment she wanted to spend the rest of her life with him and immediately felt ridiculous for having that romance-novel thought.

"What's going on there?" Meg asked perfunctorily. Not only didn't she care what was going on in Barton, but she actively did not want to know. Her queasiness surged.

"Oh, well, let's see," her mother said in a gush that made Meg realize they'd both been holding their breath. "Mrs. Tropez came in for a root canal yesterday. They told me Dr. Imbroglio was in with her for two full hours. We billed her twelve hundred dollars!"

Meg wondered whether privacy laws applied to the billing clerk. She was about to ask, thinking this would add a few seconds to the conversation, when she suddenly lurched from the bed and threw up in the garbage can.

"Hold on!" Meg shouted from across the room. "Just hold on!"

She puked again.

Meg's stomach had been like Swiss cheese ever since the accident and ensuing banquet of post-surgery meds, but she didn't usually vomit. She grabbed a handful of tissues from the desk and wiped her mouth.

"Hi," Meg said into the phone, speaking as calmly as she could.

"Meggie, did you just throw up?" her mother asked anxiously.

"A little," she admitted, glancing out the window. Hannah and Rosetta both appeared to be trying to touch their noses with their tongues. JD was leaning against a pole, his hands clasped behind his head, grinning at them.

"Do you have a fever?"

"How should I know?" Meg snapped and immediately regretted it.

There was a heavy silence on her mother's end.

"Sorry," she mumbled.

"Meg, do you have a boyfriend?"

Now, *now*, from hundreds of miles away, she knew what Meg was up to? Two and half years of Meg stealing and fucking and using and she never knew, but *this* she figured out?

"What does throwing up have to do with having a boyfriend? You think I caught this from someone?" Meg was irritated she'd given her mother even that much and afraid she was going to puke again. "I probably got it from Rosetta. She had a stomach flu last week." This was patently untrue.

"Meg." Her mother's voice trembled.

"What?"

"The doctor said you can*not* get pregnant."

"Jesus, Mom!"

"Meg!"

"What does that have to do with anything? I know I can't get…you know. Ugh, hang on."

Meg shoved the phone under her pillow so her mother couldn't hear and threw up again, then tossed a bunch of tissues over the disgusting mess. She needed to get off this call and go deal. She dug out the phone.

"…because you will *die*, Meg. Do you understand? Did you understand when she said that?"

"Whoa, what? What are you talking about?"

"Damn it, Meg. Do you or do you not remember Dr. Foster saying you cannot get pregnant?"

Meg couldn't remember ever hearing her mother curse before.

"It's hard to forget a doctor telling you you can't ever get pregnant," Meg said with as much sarcasm as she could muster, given that a headache was now weaving its tentacles around her temples. "I'm pretty sure I'm having my very first migraine. Yay," she added weakly.

"Meggie." AnneMarie took a deep, impatient breath. "She didn't say you can't get pregnant as in you are *unable* to get pregnant. She said you can't get pregnant as in you *must* not get pregnant because your pelvis cannot handle a pregnancy, let alone a birth. Carrying a baby would *kill* you is what she said." She was yelling now. "She did *not* say you were *unable* to get pregnant! Meg—"

"Mom." Meg mustered calm, even managed a chuckle. She had to, otherwise AnneMarie would be pounding down the door in the time it took her to drive to Pierre from Barton. "I promise you this is just a bug. Or food poisoning. Okay?"

AnneMarie was silent while Meg's stomach continued to churn and her mouth grew gummy.

"Okay," AnneMarie said doubtfully.

"But my roommates are waiting for me…" she lied.

"You'll rest and drink lots and lots of fluids?"

Meg assured her mother she would mind her hydration and managed to end the call right before she threw up again, just bile this time.

"I'm not fucking pregnant," she said weakly to the empty room.

Except that, of course, she was.

NINETEEN

It was pouring rain, but there was no way Meg was going to ask anyone to drive her or even call a cab. The cab would have cost as much as the pee-on-a-stick test she'd taken, and that was already twenty-two dollars she didn't have but spent anyway. Plus, she could imagine the look the driver would give her when she gave him the address, and she had no interest in getting that look. She had zero interest in having even one single human more than was absolutely necessary know what she was about to do. She'd even erased her online search history after looking up the number for Intentional Families so that future Meg wouldn't accidentally be reminded.

The wind insisted on popping her umbrella inside out so many times that by the time Meg was a block from the clinic, she was just aiming a crooked shield against an invisible enemy. She was soaked and her bones ached. She'd read that bones aching in wet weather was a myth, but she knew it was absolutely and completely true. Her hips hurt so badly she could hardly walk when a storm was coming. Right now, all she wanted in the world was to sit down.

A large, intact umbrella was hurrying along the sidewalk, a pair of bony, polyester-pantsed legs driving it toward her.

"Intentional Families!" a voice yelled from behind the umbrella and over the rain. Thunder drowned out the rest.

"What?" Meg yelled back.

An intense face popped out from behind the umbrella.

"Intentional Families kills babies!" The face, voice, and legs belonged to an ugly woman. She thrust a pamphlet at Meg, which became pulpy instantly. There was no reason to take it. Someone who leafleted in a downpour was a de facto moron.

"Well, that's why I'm here. To kill my baby," Meg said in a regular voice, knowing the woman couldn't hear her.

"WHAT?" She closed one eye against a blast of wind.

"Thank you!" Meg walked past her.

"Are you going into that place?" the woman yelled.

What fucking business was it of hers?

"We can help you! All they do in there is kill babies! We can take you somewhere where you have real choices!"

Meg picked up her pace, splashing even more water into her ill-chosen ankle boots. These were the people she'd seen from the car on the way to Carton and Box, back in September, but they hadn't seemed so aggressive from that vantage point.

"Come with me! You have choices!" The woman liked that word. Matching Meg's pace, she extended her umbrella over both of them, unasked, and her shoulder nearly touched Meg's. Meg fought the urge to swing sideways and knock her over. They were about the same height and weight.

They had nearly reached the entrance to the IF parking lot when Meg spotted her: Professor-not-Professor Tanisman. Sylvia. She was wearing a reflective orange vest that said IF Escort and she carried an umbrella large enough to protect her and an old guy who appeared to be telling her a joke. She kept throwing her head back and laughing, even though a bunch of the protesters were yelling at them, just a few feet away.

Meg quickly reviewed her options. She could keep walking, right past the entrance, pretend she was out for a stroll. That was ridiculous. This was hardly stroll weather, and she was twenty minutes away from anywhere a Linden student might naturally find herself, and her umbrella was too destroyed to hide her.

She could turn around. But that meant she would have come all this way and would be returning to campus soaking, freezing, and with the same enormous tiny problem expanding inside her every second.

Meg could fucking grow a pair and go inside. Could she pretend not to see Sylvia? Impossible. Glare at her as she passed, so she wouldn't dare say anything? Meg had been such an ardent, unyielding bitch in class on the topic of abortion. Now she was a hypocrite of the lowest order. The thought of Sylvia seeing her go in there was more than she could bear.

"My friend's car is right here," Polyester Lady said eagerly, waving vigorously to another old lady holding a sign that said, simply, Pray.

The car she stopped at had a bumper sticker that said We Support Our Priests. Meg pulled at the handle, but it was locked. Polyester Lady waved excitedly to her friend, who held up a key fob and clicked it in their direction. The lights flashed and Meg ducked inside quickly. She watched the two older women struggle to close their umbrellas and follow suit.

Meg leaned against the window, closed her eyes, and took a deep breath, relishing the silence. What the hell did *We Support Our Priests* mean? What was the point of that bland statement? Like saying, *I support my supermarket* or *I assist my elderly grandmother*? And then it hit her—it was about the sex abusers, as in, our priests may fondle little boys but we still love them. Motherfucker, who were these people?

The car was stuffy and smelled like damp wool and also of some fake cinnamony air freshener. The owner eased herself into the driver's seat while Meg's scrawny assailant slid into the back seat beside her. Meg moved as far from her as she could and then laid her sopping, broken umbrella on the seat between them; why the hell hadn't the woman gotten into the passenger seat?

The driver turned to look at Meg. Her eyes were bright and she looked very happy for someone who had been getting soaked all morning. Maybe she was glad for an excuse to get out of the rain.

"Hi! God bless you! I'm Caroline. What's your name?"

Meg shook her head, and Caroline looked confused. But this wasn't Polyester Lady's first rodeo.

"That's okay, honey, you don't have to tell us your name. I'm Maureen and we're so glad you're letting us help you. You won't be sorry." She moved the mangled umbrella to the floor of the car.

Meg was already sorry. Caroline fired up the car and pulled away slowly. Why the hell had Meg gotten in? Maybe they were going to kidnap her. Or kill her with their slow driving.

JD had no idea Meg was pregnant, and he had no idea she was getting an abortion today. The way Meg figured, she was saving him the emotional taxation, sparing him complicated feelings about this impossible cluster of cells.

The biddies were blathering.

"We're so glad you're considering your other options!"

"We have so much information at our clinic."

"And we can warm up and dry off! We have really good hot chocolate mix."

Meg doubted one mix was better than any other.

"What does your bumper sticker mean?" she asked, keeping her gaze focused out the window and not on them.

"Which one? Mine?" Caroline said, slowing for the stoplight that was still nearly a block away. "Oh, well, we're very supportive of our priests."

"Are there people who aren't?" Meg asked, feigning innocence.

"Well…" Caroline said vaguely. "There are some people who misunderstand them."

"Misunderstand that they abuse children?" Meg said coldly.

Caroline stiffened.

"Everyone makes mistakes," Maureen interjected, as Caroline turned the car onto the mini-highway that ran through Pierre. "We stand by our priests, and we recognize that a few bad eggs does not mean you throw away the whole carton."

Meg shrugged.

They pulled into a driveway, and she sat up, alert.

"Wait, we're here? It's around the corner?" Except for the sign that said CareNet Emergency Pregnancy Services, it looked like they were at someone's home.

"Yep!" Maureen said happily.

"You're just going to try to talk me out of an abortion,"

Meg said sullenly. "Without knowing anything about me or my situation."

Maureen bristled, but Caroline said, "We want you to know all your options before making a decision. We are going to introduce you to every resource and support system available to you, services you didn't even know existed!" She all but clapped her hands.

Maureen had turned away from Meg, her phone to her ear.

"No one's answering," she muttered.

"What, no one's at the clinic?" Meg said.

"It's okay, I have a key. Let's get you warm and dry!"

"You have a key?"

They flung open their doors. Caroline hurried around to open Meg's while Maureen picked her way along an alley, heading toward the back door of the row house.

Caroline was not as unappealing as Maureen was—her face was rounder, rosier, more grandmotherly—but there was an urgency to the way she looked at Meg that felt like she was sucking something from her. She had terrible, practical, wet shoes.

Meg pushed herself up from the seat and stepped over the stream coursing in the gutter. She could still leave. They couldn't forcibly make her stay. (Could they?) She had chosen to go with them because she was cold, because she was curious, because they seemed so happy to have brought her here.

Maureen opened the front door of the clinic and made a grand gesture for them to come in. Meg took the three front steps in one stride, leaving Caroline with her umbrella in her wake.

The waiting room had no one waiting. Meg knew it was a waiting room only because there were three chairs spaced evenly around a table that held stacks of perfectly splayed magazines she'd never heard of: *Guys* and *Devotion*. They all featured smiling dark-skinned teenagers on their covers. The room was done up in faded rose carpeting and floral wallpaper. Above one wooden-armed chair hung a framed print of a bluebird that was too small for the wall. There was a reception window, but no computer on the desk inside, only a pack of unopened Post-it notes and a pen lying beside it, at the ready. On the counter were a variety of pamphlets, all featuring pensive girls, their faces tilted to the side, gazes cast downward. On the wall was a calendar whose pages hadn't been flipped in two months.

The place was more than just empty; no one had been there in a long time. It felt like a museum exhibit of a room from another era, nothing like the hot, crowded feel to the dentist's office where her mother worked. Why was this place deserted? Meg was about to turn and run when Caroline laid her hand on her arm. Meg flinched and Caroline removed her hand.

"Just stay long enough for us to dry out your socks and shoes, make you some hot chocolate, and then you're on your way," Caroline cajoled. "There's a hand dryer in the bathroom. Here, sit and give them to me." She gestured to Meg's feet.

"Hot chocolate," Maureen repeated firmly. "There are pamphlets you can read while you wait." She nodded at the counter and scurried away along a narrow hallway that ran beside a staircase.

Meg sank down and loosened her soggy laces. With a soft

grunt, Caroline knelt before her. She tugged off Meg's shoes and peeled away her socks. It was one of the most intimate exchanges Meg had ever had with someone she didn't know. She watched Caroline for signs of a grimace, but the woman had this beatific smile plastered on her face.

"I'm not sure the shoes will dry, but I'll stuff them with newspaper," Caroline fretted. "The socks should do okay under the hand dryer."

"I can do it," Meg offered, straightening up. The thought of the older woman carrying the dripping, smelly stuff was too much.

"No, you sit. Take care of yourself and let us take care of you." Caroline headed off down the same creaky hall, the shoes and socks dangling from extended fingers.

The too-warm room and the promise of someone taking care of her nearly made Meg forget why she was there. She closed her eyes and listened to the silence inside, underscored by the steady hum of traffic outside. She took her first deep breath in a week and pictured JD's long, strong face and round brown eyes and felt her shoulders come down from her ears.

Meg relaxed enough to come to her senses. Obviously, these ladies were going to try to talk her out of an abortion, but when she explained that having a baby would kill her, she suspected they would soften their stances. She couldn't quite imagine them driving her back to the clinic, but maybe they could drop her off a block away so their friends wouldn't see them. By then, maybe Sylvia would be gone. So would Meg's appointment slot at IF, but she'd finagle something once she got inside.

There was a television on the wall that hinged out,

but Meg had had enough television at the hospital to last a lifetime. Like the Barton classmates' dads who had fought in Iraq and refused to go to a beach ever again, Meg felt the same about TV: it only brought back memories of combat. She half stood to reach for a copy of the intriguingly named *Guys*, when she noticed a pamphlet propped against the unmanned receptionist's window announcing Sexual Integrity Workshops.

She slid one from the Plexiglas display.

```
Our Sexual Integrity Workshops are taught
from a sexual risk avoidance perspective
(abstinence-only).
```

Meg laughed out loud and tried to picture that workshop. *Kids, don't have sex. Okay, all done. Here's your hot chocolate.*

```
Using an interactive approach, we explore
healthy choices for our sexuality and the
consequences of engaging in high-risk behavior.
```

Meg could totally *teach* this class. In her sleep. She wondered how much they'd pay her.

```
Through the use of stories, video, statistics,
games, and discussion, the participants will
learn how to make positive choices for their
futures by examining the components of healthy
relationships and the far-reaching results of
the choices we make. Those that have made past
decisions they regret will be equipped and
encouraged to change their direction from one
of despair to one of hope.
```

She really was their poster child for facing regret and changing direction from despair to hope. What games could they possibly play? She pictured Candy Land with STDs instead of candy canes. Meg turned the page, and there was a list of topics covered:

```
Making Good Decisions
Healthy Relationships
Character Workshops
Secondary Virginity
```

Meg guffawed. Did a doctor go up in there and solder your hymen closed? Why the fuck would anyone want to lose their virginity again? It was bad enough the first time, although she'd been so high she barely remembered it, just the pain and light trickle of blood afterward to confirm it had happened.

In a funny way, though, Meg kind of knew what the pamphlet was getting at. When she'd first had sex with JD, it was as though she was doing it for the first time. Like the Eskimos and snow, there should be a huge variety of words for sex: what she'd done with Troy and Baxter was a universe away from what she did with JD. She giggled as she considered asking these ladies whether she should try for a shot at tertiary virginity.

"What's so funny?" Maureen glided in carefully, holding a mug out in front of her.

"Secondary virginity," Meg said.

Maureen frowned.

"It's something to consider."

"If you say so."

She set down the hot chocolate. There was a slick of tiny marshmallows across the top.

Caroline came in behind her and sat beside Meg.

"So!" she said.

Maureen selected a chair across from them and picked up a remote control from behind a fake plant.

"So," Meg echoed, yielding nothing.

"I like to start by showing you a video of what your baby looks like right now."

Meg stiffened.

"It's not a baby yet."

"We'll get to that."

"How can you have a video of my ba—my cell cluster? Don't I need an ultrasound?"

"Yes!" Caroline said. "We're going to give you a referral for a free one at a doctor's office—"

"This isn't a doctor's office?"

"We can give you a free, lab-quality pregnancy test," Maureen said.

"I already took a pregnancy test. I paid twenty-two dollars for it."

Maureen clicked on the TV and a lot of gray shapes filled the screen.

"How far along are you?"

Meg shrugged.

"How late is your period?" Caroline tried.

"My period isn't very regular, but my last one was…" She squinted, remembering that it had come during a midterm for Caribbean Lit, which would have been mid-October so… "Sevenish weeks ago?"

"Wonderful!" Maureen said. "So your baby looks like this right now!"

"It's not a baby," Meg repeated and followed her gaze to the television. She had no idea what she was looking at.

"See this?" Maureen stood up and pointed to a tiny, pulsing white blob.

"Yeah."

"That's the heartbeat!" Caroline exclaimed.

"It's not *my* embryo's heartbeat," Meg reminded them, trying to rein in their misplaced excitement.

"Listen," Maureen said and leaned forward. She clearly wanted to take Meg's hands in hers, seemed, in fact, to be awkwardly following some sort of training protocol, but she couldn't quite reach. Meg wasn't going to make it easier for her. She did not like her. "We are client advocates and we're here to tell you all the choices and possibilities and support services available to you."

"You said that already."

She looked at Meg blankly.

"In the car."

Caroline risked patting her hand. Meg let her, purely as a rebuke to Maureen.

"We have teen mom groups that meet here—"

"What!" Meg cried. "I am *not* going to be a teen mom."

"*And* we have adoption services," Caroline continued. "You could make some couple out there very happy. *Your* baby would be snapped right up."

Meg thought about her mom, and how she had wanted Meg so badly, even if it drove away her own husband. Meg had come to believe in the years since the "accident" that

AnneMarie really did want her, even if there hadn't been a seventy-five-thousand-dollar bonus. Out of nowhere, Meg teared up. What the fuck, fucking hormones.

"Yes, adoption is a wonderful option!" Maureen pounced, in rhyme. "And we will find you the absolute best prenatal care available."

"I have less than no money," Meg told her sourly.

"It doesn't matter," Caroline said. "Everything would be paid for by the adoptive parents."

"Uh-huh." Meg was biding her time until she could go in for the kill. So to speak.

"It's important to remember the side effects of abortion," Maureen intoned. Caroline frowned slightly at her, but Maureen didn't notice. "Survivors of abortion often fall prey to drug and alcohol abuse—"

Meg chortled, but Maureen plowed ahead.

"—anger—"

Meg laughed again and Maureen pressed her lips together.

"—suicidal thoughts, relationship problems, sexual dysfunction, and anniversary grief." She sat back, having made it through her rehearsed litany.

"Wouldn't sexual dysfunction be a plus? It would really help maintain the new virginity," Meg said, almost enjoying herself.

Caroline cleared her throat.

"Well, so here's the thing," Meg said, glancing at the clock on the wall, then realizing it was frozen at an unlikely hour. "If I were to continue this pregnancy, I would die."

She sat back triumphantly, prepared for her words to take the wind out of their sails.

"Oh, I'm sure it feels like that, sweetheart, but we're telling you you can have a wonderful life after you bring this baby into the world," Caroline cooed.

Meg leaned forward.

"You're not understanding. I was in a car accident. My pelvis is held together with pins. I would literally burst apart and die if I carried this pregnancy for even another two months."

For a moment, there was only the sound of rain. Maureen crossed herself.

Go ahead, cross away.

"You can't really know God's plan," Caroline said tentatively.

"What do you mean?"

"You can't really know what would actually happen," she said.

"Uh, yeah, I can." Meg pulled up her shirt and showed her the tracks of scars run amok across her torso. Both women grimaced and looked away.

She glared at them.

"God has a plan and He meant for you to get pregnant. He doesn't make mistakes," Maureen said.

Meg tried to register what they were saying.

"You're saying I should just die."

"No, not at all! We're saying that God has a plan and you should trust Him."

"You realize we'd both die, me *and* the baby. Because I couldn't even carry it to viability."

Caroline shifted in her seat and glanced at Maureen, who set her mouth.

"Like we said," Maureen insisted primly, "God has a plan."

"So, when you have a cavity," Meg persisted, "you don't go to the dentist to have it filled, because that's God's plan, for your tooth to rot?"

"That's different," Caroline said. "That is not a procedure that will kill a human being."

"But it's still interfering with *God's plan*." Meg whined the last two words.

"Why don't you come to a group meeting?" Caroline was buying time. "There's one tomorrow night, right here."

"Will there be more hot chocolate?" Meg snarled, standing up. She was shaking, but tried to keep her voice steady. "Give me my fucking shoes, you fucking evil, dried-up bitches."

Even Maureen looked shocked. It was the highlight of Meg's shit day.

TWENTY

Caroline gazed at the screen, riveted. For a moment, she forgot it was a recorded video and not the actual baby growing in the belly across the table. When she'd been pregnant with Bethany and even a year later with Jonathan, ultrasound had been available in only a few places around the country and certainly wasn't an option for someone having a regular, uncomplicated pregnancy, such as she'd been blessed with both times. How could anyone not be filled with joy at the sight of that beating heart? Every single baby was a miracle.

Caroline turned to look at the sullen girl, whom she had recognized from the store, but who didn't recognize her. That was all right. Caroline didn't remember all her customers, but there had been that beautiful moment with the girl's mother. They had silently prayed for her right there at the Carton and Box register, and Caroline had known that God would keep her safe and told the mother so. She hadn't known He would do it by sending the girl straight to Caroline.

But now she could and would protect her and her heart thrilled.

Mary. The girl had finally told them her name. Caroline suspected this wasn't her real name, but it didn't matter. That this was the name she picked told Caroline something about her true heart.

Mary was alert and rude, and Caroline did her best to win her trust. Maureen, she was realizing, didn't have the best manner with a young, scared girl, so Caroline took charge, something she'd been learning to do more and more at the store, with Yuna's encouragement.

"This baby was conceived in love, wasn't it?" Caroline said after Mary cursed them out. Caroline had flinched, but hadn't wavered, even with the girl looming over them.

"What?" Mary spat.

"You didn't say you were raped. That's what a lot of the girls say."

"No, I wasn't fucking raped. I *like* having sex."

"And that's okay." It wasn't okay, but Caroline had to keep talking so Maureen wouldn't. "This baby was conceived in love."

"So?" Mary's voice was a shade less hostile, and Caroline thought she saw a way in.

Caroline wanted desperately to explain that she, too, had once been in love, deeply in love with Father Gilhool—with God? It had been one and the same—and so she knew what it was to feel that ecstasy. But she didn't want to say that part in front of Maureen.

Instead, she conjured up the awfulness of the doctor's office and the oily man who had reached up inside her and taken what she hadn't understood was there. (Was that true? Was it possible she really had understood so little? *Yes*, she assured herself. So much of her youth had been in the dark.) He had taken something of hers without asking permission, something beloved, and it had been a terrible, abrupt, incomprehensible end to her prayer sessions with Father Gilhool.

She told Mary about the fear and the pain of the procedure, both during and after, and how she never again saw the man she loved, because of the destruction of her baby. She stopped herself from calling it murder because she sensed she would lose her tentative grasp on Mary if she did.

"I was in love, too, and then…" She held up her palms: *poof, gone.*

Mary sat down.

"Why?" she asked suspiciously.

"Why," Caroline repeated. She did not know why, and sometimes when she was held hostage by insomnia, she wondered why Father Gilhool could not have left the priesthood and married her and raised that baby with her. She knew it was selfish—her needs over an entire congregation's—but surely that would have been better than murdering her beloved baby. Suppressed tears made her throat thick and achy. For a moment, she believed she could take this girl's baby and raise it, that that was what, even at the age of fifty-six, she was meant to do. "Because we couldn't recover."

"So you told him you did it?"

"He knew, yes," Caroline evaded, glancing at Maureen, who looked primly satisfied. At last, Caroline's terrible past was being put to the good use they'd all known it could be.

Mary sat back and crossed her arms.

"Well, I'm not telling him, so it won't destroy us."

Maureen leaned forward to speak, but Caroline cut her off.

"But *you'll* know and it will destroy you. That anniversary grief, Mary? It's real, except that it's not just the anniversary, it's *every single day* that you mourn your lost baby!"

Maureen nodded vigorously.

"I told you—having this baby will *literally* destroy me," Mary said, but for the first time, doubt flashed across the girl's face.

"And nobody wants that," Caroline assured her. "But doctors are wrong all the time. And bodies heal. I bet you needed crutches after the accident, right?" Caroline was having an inspiration.

"Uh, a lot more than crutches. Try a coma, breathing tubes—"

Caroline cut her off.

"Exactly. And now look at you. In college? Working?"

"Both," Mary snapped, and Caroline hurried past this potential obstacle.

"Right, fully capable and living your life. So what's to say your body hasn't healed well beyond what they predicted months…?"

"Four years…" Mary conceded.

"Four years ago."

Mary bit her lip.

"Let us find you a doctor, a *free* doctor's appointment to assess." Caroline glanced at Maureen. "Okay?"

There was a very long silence.

Mary gave a small nod, which infused Caroline with the deepest joy she had ever known, the godlike satisfaction of saving another life. Three, if you counted the future of this girl and the boy she loved.

TWENTY-ONE

It's not like Sylvia was on the lookout for wet pedestrians to scoop up. But in the torrential downpour, a girl walking slowly, no umbrella, not even trying to hurry between awnings, stood out. Sylvia did a double take, and was surprised that even with such minimal visual information, she could recognize someone she barely knew. Although there was that slight limp. She couldn't confirm it until she'd passed her, but it was definitely her student Meg Croyden.

Sylvia turned at the next corner, drove around the block, and easily caught up to her. She punched on her flashers and pulled over, hoping not to scare the hell out of the kid. She lowered her window, and the rain slashed in.

"Need a ride?" she yelled.

Meg looked horrified and shook her head vigorously, picking up her pace.

Sylvia considered driving away, feeling intrusive.

Ridiculous.

"Get in the car!" she barked with a maternal certainty that didn't often grace the interactions with her own children.

To her surprise, Meg got in the car. The rain pounded around them. She perched on the edge of the seat as if that would keep her from drenching it.

"Don't worry about it," Sylvia said. "It's just water."

"Thank you," Meg said, turning her head away to look out the window.

"You're welcome." Sylvia carefully pulled back out onto the road. There were hardly any other cars out. She glanced over. Meg looked wan and a little green.

"Are you feeling okay?" Sylvia ventured. There was so much more she wanted to ask.

Meg nodded.

I tried, Sylvia thought.

"Which dorm are you in?"

"Cushman."

That was one of the dorms that had been built after Sylvia's time.

"The one next to the gym?"

Meg shook her head. "The one behind the dining hall."

"Got it."

They passed a car wash—no business today—and a bodega with a window display that looked dusty even from this distance. Sylvia thought of and rejected several conversation openers. She thought about saying *Ready for class this afternoon?* but that seemed to violate Meg's prerogative not to be a student all the time. Asking about some other part of her life—in particular the part that had her walking miles from campus in the rain—also seemed nosy. So they would be silent.

Sylvia's mind wandered ahead to the rest of her day. Dry off and have a quick lie-down to transition from escort brain to teaching brain. Then class. Then home to the kids. She was hungry to see them, but couldn't deny she was aching to spend more than one night a week with Tony.

She was hit with her usual one-two punch when she thought of Tony. First, a shot of hormonal excitement that left her skin electrified as she remembered him inside her, followed immediately by anxiety about where this affair could possibly go. And then topped off with some self-chastising not to worry about the future and just enjoy the present. So really, a one-two-three punch.

Her familiar dog-chasing-tail mental acrobatics were interrupted by her phone, which twanged out the *Twilight Zone* theme. She had put it on there to amuse Leah. Now she blushed.

"My kids…" Sylvia stammered in apology, fumbling to answer and, as she did, realizing she was setting a terrible example of distracted driving. Not that Meg seemed to be judging, let alone paying her any attention. Sylvia would have ignored the call, but she was still in trouble from her broken promise two months earlier when she'd told Leah she was headed home and then not only didn't show up, but because of the fender bender, forgot to even call.

"Hello?" Sylvia punched the speaker icon and tossed the phone into the cupholder, gluing her eyes again to the wet, blurry road.

"Are there ghosts in the Vampire State Building?"

Meg whipped her head around to look at Sylvia, who flashed an embarrassed grin.

"Hi, Leah. It's good to start out with hello, honey."

"Hello honey, are there ghosts in the Vampire State Building?"

A smile broke out over Meg's face, and Sylvia chuckled, relieved.

"That's a tricky question. Can you give me context?"

"Seneca's sister says there are ghosts in it."

"Seneca's sister seems to be the source of a lot of information these days."

"What does that mean? Is she lying?"

Meg watched Sylvia, fascinated.

"Let's back up," Sylvia said, turning onto College Avenue. Suddenly they were in a place where the greenery was more plentiful than concrete. "First of all, it's called the Empire State Building."

"Does that mean it doesn't have ghosts?" Leah didn't miss a beat.

Here was one of the dozens of daily decisions that modern, overthinking, overwrought, overread, insufferable parents had to make: when was Sylvia supposed to lead her kids along the path to reality and when was she supposed to indulge fantasy? Both were important.

"It doesn't."

"It doesn't mean it or it doesn't have ghosts?"

Meg eyes widened and she mouthed, *How old is she?*

"Six," Sylvia said. "I mean the Empire State Building doesn't have ghosts."

"So what about the Vampire State Building?"

Meg laughed out loud.

"Who's that?" Leah demanded.

Meg clapped a hand over her mouth.

"It's okay," Sylvia said. "It's my student. Her name is Meg."

"Hi, Meg."

"Hi, Leah," Meg said, and her voice was scratchy as if she hadn't used it in a while or had been crying. Sylvia suspected the latter.

"How old are you?"

Meg smiled bashfully. "Eighteen."

There was silence.

"Leah?" Sylvia said. "You there?"

The reply dripped with bitter incredulity. "Mommy, you teach *grownups*?"

"I thought you knew that, Jelly Bean. That's what college—"

"Why would grownups need to go to school? Did she fail regular school?"

Meg honked out an unrestrained laugh.

"Quite the opposite, honey. She did so well, they let her into Linden. It's a privilege to go to college. You have to work hard to get in."

More silence. Sylvia raised her eyebrows and glanced over at Meg. They exchanged grins.

"Will you tuck me in tonight, Mommy?"

Sylvia sighed. "I told you, sweetheart, on Wednesdays I come home very, very late. After bedtime."

"But one time you were going to come back anyway."

This again.

"I know. I made a mistake. I'm sorry. What are you guys having for dinner tonight?" Sylvia pulled up alongside a brick building that looked identical to its older neighbors except it was a brighter red.

"Ordering in."

Sylvia glanced at Meg. There was something spoiled-sounding in that response.

"Okay, well, I have to go, Bean, but I'll be there when you wake up, yeah?"

"Yeah." Her little toughie sounded sad, and Sylvia reminded her aching heart that being away for one night a week not only wasn't dereliction of duty, but was good for everyone.

"You know," Sylvia said, "I'm pretty sure there *are* ghosts in the Vampire State Building."

"That's what I thought!"

Sylvia didn't know if she'd taken a cheap shot or practiced some expert parenting. Either way, Leah was cheerful again by the time Sylvia hung up.

"That was awesome," Meg said quietly, resting her hand on the door handle. Sylvia was surprised she hadn't jumped out as soon as the car stopped.

"They have their moments."

"You have more than one?"

"Yeah," Sylvia said apologetically, though she didn't know why. "I have a little boy who's three. He's pretty delicious."

Meg suddenly put her head in her hands and began to bawl. Relief flooded Sylvia. She'd known something was wrong, and helping people navigate emotion was familiar terrain: it was the currency of her friendships. Unexpressed emotion was the bigger challenge. Sylvia took a chance and stroked the back of Meg's head lightly a couple of times and then backed off. The girl sobbed for a good minute.

"It's not like I *want* to kill my baby!"

Ahhhh. That answered almost all the questions Sylvia had refrained from asking over the past ten minutes.

"Of course not," she assured her.

"You think I'm a total hypocrite."

"The opposite," Sylvia said automatically. "I think you're a very smart, thoughtful young woman who's open to multiple ideas and facing a really difficult choice."

Meg shuddered in the aftermath of her sobs.

"I didn't see you walk in, though," Sylvia said softly. "Did you make it there?"

"When I saw you in the parking lot, I turned around," Meg confessed. "And then these women drove me to their clinic."

Sylvia stiffened.

"Meg, that place wasn't really a—"

"Oh, I know." She waved a tired hand at Sylvia. "It was ridiculous. They had pamphlets on abstinence. A little late for that."

So she'd been inside The Place. Sylvia had been told about these so-called pregnancy crisis centers. They tried to pass themselves off as actual health clinics—some even mimicked the IF logo and called themselves Intend Your Family to deliberately confuse patients—but their sole purpose was to prevent abortion. Sylvia tamped down her rising fury.

"Keeping the baby *is* an option," Sylvia said, though in her head she was screaming *if you want to ruin your promising young life!*

"Well, except you know the car accident I was in?"

Sylvia nodded although she had never confirmed that the play Meg was writing for class was based on her real life.

"I'm held together—my pelvis in particular is held together with pins, so a pregnancy would actually kill me."

Sylvia nodded again.

"As in, I can't even consider putting it up for adoption

because I wouldn't get that far. I checked," Meg nearly wailed. "I double-checked with my doctor!"

"Did you tell them that?" Sylvia couldn't help asking. She should stay focused only on Meg, but this was a rare glimpse into the enemy camp.

"Yup."

"And?"

"They said it was God's plan."

"Meaning you should go ahead with the pregnancy?" Sylvia didn't even try to keep the horror out of her voice.

Meg nodded.

"That's appalling," Sylvia said.

"Well, they said doctors can be wrong, which is true, and also look how I'm a million times better than I was after the accident," she said, struggling with herself.

"And you'll keep getting better and stronger if you don't tax your body with a burden it doesn't have to carry," Sylvia added gently.

Meg nodded.

Sylvia decided to roll the dice and play devil's advocate.

"Okay, let's assume you could carry this pregnancy safely—and we have nothing to back that up…in fact it sounds like you'd die?"

"Yeah."

"But putting that aside," Sylvia said, hoping her rational tone would offset the absurdity of her words. "Do you or the"—she did not want to use the word *baby* or *father*—"guy who got you pregnant want to be parents right now?"

"No!" she cried out.

"Mm-hmm." Sylvia waited.

"But *I'm* adopted. And plus, I'm totally in love with my boyfriend."

Sylvia smiled. "That's great. Both those things are great."

"I'm *Catholic*."

Sylvia considered telling her that Catholics came to the clinic in the same numbers as any other faith, sometimes with the unofficial blessing of an enlightened priest.

"Meg," she said instead. "It's very easy to have a strict set of rules that leaves no room for doubt. Having choices is harder, not easier."

"It's just…if I had a baby now, oh my God. I'd be exactly like all these kids back in Barton, raising another dope-addicted thief."

"Well, that's a little grim," Sylvia protested.

"Uh, you have no idea," she said, and Sylvia believed her. "Plus, I'd have to drop out, drop your class."

Sylvia's heart leaped. Did that mean she liked her class? That Sylvia was being of some use to these kids and furthering their education? *Dial it back, Sylvia; she didn't go that far.*

"I mean, one day I might want to have a kid with JD…" Meg shook her head. "Except I'll never be able to have a kid. See, I just keep going around in circles." Her voice was high and strained.

"Hey," Sylvia soothed, touching Meg's arm lightly. "You *will* be able to have a kid. You'll be the one doing the adopting."

Meg looked at Sylvia, her eyes wide, her mouth hanging open.

"How have I never thought of that?" she said, dumbfounded. "I'll make up for this abortion by adopting later."

"You don't have to *make up* for anything. You would do it

because you wanted to. Let's go back to the fact that you would die if you had this baby."

"But…"

"But what?"

She hung her head. "The thing is, I'd want to abort anyway, and that's what's killing me." She gave a half-hearted laugh. "Killing me. Ha."

"Either way, you're talking about saving your own life," Sylvia reminded her. "Getting a college education, at a place like Linden no less, that's a lifesaver. No?"

Meg nodded, but started crying again.

"Does your mom know?" Sylvia asked. If Meg's play was based on truth, Sylvia knew not to say "parents."

Meg sniffed and shook her head. "I don't think so. I don't know actually. I think she might have guessed. She's totally anti-abortion. This would kill her."

"Wouldn't you dying kill her more?" Sylvia suggested gently.

Meg nodded, defeated. "I need to do this."

Sylvia said nothing.

"But now I've missed my appointment, and they only do abortions once a week. I have to wait a whole other week!" Meg wailed. "Oh my God. How am I going to get through another week of puking and waiting?"

"Hey, shhh," Sylvia soothed. "How many weeks are you?"

"The women thought I was eight weeks."

"Based on?"

"They asked me when my last period was. It was during midterms."

"Okay," Sylvia said, quickly calculating. "There's no

problem waiting another week in terms of New York law. How dangerous is it to your pelvis to wait another week? Because I'll help you get an appointment at another clinic that can do it sooner."

Meg shrugged, exhausted. "I don't know and I don't want to call my doctor. Nothing shows for a long time, right? It can't be that much of a difference."

She was tiny, and it didn't seem like she had much wiggle room, but what did Sylvia know?

"I'd feel better if you found out."

Meg wrinkled her nose with distaste, and fair enough: this wasn't about how Sylvia felt.

"I can't believe I'm really going to be a person who's had an abortion," Meg said, hanging her head.

"You'll be in good company." Sylvia reeled off her best parking lot fact. "One in three women in this country has an abortion in her life. It used to be something the family doctor did without guilt, before it became all politicized."

Meg looked at Sylvia, amazed.

"One in three? That's crazy."

"It's something to think about."

"I hope when I do have a kid, I talk to them like you talk to yours."

It was the most generous thing anyone had ever said to Sylvia.

"How do I talk to them?"

"Like you get a kick out of them."

Sylvia couldn't help smiling. "Meg. Tell me what I can do to help you."

Meg flung open the door. "Come with me next week."

TWENTY-TWO

Rosetta put her face up to Meg's window and stuck out her tongue to display a mouthful of chewed-up day-old scone. When Meg refused to look up, Rosetta and JD both pounded on the glass until she was forced to heed them. The sight of Rosetta's masticated mash made Meg nauseous. Not nauseous: nauseated. *Nauseous*, she'd learned, would mean that she made other people nauseated. Like *noxious*. Meg shook her head at them and pointed emphatically two times at her anthro textbook. Rosetta pointed emphatically at her own open mouth.

The scaffolding was coming down the next day. Rosetta, Hannah, and JD were swathed in coats and blankets in the frigid cold having a last hurrah before untwining the party lights, celebrating with Meg's pastries washed down with wine that Rosetta's mother had managed to have sent to them. She was incarcerated and they were underage: if you had money, it was made clear to Meg over and over, the rules bent over backward.

Meg was nauseated, yes, and she had a mountain of homework to do, yes, but those weren't keeping her from joining in the farewell celebration. It was the crushing embarrassment. The mortification. Because Meg was now officially a hypocrite of the highest order. Meg the pro-lifer was on the schedule for an abortion. The girl who had had an instantly infamous conservative outburst on this navel-gazing, knee-jerk lefty campus was going to become another government-funded statistic at Intentional Families, the mothership of the baby killers.

Hannah knocked on the window and made puppy eyes at Meg. Meg widened her eyes and tilted her head at her: *Et tu?*

Meg hadn't wanted to tell JD. Her thinking was: if she could avoid him knowing, she could have a shot at suppressing the entire incident, maybe for the rest of her life. Pretend like it never happened. It wouldn't be hard to avoid Sylvia after this term, Sylvia being her only witness. Meg sounded to herself like a gangster (assuming that word wasn't also taboo, like a gajillion others). She liked to think she would have come around to telling him, because of course that's what a relationship was all about, right? Trust, truth, honesty, all of it.

But JD had guessed.

"How on earth did you know?" she drawled with as much sarcasm as she could muster from inside the toilet bowl.

"I'm coming with you" was the next thing he'd said, holding her hair, rubbing her back, and skipping over the myriad arguments and accusations she'd anticipated.

"Oh my God," she'd moaned. "My mother is never going to speak to me again!"

"Why do you have to tell your mother?"

Meg hunched back on her heels, her knees aching from the tile floor. Why? Because she and her mother were a team now. Meg didn't lie to her anymore. Not much anyway. Not about important things. She started to cry, and JD held her close, not noticing or, even crazier, not minding the string of vomit that smeared across his shirt.

"It's my *mom*" was all Meg could wail, feeling herself separate from AnneMarie. But it was true. She would not be telling her about this because it was already shitty enough that Meg was choosing her own life over the baby's; she didn't have to make her mother suffer through the choice, too. No, Meg would not be telling AnneMarie about this. Not ever. "My mom."

Now all three of them started banging on the window.

"Okay. OKAY." Meg tossed her textbook onto her bed and shrugged on her coat. It wouldn't be warm enough, so she wrapped her comforter around her, too. Despite her nausea, despite her shame, despite the fact that she was fucking pregnant, there was no getting around the fact that she loved that her roommates and her boyfriend wouldn't leave her alone, that they wanted her out there. It was…fun. She was having fun. She wasn't sure she'd ever had fun before Linden. Even if she also sort of loathed the place all at the same time.

She stood on her desk and used both hands to unlock the old window. As soon as she did, it sprang up an inch and a gust of wind blew papers and a box of tissues across her floor. She took JD's proffered hand and gingerly stepped through. Imagine if she was really pregnant, like keeping-it-pregnant, and they got married and he treated her this gently for the rest of their lives.

"It's freezing out here!" Meg protested.

"You're just too skinny," Rosetta said, handing her a plastic cup of wine.

Two months ago, Meg's hackles would have been up, but now she knew that this was the highest compliment Rosetta could pay. She guzzled her wine, glancing guiltily at JD. He shrugged permissively.

"A toast to our front porch!" Hannah held up a coffee mug. Wine sloshed over the side. "We will miss you, dangerous, illegal-to-be-on scaffolding!"

"So many memories," Rosetta said dramatically.

"We need a ceremonial…ceremony to bid adieu," Hannah slurred.

"Hannah Goldberg, are you drunk?" JD teased.

"Entirely possible. You know we Asians can't hold our alcohol."

"Are you allowed to say that?" Meg asked.

"She can. You can't," Rosetta clarified. "Ready?"

"For what? Oh!"

The three suitemates had composed a prayer. An ode. A chant. They disagreed about what it was, but they all intoned together:

Renovation, never be complete
Without you, we could not meet
Oh, scaffolding, stay where you are
You give us the brightest spot on campus by far.

Meg turned suddenly and threw up over the railing.

"Oh, Meggie," Hannah wailed, and she reminded Meg

of AnneMarie. "It's gonna be okay! There will be other scaffoldings. Maybe not here, but maybe next year? In the, what are they called? Tenth grade? No, sophomore! Sophomore dorms?"

Rosetta and JD had immediately looked over the side to check for luckless targets.

"Whew," JD said.

Rosetta turned back and narrowed her eyes at Meg.

"You. Are. Preggers."

Meg felt herself gape like a fish.

"Rosetta," JD warned.

"Welcome to the club. That's all I was going to say." Rosetta held up her glass.

"Wait, what?" Hannah said. "What's going on? Who's pregnant? Meg? You? Congratulations?"

Rosetta gave Hannah a less-than-gentle shove. "No, not congratulations, idiot, just, shit."

"Please, please don't tell anyone," Meg begged, wiping her mouth. "It would kill my mom. And also, you know…"

"Meg," Hannah said firmly, grasping for facts she knew to be true. "Your mom will notice you have a baby whether you tell her or not."

"Oh my God, you're *so* drunk," Rosetta told her, taking Hannah's cup from her. "She's not keeping it, dumbass. When's your appointment? Do you want us to go with you?"

"How can you be so casual?" Meg snapped. "It's not a fucking dentist's appointment, Ro. It's a big fucking deal!"

"Only if you make it a big fucking deal." Rosetta shrugged. "Do you really think no one else in your uber-Catholic, Bruce Springsteeny town hasn't had an abortion? You think it's just us elitists who slip up?"

"I didn't slip up!" Meg wailed, but raising her voice had caused another surge of nausea and she clamped her lips together.

"It is funny, well, not funny exactly," JD mused, pulling Meg's blanket back up around her shoulders. "It's the townies like Meg and me who get more abortions but are quote unquote against them, and you richies probably get fewer, but get all political to protect them."

Hannah put a heavy arm on JD. "Don't call yourself a townie, JD." It sounded like *Jadey*. "You're so much more than that."

JD patted her hand and tried not to laugh. "Thanks, Hannah. I'm pretty comfortable with my roots. Promise."

"Meggie." Hannah burped and leaned across JD, breathing heavily into Meg's face. "We are here for you. Do you understand? We are your roommates and you are *pregnant* and you are having an *abortion* and we are with you. Do you understand?"

As distraught and sick as she was, Meg felt the corners of her mouth turn upward. She would be forever grateful to innocent, artless Hannah, who would not be able to hide her glee at the front-row seat she now had to A Formative College Experience. Meg suddenly felt exhausted from the relief of them knowing.

"Thanks, but please, *please* don't tell anyone," Meg repeated. She held up a hand to preempt Rosetta's righteous indignation. "Stop. I realize this is like flossing for you or whatever—"

"I wouldn't go that far." Rosetta was miffed.

"Whatever. Tooth pulled, bikini wax, wart removal, not that a baby is a wart, but my point is that I don't want to be the best gossip on campus this week."

"You mean you don't want to be the super bitch anti-choicer who made a huge stink and then went to the clinic?"

"Don't mince words, Ro," JD said, a shard of anger in his voice.

"It's fine," Meg said, surprising everyone, including herself. She was too tired and queasy to be offended, especially since, just as she understood that Rosetta calling her skinny was a compliment, she understood that Rosetta was, in her brassy way, sympathizing with Meg by articulating her unpleasant conundrum. "Yeah, that's exactly what I don't want to be."

"Yeah," Rosetta confirmed.

"And also the Catholic girl who got an abortion."

"I'm pretty sure those are a dime a dozen."

"I know," she said in a small voice, her throat tightening. "It's just that my mom doesn't know that." She finally broke down against JD in racking sobs.

Her roommates and boyfriend let her cry until they were all too cold to stay out in the dark and the wind any longer.

TWENTY-THREE

Caroline and Maureen bounced lightly on their rear ends on the full-size beds. They giggled as if they were teenage girls breaking the rules. They weren't *technically* breaking the rules. The church had paid for this hotel room on behalf of the bus driver, but it turned out the driver's mother lived nearby, and so he'd gone to spend the day with her. Caroline and Maureen, having risen at five that morning in their homes in Pierre and arrived with the sun in Albany, were exhausted by noon.

They were also exhilarated. Caroline had personally spoken with one actual congressman, one actual senator (state senator, but still), and aides from two other representatives' offices. Each had listened to her in the same way that Maureen listened to her: showing great interest and with undistracted attention. Each had taken notes and assured her that protecting unborn lives was at the top of either their or their bosses' agendas. Volunteering in front of the clinic so often made Caroline feel as though she and her fellow church members were alone in their convictions, but today she had understood that many, many people in the government—young, old, male, female, pretty, homely—felt as she did. The day had filled her with confidence and a novel sense of belonging, and given her the unprecedented feeling that someone had her back. Even during the best years of her marriage, she'd never been quite sure where she had stood with Christopher. She had floated along on assumptions.

Senator Lantana was the most sympathetic and the most emphatic. He represented two counties all the way to the west, along the Pennsylvania border, that Caroline had never heard of. She was reassured to see a framed print of the poem "Footprints in the Sand" hanging on his wall. She kept a copy in her purse. It was wonderful to see a man not only admit, but broadcast his own need for spiritual support, a need to be carried sometimes by the Lord.

Caroline shot a grateful smile at her friend, who had worked off one shoe and was massaging her foot. It was not an exaggeration to say that she had felt carried by Maureen these past few months. Caroline had been at a low point—her family, her marriage, her lack of direction—and Maureen had shown her a whole new life. She wanted to say this, or something close to this, to Maureen, but couldn't find either the courage or the words that would convey gratitude instead of desperation.

Caroline shook herself and exhaled loudly. This whole day had already been an enormous success, and they still had hours ahead of them to urge like-minded politicians to withhold state and federal funding from Intentional Families. Donald had repeatedly emphasized to her that IF got rich off abortions—her own tax dollars lined the pockets of that murderous doctor—and Caroline was fairly bursting at this further injustice that had been forced upon her. It was intolerable.

"Whew!" Maureen exhaled at the same time. "You, Caroline, are on fire. You are so good with these politicians. Are you sure you've never lobbied before?" She winked.

"Believe me," Caroline said, flattered, "the only lobbying I've done is meeting you for tea in the lobby of the Pierre Grand."

"You have a real knack for connecting with them."

"We were lucky to be able to tell them about our save last week. To highlight the crisis center," Caroline said modestly. It was true, though, that she was the one who thought to tell the politicians about the girl, Mary, and how they had saved her baby. With each meeting, she'd streamlined the story further and begun to urge these politicians not only to defund IF, but to divert those funds to CareNet. Maureen hadn't stopped her.

"I'm going to close my eyes for just five minutes." Maureen scooted back until she was leaning against the headboard.

Caroline nodded and ran her hand along the brown quilt, exquisitely happy. She knew she should rest, too, but she was too ramped up. Also, if she dozed now, she feared she'd be groggy for their afternoon sessions: two more congressmen and two more state assembly people plus a short vigil on the Capitol steps before they departed, if time permitted. Caroline had helped create the itinerary. It was a little overpacked, she had to admit, especially since she had to report to work the next morning. Just six months ago, she couldn't have imagined her life so full.

Caroline used the toilet, then splashed some cold water on her face. The hand towels were rough and clean and smelled reassuringly of bleach. When she came back out, Maureen was snoring lightly. Caroline glanced at her watch. She wasn't sure what to do with herself. Usually, she would read her Bible, but they'd left their heavier items on the bus. She smacked her hand to her forehead, as if she were performing for someone, and quietly pulled open the nightstand drawer. The wood stuck a bit and when she yanked it, some paint flakes floated to the carpet. Glancing over to see whether she had disturbed Maureen, Caroline knelt down to gather the flakes and deposit them in the wastebasket. Sure enough, there was the Good Book, looking up at her from the drawer.

With a grunt of effort, Caroline sat back on the bed and did what she did in church, opening the book at random to let His spirit guide her. She laid the vinyl-bound volume on her lap and immediately it fell open to where an index card had been placed. In purple, heavily curlicued script, someone had written:

Think for yourself: does this really make sense to you?
Puzzled, Caroline flipped over the card.
Consider facts. Consider truth. Consider atheism.
She gasped and slammed the book closed on the card. For a crazy moment, she thought that the card came with the volume, that it was some horrible, alternative version that everyone but her knew was out there, something she didn't know existed because she didn't do Facebook or read the news online or purchase anything off websites. (She had arranged this very trip with nothing but phone calls.) Did people *do* this now?

Fearfully, as though vermin might crawl out, she let the book fall open again to where the card was. With the tips of her thumb and finger, she lifted it out by a corner and laid it on the bedside table. Then she held the volume by its spine and shook it over the carpet. Nothing else emerged.

Tears sprang to her eyes, out of shame for her gullibility, out of anger at the needless cruelty contained in that flowery writing. Why couldn't people just leave things be? Why was there so much questioning and so little faith?

She closed the book and returned it to the drawer. Suddenly, Caroline was tired. And angry that she was tired: she was letting a malicious stranger derail her. She willed Maureen to wake up and distract her with her chattering. Maureen never suffered a moment's doubt about anything. But Maureen continued to snore, mouth slightly agape.

There was some pretty art on the wall—the hotel theme was seashells, though she couldn't imagine why—and she tried to locate serenity, as Father Flechette had taught his flock to do if they were distressed.

Caroline studied the closeup of the pile of opalescent seashells. They really were beautiful, she coaxed herself. God had created every whirl—or was it whorl?—and He put the color in all of them and…of course! Seashells were found on beaches, and she had just seen the senator's copy of "Footprints in the Sand." This was God's way of reminding her that He was in this room with her, guiding her and protecting her. No one could sully His Word, certainly not with a silly little index card. She pulled her purse onto her lap and fished out the parable from its zippered pocket.

"One night I dreamed I was walking along the beach with the Lord." The opening line was like a parachute, slowing and then settling Caroline's disquiet. The walker in the poem notices that sometimes there was only one set of footprints in the sand instead of two, and she beseeches the Lord: why

did He abandon her when she most needed Him? His answer caused Caroline to sigh with pleasure: *"The times when you have seen only one set of footprints, is when I carried you."*

She clasped her hands together with quiet delight and tucked the story back in its safe place. With a moment's hesitation, she tore the index card in two and chucked the pieces toward the trash. They floated down next to it, and she hastily crouched to pick them up and deposit them in their rightful place. Then she smoothed out the bedspread and was about to touch Maureen's shoulder to wake her when a tinny version of the "Hallelujah" chorus chirruped from the other nightstand. Maureen's eyes flew open. She reached automatically for her phone and glanced at the caller name, groaning with the effort of rising to consciousness.

"Donald. You answer." She thrust the phone at Caroline and closed her eyes again.

Dutifully, Caroline flipped open Maureen's phone, the one she said her kids teased her for using, but which she refused to abandon. Caroline felt a pang of envy whenever Maureen mentioned any ongoing filial skirmish: she would gladly take some good-natured ribbing from her kids instead of being discounted by them entirely.

"Hello, Donald. This is Caroline."

"Caroline, are you sitting down?"

Caroline frowned, then pulled out the chair by the desk.

"Now I am. Is everything all right?"

"No, Caroline, no. Everything is not all right." Donald had a croaky voice that sounded like his vocal cords were fraying threads. "The girl came back! She came back and I couldn't stop that…that…*witch*—God forgive me—from taking her inside. And she stayed in there with her! I think she may have performed the abortion herself because she might be a doctor. I haven't mentioned that to you or Maureen yet, but I have my reasons for believing that. A lot of those Jews and Pakistanis become doctors, and she's friends with Irving and he's a Jewish doctor, I think—"

"Hold on, Donald, hold on," Caroline said, willing herself, as she often did, to like Donald. She set her mouth in a determined smile. "I'm not exactly, I mean, what? I don't follow."

"That girl!" Donald squeaked impatiently. "The one you and Maureen took to CareNet last week. The baby you saved. *You saved,*" he added for emphasis. "That girl came back and she went inside and that escort went in with her. She brought her! And she had a big shoulder bag and you know what that's for, don't you?"

Caroline put her hand over her aching heart and let her elbows sink down until they rested on her lap.

"She's going to take the body parts home with her. She can get money for them, you know. Have I told you about the black market for the baby parts? The white baby parts. Those racists aren't interested in the Black baby parts."

"Yes," Caroline said, wishing she could hang up. Donald must be mistaken about the girl. It couldn't be Mary. "You've told me."

"But I haven't told you about the boyfriend! He came this time. Walking on the other side of the girl—the volunteer killer is on one side, boyfriend's on the other—and then he sends them on ahead into the clinic, and— Are you still there, Caroline? Can you hear me?"

"I can hear you."

"Get this. He comes with these, well, I shouldn't even tell you. It's too disgusting for a lady." Donald tsked and sighed loudly into the phone.

Caroline looked out the window, across the hotel parking lot. She could make out the dome of the Capitol. "Go ahead, Donald."

"He comes with these signs that he's made. Not exactly signs, but a set of messages that he puts one in front of the other, you know like they do on TV shows, where one person stands to the side of the camera and flips through the script for the person on air who's reading it? So this guy, scruffy, real ugly piece of work, God bless his soul, he stands there and holds up the first one. Just stands there, real still, distracting us while the killer takes the girl inside. And so me and Mike and John and Sharon and Iris come toward him because we're confused because the first, whaddya call it—placard! The first placard says 'Adopt.' And then he pulls it away and the second says 'Feed the hungry.' And we're thinking *what*? Of course we feed the hungry at the soup kitchen, and Sharon's cousin-once-removed just adopted a baby. So then then the third says, can you believe this, 'Thou shalt not kill'!" *He's* telling *us* not to kill!"

"Donald—"

"Wait. The *next* placard says 'So get down on bended knees, fellow Christians dot dot dot...'"

Caroline waited.

"And, and..." Donald finally faltered. "The last card says 'and suck my C-word!' I mean, it didn't say C-word, it actually had the C-word. Do you know what the C-word is?"

"Yes, I think I do." Caroline wondered why they had all stuck around reading the placards, though she could see how curiosity might have gotten the better of them. At the same time, Caroline didn't have a lot of confidence in the accuracy of Donald's reporting. "Are you sure it was the same girl?" She felt a prickle of hope that Donald had it wrong. It was still terrible that *this* baby would be killed, but at least it wouldn't be Mary's baby, the baby she, Caroline, had saved.

"Oh, I'm sure," Donald said with satisfaction. "He keeps coming out to yell at us about you and Maureen."

Caroline felt a zap of stress in her belly.

"He says, 'You tell those kidnapping bitches, I mean B-words, to keep their F-word-ing hands off my girlfriend. They could have killed her, you dumb F-words! If she had a baby, she would die.' Most ignorant thing I've ever heard," Donald commented. "God made women, especially young women, perfectly designed to give birth."

Caroline slumped back in the chair. She wondered how he could remember the exchange in such detail, but she knew that it was indeed Mary who had returned. A wave of fury toward the kike (God forgive her) volunteer nearly suffocated her. Caroline had no doubt that without that evil woman's encouragement, Mary wouldn't have gone into the clinic that morning.

"So how's it going up there?" Donald inquired cheerfully. Caroline handed the phone to Maureen, who had dragged herself up from the depths of sleep.

She knelt in front of the window and crossed herself. Why had God chosen today of all days to keep Caroline from the clinic? In the store, back in September, she had assured this girl's mother, the one with the cross, that God would protect her daughter. And then God sent Mary to Caroline for protection. It had all been so clear. Had He changed His mind? Caroline shook her head to expel the ridiculous thought. God didn't make mistakes. God had a plan. He just hadn't revealed it to Caroline. She might never know His plan, and she would have to make peace with that thought.

Maureen ended the call and joined Caroline in prayer, and Caroline felt a bit better. But the day went downhill from there. First, they had a meeting in a stuffy office with a young, handsome, sharp-jawed assemblyman who introduced himself as an avid supporter of SNAP. When Caroline and Maureen showed no sign of familiarity, he clarified that SNAP stood for Survivors' Network of those Abused by Priests. He said it was morally imperative as well as politically savvy to fight for both unborn children as well as abused children and that it delighted him to confuse the opposition. Although Maureen had gently elbowed Caroline, urging her to tell the CareNet story (omitting the recent update), Caroline found herself at a loss for words and could only shake her head. An aide thought Caroline looked pale and offered her a glass of water. She gulped it down, determined to keep the man's words at bay.

"I don't know what gobbledygook he was speaking," Maureen said definitively when they left his office, and Caroline envied her clear-cut approach: new information either slotted into Maureen's view of things or it didn't, in which case she simply didn't see it.

The next meeting was no better. Instead of the assemblywoman they'd been promised, they were met by a petite, sweet-voiced Black girl wearing a delicate silver cross around her neck. The two older women relaxed, pleased to have a chance to bond cross-racially. After listening and nodding and taking copious notes, the girl asked them, as if the thought were just occurring to her for the first time, whether they still opposed abortion in cases of rape or incest.

Maureen and Caroline exchanged knowing glances. Caroline confidently extracted from her bag of lobbying literature ("lobby lit," she was already calling it) a sheet of paper.

"Of course, we don't expect a twelve-year-old rape victim to raise the baby, but we can help her find a home for it," Caroline said as she handed the aide the black-and-white printout. "We really can."

"I'm sure if it's a white baby, you can," the girl murmured, skimming the text. Caroline sat back, knowing how beautiful this piece of writing was, confident it would help the young aide answer her own question.

God does not allow His people to choose when morality applies. There are no reasons for which God would ordain the taking of an innocent life. God agonizes over a young girl who is raped. He longs for her to turn to Him so that He can show her His mercy and love in the midst of her pain. But, never does He want her to end the innocent life of a baby. Murder is not only wrong, but the act would also only intensify the agony that the woman suffers already.

The aide's eyes widened.

"Where is this from?" she asked.

"A website called Rapture Ready," Maureen said, pleased.

"So, this isn't actually the Bible. It doesn't cite any verse."

"Well, no," Caroline jumped in. "But it's all very accurate."

"So you're saying God would make a child who has already suffered a rape, maybe even at the hands of a man who was her guardian, to then go through the pain of childbirth, and perhaps raise a baby who is also her sibling?"

Caroline pictured the seashells from the hotel picture. Surely, God was testing her, but she didn't understand what she was supposed to do.

"I think we're all done here," Maureen said crisply. "We're very clear about right and wrong, and we thought Assemblywoman Shaunessy was, too. We'll send her a follow-up note letting her know how this meeting went."

"Please feel free," the aide said softly, politely, but she did not rise from her seat when they stood to leave.

Caroline was guiltily grateful that there was no time at the end of the day for a vigil on the Capitol steps. She sank into her seat on the bus and promptly fell asleep. She awoke to Maureen kneeling backward on the seat beside hers, giving a rousing account of their afternoon to the others.

"We will tell the congresswoman that she has an infidel in her employ!" Maureen shook her fist, extremely pleased with this line she had hit on and which she would repeat for days and years to come. "An infidel in her employ!"

Caroline closed her eyes quickly, so no one would know she had awakened. She knew she was too tired to assess the day accurately. She hoped that with time she would come to regard it as a success—the morning had been great, she reminded herself wearily. Her thoughts floated to the following day, and she was comforted by the thought of spending it in that bright, beautiful store, helping Yuna set out more Christmas displays. She'd seen some of the recent arrivals in the storeroom and was excited that she would get to handle the glass bowls filled with gleaming colored ornaments, the red and green high-thread-count linens that were pristine and crisp, and the brushed-steel flatware that lay smoothly in her hand with satisfying weight. She'd set a Christmas table as though it were her own, only better, with enormous bouquets of fake birch branches wound with delicate fairy lights, standing up from oversized hand-blown glass vases. Headquarters sent instructions with photos of exactly how the displays should look, and they matched Caroline's idea of a perfect Christmas.

All the items were celebratory and brand new, unsullied by mistakes, free from the taint of a past.

TWENTY-FOUR

Sylvia still wasn't comfortable letting Tony see how her breasts became empty sacks when she turned on her side, so she lay back with her arms over her head: the ladies' most flattering angle. He stretched and let his long legs press up against hers. That felt as delicious as anything they'd just been doing.

"I'll miss sex and food when I'm dead," he murmured, and Sylvia laughed.

"One more than the other?"

"Is it showing my age if I say food?" he said sheepishly.

"Maybe," Sylvia said, "but I'm with you. No peanut butter or cheese in the afterlife, I hear."

"That's what you'd miss?" He elbowed her gently. "Not wine and truffles?"

"I'm not the sophisticate you would have me be. You're lucky I didn't say Suzie Qs."

"Oh, well, those are amazing." He nodded mock-seriously and let his eyes drift closed again. After a moment, he said, "What are you going to do with your body when you die?"

"Kind of hurrying things along there, aren't you?" Sylvia said, trying to sound light, but a little shocked. This topic was not the stuff of a two-month fling. If that's what this was. They hadn't discussed what this was. "My dad was cremated, and my mom says when her time comes I'm supposed to mix her with him. I guess I'll add myself to the family ash heap. What about you?" She braced herself for a full-on Catholic interment.

"Something earth-friendly. I'm still researching it."

"Like being left on a mountain for carrion?"

"Maybe not that drastic. I was just thinking of forgoing embalming, allowing myself to disintegrate in a biodegradable cardboard coffin. That's a thing."

Sylvia nodded, unsure where to go with this. She doubted they'd be in each other's lives when this part of the future arrived.

"Aren't Jews supposed to not be cremated?" he asked.

It wasn't so hard to explain—Jewish by heritage, atheist by religion—but Sylvia didn't feel like explaining, and that was one of the many ways she knew that this, whatever this was—relationship, encounter, affair—was site-specific and time-limited and would not last beyond the end of this school year. It took a very long time to get to know someone (Ethan had had a few years' running start with Lisette), and while Tony might have been worth getting to know, she wasn't ready to do the heavy lifting.

Sylvia was still very much in mourning for her marriage, if not for Ethan himself, though she struggled to distinguish between the two. In bed at night, Ethan used to watch sports on TV while Sylvia watched *Brideshead Revisited* (he called it *Poofters and Palaces*) on her laptop beside him. During commercials, he'd bury his lips in her hair and admire the real estate porn quotient of the show. It may not have been what the guides recommended, but it was a cozy setup, and it was theirs and it was one of a thousand little vignettes that made them who they were as a couple. To re-create that sheer volume was daunting.

Sylvia had spent the semester hoping she would figure out how to forge a new path out of her shattered marriage. But twelve weeks of playing the role of a professor and sleeping with a new guy were not going to confer instant clarity.

"It's a longer conversation," Sylvia said, sitting up and swinging her feet onto the floor. "As fascinating as this topic is, I gotta go grade a bunch of sophomoric plays and then buy a Secret Santa gift." She was guiltily relieved that she had genuine tasks calling her away, even if one was for a dreaded department holiday party.

"Isn't the culturally sensitive term 'Secret Solstice' gift?"

"Aren't we too old for grab bag gifts?" Sylvia countered, reaching for her clothes. She foresaw a bounty of scented soaps in her immediate future.

The semester was all over but the grading, and the grading was proving to be the hardest part of what had been a very hard, eye-opening few months. In addition to dealing with Lily, who had emailed to insist that Sylvia "couldn't let her fail," and Aaron's *mother*, who seemed to think it was normal to contact her son's college professor, as if he were in nursery school (and even then, weren't you paying the nursery school to handle any problems that arose between 9 a.m. and 3 p.m.?), now she had to actually put a grade on these kids' creative endeavors. And as devastatingly third-rate as some of their final plays were, Sylvia didn't feel it was her place to crush their fragile writer egos. She had reluctantly given Mason's "Sniffing My Fingers" an A-, but felt compelled to scrawl "for effort" alongside the grade.

Sylvia left Tony's tidy split-level and headed back to campus. Since meeting him, she hadn't spent a single Tuesday night at her grim quarters in Basement Vistas; nasty David Ketchum had been right about the lodgings. They were worth avoiding. She drove the five miles as slowly as she could, putting off the task ahead. There was another reason she was dreading grading: Meg Croyden. The week before, Sylvia had accompanied her and her boyfriend to the clinic for her abortion, and in doing so had left the line between student and teacher far behind. Now she had to give a formal assessment of Meg's play, and how could she do that impartially? It didn't help that even before she shepherded her through her crisis Sylvia had held Meg's to be by far the best work in the class. It would have been easier to grade if she'd been a terrible playwright; Sylvia would have had more confidence in her ability to be fair.

She pulled into the parking lot of the science building and turned off the car. The stack of plays menaced from the passenger seat. Sylvia's plan was to sit herself down in the café and not get up until she had done a first pass on all the scripts. She groaned out loud as she ran a thumb along the pages. Hundreds of pages. And they'd submitted only first halves of plays, as a semester wasn't enough time to write a complete play. And still, Sylvia would do anything, *anything*, to avoid this onerous task.

Something brightly colored caught her eye. She wrenched herself around and extracted from the floor under the passenger seat a long red knitted scarf, now breaded with Cheerio dust and bits of dead leaves. Her immediate thoughts:

1) Meg had dropped this.

2) It was very cold out.

3) Meg was headed home for winter break the following day, a home that was in an even colder region than Pierre.

4) Most likely, her mother or some other relative had knitted this for her.

5) Aforementioned relative would no doubt be hurt if Meg didn't show up to Christmas wearing it.

This is what Sylvia argued to herself as she dialed Meg's number, excited by the prospect of delaying grading. She had texted Meg a quick check-in the day before, but didn't want to assume that she was now a part of the girl's story. Meg might have wanted to forget the whole day and was entitled to do so.

"Hi, Sylvia." She answered on the second ring: not avoiding her. It felt oddly the same as after a first hookup—neither person is sure what the night meant to the other, neither knows how to move forward or whether the other one even wants to. Sylvia wasn't sure whether their experiences matched up, whether they had reason to stay in touch.

"Hey, Meg," Sylvia said, trying to convey in those two syllables trustworthiness, steadfastness, cheer, and an absence of expectation. "I just found your scarf in my car. Do you want me to bring it to you?"

"Scarf?" she said, and Sylvia's mood sank. She was not going to be rescued from grading. "I don't think I had a scarf. Hang on. JD?" Sylvia heard her turn away from her phone, then come back, her voice filling Sylvia's ear. "It's JD's, but he says not to worry about it."

"Oh, okay," Sylvia said, muffling her disappointment.

"Hey, how are you feeling?" Casual, as though inquiring about a cold.

"Pretty good. A few cramps and practically no bleeding."

"That's great!" Sylvia said, too enthusiastically. "So should I drop off the scarf at your dorm or…?" Pathetic.

"We're heading to Carton and Box right now to get JD some glasses. Drinking glasses, I mean. Wanna meet us there? You could bring the scarf with you." Her voice was matter-of-fact, and Sylvia didn't think it was an act, unless her entire affect was the result of years of playing it cool. Which still didn't make it an act.

"I'd love to!" Sylvia said quickly. "I'll meet you there. Half an hour?" She wasn't about to suggest carpooling. Too pushy.

"Sounds good." Meg didn't seem to be weighing her words at all.

Okay. She'd pick up a grab bag present at Carton and Box, give JD his scarf, and then get right down to grading. Sylvia was merely reversing the order of the day's tasks. She pulled out of the parking lot and threaded her way through the fifteen-mile-per-hour roads of campus until she reached the streets of Pierre.

For Sylvia, the day of Meg's abortion had been extraordinary and memorable. Before last Wednesday, she'd only ever been inside the clinic's human resource office and the waiting room. She'd never been buzzed into the hallway that held the exam rooms, to the cheerful, regular old medical suite. It was easy to remember there that abortion had been a routine procedure, before the assholes outside had gummed up the works with religion.

Meg's boyfriend, JD, turned out to be a tall, quiet-spoken

guy who wisecracked when you least expected it. Sylvia had gathered that he was in his twenties and wondered if the age difference might translate into too much emotional gravitas for a first-year. None of her business, and anyway, it was clear he adored her. Sylvia and JD sat with Meg in the waiting room while she was called in no fewer than three times to meet with various nurses and social workers to triple-check that she was absolutely, one hundred percent certain this was what she wanted to do. Neither of them was allowed in with her to those meetings. It was a wonder anyone went through with an abortion; with so many opportunities to back out, it came to seem like a suggestion that you should.

Meg had tried to insist that JD not miss work for this, but he told her in no uncertain terms that he was going to be with her every step of the way. After learning about her experience the week before, he said he couldn't trust her not to risk her life by putting this off for even one more day. The poor boy looked terrified at the thought of losing her, but as terrified as he was, he couldn't see her afterward because he had a history of fainting at the sight of blood. Even though it was explained to him that there would be no blood in the recovery room, he remained glued to his uncomfortable orange plastic seat in the waiting room.

So Sylvia went back there by herself. The mood in the recovery room was light and chatty. The walls were painted two different primary colors, not what Sylvia would have chosen, but perhaps it was to distract from the fact that the room lacked windows. There were two other women besides Meg sipping ginger ale in recliners, while a nurse entered information into a laptop, hopping up every few minutes to take a blood pressure reading. One patient looked to be about Meg's age and had ten times as much to say.

"How dare they judge me?" she was opining to her captive audience when Sylvia was allowed to come in to see Meg. She would learn that this patient's given name was Destiny, but she preferred to be called Barbara. "How *dare* they! They don't know me. They don't know my story. They don't know a damned thing about me!" She shifted huffily in her seat, energized by her own outrage.

"And it turns out they wouldn't care even if they did," Meg replied, and waved a grateful greeting to Sylvia.

"Let me guess," Sylvia said by way of hello. "We're talking about the protesters outside?"

"She's one of the escorts," Meg told the room with what, to Sylvia, was unmistakable pride. "The people in the vests who help you get inside."

"Well, miss, I thank you, I really do. They call themselves Christians, but they don't know the first thing about being a Christian!"

"I often tell them I hope God forgives their ignorance," Sylvia agreed.

Barbara's eyes went wide. "Exactly! That's exactly right!" And then Sylvia felt guilty, because this retort that she tossed at the protesters was a mockery designed solely to infuriate them. She had no desire to mock this girl's beliefs.

"Don't you wonder how many of them have daughters who've had abortions? Or even had them themselves? They probably tell themselves it's something else," mused the third patient in the room. She was a neatly coiffed woman not much younger than Sylvia, wearing a wedding ring and dressed as though she was heading to chair a board meeting after this. "They have got to be the biggest hypocrites to walk the face of the earth."

"They live in a world of black and white!" shouted Barbara. "They've been taught that grays are something to fear. What they are are a bunch of cowards."

Sylvia sat down next to Meg and patted her hand tentatively.

"That's exactly what you've said about them," Meg commented.

"How are you doing?"

Meg gave her a wan smile. "I'm so relieved, I'm practically giddy, and I feel guilty for feeling so relieved."

The comment was meant for Sylvia, but the room was small.

"Don't feel guilty, girl!" Barbara exclaimed. "I'm gonna throw myself a party. I just saved my entire future and the future of my baby girl. She don't need no sibling taking food from her mouth. You hear me?"

Meg smiled. Sylvia had never seen her so mellow. Must have been the meds. She stifled a grin, not knowing that Meg had refused to take anything but ibuprofen.

"Definitely do not waste your time on guilt," instructed the other woman, whom the nurse kept addressing as Mrs. S. "If anyone should feel guilty it's me. You two are children with your whole lives in front of you. I already have two kids and plenty of, what do we modestly call it now, *resources*." She scowled at her plastic cup of ginger ale. "I could easily have managed a third child, in practical terms. But I just didn't want one." She looked around the room defiantly. "Plain and simple. It wasn't in the plan. And I have no intention of feeling guilty," she said in a way that made Sylvia pretty certain she was fighting more guilt than anyone else in the room.

"Damn," murmured Barbara.

Sylvia stood back to make room for the nurse to wrap a blood pressure cuff around Meg's arm. Meg leaned back and closed her eyes.

"How's JD holding up?"

"A little pale, but fine."

"He's always a little pale."

Sylvia grinned.

"You wanna hear something weird?"

"Always."

"I'm glad I got pregnant. I know that's creepy, but I like knowing that I was able to, even if I'm never going to be able to give birth. It made me feel…feminine."

"That makes total sense," Sylvia told her and meant it.

Meg briefly opened one eye, took Sylvia's hand in hers, then settled back.

"Is there anything I can get for you?" Sylvia said, happier than she'd been in a long time. "Do for you?"

"Nope. Just you being here is awesome."

And it struck Sylvia that she was being permitted to do for Meg what her sister, Maddie, had not let her do: simply be there.

Overwhelming gratitude formed a lump in her throat, and she reached for a tissue as unobtrusively as she could, hoping Meg wouldn't catch her tearing up. She wondered if this was how a doula felt, because this felt like a birth, Meg's rebirth, the reclamation of her life.

Suddenly, the married-with-children patient covered her mouth.

"Feeling okay, Mrs. S.?" the nurse said, scooping up a plastic bin and arriving at her side in one swift motion.

But Mrs. S. was laughing. "The radio," she said, nearly choking. "The radio!"

The volume was low, and they all strained over Mrs. S.'s outburst to hear what was playing on the Best of Yesterday station. Sylvia's eyes grew wide with amused shock, and Meg cackled along with Mrs. S. and Barbara as the unmistakable *whump, whump, whump* of Queen's "Another One Bites the Dust" filled the recovery room.

TWENTY-FIVE

Meg stood just inside the range of the sliding door sensors while JD parked his car. He was being so sweet, not letting her walk across the store's parking lot in the cold. She had a feeling he would have been this chivalrous even if she wasn't recovering, but this way they could both enjoy his gesture without feeling dopey.

The store was warm, and Meg unzipped her puffy North Face parka (borrowed from Hannah) and the Patagonia fleece (borrowed from Rosetta) she wore under it. Her arm brushed a towering fake Christmas tree bedecked with square and conical metallic baubles, and she quickly reached out to steady one that threatened to slide off and shatter. She hoped Sylvia would get there soon. It embarrassed Meg how eager she was to see her teacher. She hadn't wanted to call her, didn't want Sylvia to think she was somehow obligated to Meg just because she'd gotten snagged in Meg's drama. Another idiot teenager knocked up.

Meg peered through the oversize windows, willing flakes to fall from the sky. The first snow of the season had been predicted by forecasters, and it was expected to be a blizzard, for which Meg was ashamedly grateful. A blizzard would prevent her from making the four-hour slog home to Barton tomorrow, and if the snow was bad enough, it could shave off a few days from the long visit with her mother that lay ahead. Meg had told JD she was dreading the visit because she still felt guilty about the secret she was keeping from her religious mother, which was part of the truth.

The whole truth was that sometime after she'd arrived at Linden, even before she'd learned she was pregnant, her conversations with AnneMarie had become increasingly difficult to sustain, and not just because the number of secrets was growing. Meg still hadn't told her about JD, but she didn't think this omission was the sole source of the tension. It was more that they seemed to be speaking, if not different languages, then different dialects. Complaining about snotty Alicia from playwriting class, Meg had breezily parroted Rosetta, who knew everyone, telling her mother that only the best cheeses preceded Alicia's index finger. As soon as the words were out, Meg knew she'd have to explain, and anger fueled by unbearable sadness welled up in her before her mother could even make her bewildered request for clarification. Another time she'd made a joke about someone who probably baked placenta chip muffins and had again instantly regretted the comment for the gulf it exposed.

Through the glass door, she watched as her boyfriend and her professor greeted each other in the parking lot with a long embrace. How had she gotten here in such a short time? Four months ago, she hadn't known either of them, and now they were two of the most important people in her life. The others, to her amazement, were Hannah and Rosetta, who had become her campus family. After returning from a day spent in far flung corners of Linden—Rosetta had become preoccupied with making light bulbs in the college's maker space, while Hannah had discovered capoeira—Meg felt her guard come down in a way she had only ever felt in the company of her mother during her post-accident years. It terrified her. They could so easily turn on her, mock her, and now, they had something over her. She had no choice but to trust them.

Meg often thought about Michelle, especially when the three of them had lounged around the now-gone scaffolding. Michelle, the missing fourth suitemate, her roommate, who hadn't been able to make it to Linden. *Did she know what she was missing?* Meg would wonder as she looked out across the campus that was starting not to feel so hostile. Could she even imagine what life was like here? Meg couldn't have, not in a million years. When she dodged earthworms emerging on the campus flagstones after a rainstorm, she wondered whether Michelle also would have squealed if she'd squashed one of the slimy critters. When she reached for a chocolate pudding from the stainless steel dessert shelf in the cafeteria, she imagined Michelle sliding her tray along the rails behind her. When she turned the lock to her bedroom so she and JD could make love, she wondered whether Michelle would have begrudged her her boyfriend.

Cold wind sent JD and Sylvia barreling toward the entrance and arriving in a tumult.

"It's like when someone explains derivatives!" Sylvia was shouting over the gust as the doors slid open. "I immediately feel boredom and panic. Panic about how bored I'm going to be."

"We were each listening to Brian Lehrer interview the

baseball commissioner," JD explained, breathing hard. He enfolded Meg in his arms.

"Look, I know first, second, third base, home plate. And a fair amount of 'Who's on First?' Don't start saying other words to me," Sylvia said, rubbing her arms vigorously. "Hiya, kiddo!" she said, a big smile warming her face. From JD's embrace, Meg gave her a little girl's wave.

"Hey, Sylvia," she said shyly. What was their interaction supposed to be like now that they were no longer teacher and student and no longer in crisis mode? Meg's emergency had come with a ready-made protocol that all three of them had known instinctively how to follow. But what about afterward? What was the universal etiquette for housewares shopping with the former professor who hadn't yet graded your final project, but who had helped you get your abortion?

"I promise I'm not going to crash your party," Sylvia said, reading Meg's mind. "I just need to find something for a Secret Santa exchange for tonight. We have a twenty-dollar limit." Her gaze swept across the merry displays of plates and flatware and lemon-colored lemon squeezers and avocado-colored containers that were the shape of a platonic half avocado. "The problem is I want everything here. And the life that goes with it."

Meg was familiar with the gaps in her own life, but never imagined there was anything lacking in Sylvia's life, let alone anything that Carton and Box could fill. She realized she didn't know much about her teacher, beyond the fact that she had two funny kids and two friends who had visited her from the city. Meg pictured a breezy, urban life that was full and perfect, or if not perfect then stippled with enviable imperfections like high taxes (that she could still afford) or not enough time to help her kid with a science project because she was busy directing a television show. Meg assumed there was a husband, though it occurred to her that Sylvia had never mentioned him. Was there a wife? The thought made Meg's stomach catch even though one semester at Linden was enough for her to know that was a sentiment she should vanquish. She hoped Sylvia wasn't gay, but couldn't have said why it mattered.

JD must have been wondering the same thing because he said, "What kind of life would that be?"

"Oh." Sylvia waved her hand breezily, suddenly embarrassed. "I don't know, all matchy-matchy and bright, with nothing chipped or missing. Natural looking, but not obnoxiously environmental. Like, somewhere between a sustainably harvested kale jeans kind of person, but not all the way to a disposable plastic bottle kind of person."

JD and Meg looked at her.

"Never mind," Sylvia said, embarrassed.

"No, I get it," Meg said, and she thought she did.

The three of them drifted toward the shelves that held hundreds of drinking glasses: tall, short, curved, square, triangular, all lit from above so that they rivaled the Christmas decorations in radiance.

"This is kind of what I mean," Sylvia said. "I want all these glasses. But I would only need to buy six or eight. And six or eight isn't going to make me feel the way this display feels."

"Ah," Meg said, because now she did understand, but had thought only people like her felt that way in stores like this. She hadn't known someone like Sylvia could be left wanting by a chain store.

"Anything I can help you with?" said a young woman with a gap between her front teeth and a name tag that read Yuna.

"Just checking out the glasses," JD told her, and she looked up at him, startled. She had addressed her question to Sylvia.

"Well, we have *literally* twenty-six different choices this holiday season, so I can help you narrow it down." Yuna put air quotes around "literally," and Meg glanced at Sylvia just as Sylvia was glancing at her; Yuna noticed their silent exchange. "What?" she said attempting a cutesy voice. "What'd I say?"

"Nothing," Sylvia assured her, but JD said, "You put up air quotes when you said 'literally.'"

Again, Yuna seemed surprised by his presence.

"What?"

"Air quotes," he said, demonstrating. "It doesn't make sense to put the word *literally* in quotes. Quotes literally mean it's not literal."

Yuna looked confused, and Meg felt sorry for her. She elbowed JD gently.

"He's kidding around. He has a weird sense of humor. Which glasses do you like?"

"Jonathan?" a voice said.

Meg, Sylvia, and JD turned.

All three of them recognized the voice, but one knew it better than he knew his own.

"Mother," said JD.

TWENTY-SIX

"Jonathan," Caroline said, putting her hand to her heart. She moved to hug him, but he stepped back. Embarrassed, she glanced at the people with him, who had also stepped away.

She registered the girl first. The Girl. Mary. Caroline drew in her breath.

"You," she said softly.

"You," Mary spat back.

"You two know each other?" JD said, horrified.

"You went back," Caroline said, her gaze fixed on Meg. "Why did you go back to that terrible place? Why did you kill your baby?"

"What the fuck?" JD said, dumbfounded.

"This is your *mother*?" Meg said to JD. "She's the one who tried to keep me from getting it done."

"You?" JD growled at his mother. "You're the freak who would have killed my girlfriend?"

"Your girl—? Oh, dear God." Caroline felt faint as a realization dawned on her. "Jonathan, that was *your* baby?"

Caroline looked around for something to lean on and could find only Yuna. Caroline clamped her hand on the young woman's shoulder. It was then that she registered the other person with them.

The devil's own henchman. Henchwoman. The so-called *escort*. Caroline sucked in her breath.

"What in God's name," she demanded weakly, "are you doing with *her*?"

JD drew himself up to his full, substantial height, and his face grew red.

"This is my girlfriend, Mother, and you're off to a shit start if this is your idea of a greeting."

"Not her," Caroline nearly whispered. "*Her.*" She put her hand to her lips and extended one finger at Sylvia, feeling her heart begin to beat uncomfortably hard.

Jonathan looked confused. "Sylvia? She's our friend."

"No, no, no." Caroline's voice rose with each syllable so that she began to keen.

"Mother, shush." JD glanced around. Other customers were staring. "What is the matter with you?"

"NO. NO!" Caroline turned on Sylvia, the rage of a life spent denying and being denied rising with bile in her chest. "You goddamned devil. You heathen murderer! You killed my grandbaby."

From the moment Sylvia had begun facing off with the blockheads in the parking lot, she had long dreaded an encounter with any of the protesters away from the clinic, dreaded crossing paths with them in real life. She was a little scared, a little horrified by the idea, but mostly she felt it would be an intolerable invasion of her privacy.

"She's one of our protesters," she explained to JD, who looked stricken. "She's your *mother*?"

"Don't you dare call me *your* protester!" Caroline cried out, aware of, but for the first time in her life unafraid of, making a spectacle.

"Um," said Yuna as Caroline stared Sylvia straight in the face.

"You killed my grandchild." Caroline's voice was low and hoarse.

Sylvia's heartbeat, already uncomfortably fast, kicked up another gear even though she knew this was a crazy person and all she had to do was stay physically safe.

"How do you figure?" Sylvia attempted condescension and glanced at Meg for backup, but Meg's face was screwed up in fury.

"Sylvia saved my life, you fucking witch!" Meg cried out, and JD turned to wrap his arms around her, to hold her back. "You're the one who tried to kill me!"

"Um," said Yuna again.

Caroline, still inches from Sylvia, turned to the flailing Meg, her face twisted in fury. "*You.* You have some nerve. You were carrying *my grandchild.* MY grandchild! My flesh and blood. Right, Jonathan? Right? And *you*"—she turned back to Sylvia and thrust her finger in her face—"*you* brought her back. Oh, sweet Jesus, that was my baby inside her. *My baby!*"

Caroline felt the relief of throwing propriety and civility and control to the winds—not unlike going ahead and peeing in her pants as a little girl when the pressure overcame all else, imminent shame be damned. Caroline howled, unearthly sounds escaping from a place inside her that had always been locked, screwed down tight, airless. She didn't recognize her own voice because it wasn't hers anymore. It was the voice of someone who had been forsaken by her parents, and then her kids, and then her husband. It was the voice of someone who had lost the one human soul who would have loved her, lost the little soul before she even met it.

Caroline covered her ears and closed her eyes and screamed. She screamed and screamed and screamed, until her throat felt scraped as raw as her soul.

When she opened her eyes, she found the devil herself collapsed at her feet.

"Call 911, CALL 911!" Yuna cried out, dropping to her knees beside Sylvia, who had crumpled with one leg sticking out at an unnatural angle, and her head resting on JD's enormous, booted foot.

JD and Meg stood frozen, shocked into forgetting their own agency.

Yuna put her fingers to Sylvia's neck.

"I don't know how to do this! I don't know what I'm doing!" she wailed. "Does anyone know CPR? Call 911!"

Annie the CPR doll and her beguiling, grotesque lips. The smell of mildew and stale Pringles. Empty Tab cans and Stella D'oro packages at the side of the sink, the maroon countertops peeling beneath. The steady flow of adrenaline pumped by the air she shared with Father Gilhool, the feeling of being cherished, wanted—the only time she would ever feel that, though she didn't know it then, at fourteen. The only time she would feel alive inside her body.

"I know CPR," Caroline heard herself say dully as she put her hand on Yuna's shoulder and eased herself into genuflection, bending over Sylvia's slack, graying face. "I know it."

TWENTY-SEVEN

Sylvia felt relaxed, more rested and alert than she'd felt in years. She was happy and focused. This was her favorite part of the play rehearsal process—the midpoint in the schedule when everyone was familiar with the script, excited by the direction the production was going, feeling the richness of the project, basking in the team love, but still well before the panic of opening night, for which they would suddenly feel utterly, inexplicably unprepared, and also before the tedium, the long hours, and the bad tempers of tech week. She sprawled out in the empty house, her shoeless feet propped on the seat in front of her, script and notes and the dramaturg's materials spread around like a nest. The lighting women at their tech table behind her, programming cues, calling out in their inscrutable code to someone hanging from the grid clutching a can, a rainbow of gels within reach, their voices echoing in the empty theater. She could see a remnant set piece from the last production—was it a diner booth or a train seat?—jutting out from backstage, quickly becoming a repository for take-out containers and Styrofoam cups.

Being in a theater during rehearsal was like being with a celebrity in her pajamas—you felt privileged by the intimacy.

And when she was onstage, in full makeup and costume, you could think, yeah, but just a few hours ago, your skin was pasty and your Spanx were still in the drawer. This was when behind-the-scenes got its moment in the spotlight. Everyone there had a purpose, and no one required a mission statement. It was mutually understood that everyone there was in thrall to this ephemeral activity, catering to the hardwired human need to be told a story.

Sylvia tried to push herself up out of her slouch, to call out to her actors, but found she couldn't. Something was holding her down, weighting her back into the seats. The stage was thrust into total darkness. She grasped for the name of the show she was working, an actor's name, a character's name that she could shout. Iago? Beneatha? Stella? Why couldn't she remember what she was directing? And now the seat was shaking, the theater was shaking, she was shaking. She strained to look up, to make sure the gaffer wasn't going to fall from her perch.

She found herself looking into Ruth's amused face, bright sunlight making her squint, the smell of antiseptic burning her nostrils.

"Directing in your dreams?" she asked.

Deflated, Sylvia remembered where she was. Saint Francis Hospital in Pierre, recovering from a heart attack, of all ridiculous things. She closed her eyes, willing herself back into the dark theater.

"Hey, hey, don't go back to sleep. We want to see you," Ellie chided. "And the doctor wants you up and about."

"He looks like he's straight off a billboard," Ruth added.

Sylvia tried to respond, but her throat was dry. Ruth

handed her a can of ginger ale, and she pulled herself up to sip at it.

"Handsome billboard or 'if you've been in an accident, call'…billboard?" she managed to croak.

"The latter," Ellie said.

"Is Ethan coming?" Sylvia asked, surprising all of them, including herself. Ellie glanced at Ruth.

"He wasn't sure whether you'd want him to bring the kids."

"That's not an answer."

"Syl. What do you want? For him to sit at your bedside and realize he almost lost you and get back together with you?" Ellie pleaded.

Sylvia closed her eyes against her friends.

"I used to keep fresh reading material in the bathrooms for us," she told them bitterly. "Like, actually rotate out the old *New Yorkers*. I wonder if Lisette does that. Or if she doesn't, does he even notice?"

"So you don't want to get back together with him," Ruth said.

Sylvia tried to shift in the bed. "Maybe it's exactly what I want."

"Well, you can't have it."

"I'm sorry, who invited her?" Sylvia said, mustering what energy she could to glare at Ellie.

"Ruth," Ellie implored. "Give her a break. The woman almost died."

"I did *not* almost die," Sylvia said and was immediately embarrassed by her petulance. "I sound like Leah."

"There *is* someone who would like to see you," Ellie said carefully, "but only if you're up for it." Sylvia came awake another notch.

"Who, Tony? Meg?" She sank back down. It was probably Mariella, wanting to know when her grading would be done. Was it possible she'd summoned a heart attack to avoid grading?

"No," Ruth said. "The woman who gave you CPR, who saved you."

Sylvia's pulse ticked up, and she glanced at the screen to witness it etched on her record.

"What? No! I don't want to see her. I mean…*no*. Do I have to? Can I write her a thank-you note instead?"

"A question for Emily Post," Ruth mused.

"You know who she is, right?" Sylvia asked, feeling warm.

"Oh yeah," Ellie said. "Meg told us the whole story."

"The *whole* story?" Sylvia said.

"Everything," Ellie confirmed.

"Like, including the bit about how the embryo would have been her grandchild?"

"Uh-huh."

Sylvia drummed her fingers on the bed's siderail. "I don't want to see her."

"Understandable."

"Why the fuck is she here? She changed her mind and wants to do away with me?"

Ellie shrugged. "Is it possible she wants to make sure you're okay? Or, you know, see her handiwork? It's not every day a person gets to save another person's life."

Sylvia groaned.

"What? It's true."

"Now I'm indebted to her! For fucking ever. The last thing

in the world I want to be. Why couldn't it have been anyone, literally anyone else who saved me?"

Ellie adjusted the heavy yellow drapery bunched at the edges of the windows. "Why do they have blackout curtains here, but they'll turn on the overhead lights at three in the morning to take your temperature?"

"Some people, not me, of course," Ruth said to Sylvia, "might think you sounded a little ungrateful."

"No," Ellie said before Sylvia could respond. "Sylvia *is* grateful and that's what's bugging her. She doesn't want to feel grateful to that woman."

Sylvia pointed at Ellie. "What she said. Also, I keep thinking, you know, if the situation were reversed, would I have…?" She trailed off.

"Well, you couldn't have, because you don't know CPR, so it's moot." Ruth brushed away the concern. Sylvia glanced at Ellie, who shrugged. What would it be like to have such clear solutions for every hurdle?

"What's moot is discussing whether I'm going to see her," Sylvia conceded. "It's not like I'm *not* going to let her in here."

"We're too civilized for that," Ellie agreed.

"How do I look?"

"That's your concern?"

"My pride didn't have a heart attack."

"You look fine," Ellie soothed. "But here, why don't you…" She handed Sylvia the hairbrush she'd been instructed to collect at Basement Vistas. Sylvia ran it through her hair, then tossed it aside.

"Who am I kidding? Let's get this over with. Bring her in."

"She's not your executioner," Ruth muttered as she pulled

open the heavy door. She looked up and down the hallway. "Not here," she announced.

"Go to the lounge at the end of the hall," Ellie instructed impatiently.

Ruth huffed and left in search of Caroline the Savior. Sylvia found herself relieved to have a respite from her friend.

"Ruth is getting to be more Ruth, isn't she?" Ellie commented.

Sylvia nodded, glad she hadn't been the one to say anything. Her observation wouldn't have been so benign.

"Do you think I would have saved her if she'd dropped at my feet?" Sylvia asked in a small voice. "I mean, assuming I knew CPR?"

Ellie sighed as if the weight of the question were pushing the breath out of her. She studied the perforated panels in the ceiling.

"I do," she said decisively. "I really think you would have."

Sylvia shot Ellie a grateful smile. Even if she suspected otherwise, it cost her friend nothing to give this generous answer. She leaned back against her pillow and looked out the window. A private room, a view of snow-covered trees and of blue sky, nurses who appeared not to be overworked: being hospitalized outside the city had benefits utterly novel to her.

There was a faint tapping at the door. Sylvia and Ellie exchanged glances.

"Come in?" Sylvia called out weakly.

"Everyone decent?" Ruth said from the other side.

Sylvia rolled her eyes at Ellie, but her stomach tightened.

"Come on in."

"What?"

"Enter!"

Ruth pushed open the door and gave them a brave smile. Behind her was the protester. Sylvia's savior. Caroline.

Caroline looked smaller and less threatening than she ever had before. She didn't have her cabal with her, Sylvia thought.

"Hi," Sylvia said with a minimal wave.

"Hi," Caroline said.

Ellie stood and steered Ruth back out the door. "We'll be right outside if you need us."

Sylvia thought Caroline might be offended or at least amused by Ellie's menacing undertone, but she appeared too nervous to notice. What did she have to be nervous about? You couldn't take a higher road than she had. It pissed off Sylvia to think she had given Caroline such an extraordinary opportunity to be ethically mighty. She knew Caroline would attribute her heroism to her Christianity, and Sylvia wanted so badly for Caroline to understand that nonreligious people would have done the same. Except. The uncertainty niggled at Sylvia about what she herself would have done had it been Caroline who had collapsed. She knew that had it been just about anyone else on the planet—a homeless person, a farebeater on the subway, even horrible David Ketchum—she would have jumped into action. But the idea of saving the life of someone who wanted to run roughshod over the lives of others gave her pause.

What if it had been a pedophile at her feet? A white supremacist? The list began to whittle down until Sylvia felt her moral compass spinning wildly.

Caroline remained standing by the door.

"Feel free to sit," Sylvia said, gesturing to a chair.

Caroline pulled the vinyl-upholstered chair a few inches farther away from Sylvia's bed and perched delicately at the edge, her purse propped on her lap, ready to run at any moment. She had the moral advantage *and* the mobility advantage, Sylvia thought sourly. *Straighten up,* she chastised herself.

"How are you feeling?" Caroline asked.

In the clinic parking lot, Sylvia had come to loathe Caroline's voice, and now she flinched at the sound of it, up close and personal.

"Much better," Sylvia lied, though she didn't know why she was bothering to lie. She was tired, so tired. "Miracle of modern medicine. I have a couple of stents. Lots of blockage cleared."

Caroline nodded and squinted at her purse.

"I came to apologize," she said in a small voice.

Sylvia was taken aback.

"What do you have to apologize for?" Unable to resist, she added, "Saving me?"

Caroline either ignored or didn't understand the sting. "I'm afraid that I upset you so much you had a heart attack." She sat back as though she'd been carrying those words around for days and was finally relieved of her burden.

"Oh," Sylvia said, considering this. On the one hand, the woman wasn't completely off the mark. Her angry accusations in the store had definitely triggered Sylvia's cardiac arrest. On the other hand, the doctors said she'd been a time bomb for years and appeared to have had some smaller stealth heart attacks, a concept with which Sylvia was still grappling. The idea that she was so deaf to her own body was terrifying and mystifying. How were you supposed to be attuned to yourself without becoming Sylvia's least favorite kind of person, a hypochondriac? No, her least favorite were anti-choice protesters.

The monitor broadcast the rise in her blood pressure. Thank God this town crier of a machine, telling all her secrets, wasn't connected to her in regular life.

"Well," Sylvia said, modulating the urge to heap upon this woman glorious guilt for the rest of her life. "It was going to happen eventually; *something* was going to trigger it." There, that was good. Truthful.

Caroline looked duly discomfited.

Sylvia steeled herself against the urge to make sure no one felt uncomfortable in her presence. She would remain silent.

"Sylvia, I'm so terribly, terribly sorry that I was that trigger. Truly. It's going to haunt me for the rest of my life."

Sylvia knew she shouldn't be surprised that, during the course of these exceptional events, Caroline had learned her name, but it still felt like a trespass to hear it cross the woman's lips. Though Caroline had given her mouth-to-mouth, so they'd already been as intimate as Sylvia had been with a dozen guys before Ethan. She shifted in her bed. God, she was sore. On top of everything else, she had bruises on her hip from the collapse.

"I don't know that you need to be haunted by it," Sylvia said, impatience leaking over her words. "You did save my life. If someone else had triggered the inevitable, there's a good chance they wouldn't have known CPR, or used it, or whatever." Sylvia stopped. She didn't want Caroline to feel *too* good about herself.

Caroline's eyes widened slightly, this possibility not having occurred to her.

"I guess that's true."

Sylvia sniffed dismissively and felt very, very small. This was how she knew there was no god—a real god would punish her for being so graceless in this of all moments.

"I need you to understand something," Caroline suddenly said, looking straight into Sylvia's eyes, and Sylvia resisted the cowardly impulse to look away. "I pray for you every day."

"That really isn't necessary," Sylvia retorted automatically.

"I pray for your soul. I pray for you to find peace within your heart."

"I have plenty of peace."

"I don't think you understand the joy of letting Christ into your life," Caroline gently persisted.

Sylvia flinched at the name. It was such a bold and personal utterance as to be a nearly sensual word. It was also absurd.

"You have to understand that, to me, that's like saying I should let the tooth fairy into my life."

Caroline looked at her sadly. "I know that's how you feel, and that's why I pray."

Always an answer.

"Do you read books other than the Bible?" Sylvia asked her, eyeing the stack her friends had supplied.

"Occasionally."

"Books that aren't *about* the Bible, or advice on how to get the most out of it, or whatever those books are on the rack at the drug store." Caroline looked surprised, and Sylvia knew that's exactly what she bought and where she bought them.

"No, not really. Not since school."

"So how would you even know what other possibilities are out there for finding peace? Aren't Christians supposed to practice humility? That doesn't seem very humble, assuming you know the best for every single person on this very varied planet."

Caroline was flustered. Good. Forget her heart and staying calm. Sylvia had had it with these noxious proselytizers preying on—and praying on—people who were struggling, offering them a fairy tale as a solution. They were as bad as drug dealers. And somehow blind to all the good committed by nonbelievers. Sylvia had a thought.

"You want everyone to accept Jesus Christ as their savior, not that all of us feel we need saving, thanks, but you also parrot stuff about tolerance of other faiths. So, which is it? Are you lying when you say the Jews and the Muslims are your brothers and sisters—and by the way, it's not just three men in the room, there are hundreds of religions out there—or is it kind of a tiered thing? If they believe in Allah, that's way better than us nonbelievers but nowhere near as good as you?"

Sylvia's monitor was beeping fast now, and Caroline's eyes grew wide.

"Please, Sylvia, calm down."

"Stop saying my name!" Sylvia spat, knowing this was far from her greatest moment.

Caroline studied her. "I want everyone to understand the joy of being saved by Christ," she said quietly, "and I want everyone, *everyone* to spend the rest of eternity in Heaven."

Sylvia shook her head. "But *you* saved me. Not Christ. People are saved by other people, not historical figures or imaginary woo-woo ghosts."

"It's God working through me to save you."

Sylvia chuckled. "It's like the joke about the drowning man."

Caroline's mouth set in a prim line. "I don't know that one."

"Oh," Sylvia said, waving her hand, not in the mood to launch into a long telling. "You know, a guy is drowning and a rowboat comes along and throws a life preserver, but the guy ignores it and says, 'No, no, God will save me.' Then a big ship comes along and sends out a, whaddya call it, you know, like a rescue boat, and the guy goes again, 'No, no, God will save me.'"

Caroline looked perplexed, and Sylvia wondered if her people ever told jokes. She barreled on.

"So then a helicopter comes and drops a rope ladder thing, but again, 'No, no, I don't need the ladder, God will save me.' Finally, the guy is tiring and really about to drown, and he cries out, 'God, I've had such faith, I've waited and waited and trusted in you, why have you forsaken me?' And God says, 'Dude, I sent you a life preserver, a rescue boat, and a helicopter, what else do you want?'"

Sylvia sat back, exhausted. That was the most she'd spoken in days. And it looked like it had gone over Caroline's head.

"I think that joke just proves what I said, right?" Caroline said doubtfully.

Sylvia frowned and then guffawed. "Yeah, actually, it totally does. I don't know why I told it."

"It's a funny joke," Caroline said. With some effort, she pushed up on the armchair and stood. She moved like an old lady, though Sylvia guessed she was only in her fifties. What the hell had she come for and had she gotten it? Sylvia was tired and was mad that she was tired. She wanted to recover instantly, wanted to put this behind her, didn't want to be someone who'd had a heart attack. The phrase as applied to her sounded as atonal as the suggestion she accept Christ. Poor Christ probably would have preferred a heart attack to bleeding to death from crucifixion. Sylvia was getting drowsy. What was wrong with these people, wearing an instrument of the most gruesome torture imaginable around their necks all the time? If someone wore an image of a cat nailed to a cross, people would be horrified, but a man, that was fine. She sniffed. She was going to start wearing a necklace with a revolver as a pendant. No, that wasn't the same. She'd need to wear that medieval contraption that stretched people until they burst. What did those look like? She pictured a massage table…

"What are *you* doing here?" a voice growled.

Sylvia woke with a start, embarrassed. She forgot for a moment where she was and why someone would be mad she was there. She focused her eyes and saw tiny Meg, every muscle tensed, glaring up at Caroline at the door of this—*her*—hospital room.

Caroline stepped back from the fury, protecting her heart with her hand.

"I was checking on her," Caroline said defensively, almost petulantly.

"Well, *don't*," Meg said.

Caroline took a steady breath, as if restraining herself. She had one hand on the doorknob, and Sylvia thought, *Go already! You are not welcome here.* But the older woman lingered, unable to take her eyes off Meg. Meg took a step back, away from the scrutiny.

"What?" she spat.

Caroline shrugged helplessly, and Sylvia felt a zephyr of sympathy. She tried to imagine some girl carrying Nathaniel's baby and then aborting, but Nathaniel was currently three, and so she was unable to conjure the parallel without revulsion.

"Here's what I don't understand," Meg snarled. "You were completely willing to let *me* die by making me keep that bunch of cells, but you intercepted and saved her life. Why? Why do you get to play God and decide who lives and who dies?"

"It's not a bunch of cells!" Caroline cried out. "It's a human being. My grandchild already had ten fingers and ten toes." Her voice quivered, and she sniffed violently to hold back tears.

Meg reached down and tugged off her puffy moon boots and the socks beneath. She threw them to the side and thrust one foot at Caroline.

"What the fuck do you call these?"

Sylvia wanted to cheer.

Caroline grew pale, and Sylvia hoped she wasn't about to have a heart attack. *Don't steal my thunder*, she found herself thinking and clapped her hand over mouth to keep from laughing at herself.

"How can you laugh?" Caroline wailed, turning on her. "Why have you no respect for the sanctity of life?"

Sylvia felt the familiar rush of fury toward this word-twisting, undereducated, limited woman. She was about to erupt, but caught herself. This was not the time nor the place, but nowhere was the time or place. Sylvia would never be able to see the world through this woman's eyes, no matter how hard she tried, and vice versa, though Sylvia suspected Caroline never tried. Sylvia, on the other hand, spent most of her time in the parking lot trying to fathom Caroline's ilk, no matter how revolting and inhumane the consequences of their world view: unloved children and shattered lives.

"I ask the same of you," Sylvia said.

Caroline shook her head, not in disagreement, but with a genuine lack of comprehension.

The door to the room flew open, nearly knocking Caroline over. In came Irving.

He looked at Sylvia, pale and tired in the hospital bed, then to Caroline, and then to Meg standing on the cold floor in bare feet.

"If I'd known we were doing pedis, I woulda brought my nail polish!"

Irving's arrival was too much for Caroline. With a grimace, she put her head down and left.

"Something I said?" Irving said.

"No, your mere existence," Sylvia said, surprising herself by holding out her hand to her new friend for whom she felt a wave of familial affection. He grasped it in his.

"The feeling, as they say in Brooklyn, is mutual."

"I don't think Brooklyn can claim ownership of that expression."

Meg looked back and forth between them, looking smaller than ever. Sylvia held out her other hand to her, and Meg approached without thinking and took it. What a family.

TWENTY-EIGHT

Ignoring Christopher's hushed warnings, Caroline grasped the polished walnut banister, and made her way up the wide stairs. Bethany and Anya referred to this hulking, drafty, creaky Victorian as charming, but Caroline thought it could do with a sizeable injection of insulation and wall-to-wall carpeting, an opinion she was smart enough to keep to herself. God forbid she say anything that could be interpreted as a suggestion.

At the moment, though, she hoped her noisy footsteps might rouse little Grace. Her pink-cheeked delight had been sleeping for over two hours, and Caroline missed her. She got to see the baby only once a week for six precious hours that she looked forward to from the moment she left her.

Caroline made her way down the hall, past the riotous collages Anya did that Caroline didn't understand (and kept quiet about that, too), and gently pushed open the door to Grace's room. Caroline's breath left her as it always did when she first laid eyes on the child. The baby was sleeping in her favored position, with her rump high in the air, her face turned to one side, rosy and chubby and peaceful. This afternoon, time and season conspired with the sun to illuminate the baby's face until even the most blasphemous apostate would be persuaded that angels existed among us.

Caroline placed her palm on her granddaughter's back and closed her eyes with pleasure. Warm, solid, so much humanity and promise in that dense little bundle. She sang softly.

"Ri-ise and shi-ine, and give God your glory glory, ri-ise and shi-ine and give God your glory glory, children of the Lo-ord."

She was forbidden to read any of the Bible to the baby, nor was she allowed to pray with her or near her, humiliating terms to which Caroline had acquiesced. But surely a lighthearted song about Noah's ark—animals!—would not sully the atheism of a six-month-old. Caroline rolled her eyes at the empty room. The décor was minimal, not uncozy, but a far cry from the lacy valences and embroidered pillows that Caroline had preferred for her own babies. Grace puckered her rosebud lips and suckled at the air.

"Dang," Caroline cursed and hurried to the top of the stairs to call down to Christopher. But he was halfway up, holding aloft the forgotten bottle of warmed milk. She smiled at him gratefully. "Thank you," she whispered, returning to the room.

Grace's blue eyes were wide open. She blinked at the world. What did she think each time she opened her eyes?

"Hello, sweet girl," Caroline cooed.

"Ayah," Grace said.

Caroline set the bottle down and reached for her baby, who reached back for her.

"The Lord said to Noah, there's gonna be a floody floody, Lord said to Noah, there's gonna be a floody floody, get your children out of the muddy muddy, children of the Lo-ord."

"Ayah, ayah!" Grace sang.

They settled into the glider, the one piece of furniture Caroline would have liked to have had when she was a young mother. The rest—the so-called Diaper Genie (the poop still stank), the wipes warmer—were all designed to make new mothers feel they were negligent if they didn't have them. Again, Caroline kept her mouth shut about the unnecessary expense. Money didn't seem to be a problem for Bethany and Anya. Anya drew a large salary from a company that went to other companies and instructed them on whom to fire. Bethany was a tenured professor of engineering at SUNY New Paltz, her alma mater.

Grace reached for the bottle and lay back in Caroline's arms.

"The animals, they came on, they came on by twosies twosies, animals, they came on, they came on by twosies twosies, el-e-phants and kang-aroosies roosies, children of the Lo-ord!"

Grace kicked her feet and reached up with her free hand to stroke Caroline's face. Caroline's insides melted, and she thought she might explode with joy.

The floor creaked, and she and the baby looked to the doorway, where Christopher had appeared.

"Caroline," he admonished gently.

"Oh, for Pete's sake, it's a children's song." She waved away his objection with a smile. She knew he wouldn't report her. He had been happier, more attentive, even occasionally de-monstrably affectionate with Caroline since she had achieved this tentative peace with Bethany.

Caroline wasn't sure that she would ever live down the shame of having turned against her own flesh and blood, but she was trying as hard as she knew how. She had been greatly rewarded, and not only with these visits to Grace: Christopher had noticed her change of heart and moved back home!

"I missed your cooking," he teased during their brief, uncomfortable discussion about the six-month hiatus in their marriage, and that was okay with her. The whole episode had been embarrassing, and they both wanted to put it behind them without fanfare. Each morning, though, Caroline could scarcely believe her eyes when she found Christopher beside her once more.

When he left, he had called her strong, but she knew he was the strong one. Christopher was as good a Christian as anyone she'd ever known, and he understood that God made Bethany the way she was and so hadn't sacrificed his child or his grandchild for his beliefs. Isn't that what Caroline had done? Sacrificed her family because of what was essentially a lack of faith in God's plan? Stupid, so stupid!

The first thing Caroline did after saving that woman's life was track down Bethany. It hadn't been hard to find her, but it had necessitated a mortifying conversation with Maureen, who, of course, knew exactly how to reach Caroline's daughter, and had not concealed her titillation at the role she was called upon to play in the reunion. It irked Caroline no end.

On the phone, Bethany's voice was deep and assured, and, even though she knew it would irritate Bethany, Caroline burst into tears. She hadn't seen or spoken to her own daughter for eleven years. How on earth had she ever thought that was right?

"Would you like to meet at the diner, for old time's sake?" Caroline had suggested, after bringing her own voice under control. It would be especially poetic to go to the last place they laid eyes on each other.

Bethany had issued forth an immediate guttural rejection. "Uh, no. Why don't you say what you have to say to me and we can go from there."

"Now?" Caroline was caught off guard. She thought she would have more time to fine-tune her apology.

"Yes." Bethany sounded slightly distracted, as if she might even be doing something else at the same time, multitasking during her first conversation with her mother in over a decade. Caroline took a deep breath and prostrated herself as best she could over a phone call. She apologized for turning Bethany out, for not accepting her as she was, for not understanding God's plan. There was a faint grunt on the other end of the line so she quickly summoned up what courage she had left.

"Can I meet your baby?" Caroline asked, aiming to sound humble, but not weak, which she sensed would not curry favor. She listened to her daughter's silence, her pulse beating uncomfortably in her temples.

"Yeah, okay," Bethany said.

The speed with which Bethany agreed was a punch in the gut: the ball had been in Caroline's court this whole time. Her daughter's heart had been open to even the slightest of overtures. Caroline felt like dirt, absolute dirt.

"It rai-ained and pou-oured for forty daysey daysies, rai-ained and pou-oured for forty daysey daysies, nearly drove those animals crazies crazies, children of the Lo-ord," Christopher joined in softly. He, too, had been eager to make amends.

All Caroline had to do was tell him she'd accepted Bethany as she was (Caroline tried not to dwell on whether she had truly accomplished this), and he had asked to come home.

There were so many things Caroline wasn't allowed to think: that she was relieved the baby had come from Bethany's womb and not Anya's and knew she wouldn't feel Grace was her grandchild otherwise; that she was, in the same way, relieved the breast milk she now fed Grace came from her own daughter; relieved the baby's father was white, never mind that Caroline, let alone Grace, would never know who he was. She also wasn't supposed to wish that her daughter wasn't gay, but she did wish that, prayed every day for Bethany to have a change of heart. *God loves you just the way you are, but He loves you too much to let you stay that way.*

Was it because she had these thoughts that she was still being punished? Ashamed, Caroline tiptoed around the jagged edges of Jonathan's silence and the fact that she couldn't seem to have a relationship with both her children at the same time. After eleven years of the silent treatment by Bethany, it was now Jonathan's turn to shut her out. She thought of the strange story—a joke she had called it—Sylvia Tanisman had told her in the hospital, about God saving through people. He punished through people, too.

She still didn't see much of Bethany. Her daughter left the house as soon as she had briefed Caroline and Christopher on the day's instructions, which rarely varied, and arrived home minutes before they were scheduled to leave. They almost never laid eyes on Anya, who left early and came home after Caroline and Christopher had gone home. That was fine with Caroline, though the two times she had witnessed the couple together with the baby, she was struck by their easy choreography and the natural generosity they exuded as a unit. She was certain she had never felt that relaxed with Christopher in all their thirty-four years. But this generation was so different in so many ways, informality being the biggest distinguisher.

Caroline pulled the bottle away and leaned Grace forward against the full span of her hand, spreading a burp cloth over vulnerable areas in one easy motion. These movements came back to her so naturally, as if she had been feeding babies just yesterday. She shook her head at the piles of instructional books that were everywhere in this house, futile amulets against whatever God had planned.

Cribsheet: A Data-Driven Guide to Better, More Relaxed Parenting

Strategies for Smarter Cookies

Education Begins at Birth

Five Simple Steps to Sleep

Attachment Parenting

Weaning without Guilt

The Danish Way of Parenting

The Secret to Loving Children Effectively

Caroline had managed just fine without this inane library that seemed designed to stoke fear and insecurity.

"Ayah?" said Grace.

"Yes, beautiful," Caroline cooed at her. "More is coming,

just as soon as you—"

Obligingly, Grace let out a little honk and sighed, eliciting chuckles from her grandparents.

"How about some tea?" Christopher said softly. "I'll have it ready when you come down."

Caroline momentarily considered reminding him of the household rule that no hot beverages were to be consumed while the baby was awake. She decided she was too pleased that he had committed a no-no—it was usually Caroline who was admonished for such transgressions—and also knew the rule was absurd.

"That would be lovely." She smiled shyly back at him, knowing that his return was God's work, too. *Indeed, there is not a righteous man on earth who continually does good and who never sins.* Lately, Caroline held close this verse from Ecclesiastes. She had sinned, but that did not mean she did not deserve her husband by her side.

Grace finished her bottle and let out a triumphant "Ayah!"

Grasping her baby tightly in one arm and the banister in the other, Caroline slowly, slowly eased them both down the stairs. She would never ever admit to Bethany, or Christopher for that matter, that this part of the child-minding made her very nervous. Caroline would simply continue to use every ounce of her concentration and strength to get Grace safely down once a week. So far so good, and it was the one benefit of rarely crossing paths with her daughter, never to be witnessed in this vulnerable stance.

Christopher had set up the couch pillows on the floor to help pen in Grace while she played and to cushion the occasional faceplants, which only delighted her. Caroline eased the baby down onto a plush blanket and immediately placed in her hands an old Fisher Price airplane. Caroline had been more delighted than she cared to admit by the gratitude Bethany and Anya had expressed when Caroline produced some of the old toys she'd saved. She'd been afraid that her proffering would be disqualified for being made of accursed plastic, but apparently the status of being enduring and reusable triumphed. Grace also loved the school bus and the Kenner tree house that popped closed with a satisfying click when you pressed down the canopy.

Caroline placed one hand on the overstuffed couch pillow and awkwardly folded herself onto the floor beside Grace.

"Ayah, ayah, AYAH!"

Sunshine flooded through the curtainless windows and lit up the collection of framed photographs atop the baby grand piano. Anya had gone to a conservatory before realizing she didn't want to be a starving artist. Now she painted and played on her own time, while providing for her family, of which Caroline approved and which contributed to her sense that Anya was the man in the couple. Christopher had told her she was absolutely not supposed to think that let alone ever say it, but really. Anya only wore pants, she kept her hair cropped short, and had no plans to incubate a baby, ever. So what else was Caroline supposed to think? She clearly could not have landed a man, but Bethany certainly could have.

"Here we go!" Christopher singsonged. One thing the girls had in their house was an extraordinary collection of teas, many of which Caroline had never heard of. She and Christopher had decided to sample a new one each week. He carried in a tray with two mugs, spoons clinking against porcelain, a drab green sugar bowl Caroline would never have owned, and a small pitcher that said Creamah. She didn't understand the misspelling, and supposed it was a joke lost on her. He set down the tray on the mantel, far from Grace, Caroline noted with satisfaction.

"And what have we today?" Caroline said lightly.

Christopher squinted at a tea bag, and when he couldn't make out the tiny letters, he squinted at the ceiling. "Lapsang Souchang. Or Lapchang Souchan. Something like that. In any case, a black tea."

"Are you sure that isn't racist, calling a tea black?" Caroline was only half teasing.

"Truthfully, I don't rightly know, ma'am." Christopher bowed to her, and she giggled. "Could well be."

Grace stopped rolling the bus for a moment and studied them. "Ayah," she declared seriously.

"Yes," Christopher agreed. "It's a minefield." He wrapped each tea bag around a spoon and squeezed, then unwound them and plopped them on the tray. He stirred in one spoonful of sugar for her and one and a half for himself. He put a splash of cream in both cups and gave them a final stir. He closed his eyes.

"Thank you, Lord, for this modest repast we are about to receive. We are grateful to you for every sip and every morsel, for friends and family and especially for Grace. Amen."

"Amen," Caroline said, trying to hide her hurt that he had said the prayer without alerting her.

Christopher opened his eyes in surprise.

"I'm sorry! I got used to, you know. Squeezing in a quick prayer so the girls wouldn't catch me." He smiled sheepishly. "I had to say them on the sly."

Relief flooded Caroline. He was still saying grace. He did it even in this house, without fear of reprisal. He wasn't excluding her. She crossed herself quickly and accepted a cup from him, taking care to give a wide berth to Grace.

"I hope they don't have one of those nanny cams set up in a teddy bear or something like that," Christopher commented, furrowing his brow as he blew on his tea.

Caroline shuddered at the thought that Bethany would harbor such distrust. But, who knew? If one of those devilish parenting guides had suggested it, she—or Anya more likely— might well have set one up.

Together, they cast their eyes around the room, then tittered nervously.

"Wouldn't even know what to look for," Christopher concluded, and Caroline felt they were on the same side.

Caroline permitted nothing to interfere with these Wednesday visits even though it meant she could no longer join Protect Life outside Intentional Families. She told Maureen her schedule had changed, which had the benefit of being true and convenient. She had tried to summon disappointment. She assured them and herself that she would keep those unborn babies in her prayers, and she had. One unborn baby, in particular. But the truth was that she had come to dread protesting. She was on edge from the moment she left her house to the moment she drove away from the clinic. She disliked approaching strangers and disliked being reviled by people who didn't even know her. She felt she was doing a world of good here in this house for Grace, certainly more than she ever could do in downtown Pierre.

Grace wobbled, and Caroline reached out to steady her. Grace rolled the airplane over her hand, and Caroline winced, then smiled apologetically for wincing.

Caroline didn't know how much Bethany knew of what had happened at the clinic. The children were close—could she take pride or, she corrected herself, pleasure in their relationship with each other? Either Jonathan had kept the whole terrible story to himself or, equally miraculous, Bethany knew the story and had allowed Caroline back into her life anyway. Or maybe—and here Caroline knew she was definitely venturing into sinful pride territory—Bethany knew Caroline had saved that woman's life. Not *that woman*, she corrected herself. Sylvia. But maybe the fact that Caroline had saved her life, the life of someone she deeply disagreed with, had won her favor in her daughter's eyes. She couldn't imagine asking her, though, not in a million years.

Christopher, unable to sit on the floor, pulled the butterfly chair closer to Grace and Caroline. The chair was covered in a white canvas sling that had a rip in it, and Caroline wondered whether Bethany and Anya knew it was torn and purposely chose not to repair it. Maybe that was part of the look. Christopher set his mug on a low side table, squatted as deeply as he could, then took a leap of faith and let himself fall backward the rest of the way into the uninviting seat. He flung out his arms to steady himself, and his right hand sent his tea flying.

At home that night, lying in bed beside him, Caroline shuddered over and over at the close call, seeing the scalding liquid spray behind Christopher. Grace had been oblivious, and there had been no need to tell Bethany about the incident, but Caroline was unable to stop worrying the memory the way she might tongue a troublesome tooth. Why on earth had Christopher chosen that chair and not the sturdy armchair? Tortured by the nonstop replay of the scene, Caroline finally had to make her way to the kitchen to warm some milk. The microwave clock glowed 3:05.

As she stirred the milk to heat it evenly, the answer hit her. Christopher had been able to move the butterfly chair, whereas the armchair would have been too heavy.

He had done it to be closer to Caroline.

TWENTY-NINE

"Are you okay? Are you okay?" Sylvia yelled at the creepy doll as she shook the rubbery shoulders, feeling more than a little ridiculous.

The doll did not answer, so Sylvia checked for a pulse. "No pulse," she announced to the room. "Call 911!"

Sylvia felt all eyes on her as she loomed up on her knees to begin chest compressions. It took quite a bit of strength, and, as she had on the previous two turns on the Annie doll, Sylvia wondered from where that frumpy, slow-moving woman—*Caroline*—had summoned the strength to pump her heart. Sylvia's fellow trainees paid overly close attention to her turn because Sylvia, having actually suffered a heart attack, was apparently steeped in authenticity. She suppressed a smile, which wasn't hard because the moment was coming when she'd have to lower her mouth to the doll's.

"Ten, eleven, twelve…" she huffed softly when her phone rang. She glanced over at her purse, then pleadingly at the Red Cross instructor, who firmly shook his head. The phone stopped ringing. Sylvia hurried through the rest of the compressions.

"Slower," said the instructor, an underpaid man in a room full of women. Sylvia wondered at the dynamic, wondered why this doll was always female. Had no one invented a male CPR doll? The pairing of human men with female dolls danced across her imagination and instantly made her queasy. Her phone rang again. Fuck it, what was this guy going to do, fail her? She stood up and, with a thin apology, grabbed her phone from her purse. She stepped out of the break room being used for the First Aid class, into the hallway she now knew so well. She flashed a smile at Melissa, her favorite nurse, the one who had trained her to work the recovery room.

"Ethan?" she said, her heart leaping at his name and number. "Is everything okay?"

"Mommy," Leah stated firmly.

"Hi, Jelly Bean," Sylvia said, trying not to sound disappointed. Why, oh why did she still look forward to hearing his voice? When would that end? Would it end?

"I told Seneca's sister the Chrysler Building was named for Christ, but she says I'm wrong. Tell her *she's* wrong."

"Wait, Bean, don't put me on speakerphone!" The connection went identifiably fuzzy as Sylvia's voice was broadcast into some room somewhere, with unknown people listening in. She hated speakerphone.

"Too late. Tell her."

"Well, wait, it's *not* named for him."

Leah's voice quickly became intimate again, and Sylvia unclenched. "Really?" she said in a way that was fascinated and not upset, as Sylvia had anticipated. "That's a first. That guy puts his name on everything."

Sylvia burst out laughing, felt a wave of adoration for her munchkin, but not a wave of longing. She would see Leah and Nathaniel tonight, when she returned home. To everyone's surprise, but hers most of all, Sylvia had agreed to stay on for the spring semester, even though Linden had offered to let her out of her contract.

"Okay, kiddo, let me call you later. I'm in the middle of something."

"A class?"

"Yes, but one I'm taking, not teaching."

"*You're* in college, Mommy?" Leah said incredulously.

"No, no," Sylvia hurried to forestall a tsunami of misinformation. "It's just a short class on…" She had to tread carefully, not having told her children she'd had a heart attack, only that she needed to rest up in Pierre because she'd been a little bit sick. "It's actually a class on how to save someone's life if they're having an emergency."

"Like for superheroes?"

"Yes, but no flying lessons."

"Oh."

There was an urgent tapping on the classroom door, and one of the other students—a new escort who had joined the team over the winter break while Sylvia had been back home— beckoned her inside. She held up a finger in response.

"I have to go back in, but I'll call. I promise."

"Promise?" Kids might be very forgiving, or so she was told, but they did not forget. Whereas Sylvia, as she aged, found herself forgiving only *because* she forgot. She chuckled.

"What's so funny?" Leah demanded, trying to prolong the conversation.

"Just silly thoughts. Gotta go, love." Sylvia made kissing noises into her phone and disconnected the call. It looked harsh to others, but it was the only way she could extricate herself from her exacting boss.

Sylvia returned to the break room in time to see the new escort giving the doll mouth-to-mouth resuscitation, and her first instinct was to avert her eyes. Sylvia was not taking this class because of a heightened awareness of heart attacks and sense of gratitude, or rather, those were not her *only* motivations. She did feel aware and grateful, she assured herself. But she also knew she was pursuing certification in First Aid and CPR because she didn't want the zealots outside the clinic to corner the market on saving lives. Leave it to Sylvia to turn an act of selflessness into something tinged with pettiness and a touch of anger, but there it was. Ruth had understood completely.

"Sylvia," the instructor said. He wiped off the doll's mouth with an alcohol-saturated cloth and looked at her expectantly. "You may finish your turn. I'd hate to see you have to pay for a new certification class," he added, not hiding how delighted he'd be if this came to pass. Before the heart attack, wanky little power-seekers like this twerp, the kind of people who gave waiters needless grief, would have sent her into a tailspin of loathing and despair over human nature, but now she just smiled at him. A fake smile, but the fakeness held power. In the words of all her students at one time or another: whatever. It wasn't so much that she had a new lease on life because of the heart attack, it was that she had survived the humiliation of being rescued by someone she loathed.

As Sylvia knelt over the doll again, it occurred to her that she had also survived being cared for by people she didn't know very well and had resisted dissolving into a puddle of indebtedness. Was it possible that the stent propping open her previously clogged artery was in fact pulsing out superpowers?

When she was released from the hospital, it had been her colleague Mariella Corkenthorp who had picked her up, and it was Mariella and her husband and his fake plants who had taken her into their charming, rambling Victorian, over Sylvia's weak objections. Because in fact she couldn't imagine recuperating in her dismal room at Basement Vistas any more than she could imagine imposing on Meg and JD or, especially, Tony to nurse her back to health. They hadn't yet reached the drive-me-home-after-my-heart-attack stage of their relationship.

Sylvia laughed out loud as she screwed her eyes shut and put her lips on Annie's.

"People express their nervousness in different ways," the asshole observed.

Mariella, perching at the edge of the driver's seat, both hands gripping the wheel at the ten and two position, back ramrod straight, alert to all danger for the whole of the three-mile trip, had made it seem like Sylvia was doing her a favor. There were worse things than a kind and eager person. She'd announced that "we" had a surprise for Sylvia.

"Who's we?"

"The department." Mariella waited.

"I don't think I have the energy to guess," Sylvia had told her apologetically. She leaned her head back against the seat and managed a polite smile. The car smelled, predictably, like patchouli.

"Oh, of course. Well…" Mariella gave her full attention

to braking at a red light, and Sylvia wondered whether she always drove quite this cautiously or whether she felt Sylvia was delicate cargo. Mariella turned to Sylvia, beaming. "We graded your final scripts for you!"

Sylvia's stomach dropped. Instead of being thrilled, she had been mortified. Her colleagues would see what sophistry and drivel her students had produced under her substandard tutelage.

"Wow."

"Don't thank me," Mariella burbled, though Sylvia had not thanked her. "It was all David's idea!"

"David Ketchum?" Sylvia had said incredulously. He hated her. Or so she thought. He probably was grabbing at the chance to see how bad the work was, she realized.

"Yep," Mariella said breathlessly. "And Sylvia." Sylvia had waited dutifully, dreading what was coming next. "We were all so doggone impressed."

"What?"

"Even Felix, and you know what a tough customer he is." Felix was the fusty, faux-British-accented chair of the department.

"What do you mean by impressed?" Sylvia tread cautiously.

"The quality of the work you got those kids to produce was, well, it was magnificent!"

"Magnificent." Sylvia turned the word over in her mouth. She had never used that word in her life. It was a word for fairy tales. "David thought they were good?" she confirmed.

"All of us," Mariella said firmly. "The students really found their voices."

"Uh-huh." Sylvia had coughed so she wouldn't laugh. At

the time, she'd taken this as further evidence that she was not cut out for this: her expectations of the students were too high, too professional apparently.

Now, Sylvia blew two breaths into the doll's mouth and, disturbingly, the chest inflated.

"Good, good," said the instructor. "Again."

So Sylvia was once again subjecting herself to student screeds like *Mirror, Mirror*, about a woman who sued herself, a transparent conceit that allowed its author to fashion not just one but two protagonists in her likeness. Mostly, it had been Mariella who had pushed Sylvia to return. It turned out that there was no way to say no to her, and Sylvia had come to understand how someone as seemingly soft and bubbly as Mariella achieved as much as she had in her career. She railroaded everyone with generosity to gain control and got exactly what she wanted. Mariella was a force to be reckoned with.

Sylvia looked at the instructor expectantly, awaiting her fate, trying to look like she cared. He paused, enjoying all eyes on him, then solemnly handed her an alcohol wipe, a blessing from on high that she had performed to his standards. She hoped she was not rolling her eyes.

Sylvia also returned to Linden because her teaching hadn't been awful, because she wasn't ready to commit Meg to being a brief chapter in her past, because Ethan had made it painfully clear that even a heart attack would not awaken anything in him, because even Maddie had not felt compelled to jump on a plane, and yes, because Tony was here. She now stayed with him every Tuesday night without worrying about their future or what it meant. She allowed herself to enjoy the fact that she enjoyed sex with him and he seemed to have no complaints about her, and they never ran out of things to talk about. Perhaps all relationships should be conducted on a weekly basis. But mostly, Sylvia returned to Pierre because of the clinic.

She wiped down the doll and blocked out the instructor's wrap-up by studying the break room, trying to commit it to memory for a future time when this strange year receded further and further from her grasp: the government-mandated postings, the remnants of hardening birthday cake, the staff graffiti ("if men could get pregnant, abortion would be a sacrament").

She filed out with the rest of the volunteers. Feeling pleasantly proprietary, Sylvia adjusted a folder that was askew in a rack on a narrow counter and paused. She had grown to love this fluorescent, antiseptic, unglamorous-in-every-way hallway. When she was in that windowless recovery room at the end of it, holding a patient's hand, chatting about the weather or birth control options, attaching a blood pressure cuff, listening to their stories, she thought about nothing else. Not Leah and Nathaniel, not Ethan, not her class, not the work offers starting to come again from LA. She didn't even think about Tony. She was so certain that this was where she was meant to be and that it was what she was meant to be doing. Tipping ginger ale into a plastic cup for a nauseated patient allowed her to directly protect the progress of an enlightened society. She wouldn't ever utter aloud something so insufferably pompous, not even to Mariella—especially not to Mariella, whose delight would be unbearable—but that was exactly how she felt.

Waving goodbye to the receptionist through the Plexiglas, the receptionist who still didn't smile at her with any recognition and likely never would, Sylvia braced herself for the trip across the parking lot and past the protesters. She continued to park around the corner, both to save a space for patients and also to keep the ancient cult members from recognizing her car, and she experienced a rush of unwelcome adrenaline whenever she had to pass through the group. Remarkably, Caroline seemed not to have told any of them what had happened, a nugget that Sylvia was still digesting. She had anticipated having to ward off relentless demands that she recognize her blasphemous irony and express eternal gratitude. Sylvia found she was even more grateful to Caroline for her reticence than she had been for the CPR. No, that wasn't right. Not more grateful. More connected. This act of generosity—the not telling—was the first time ever that Sylvia felt she and Caroline understood each other. It was unsettling.

"We know what's in that bag!" Donald yelled in Sylvia's direction.

Sylvia looked behind her.

"In that bag," he croaked, nodding to Sylvia.

Sylvia pointed to her own shoulder bag, in which she had two unread scripts, a pair of sneakers, and a jog bra in the unlikely event that the urge to exercise hit her, and a small purse, which held a whole other universe of essential and nonessential items. She laughed.

"You do?"

"I know you hide the body parts in that bag of yours."

"I do?" Sylvia stalled. This was a whole new level of creepy crazy.

"You've got the dead baby parts in there!" he insisted.

Sylvia noticed two of the other protesters drift discreetly away from him. She had so many questions for Donald, none of which was askable. Wouldn't the bag be dripping? To whom was she bringing these parts and why? Was it for money? For a satanic ritual? Instead, she shocked both of them by approaching him and opening her bag. At first he shrank back from her, and she wondered why she hadn't thought to physically menace him before. He was frail and old and she was young (yes, young!) and strong, unused running shoes and heart attack notwithstanding, and her mere proximity to him was threatening.

"Go ahead," she said, calling his bluff.

But he reached out and she watched as his crepey hand touched her belongings one by one. Her vision hyper-magnified, and she would forever remember the raised veins on his fingers and eczema patches on his knuckles. She watched him move each sneaker. She glanced at his face, closer than it had ever been. His hair was thin, his eyes rheumy and vacant. But still he continued to root around her bag, once with enough force that she felt the pull of it on her own outstretched arms.

Like a TSA agent, he silently tapped on the purse inside the shoulder bag and nodded. She was to open it, too, for inspection. Disbelieving, Sylvia watched herself unzip the bag, saw him handle a Chapstick, a pack of tissues, sunglasses, all of which she knew she would have to either throw away or sterilize.

Finally, he stepped back and for one moment, Sylvia thought, *This is it. This has pierced his fantasy. He has to recognize that he's crazy, a liar, perpetuating incredible, damaging myths.*

"The other girl. She brought it out the other door," Donald concluded, not the least bit embarrassed.

Sylvia closed up her bags. The quickest route to her car was to the left, but instead, she intentionally headed right so that she would pass him. She veered revoltingly close to him, nearly brushing his shoulder. To her great satisfaction, he shrank away. When she was halfway down the block, he resumed yelling at her.

It didn't matter. She'd be back next week.

THIRTY

Meg shut the door to JD's car and pulled her coat tightly around her. She tread carefully, her steps alternately punching through the snow crust and sliding along the top of it. She waggled her fingers at JD, embarrassed by her ugly gait. A blast of wind threw her off balance, and she stumbled against Sylvia's car, grabbing the door handle to keep from hitting the ground. Just what she needed—a rebroken hip.

Meg fumbled with the buttons on the fob until the car shrieked its welcome. After a moment's hesitation, she pulled open the door and slid in.

She ran her hands over the steering wheel, bruisingly cold even through her thick gloves. Busied herself with adjusting the mirror, the seat, studying the dials and gauges. She was suffused with an old memory of panic that the car wouldn't start. Meg and her mother had become experts at jump-starting, as had most everyone in Barton. At Linden, she met for the first time students who didn't know the difference between the red and black jumper cables, and who had cars that were not beaters they'd saved for, but shiny new gifts bestowed on them because they'd acquired a high school diploma.

Part of her hoped the car wouldn't start. It had been over four years since Meg had been behind the wheel; she hadn't operated a car since the day of her rebirth. The license in her wallet was still the fake one she'd bought when she was fourteen. She guffawed to herself, but finally, it was too cold to just sit, and JD would start to wonder what was wrong. She put her foot on the brake and turned the key, holding her breath.

Of course, she thought, laughing out loud, as Sylvia's Honda purred to life. This was what it was like to have enough money. Cars started, even after two nights in frigid temperatures.

Sitting in the driver's seat felt like an intrusion on Sylvia's privacy. Meg tried not to register the brand of gum (Trident) tossed on the console, tried not to think *Sylvia chews gum?*, tried not to notice the grime and leaves and bits of tissue stuck to the floor mats, tried not to imagine Sylvia checking herself in the same rearview mirror Meg glanced in now. Did someone Sylvia's age still care what she looked like?

On the passenger seat was a stack of scripts, unmistakably her class's final work. Meg didn't even hesitate; she riffled through the stack in search of grades and comments, but they were free of markings. Meg briefly wondered whether there was another set of copies somewhere else that Sylvia had begun grading. Weren't grades due in just a few days?

A splash of color caught Meg's eye, and she turned to look at the back seat. JD's red scarf was coiled there, the reason Sylvia had come to meet them at Carton and Box two days earlier. What if Sylvia hadn't noticed the scarf? What if she hadn't called Meg, hadn't come to meet them? What if she'd had her heart attack home alone? What if she hadn't had the heart attack in front of JD's mother, the satanic savior who had tried to keep Meg from having an abortion, but who had saved Sylvia's life?

Meg shuddered and pulled the scarf to her face and breathed in the scent. She couldn't get enough of JD, couldn't believe how much she wanted to be with him every minute of every day, couldn't get over how she never got sick of him. Everyone else in the world eventually got on her nerves and made her look for the exit, but not him. She waved the scarf at him through the window and blew a kiss, a gesture that only months ago she never in a million years would have considered making.

Trembling, Meg put the car in reverse and looked over her shoulder. The store wouldn't open for another hour, and she was grateful the Carton and Box parking lot was empty. She hesitated before taking her foot off the brake. When had she morphed into someone other people trusted to drive their cars? For the first time in her life, Meg was able to do favors.

JD honked and held up both palms out to the side, questioning. Meg put up one finger: *Just wait.*

Ridiculously, she wanted to talk to Sylvia's car, to tell the little blue Civic how grateful she was to its owner. Grateful to Sylvia for taking her to the clinic, for staying with her, for not judging her. Not just not judging her: operating completely outside the idea that Meg was even in a situation that anyone ought to judge.

She waggled the rearview mirror again, fidgeted the side-view mirror, took a shaky breath, and let up on the brake, inching back as slowly as the car would permit. Her heart was pounding, and she began to sweat through her layers.

Who could guarantee she wouldn't turn the steering wheel into a wall again?

Meg depressed the brake fully and shifted the car into park. Sylvia didn't know the circumstances of Meg's crash, but JD did. He would understand. She put her hand on the door handle, but as soon as she made contact, Missing Michelle again popped into her mind. Meg felt desperate to know what Michelle was doing. Did she still think of life in semesters? Was she waiting tables? Attending community college? Trapped in a mental health facility?

Meg crossed her arms over the steering wheel and rested her head. Immediately, JD was at her side, sliding into the passenger seat. He placed his palm gently on her back.

"There's no cosmic rule that says you have to do this."

Meg shook her head, her nose rubbing against her sleeve.

"I know. But I'm going to."

"Because you're scrappy?"

Meg gave a courteous, half-hearted chuckle. Two different professors had used the adjective to describe her, leading Meg to conclude it was code for *upstate trash*.

"No, because I just fucking can."

"That sounds pretty darn scrappy."

Meg groaned. "I just need a minute."

"Okay."

Meg instinctively touched two fingers to the center of her collarbone, but the gold cross she had worn for so many years was no longer there. It was stashed in the top drawer of her dorm room dresser while she worked out what its purpose was and what her intention was in wearing it. She had been weighing whether to put it on when she returned home to Barton, but wasn't even sure what her criteria were for deciding. It would be so much easier, of course, just to wear it. No questions from her mother. No hurt, uncomprehending looks. To leave it off was to actively injure her mother. And here she was, still reaching for it anyway.

She could keep things smooth by lying (by omission, but still). Or she could let AnneMarie see who her daughter was becoming. As unsatisfying as it would be, the right thing to do probably lay somewhere in the middle, requiring lots more effort and balance. Meg groaned out loud. It was a shit ton of work to effect change slowly and gently, and it was also entirely against her nature.

"Megster?" JD said.

She looked at him pleadingly, longingly. She was desperate for guidance.

"Think you could fast-track this little milestone? I'm starving."

Meg chortled and pulled him to her. That was all it took to shake her out of her self-important, overexamined self. When had she become so ridiculous? Start the damn car and go.

"I love you," she told him. For the first time. She felt him tense up, but she wasn't scared. He pulled back to look at her.

"Well, guess what. I love you, too."

She laughed. "Guess what?"

He swatted at her, and she grabbed his wrist and kissed him.

"Okay," he said, all business. "If I get out of this car, are you going to start driving?"

Meg nodded dutifully. "But where to? Hospital? Her place?"

As if to answer her question, from inside her jacket pocket (Hannah's jacket pocket), Meg's phone rang.

"Hannah and I are starving," Rosetta said when Meg answered.

"Hunger is in the air," Meg observed cryptically.

"Poetic. Her parents are picking her up in two hours. Our last chance to be together before three and a half weeks of hell aka family time."

"Be still my heart! Is stone-cold Rosetta Stone becoming sentimental?"

"Fuck you, Croyden. Meet us at Gloria's."

"No fucking way," Meg told her, noticing that she rarely cursed anymore, usually only when Rosetta cursed first. "I hate that place and I hate Gloria. You know I won't go there."

JD nodded as he deciphered the gist of the conversation.

"Get over yourself. See you in fifteen minutes."

Rosetta hung up and Meg looked at her phone, marveling over how little Rosetta had changed this term while she, Meg, felt as though she were continents away from whom she'd been in September. Of course, Rosetta now ate food instead of sniffing leaves, which, Meg realized, probably represented some deeper shifts within.

"We're going to Gloria's."

JD raised his eyebrows in a query.

"Rosetta," she explained, and he nodded, understanding all instantly. Meg's heart soared.

He opened his door and the wind barreled in. "You've got this," he told Meg. "And I'll be right behind you the whole way."

They left Sylvia's car outside Alumni House, parked JD's truck in a visitor's spot, and crossed the street to Gloria's, holding hands. Outside the diner, Meg turned to JD.

"I can't go three weeks without you!" she wailed and was immediately chagrined. First she goes ahead and blurts out the L-word and then she unleashes a torrent of neediness on him. What the hell was wrong with her? JD was going to regret telling her he loved her back.

"So why don't I come up to Barton with you for some of it?" he said simply, unfazed as ever.

Meg shivered with relief. She was working hard to get comfortable with the idea of being happy. She had done the opposite of everything someone could do to land herself a real boyfriend while also being here at Linden, learning the history of Hispaniola and understanding how Aristotle could show up in both a math and writing class, and that was how she knew for sure, without a doubt, right there outside the disgusting, ridiculous diner she hated, that there was no god. Why should she, Margaret Anne Croyden, former addict and bathroom-born mistake, have gotten this gilded second chance when there were people who had worked harder, behaved better, and prayed more who still were scrambling to find an open door?

While JD waited for an answer, he opened the fogged-up door, and pulled her with him into the tight space near the first booth, where they were instantly overheated. Despite the close, oily air, Meg felt the weight of a lifetime, her lifetime, lift. Her head was clear, and she felt overwhelming gratitude for the clarity. Her confirmation that there was no god meant she could wear her cross home because she no longer had to struggle. She had nothing to prove. Meg could afford this gesture of kindness toward her mother. But she also knew that she would bring JD home, and he would sleep in her room with her, in her bed, and she would not pretend to her mother about this.

Rosetta and Hannah spotted them and began waving and shouting as if they hadn't seen Meg in years, and drawing the ire of Gloria, who promptly told them to shut up.

Meg slipped past Gloria, and into the booth beside Rosetta while JD sat beside Hannah.

"Guess what Meg just did," he said proudly and Meg startled. Was he going to announce that she'd said she loved him? She held up her hand to stop him. "She drove!"

Meg grinned as much from her own idiocy as from pride.

"No way!" Hannah beamed like a proud mama.

"Jesus, finally," Rosetta drawled. "Now I can drink off campus and you can drive me home."

"It's not like I suddenly have a car," Meg reminded her.

"Yeah, but I do, dumbass," Rosetta said. "You'll drive mine."

Hannah leaned across the table and said conspiratorially, "It's a sweet ride."

"Okay, homey, good to know," Meg teased.

"What'll it be?" Gloria stood at their booth, one hand on the banquette, presenting only her profile, as if she had better things to do elsewhere.

"You'd better be treating, Stone," Meg suddenly decided. "This wasn't my choice."

"Deal. Order the works."

"No way," Meg said. "The food here is the worst I've ever had." She experienced the inestimable satisfaction of Gloria turning her head and actually seeing her for the first time. When their eyes met, Meg told her, "Just coffee, thanks."

THE END

ACKNOWLEDGMENTS

Many people buoyed me and this book, which has been oh-so-timely for too many years. For unparalleled editing guidance that finally brought *This Was Not the Plan* to "Yes!" I owe a debt of gratitude to Gay Daly. I also give my heartfelt thanks to the members of my reading group, who let me present a draft as one of our reads. Jean Kouremetis, in particular, gave me the benefit of extra time and the attention of her next-level brain.

This story would not have existed if not for Ira Hochman, a one-man Borscht Belt show and one of the most honorable and well-read people I know, all wrapped up in a truly delightful person. Thank you for letting me steal your lines, which poured forth during our hours together in sweltering heat and freezing cold.

Without my beloved family, friends (who are my family), and neighbors (who are my friends), I would not feel safe enough to slip away into the unpredictable land of fiction each day. I cannot list everyone who makes my world go round without sounding like a yearbook page, so you will have to trust you know who you are.

However…Mom, Sacha, Talia, and Gabriel: you are my everything.

ABOUT THE AUTHOR

Daphne Uviller is the author of the Zephyr Zuckerman series *Super in the City, Hotel No Tell*, and *Wife of the Day*, which were optioned for television by Silver Lake Entertainment, and she is the co-editor with Deborah Siegel of the anthology *Only Child: Writers on the Singular Joys and Solitary Sorrows of Growing Up Solo.* She has one husband, one dog, and two teenagers, and she lives near the glorious Hudson River.